HALF SEVEN ON A THURSDAY

In life, there's no such thing as a dress rehearsal...

When Edward Bull agrees to direct the amateur production of *Death by Dying,* he thinks it will take his mind off his wife's recent affair. However, he is soon to discover that all the real drama is taking place off stage. Among his cast there is Maria, trapped in a loveless marriage to an older man, and her sister Ellen, scarred after a tragic motorbike accident. There's handsome, charming Robert, who glides through life, there's outspoken Theo, gentle Harry and independent Judith, each with their own stories. As the weeks pass their lives intertwine, until opening night draws near...

HALF SEVEN ON A THURSDAY

HALF SEVEN ON A THURSDAY

by

Roisin Meaney

Magna Large Print Books
Long Preston, North Yorkshire,
BD23 4ND, England.

British Library Cataloguing in Publication Data.

Meaney, Roisin
    Half seven on a Thursday.

    A catalogue record of this book is
    available from the British Library

    ISBN   978-0-7505-3421-5

First published in Great Britain in 2009 by Hachette Books Ireland
An Hachette UK company

Published in Large Print 2011 by arrangement with
Headline Publishing Group Ltd.

Magna Large Print is an imprint of Library Magna Books Ltd.

Printed and bound in Great Britain by
T.J. (International) Ltd., Cornwall, PL28 8RW

For the Granary Players,
who were my inspiration.

Actors Wanted

Male and female adult actors required for upcoming production of new three-act murder mystery play by local playwright. Previous acting experience desirable but not essential. Rehearsals on Thursday evenings for approximately six weeks, leading to a week-long run in the Arts Centre in early June. Auditions upstairs in Mc-Millan's Pub, Quinn Street, this Thursday, 24 April at 8:30 p.m sharp.

The Portmaine Herald, Monday, 21 April 2008

Audition Night: Thursday, 24 April

McMillan's Pub

Her hair, Edward saw immediately, was exactly what he'd had in mind for Dorothy. Long, a good foot past her shoulders, iron-straight, a satiny sheen on it even in this gloomy light, and the precise colour – as far as he could make out – of the soft flesh of a perfectly ripe nectarine, that beautiful rosy-orange shade you seldom saw on a woman's head now.

Her figure was somewhat disappointing. He would have liked her a couple of inches taller, a little more willowy – and younger too, at least five years younger; Dorothy was supposed to be in her late twenties.

But the hair was perfect.

He leaned forward and watched intently as she picked her way through the haphazardly arranged mismatched chairs and low tables.

'Are you limping?' he asked.

She started violently, her wonderful hair arcing across her face as she swung towards the sound of his voice, hand flying to her chest. 'Jesus! You scared the shit out of me!'

Charming; such polite vocabulary. Edward reached across and tilted the dusty green shade of the table lamp nearest to him, throwing a fraction more light into the room.

'Sorry. I don't usually make much noise when I'm on my own.'

She squinted at him suspiciously, palm still pressed against the bare skin above her top. 'Why is it so *dark* in here?' She looked at the bunched lace curtains on the row of narrow windows. 'If they took those horrible things down, we could see what we were doing.' She turned back to Edward. 'You here for the auditions? Is this where they're on?'

Edward nodded. 'I am. It is.' He glanced at his watch. 'You're three minutes late.'

Her mouth opened a fraction wider. 'What?' She looked at her own watch, holding it close to her face. 'You're joking, right?'

'I am, yes.'

He wasn't. He indicated a nearby chair. 'Why don't you sit down?' He wondered if anyone else was going to turn up, and if so, why they couldn't be bothered to be on time. Hadn't they read '8:30 sharp'?

She dropped her bag onto the floor and sat. She wore a navy skirt to her knees, that held for Edward a vaguely uncomfortable suggestion of a school uniform, and a cream top. She pushed out her bottom lip and blew her fringe out of her eyes.

'My sister's coming. She's gone to the loo.'

Great: a brace of cursing females. Probably put a hex on him if he didn't cast them. For the life of him, Edward couldn't remember what exactly had possessed him to take on this ridiculous project.

'So, are you an actor or what?' She tucked her hair behind her ear and it immediately slithered forward again. A brief, painful echo of his wife whistled past him. Women and their hair, always fiddling with it. He smelled oranges.

'No – I'm going to be directing.'

'Oh – right.' And before either of them had a

16

chance to say any more they heard footsteps on the stairs. Both of them turned towards the open doorway 'Here's Maria.'

But a man appeared instead of Maria. A burly, shambling, tousle-headed male of around, Edward guessed, twenty-five. Blinking into the gloom, pushing something into the pocket of his jeans.

Moving cautiously until he spotted them at the far side, his solid thigh bumping against a small table as he approached, his hand reaching out to stop its sideways tilt. A tight, polite smile on his big, broad face.

'Hello. I'm here for the auditions.'

A softer voice than you'd expect from that frame. Looking from one to the other uncertainly, large hands hanging awkwardly at his sides.

Edward regarded him solemnly, sweeping his gaze past the knobbled, rusty orange sweatshirt – surely too heavy on this unseasonably warm evening? – the frayed, baggy jeans, the ridiculous shoes that were supposed to suggest that you'd just moored your boat around the corner.

Much too young for the writer. Pity, that mop would probably have suited Jack McCarthy. They could try ageing him a bit, see what he looked like in tweeds.

Or possibly the gardener – yes, of course, the gardener would be a much better fit. Wellingtons and a rake, and one of those woolly hats. Yes. Maybe.

'Have a seat,' Edward said. 'We're waiting for a few more to turn up.'

He'd deliberately put 8:30 sharp – he hated to

be kept waiting – and now it was nearly twenty to nine. He'd give it five more minutes, and then he'd abort the whole ridiculous business. The redhead would probably swear at him again, but it couldn't be helped.

More footsteps outside as the big man sank into a too-low, creaking armchair, and Edward turned and watched Penelope McCarthy walk in.

Made for the part. The right age for Penelope, mid-thirties or thereabouts, tall enough and thin enough, if she could just carry off the air of superiority, the cool hauteur that he needed for the writer's sister.

He tried to picture her in pearls and one of those skirts that women shouldn't be able to walk in. High heels, of course, and a cigarette, maybe, in a holder. He wondered if she smoked. She'd have to be a smoker in reality – you could always tell the ones who weren't.

'Over here.'

The redhead was gesturing her into a chair. How could they possibly be sisters? Edward couldn't see a resemblance. Maybe one was adopted.

He studied the newcomer again. Pink blouse buttoned almost to her chin, loose grey trousers, flat black shoes. No hips and not much of a chest – the sister had all the curves. Red in her hair too, but a much darker, almost mahogany shade. Pulled away from her face, emphasising the high cheekbones, the pointed chin. Not plain exactly, but nothing to stop you in your tracks.

He'd seen her somewhere before, he was sure. Worked in a shop, maybe – or he'd buried someone belonging to her, back when he had a job.

He cleared his throat. With three of them there, he probably should introduce himself. 'Edward Bull is my name, I'll be directing' – another pointed look at his watch '–that is, if enough people turn up to cast the play.'

The second sister offered her hand. 'Maria. Talty.'

She made them sound like two separate sentences. Her voice was lower in pitch than Edward had been expecting from that fragile frame. Her hand was cool. She glanced towards the other man, who immediately lunged forward in his armchair, arm outstretched, causing it to creak violently.

'Harry Buckley. Pleased to meet you.' He nodded at Edward and the redhead, both too far away for a handshake.

'Ellen Greene,' the redhead said, flapping her fingers at them. Unlike her sister, she wore no wedding ring. If asked to guess, Edward would have taken her for the married one. She crossed her legs. Edward's glance swept over them – good knees – before he could stop himself.

'So, how many do you need?' she asked him.

'Sorry?'

'People, for this play of yours. How many are in it?'

'Six,' he told her. 'And,' he added, 'it's not my play – I'm simply the director.' God forbid that anyone would hold him responsible for it.

As he spoke there were voices on the stairs, and a second later a man and a woman came through the doorway.

'Hello. Is this where the auditions are on?' The

man strode in. 'We asked downstairs and they sent us up here.'

The woman followed him into the room. 'It's a bit dark, isn't it?'

'I said the same thing,' Ellen told her.

She looked fiftyish, around the right age for the housekeeper, but nothing else about her did anything to inspire Edward. Not the bobbed, pale brown hair or the eager-to-please expression on the soft, round face. Certainly not the shapeless, dark cardigan over the horrendous flowery skirt, although of course clothes didn't matter a damn. But where was the presence he wanted for Betty? Where was the character, the steel he needed to make her a credible murderer?

The man was slightly more promising. Good-looking, which never hurt, early forties by the look of him, right age for Jack McCarthy. Well able to carry off the country squire look. And well able too, Edward guessed, to flirt with young, innocent Dorothy Williams.

'Edward Bull,' he told them. 'Director.'

'Robert McInerney.' His handshake was solid. 'And I have no idea who this charming lady is – we met on the way in.'

'Judith O'Sullivan.'

She had a nice smile, her whole face crinkling with it. Edward made the rest of the introductions – twenty-three years of dealing with bereaved people had left him good with names – and then bent towards his briefcase. 'We may as well get started. Hopefully a few others will–'

Someone thumped suddenly up the stairs, drowning out the end of his sentence. They all

20

turned to look as a woman burst through the doorway and clumped heavily across the room. What on earth was she wearing on her feet?

Thick, unusually curved heels, soles at least three inches high, shiny uppers that covered her ankles and laced across the front. They looked like they had come straight off the feet of some demented fairytale witch, except that they were purple instead of black.

Above the shoes she wore a loosely cut green dress that fell to just below her knees, in the kind of material that made Edward's teeth sore, and she'd dyed her hair the horrible false, sharp pink of the candyfloss he'd tasted once as a child, fascinated by the feathery look of it but immediately revolted by its cloying grittiness in his mouth.

Her features weren't regular enough to be pretty – wide, slightly hooked nose, pale eyes a fraction too far apart, overlarge teeth between alarmingly purple lips – but she was striking in a slightly off-kilter way.

If Edward was stuck, she might just do for the postmistress, but the pink hair would have to go. She was far too old for it, for one thing – had to be at least thirty.

'Sorry, have you started?' She looked at the bundle of scripts in Edward's hand. 'My baby is teething and it took forever to get her to sleep.'

Edward shook his head. 'No, we were just about–'

'Oh, good. I'm Theo DeCourcy, by the way.' She sank into a chair and crossed one awful, witchy shoe over the other. 'I've no acting experience whatsoever, but this sounded interesting.'

She stuck out a hand – covered in a ridiculous lacy fingerless glove – and Edward obediently put a script into it. She peered around the room. 'Is it me, or is it really dark in here?'

And a second later: *Death by Dying?* What kind of a name is that?'

An hour and forty minutes later there were far too many people scattered throughout the long, narrow room, sprawled on chairs, perched on window sills or simply propped against walls. They'd pushed open what windows would budge, but it was still uncomfortably warm. Layers were peeled off, sleeves were pushed up, and the six by now slightly wilting scripts were being flapped enthusiastically in front of damp, rosy faces.

Someone had discovered a central light whose bare bulb was harsh and unflattering, but which at least made the lines of dialogue easier to read. Edward had made sure that everyone tried out for at least one part, cringing quietly as words were mispronounced or skipped altogether, as cues were missed, as conversations were reduced to a series of halting, unconnected phrases by people who he fervently wished had stayed at home.

'Right.' He stopped scribbling and put down his biro and stood up. It took a good fifteen seconds for the whispers and mutters and fidgeting to die down, for all the faces to turn towards him.

He'd never been comfortable talking to a crowd, never at ease with attention focused on him. He wished someone would flick the light switch and send them all into the gloom again. He cleared his throat and looked down at the notes he didn't need.

'First of all, has everyone signed this?' He held up the sheet he'd sent around, collecting names and contact numbers. Experience had taught him the importance of back-up – who knew what problems might arise within his chosen cast?

A general nodding. Edward slid the sheet into his briefcase and continued. 'As you all know, there are only six parts in this play, so apologies to those who'll go home without one.'

Not a sound. A bead of sweat trickled unpleasantly down his back.

'At this stage, before I announce the cast' – Lord, how pompous that sounded – 'I'd like to repeat that I will expect complete commitment from each and every one of you.' His stern gaze left nobody out. 'If anyone feels at this stage that there's the smallest chance of their not turning up here *every* Thursday evening – and probably two or three extra evenings in the week before production' – he gave this a second to sink in – 'I would like them to please leave now.'

His words created a small, self-conscious ripple. Feet shuffled. A throat was cleared. A few heads swung around, searching for deserters. Nobody got up, nobody headed for the door.

Edward went back to his notes. 'In that case, thank you all for coming, and I would like the following people to remain behind please.'

He called out the six names and stayed standing through the subsequent clatter of chairs being pushed back and jackets being gathered up and the general bustle of the room emptying out, until they were left, finally, to themselves.

Edward dropped his notes into his briefcase and turned to face them. 'I hope none of you are afraid of hard work,' he said. 'Despite the fact that this is an amateur production and none of you will be getting paid, I expect you to give as much commitment as if you were all on Hollywood salaries.'

They smiled politely. It had sounded funnier at home.

'I speak as I find,' he told them. 'If I'm not happy, you'll know about it. I will be fair but demanding, and as director, my decision on any queries that arise will be final. I expect lines to be learnt promptly, and I expect you to turn up to rehearsals *on time* – particularly as I was the only person here at eight-thirty tonight.'

He let that bit sink in too. No harm to lay down the law from the start.

'Now,' he said, 'any comments before I give out the parts?'

And immediately they all began to speak at the same time.

'What character am I playing?' asked Theo DeCourcy. 'I hope it's not the postmistress – she's not very exciting, is she?'

'I'd just like to say thanks very much,' said Harry Buckley. 'I never thought I'd be offered a part.'

'I was sure you weren't going to cast me,' said Ellen Greene. 'You kept cutting me off when I was reading – I thought you hated me.'

'What time are the rehearsals?' asked Robert McInerney. 'It's just that Thursday is our late opening, and if we're busy it might be tricky to be here much before eight.'

'I hope I won't have too many lines to learn,' said Maria Talty. 'My memory is hopeless. I'll do my best, of course, but it might take a while.'

'I can paint backdrops too,' said Judith O'Sullivan. 'If you need that done, I mean – just a thought. I'm an art teacher, you see.'

Edward listened to the babble of their voices. He had barely six weeks, maybe ten rehearsals altogether, to shape this best-of-a-bad-lot collection into some kind of a team. Only one of them had any acting experience; two, possibly three, out of the six could be called attractive; and one already showed distinct signs of lacking commitment.

Not to mention the fact that the play was mediocre at best, the first effort of a young, inexperienced local man. Talk about mission impossible.

'Rehearsals,' he told them, 'will take place at seven-thirty *sharp* each Thursday,' – looking pointedly at Robert – 'and will last approximately two hours, possibly longer. You will be expected to learn your lines on time' – a glance in Maria's direction – 'and parts' – to Theo – 'are not negotiable.'

He began to distribute fresh scripts, thinking with longing of the very large brandy with his name on it in the pub downstairs.

'He was like Hitchcock,' Ellen said, 'sitting there in his armchair, not making a sound. I nearly got a heart attack when he spoke.' She stopped suddenly. 'I just remembered – he asked me if I was limping.' She looked indignantly at Maria. 'The nerve.'

'Watch the road.' Maria pushed her seatbelt

into its casing and tucked her blouse down under it. 'Well, you do limp.'

'I do not. Well, barely. Most people don't even notice.'

'He did, obviously, the minute you walked in.'

'Well I don't know why he asked then, if he could see it. I didn't tell him anyway. It's none of his bloody business. I have the part now – he can't very well take it away from me.'

'I never thought we'd get parts,' Maria said. 'I didn't even want one.'

'Me neither ... but I kind of got into it.'

Maria frowned. 'I thought you were dying for a part. That's what you said when you rang and practically begged me to go with you. That's the only reason I came along.'

'Oh, I was,' Ellen said quickly. 'I mean, I love the *idea* of being in a play – I'm just not too sure that *this* play is the one I'd choose. You were brilliant as Penelope though, much better than anyone else. I wasn't surprised when he picked you.'

They drove in silence for a few minutes, past the community centre, through the roundabout, across the city's newest bridge, up the hill and towards the housing development where Maria lived.

Ellen shifted gear as they turned into the wide avenue of red brick houses. 'You don't hate the thought of it, do you? I wouldn't like to think I'd forced you into it.'

'Actually,' Maria said slowly, 'I don't. I thought I would, but I don't.'

'Good.' They pulled up in front of Maria's house. 'But honestly, sitting there like God

Almighty, judging us all.'

Maria laughed. 'Ellen, he *is* the director – it's his job.'

'I'd say he loves laying down the law.'

'He's quite attractive though, you have to admit that. He reminds me a bit of Tommy Lee Jones.'

'I don't care what he looks like, he'll still be bossing us around every Thursday. So what do *you* think of the play anyway? It's a bit corny, isn't it?'

Maria unbuckled her seatbelt and reached for her bag on the floor of the car. 'I'm surprised it's a new one – it seems kind of dated to me. It reminds me of the old black and white films we used to watch on Sunday afternoons.'

'Wait till Mam and Dad hear we're both in a play. Wait till I tell them I'm the murder victim.'

Maria laughed. 'You've got a great part. I only have a few scenes, not important at all.'

'I think Penelope is interesting, and you've some good bitchy lines. Wonder what Herr Direktor thinks of it.'

'I presume he likes it, if he's agreed to direct it.' Maria opened the car door. 'Want to come in for a cuppa?'

Ellen hesitated. 'I don't think so, thanks. I've a pile of ironing waiting at home.'

Like ironing had ever stopped her staying out; like Maria was fooled for a second. But the offer was always made, and always refused.

'OK. See you Sunday.'

'See you.' Ellen watched her sister walking up the path of number fourteen, rummaging in her bag. Pushing her key into the door, turning to wave.

Driving home, Ellen felt vindicated. Playing the sympathy card, making out that she'd needed Maria's moral support to go to the auditions, had made her feel vaguely guilty. She could easily have gone to McMillan's on her own – if she'd had the slightest interest in being in a play, which she hadn't. But of course she was doing it for Maria, not the other way around. Her sister needed something like this, some kind of escape from that awful life of hers, even if it was just for a couple of hours a week, and now she had it. And by the sound of it, Maria was quite happy with the outcome, so Ellen's plan had worked beautifully.

The only problem was that now she was tied – they were both tied – to being ordered around for the next six weeks by a man who clearly revelled in telling everyone else what to do, and Ellen wasn't at all sure how she'd cope with that. She didn't relish the idea of learning lines, of having to stand up in front of the others every Thursday and put on an act.

She'd just have to keep reminding herself why she was there, and hopefully the experience would bring Maria out of herself a bit, help her to make a few friends who'd distract her from her problems at home, more than that dreary little bookshop could. Although it was doubtful that Maria would have much in common with that loud pink-haired woman, and the other one was a bit long in the tooth, but still.

As she turned down a narrow side street, the open doorway of a pub and the scattered smokers around it caught Ellen's eye. She glanced at the dashboard clock – five past eleven. Plenty of time.

She pulled into a space and checked her reflection, ran lipstick across her mouth, dipped her head and swung it back and tousled her hair with her fingers. Undid another button on her top.

She walked slowly into the pub, disguising the limp as much as she could – not that it ever bothered them – and tried to remember when she'd changed the sheets on her bed.

As he drew up to the edge of the path and swung his leg over the crossbar, the bottom of Harry's jeans caught on the carrier, and the resulting loss of equilibrium sent bicycle and rider crashing heavily to the ground.

'Blast!' He scrambled to his feet, already feeling the sting of a palm that had slapped hard onto the concrete, and an ominous throb in one hip. 'Damn and blast!' He gave a quick look around and saw nobody – thank God.

He should have put on the clips. So what if they'd seen him, who cared if they thought bicycle clips were naff? They were nothing to him, they were complete strangers to him – apart from Judith, whose face he'd recognised as soon as she'd walked in. He was good with faces.

But he'd left the blasted clips in his pocket, too self-conscious to use them in front of the others, and now it served him right.

The stupid thing was, they probably hadn't even noticed him. By the time he'd unlocked the bike, they were more than likely walking towards their cars, not looking in his direction at all, not in the least bothered whether he wore bicycle clips or not.

He examined his palm. Not a bad graze, bit of Savlon on it when he went in. He massaged his hip – stiff in the morning probably, but he'd live.

He hauled the bike up and wheeled it in through the gate, hearing the wheeze of a mud-guard scraping every so often against the front tyre. In the shed he took the script from the carrier and smoothed it out.

Imagine, him in a play. Wait till he told Ma.

Eve was in the kitchen, in George's dark blue pyjama top and a pair of grey leggings. Harry liked her short blonde choppy fringe, the contrast with her heavy dark eyebrows.

'Hi Harry.' She held up a slice of brown bread. 'I'm making toasties – want one?' A block of orange cheddar sat on the worktop beside the sliced pan.

Harry shook his head, moving past her towards the door into the hall. 'No thanks, think I'll just–'

'Oh, hey, how did you get on?' She was bare-foot, her toenails painted a deep pink. 'Did you get a part?'

Harry grinned, feeling the heat in his face. 'I did, yeah. I'm–'

'Oh, that's brilliant – wait till I tell George.' She turned back to the worktop and began slicing thick wedges of cheese. 'Well done you.'

'Thanks ... well, I'm off to bed. See you tomor-row.' Harry left the kitchen and went upstairs. Passing their bedroom door, he heard Amy Wine-house singing about not going to rehab.

He imagined the conversation when Eve brought up the toasties. 'Guess what – Harry got a part in the play. Can you believe it?'

'You're joking.' George lowering his book and looking over his John Lennon glasses at her.

'No, he really did.'

And they'd wonder – in a nice way, though – how on earth he'd managed it.

In the bathroom he cleaned his hand and rubbed Savlon on the graze. He pulled down his jeans and examined the slightly pinker patch of skin on his hip.

He hardly knew what had possessed him to go along to the auditions. He'd never stood on a stage in his life, never had the slightest inclination to act in anything.

But for some reason, the ad in the paper had stayed with him. In the days that followed, he'd begun to find the idea intriguing. He'd imagined standing up on a stage in front of lots of people, not as Harry Buckley in the library who you wouldn't look twice at, but as someone different. Someone who wasn't afraid to say what he felt, or who wouldn't let anyone walk all over him.

Not that it mattered, though, what the character was like – he could be as obnoxious as anything. The main thing was that he wouldn't be Harry. It was his chance to try out another person's skin, maybe the only chance he'd ever get.

Oh, he knew it would only be for a few weeks, and that it was all pretend anyway, and when it was over he'd have to go back to being himself again and nothing would have changed. But wouldn't it be something?

And before you knew it, before he could give himself time to change his mind, he was heading into McMillan's on Thursday evening, walking past the little knots of late office workers and early evening drinkers, and up the narrow stairs whose carpet disappeared when you turned the corner, even as the little voice that he'd managed to stifle up till then began to whisper: What do you think you're doing? You can't seriously imagine that anyone will want you – you're having a laugh, aren't you?

But it was too late by then, because he was through the doorway and into the long, badly lit room, and two people were sitting at the other end, watching as he blundered towards them, almost knocking over one of those tiny little spindly-legged tables that made him feel even more like Gulliver in Lilliput.

And the more people who'd shown up, the more nervous he'd become, the more certain that he was wasting his time. And then, miraculously, he'd landed the part of Tom the gardener, silently attracted to poor, doomed Dorothy.

It wasn't a very big part, which was probably just as well. Not too many lines to learn, not too much of the spotlight resting on him. And Tom's character wasn't a million miles away from Harry's own, which probably helped. His nervous stuttering hadn't mattered, might even have added to the part. So for the next six Thursdays Harry Buckley would disappear and be replaced by Tom Drury.

He leaned against the door of his bedroom and examined the script. *Death by Dying,* it said on the cover. *A play for theatre by Jonathan Crosby.*

He thought again about telling Ma on Sunday.

She'd have to react to that, wouldn't she? Usually he had nothing interesting to tell her; it was no wonder she didn't say much. This would be different.

He turned the cover over and began to read, his eyes flying back and forth.

She stood in the hall and listened. No sound from upstairs. A burst of laughter, too loud, from the sitting room. She walked in.

'Turn that down a bit, will you? Guess what.'

Ben was lying on the couch, spread out the length of it. 'Hey.'

He reached for the remote control on the floor and pressed the mute button. He opened his arms and Theo dropped her bag, kicked off her purple shoes and lowered herself onto his body. Their faces were almost touching.

'Guess what,' she said again.

He tugged at the ends of her pink hair. 'You got a part.'

She grinned. 'I did.'

'Fantastic.' He pressed a loud kiss on her mouth. 'Good girl. I knew you would.'

'How was Chrissy?'

'Didn't stir.'

She looked sternly at him. 'And how would you know, with that TV blaring?'

'Relax, woman.' He tugged gently on her hair again. 'Sean is keeping an ear out.'

'OK.' Theo slid off him and stood up. 'I'm starving. What's left?'

He reached again for the remote control. 'There's soup in the fridge. And maybe pizza, unless Sean's been down.'

Usually when she wasn't working late the three of them ate dinner around eight, after Chrissy had been put down for the night, but with the auditions this evening she'd eaten earlier, and now the hollow feeling in her stomach was almost an ache.

In the kitchen she took the pizza box from the fridge and lifted out the one remaining slice and picked off the pepperoni discs and threw them into the bin, and replaced them with blobs of mayonnaise.

As she chewed she searched the fridge again and pulled out the Pyrex jug. She took off the tinfoil lid and sniffed at the grey liquid – mushroom, not her favourite. She emptied the soup into a bowl and put it in the microwave and went back to the pizza, leaning against the fridge as she ate.

Funny how things worked out. Sean and herself alone for years, not a sign of a man for her – or not any she'd be interested in. She'd begun to assume, once thirty had come and gone, that this was her lot, that she'd had her ration of romance early on.

And then Ben Talbot had sat beside her at a cousin's wedding three years ago, and Chrissy had happened late last year. Not exactly planned, but not unwanted either. And here Theo was again, nearly eighteen years after Sean, back to the broken nights and the nappies and the bottles. Only this time she wasn't fifteen, pregnant and deserted by the boy she'd been stupid enough to think had loved her. Now she had Ben, and everything was different.

And Ben had Gemima – but that was another

story, and one she didn't feel like thinking about tonight.

The microwave pinged and she threw the pizza crust into the bin and lifted out the steaming soup. As she took a spoon from the drawer she caught sight of her reflection in the darkened kitchen window.

Time for a new look – she was getting tired of pink hair. She pulled off the wig and ran a hand over the stubby brown fuzz that Caroline shaved every three weeks. Like a concentration camp survivor, she looked – well, from the chin up maybe. Her face had always been the thinnest part of her, unfortunately.

It had begun soon after Chrissy was born, when Theo was just beginning to remember the whole huge upheaval caused by the arrival of one tiny new human. When she and Ben were taking turns to snatch an hour's sleep, when they grabbed what food they could in between feeding and changing and rocking and washing The Baby Who Never Ever Slept.

When she'd first begun to notice the hair loss, remembering something similar happening after Sean was born, Theo hadn't been too bothered.

'My hair is falling out,' she'd said to Caroline when she'd finally found the hour and a half she needed to get to the salon. 'I'd forgotten about that.'

'After I had the twins,' Caroline had told her, 'it came out in handfuls. I got the fright of my life. Nobody had warned me.'

But six weeks later, it was still happening, a fresh scattering on her pillow every morning.

More coming out every time she brushed it or put a hand through it.

'I think maybe you should let your doctor have a look,' Caroline had said when she'd seen her again. 'It should have stopped by now.'

And the diagnosis, when it finally came, had been like a death sentence. Oh, she knew it could have been so much worse. She could really have been dying; she could have found herself sitting in Dr O'Meara's surgery listening to him saying, 'I'm terribly sorry, Theo, but you've got six months at the most.'

But still, to lose her hair. She'd always looked after it, sniffing shampoos in chemists like a demented bloodhound, suffering through a final cold rinse so it would shine, slathering in deep conditioning treatments anytime it needed pampering.

She hadn't known how to tell Ben, except the only way she'd always told him things: straight out.

'I'm going bald,' she'd said. 'I have alopecia. It's all going to come out.'

'Are you sick?' he'd asked. 'Is this something serious?'

'No,' she'd said, because she couldn't explain how serious it was without sounding vain. 'It won't make me sick, just ugly.'

And of course he'd put his arms around her and told her exactly how beautiful she was, with or without hair.

'In fact,' he'd said, 'I didn't like to say anything before this, but I have a thing for bald women. Sexy, bald women with shiny heads.'

'I love you,' she'd said, pressing her lips to his stubbly face. 'I seriously love you.'

It had been harder with Sean, who hadn't known how to take it.

'Think of me as an older and wiser Sinead O'Connor,' Theo had suggested, but he hadn't smiled.

'How did you get it?'

'I was just unlucky,' she'd told him. 'My hormones let me down.'

'Will it grow back?'

'Maybe,' she'd lied. 'We'll just have to wait and see.'

'But I'm getting a wig,' she'd told both of her men.

'Fine,' Ben had said, 'as long as it's not pink. Right, Sean?'

And as soon as he'd said it, it was the only colour Theo wanted. She wasn't trying to be awkward, but suddenly a head of pink hair was all she could think about.

'What would you think of a pink wig?' she'd asked Caroline at her next visit. By now, Caroline was cutting it very short so it didn't look so thin.

'Pink.' Caroline had considered. 'Let's have a look.' She'd got a book that was filled with bunches of different coloured hair, and they'd picked out a shade that reminded Theo of the vivid Liquorice Allsorts she'd devoured through both her pregnancies.

Sean, surprisingly, had been fine with the pink hair – probably would have been happy with any colour in preference to a bald mother. And Ben had loved it.

'You should have gone pink years ago,' he'd said. 'You look like Uma Thurman.'

'She doesn't have pink hair.'

'Well, no, but remember the black in *Pulp Fiction?*'

'That doesn't make sense. You just fancy her.'

'True,' he'd admitted, 'but I'd fancy her more if she had pink hair.'

Chrissy hadn't seemed to notice, which was probably good. And after a few weeks, it was like Theo's hair had always been pink.

She'd asked Ben to tell Gemima, knowing they'd have to say something.

'It'll be better coming from you,' she'd said. 'Don't make a big thing of it, tell her I'm fine about it.' Because the last thing she wanted was for her future stepdaughter to look at her with pity.

So Ben had told Gemima, who had never once referred to it with Theo, which was exactly what Theo had been expecting. The first time Gemima saw Theo's wig she kept darting glances at it, but no mention was made.

Theo wondered afterwards how Gemima had broken the news to her mother. Had Miep laughed at the thought of Ben's new woman going bald? Did they smirk together when Gemima mentioned the pink wig?

Not that Theo cared – what was Miep to her, but the woman Ben had married when he was young and foolish, and divorced as soon as he got sense? Let them laugh, it didn't bother her in the least. Theo got a kick out of having pink hair, that was all that mattered.

But now she was ready for a change. She'd call in and talk to Caroline next week. Maybe it was time to go blonde, see how much fun they really had.

She threw the wig on the draining board and dipped her spoon into the soup and stirred, and wondered again why exactly at the age of thirty-four she'd decided to try her hand at acting.

The idea had intrigued her when she'd read the ad. The thought of walking across a stage with everyone looking at you, wearing clothes that didn't belong to you, trying to remember your lines, trying to say them as if you meant them – it all sounded like it might be a laugh.

'Do you think I'd be good at acting?' she'd asked Ben.

He hadn't batted an eyelid. 'Absolutely.'

'Really? I'm thinking of auditioning for a part in a new play.'

'What kind of a play? Is there full frontal nudity?'

She'd shown him the ad.

'I'd say go for it. As long as they don't make you the helpless victim – you'd never pull that off.'

So she'd gone, and she'd been offered a part. Who cared if the play was a bit clichéd, and the postmistress – who was bit of a cow, but not enough to get your teeth into properly – had probably the smallest part of all? She'd give it a go, and hopefully she'd enjoy it.

She wasn't sure what to make of the director. He'd done his best to put the wind up them – must be a headmaster or something by day, used to bossing everyone around – but Theo didn't scare easily.

She didn't know any of the others, apart from Caroline's ex, who she recognised from the salon – you'd remember that good-looking face. And she knew he was Caroline's ex because the friend who'd recommended Caroline to Theo had mentioned it.

He and Caroline had split up long before Theo started going to the salon, and Theo had no idea why. But she wouldn't be surprised if he was a bit of a lad – he had that look about him, the look of a man who enjoyed women.

He'd shown no sign of recognising Theo at the auditions, and she'd said nothing. No point in getting too friendly with any of them until she had them figured out.

She pulled on the wig again and left the kitchen, and immediately she heard a wail from upstairs. She stood for a minute in the hall, and when no doors opened, she put the bowl of soup on the phone table and walked towards the stairs.

Robert belched as he opened the door of Mc-Millan's. The cool evening air hit him, a welcome change from the stuffy upstairs room, and to a lesser extent from the pub itself. Drinking alone on a Thursday night – he'd pretended not to notice Edward Bull nursing a glass at a table in the opposite corner – and home to bed by himself; must be losing his touch.

He had to admit that he'd enjoyed this evening. He'd gone along with his tongue firmly in his cheek – if you looked at it in a certain light, the idea of acting in a play had a vaguely naff feel to it. He was certain he'd never have considered it if it hadn't been for Mrs Salmon.

'There was an ad in the *Herald*,' she'd told him at her six-weekly trim. 'They're looking for actors. I said to John, I bet your Robert will try out. You have an actor's face if ever I saw one. Did you never think of going for acting?'

'Never,' Robert had told her truthfully. 'I wouldn't have a clue how to act.'

'Listen, half of them don't. That fellow in *Coronation Street,* the one married to the blonde, he hasn't a notion. I wouldn't let that stop you.'

'I'm not sure I'd have the time—'

'Ah, go on with you, it said only once a week for the rehearsals. You'd have a laugh – and those boys of yours would be so proud to see their daddy on the stage.'

Robert had smiled. 'You think?'

'Of course they would – they'd love it.'

'I'll have a think about it,' he'd promised.

And he had thought about it after Mrs Salmon had left. He'd rummaged through the magazines in the salon until he'd come across a copy of *The Portmaine Herald,* and he'd flicked through the pages and found the ad.

'I'm thinking of trying out for a play,' he'd told Caroline in the staff kitchen.

She'd laughed. 'Why am I not surprised? The boys will be tickled pink.'

'Don't tell them,' he'd said quickly. 'In case I don't get it.'

'When is this happening?'

'Thursday. I'll have to leave a bit early.'

'Well,' she'd said, 'you're the boss.'

'You don't mind?'

41

'Why should I mind?'

'Because you're the boss too,' he'd pointed out. 'You could wag a finger at me and tell me I'm being very irresponsible.'

She'd smiled. 'And you'd listen, of course. Go to your play, if it keeps you happy. You can work twice as hard on Fridays to make up. And if you get the part, we'll all come and clap loudly.'

He'd liked the idea of that, the boys and Caroline sitting in the audience, watching him. He thought about it again, now that he'd landed himself a part, and found that he still liked it.

He checked his watch as he reached the car: too late to text the boys. Didn't matter, he'd see them tomorrow. He pulled his phone out of the glove compartment – maybe they'd sent him a message before they'd gone to bed. But there was no message waiting for him. He threw his script onto the passenger seat and turned the key.

Tomorrow. He could wait till then. He'd see Caroline first thing.

But as he drove out of the car park, he turned left instead of right. You turned right for the dual carriageway that led to the parade of shops behind the fire station, you turned right for his little flat above the salon. You turned left for Caroline's house.

His house, then their house, and now Caroline's house. He'd bought it eighteen years ago with a bank loan that had kept him awake for several months, until the profits in the salon had steadied enough for him to relax. It had been his house for seven years, until Caroline had joined the salon as a junior stylist, and it had taken all of five weeks for them to decide that it wasn't enough just to be together all day.

So it had become their house, where she'd missed a period almost at once, where they'd lain in bed at night and squabbled about baby names, just so they could make up afterwards. Where, eight and a half months pregnant – and enormous with the twins – she'd brought him breakfast in bed for his birthday.

Now, nine years after he'd left it to her and the boys, it was definitely Caroline's house. He didn't grudge it to her; he knew the only person to blame for his not still living there was himself. But he'd gone beyond all that – they were both past that now. They'd moved on ages ago.

He drove along the quays, saw the river sparkling with reflected streetlights. It looked much cleaner at night, when you couldn't see how brown it was. Past the new shopping centre, everyone hoping for a Marks & Spencer that hadn't arrived. Down a side street, towards a pub emptying out for the night.

As he drew nearer, a couple came through the door and turned onto the path in front of him. The man's arm slung around her shoulders, her hand in the back pocket of his jeans. It was the long strawberry-blonde hair he remembered – and yes, there was the slight limp he'd noticed as she'd walked out of McMillan's upstairs room ahead of him earlier. Her boyfriend looked a fair bit younger, hardly out of his teens.

Robert drove past them and down Caroline's street, and swung the car in through the gate and up the short drive. The light was still on in the sitting room, as he'd assumed it would be. She never went to bed before midnight.

He tapped on the window, not chancing the doorbell with the boys asleep. 'Only me,' he called softly, and a second later she appeared at the front door.

'What time d'you call this?' But she wasn't annoyed. She wore a short pale blue dress that showed off her legs. He used to tell her that he'd fallen in love with her legs first, before the rest of her.

'I was passing,' he said, 'and I just wanted to tell you that I got a part.' Silly, how pleased he was. Like his son Noah after a good hurling match.

She smiled back at him. 'Good for you. The lads'll be chuffed. Come in for a minute.' She stood back and he walked past her into the hall.

She made coffee in the kitchen she'd painted a sea green, that worked beautifully with the cream units. He stood by the breakfast bar and watched her pouring full-fat milk into her cup, scattering chocolate digestives onto a plate. Never counted a calorie, ate whatever she fancied, and not a spare ounce on her. He bet the other stylists hated that.

'So tell me,' she said, 'are you the hero or the villain?'

'I'm a famous writer who has a murder take place in his house. You'll have to wait and see whether I did it or not.'

'A famous writer.' She sipped her coffee. 'Lots of lines to learn?'

'A fair few. Haven't really had a proper read of it yet – he just got us to run through a few scenes tonight.'

'Did many turn up?'

'Loads; the place was packed.'

'Anyone we know?'

He shook his head. 'Although I thought one woman looked familiar.'

Caroline lifted an eyebrow. 'Only one?'

Robert smiled. 'Not in a social sense – I think she must work somewhere in town. I know her face from somewhere.'

Caroline took a biscuit from the plate and bit into it. 'So have you decided where you're taking my sons for the weekend?' Her running joke, claiming the boys for herself.

'I thought Dingle – they said they've never seen the dolphin.' He allowed himself one Saturday in six off, and he always took the boys on an overnight trip.

'How's the forecast?'

'Fine, I think. But we'll pack the wellies.'

'You certainly will.'

It had taken them long enough to be able to talk like this, with no bitterness, no tears. To be fair, she'd never stopped him seeing the boys, not even when she couldn't bear to look at him herself, couldn't speak to him beyond what had to be said.

And she'd come back to work at the salon eventually, when he'd offered her a partnership in the business. Still full of guilt, still trying to apologise to her.

It had been awkward at the start, the other stylists not sure how to handle it – and who could blame them? Caroline had been a junior stylist up until her maternity leave almost two years before, and now she was back in the salon as one of the bosses.

A couple of their senior stylists had left, unable to come to terms with the new arrangement, uncomfortable with having to answer to a person so much younger than themselves. But after an initial shaky few months, Caroline had developed a head for business that had surprised Robert almost as much as her ability, at twenty-two, to be a wonderful first-time mother to two babies.

He rinsed his cup in the Belfast sink. 'Better let you go to bed.'

She yawned as she stood up, showing him her perfect teeth. 'You should be in bed yourself, at your age.' Another joke, the reminder that at forty-two he was a decade older than her.

They walked towards the front door, Robert pulling his jacket on.

'See you in the morning. Thanks for the coffee.' He put a hand briefly on her arm, their only physical contact these days. 'Oh, and would you mind if I told the boys? About the play, I mean?'

She smiled. 'Of course not – I wouldn't dream of stealing your thunder. Goodnight, drive carefully.'

As he drove off, Robert was conscious of a vague dissatisfaction that had been manifesting itself at odd moments recently, and which he could find absolutely no reason for. Life was good, and he intended to enjoy what it had to offer him for as long as he could. Forty-two wasn't old – with luck, he still had years ahead of him.

He had an active social life – he was well aware that some would say it was a little too active, but he wasn't one to let the opinions of others upset him. He enjoyed the company of women, always had, and there were plenty of available partners anytime he looked for one.

He hadn't been in love for a long time, which was fine by him. He wasn't looking for love or any kind of commitment – look what had happened when he'd tried that – and why would anyone grudge him a bit of fun now and again?

And best of all, he had the boys, his two reasons for living. His heart lifted as he turned onto the dual carriageway that led back into the city centre.

He couldn't wait to tell them.

Judith opened the back door and called softly. 'Here, puss. Here, puss, puss.'

The cat wasn't hers; she thought it belonged to the young Polish family three doors down. Judith didn't even know what its name was, or whether it was male or female. She suspected that it was male from the way it devoured any food she put out – surely a female would be daintier?

But whatever the gender, Judith liked to see the cat sitting on her patio, or licking its black and white body clean on her window sill. And lately she'd taken to coaxing it inside for an hour or two before she went to bed. She enjoyed the warmth of it on her lap, the gentle vibration of its purring.

There was no sign of it tonight though – probably sitting on another lap three doors down, where it belonged. Judith closed the door and filled the kettle. She shouldn't have tea this late; she'd pay for it with at least two trips to the loo in the small hours. But she needed tea tonight.

She was parched from sitting so long in that stuffy room.

She smiled at the thought of being up on a stage again. It must be well over thirty years since she'd acted in anything. She'd joined the dramatic society in college – impatient, at eighteen, to meet someone and fall in love. (Unaware, of course, that Samuel was still almost a decade away from her.)

They'd given her a part in a comedy – a farce, really – set in a Blackpool hotel. She was the receptionist, and for most of the play she stood behind a desk at the side of the stage and answered the phone in an English accent. She still remembered practising her main line – 'Good morning, the Royal Hotel, how may I be of assistance?' – any time the phone rang in the house she shared with three others.

After that she was a housemaid in a period play, and the following year she played Agnes in *Dancing at Lughnasa*. And then college was over, and she got a job teaching history and art in a secondary school in Dublin, and gradually forgot about how exciting it was to dress up and become someone else.

But the ad had reminded her, and she'd taken a chance and gone to the auditions. Thankfully, she hadn't been the only fiftysomething there – at least half the crowd had been over forty, most of them women. But the director had chosen Judith, which had made her feel foolishly delighted.

And what a part she'd been given – Betty, the cranky but seemingly harmless housekeeper, the woman nobody really noticed, the one person nobody would ever suspect was capable of stabbing someone else through the heart with a letter opener.

The play wasn't that original, nothing to get too excited about, but Betty was by far the most interesting character. She hoped none of the others had been desperate for the housekeeper's role.

Of course the rest of the cast were all younger than her, which she'd been half expecting. Not that it really mattered. It wasn't as if she was looking for love this time round; even now, all these years later, she couldn't imagine replacing Samuel, didn't believe she could ever feel the same way about anyone else.

Her mind slid away from him – it still hurt, it would always hurt – and she went back to thinking about the group of people she'd met for the first time a few hours earlier.

The dark-haired man – Robert, was it? – holding the door open as she'd walked into the pub behind him, making some joke about the Oscars. He seemed friendly, and certainly he was handsome, but maybe just a tiny bit full of himself. She wondered what he did for a living – hadn't he said something about staying open late on Thursdays? Some kind of a business then. She could imagine him running an expensive little art gallery, charming the wealthy ladies who came in to kill an hour before lunch.

And the two sisters, with the same lovely dark brown eyes – what were their names again? She couldn't remember, had always been bad with names – not a good quality for a teacher. The older sister had been surprisingly good as the writer's sister; Judith hadn't expected the

49

haughty voice when it came.

And the other woman with the pink hair, and those purple shoes – Chloe, or Theo, something like that. Imagine being that confident that you didn't give a tuppenny damn if everyone stared at your bright pink head or laughed at your way-out shoes. She might be fun, that one.

And the young man who'd got the gardener's part – she knew him from someplace, definitely. He'd hardly opened his mouth all night, and then he'd read the part so well, he'd sounded so exactly right. He was playing himself, of course, all shy and awkward. Judith would have liked to talk to him afterwards, find out why he looked familiar, but he'd gone ahead of her down the stairs, and by the time she'd reached the door he was already pedalling off on his bicycle.

No matter. They'd have plenty of time to talk at the rehearsals. Six weeks they'd be working together – hopefully they'd all get on.

In six weeks she'd be a retired teacher. The thought was sometimes terrifying. How was she to fill the rest of her life – so big and blank from where she stood, all those hours, all those days – with worthwhile experiences that made her happy?

What now, Judith O'Sullivan? Where to now?

But there was excitement too about what might be ahead, and there was hope. And in the meantime, she intended to enjoy the next six weeks.

She thought about Edward Bull – no problem remembering that name. All fierce scowls and looking at them over his glasses, but Judith wasn't fooled. His bark was loud, but she doubted that any of them would need to worry about his bite. He'd probably rant a bit if someone was late for rehearsal, but Judith didn't anticipate any serious outbursts. Then again, she could be wrong. Time would tell.

She stood and brought her cup to the sink, and smiled out at the black and white cat on the window sill that had finally answered her call.

Theo DeCourcy, he wrote in his small, cautious writing, *playing Ursula the postmistress. No previous acting experience, good strong voice. Mother of small baby – problem?*

He always made notes, liked jotting things down as he went along. Useful sometimes to check back. He thought for a minute, and then added Hair colour, underlining it twice.

He should have said something at the auditions. What if she refused point blank to change the colour? Theo DeCourcy didn't strike him as one who'd take kindly to being told what to do, but there was no way he was having a postmistress with pink hair. He'd have to pick his words carefully – not something that came easily to him. He'd had to work hard at that when he still had a job.

He turned the page and wrote *Robert McInerney, playing Jack McCarthy the writer. No previous acting experience. Looks the part, good voice, hopefully will deliver on performance.*

He paused, then added *Mentioned Thursday late opening – problem?* Edward wasn't having latecomers, he'd made that quite clear at the auditions. He'd have to come down hard on anyone

51

who didn't show up on time next Thursday.

He turned the page and wrote *Ellen Greene, playing Dorothy the journalist. No acting experience.* He'd forgotten to ask her about the limp, or rather, he'd forgotten to get back to her about it. He'd asked and she hadn't answered. Of course, it could be gone by next Thursday; she could have just sprained her ankle or something. But if it was a permanent thing they'd need to make some reference to it, explain it to the audience. He'd have to ask her about it again, no time for sensitivities.

He wrote *Limps slightly.* He thought some more. *Good hair,* he wrote. *Has a presence.*

A presence? Where had that come from? He lifted his pen to cross it out, then lowered it. He'd written it, so he must have seen something.

He wondered if he could possibly suggest that she lose a few pounds. He imagined how his wife would have reacted to such a suggestion, and decided to say nothing. He could dress her in dark colours, although he'd imagined Dorothy all pale and innocent, to contrast more starkly with the murderous Betty.

Limps slightly, good hair, has a presence – was that it? He thought back to the auditions, heard her reading Dorothy's speech to Betty in the study, the pivotal speech of the play. How the others had all listened, how you could have heard a pin drop. He wrote *Fluent reader.*

Wonderful. Just what he needed on the stage in a little over six weeks' time: a bunch of fluent readers.

He got up and crossed to the far end of the room, the part that an estate agent, trying his best, would probably call the kitchenette. He reached into the nearer of the two presses attached to the wall and pulled a three-quarters empty bottle of brandy from behind a bag of porridge.

His drink in the pub after the auditions had been spoiled somewhat by the danger of Robert McInerney turning around at any moment and spotting him. Edward Bull didn't do small talk, particularly with people he'd only just met, and who he hoped to maintain some kind of distance from as their director.

He poured a measure and went back to the notebook and wrote *Judith O'Sullivan, playing Betty the housekeeper. Shows promise.*

She'd been surprisingly good. He hadn't been expecting that from her. As she'd read, she'd seemed to intuit Betty's personality, begun to inhabit the housekeeper's character. And in the scene with Dorothy in the study, when she'd picked up the letter opener and stabbed the journalist who'd threatened to disgrace her, she'd had exactly the right tension in her voice, she'd got it spot on. She was Betty, his only possible choice.

He wrote *Previous acting experience.* She'd told him that it was years ago when she was in college, but no matter. She'd stood on a stage, she knew what it felt like to perform.

He remembered something suddenly, and wrote *Offered to paint backdrops.* Apparently she taught art in the comprehensive – funny, he wouldn't have taken her for a teacher. A librarian he'd have said, if someone had asked him to guess.

He turned the page and wrote *Harry Buckley, no acting experience.* Not bad as the gardener though, suited the part. The right note of timidity in the voice, even brought in a little stutter, which Edward had liked. As long as he managed to learn his lines and didn't go to pieces on opening night, he should be OK. He wrote *Warn him not to cut hair.* That awful shaggy look was just right for bumbling Tom.

Who was left? Oh, yes. *Maria Talty, no acting experience.* He thought about Maria, the older sister and the quieter of the two. He wondered what had brought her to the auditions – he couldn't imagine it had been her idea. Possibly dragged along by the bossy younger sister. Not that it mattered why she'd come. He felt she'd make a good Penelope. She'd manage the right mix of reserve and vulnerability.

Good diction, he wrote. *Work on posture.* She hunched her shoulders a bit, he'd have to knock that out of her. His Penelope would need to be ramrod straight.

He closed the notebook and put down his pen and ran a hand through his hair. He took off his glasses and massaged his temples and then pressed the heels of his palms to his eyes. Enough for now. There was nothing more he could do till he saw them at the first rehearsal.

He wondered how many of them would have the lines of act one learnt by next Thursday, like he'd suggested. He hadn't missed the looks of disbelief that had passed between them. He'd discover soon enough how many of them were really committed to this play.

He picked up his glass and took a sip, enjoying the fierce heat of the brandy going down. Remembering the night, just over a year ago now, he'd sat in his father-in-law's study, drinking brandy from a crystal balloon and listening to the older man telling him what a fool he was.

'Bull by name, bull by nature,' Cathal had said to him. 'Can't you let it go, Edward, for Christ's sake? My daughter made one mistake in twenty years, let it go. You're not perfect yourself.'

'I didn't cheat on her,' Edward had told him. 'I didn't fool around with the man who came to landscape the garden.' The words left a bad taste in his mouth. He washed it away with brandy. 'I was never unfaithful,' he'd said.

He'd moved out. Cathal had done his best to change his mind, but Edward was adamant. He was deaf to Sophie's apologies, blind to her tears.

'You keep the house,' he'd told her, although he was the one who'd paid the mortgage, she'd never contributed a cent to it. 'I don't want it. I don't want anything to do with you ever again.'

'Edward,' she'd wept, but he was deaf and blind and would not be moved.

He'd walked away from his job too. How could he go on working for her father?

'Don't be stupid, Edward,' Cathal had said. 'You're a year away from being made a full partner – don't throw that away too.'

'I can't stay,' Edward had told him. 'No hard feelings.'

There *had* been hard feelings – there had been plenty of those – but Cathal had been decent to him. He'd insisted on paying Edward a generous lump sum, despite Edward's protests that he didn't need it – which of course Cathal knew, having been the one who'd advised Edward to invest so wisely in the nineties.

'Take it,' he'd ordered. 'Call it early retirement, if you must. Come back if you change your mind,' he'd told Edward. 'There'll always be a job here for you.'

But they had both known that that wasn't going to happen. Bull by nature.

Now, for the first time in his life, forty-four-year-old Edward Bull was living alone, in the granny flat attached to his eighty-six-year-old Uncle Rory's house. Rory had offered the place when Edward had officially become homeless, and Edward had been happy to accept it as a stopgap while he found another house, or maybe an apartment. Just give him a month or two to take stock and get his bearings, and he'd start looking around.

'No rush,' Rory had said. 'Yours for as long as you want it. No good to me, never use it.'

'A few months,' Edward had promised. 'That's all I need.'

But that had been over a year ago, and he was still there. A month or two had become six – it had taken long enough just to straighten up the place, not inhabited since Rory's brother had died seventeen years before – and with each further day and week and month that passed, the business of finding somewhere else to live became more and more of an obstacle course in Edward's head.

The thought of trawling through estate agents' catalogues, traipsing through other people's messy lives, negotiating with solicitors and surveyors and prices – all this filled him with increasing dread.

And anyway, why move? Hadn't Rory said it was no use to him? Mightn't his uncle actually be glad to have someone so close? Wasn't it almost Edward's duty, as Rory's relative, to keep an eye on the older man?

His days took on a different shape. He spent longer in bed in the mornings, half listening to the harmless chatter of radio talk shows. He stayed up later, watching films and documentaries and reruns of the few comedies he'd been able to tolerate first time round. He ate less and drank more – a bottle of brandy hadn't lasted him a week for some time now.

Every Tuesday he took his uncle out for dinner to Gerry's Steak House on the next street, and every Friday he walked up the crazy paving path that linked his granny flat with Rory's house, and ate the simple meal Rory cooked for him.

He read every page of the daily paper and walked by the river on dry days, and occasionally met a friend or two for a drink, and twice a month or so he went fishing alone, because the man who'd introduced him to the joys of sitting by a riverbank with a rod in his hand was Sophie's sister's husband.

Edward never thought about the future, never questioned whether he was truly happy. Why bother with all that, why rock the boat? He'd made his choices and now he was living with them. Money wasn't an issue – his various investments yielded enough dividends to keep him comfortable. He sent Sophie a monthly cheque with no covering note, which she never cashed.

Sophie didn't need his money, with her share of the family business.

And then, a little over a month ago, a longtime friend had called around to the granny flat with a bottle of brandy and asked Edward, somewhere around their third glass, to direct his son's first play.

'You'd be doing us a favour,' the friend had said, not meeting Edward's slightly bloodshot eye, not letting his gaze fall on the tumble of dishes in the stainless steel sink. 'I thought of you,' he'd said, 'because I remembered how you used to love directing, you were bloody good at it. And Jonathan would be thrilled.'

He was William Crosby, managing director of Portmaine's biggest employer, the US-owned Carran Computers. He probably earned three times Edward's former salary. Uncle Rory's granny flat would fit easily into his conservatory.

William Crosby hadn't said 'This is my attempt to get you back on your feet.' But he may as well have. They'd both heard it.

And remembering the group of them setting up The Portmaine Players in their early twenties, the productions put on in damp school halls and dingy community centres, the props and costumes begged or borrowed, the terrifying thrill of first nights, the drunken parties after the set had finally been struck, Edward Bull, ex-undertaker, found himself agreeing to cast and direct Jonathan Crosby's first play.

And now he was trying very hard not to regret that decision.

He brought his empty glass over to the sink. He

opened the door that led off the living room into the tiny bedroom. He took off his clothes and dropped them on the floor; who was going to complain? He walked naked into the even smaller bathroom and regarded himself in the mirror above the sink.

You're no oil painting, he told himself. Dark, receding hair sweeping back from a wide forehead, lines carved into the skin, scoring pathways from nose to chin, scribbling out from his eyes.

Craggy, Sophie called his face. 'Sexy,' she'd said. 'Like Billy Bob Thornton. Very manly. Very rugged.' Pulling none too gently on his chest hair. 'My caveman,' she'd said, grabbing him where every man wanted to be grabbed. 'Service your woman.'

He pulled open the door of the shower cubicle and stepped inside.

Maria Talty

She stood at the sink holding the wrong peanut butter, and she listened to her husband taking the shell off his boiled egg.

Two raps, always two, the spoon held between finger and thumb by the very end of its handle, and then the softer sound of shell being picked off as he piled the pieces into a heap on the table until the entire egg sat exposed, creamy white and shiny, the eggcup she always put out ignored.

The whisper of salt being scattered, and then

59

the tiny rubbery slither of his teeth breaking through the white, the slurp as he caught the oozing yolk.

Maria unscrewed the top of the peanut butter jar and reached for the tea strainer hanging on a small hook beside the sink.

From his chair, Pat said, 'Mah?'

'Coming, lovie.'

She spooned peanut butter into the strainer and pushed it through with the back of the spoon, trapping the small nutty pieces and letting the smooth worms of paste plop onto the plate underneath. She took a knife and spread the peanut butter carefully over each of the three waiting cream crackers, every corner covered. 'Just coming now.'

She must have been miles away, picking up the wrong jar in the supermarket, not noticing the red label instead of the blue. She put the plate in front of Pat, praying that no bit of peanut had slipped through. If he came across even one, the tiniest fragment, that would be it.

'Now, darling. Eat every bit, OK?'

Pat picked up a cracker and held it to his nose. He always reminded Maria of a cat, the way he sniffed at everything before eating it.

She sat opposite Michael and raised her cup of half cold tea as he swallowed the last mouthful of egg and began spreading butter on a slice of her homemade brown bread.

'What time are you back?' She made him talk when Pat was there. Pat needed to hear conversation.

He shrugged. 'Six or half, the usual.' He reached

for the little bowl of marmalade and stuck his knife in, paying no heed to the spoon.

'It's cold this morning.'

'Mmm.'

Somebody was talking softly on the radio. Michael insisted on *Morning Ireland* at breakfast, but always so low that you couldn't hear it. On her own, Maria would have Lyric on, louder. She'd hum along if something she knew came on. Her mother used to tell her she had a sweet voice.

Pat took a tiny bite of his cream cracker, scattering crumbs. Michael glanced across at his son.

Maria said quickly, 'I got a part in the play last night.'

He'd been asleep when she got home. He hadn't moved when she'd pulled back the blankets and slid in beside him.

'Did you?' He held out his cup and she lifted the teapot and poured. 'How often will you be gone to that?'

'Once a week only. Thursday evenings for a couple of hours.' She wouldn't mention the extra ones in the last week; time enough for that. 'Pat will be in bed before I go.'

She'd have to have him in bed by seven, earlier than he was used to. She'd coax him up with a Kit Kat.

She still couldn't believe she'd been given a part in the play. All through the auditions she'd been horribly nervous, her stomach clenching as she'd listened to the others reading. Her hands almost glued together, she'd squeezed them that tightly as she'd waited in dread for the ordeal of her turn.

61

When it had come she'd had to force herself to read the lines, her voice sounding so false to her, not like her normal voice at all – which apparently was exactly what the director was looking for, because amazingly, she'd been offered the part of Penelope.

And the other people he'd chosen, that woman with the pink wig – it had to be a wig – she sounded like a right bossy boots. And the man who thought he was God's gift – she was glad she was playing his sister and not anyone who'd have to flirt with him.

The woman who'd got the housekeeper's part seemed OK, and the blonde, boyish-looking man who'd been picked for the gardener.

Maria wasn't sure what to make of Edward. She hoped he wouldn't start shouting at her if she forgot her lines. Ellen would be well able for anything like that, but Maria would hate it.

'Mah.'

She looked up. Pat was holding out his mug.

'Here, love.' As she picked up the milk jug, Michael pushed back his chair.

'Time to go.'

She poured milk, feeling the anger running through her. 'Just a second, he's nearly ready.' *Give your son two minutes to finish his breakfast, you miserable bastard.*

Imagine if she screamed it out loud at him. Imagine the satisfaction of that.

She smiled at Pat, pushing away her anger. 'Hurry up now pet, Daddy's waiting.'

Pat brought the mug to his mouth and gulped the milk noisily. Maria watched the small Adam's apple bobbing with the swallows, and wanted to let the tears pour out of her.

'Good boy.' A dribble of milk crawled from the corner of his mouth down to his chin, but she knew better than to go near it.

Standing at the path waving them off, Pat looking solemnly out at her, she watched till the Land Rover had turned the corner. She imagined the quiet journey, not a word between them. He never spoke to Pat except to give out.

He'd been so happy when his son was born, more attentive to her in the weeks following the birth than he'd been while they were going out together, while he was working up to his proposal.

'You're a fine-looking woman,' he'd told her then, and even though she knew it wasn't true, that the best you could say about her was that everything was in the right place, she liked hearing what nobody had ever said to her before.

'I'll treat you right,' he'd said, and anyone would say that he had. The fancy house with two en suites and a conservatory and a utility room bigger than her mother's kitchen. The bookshop, his present to her after they were married. 'Give you an interest,' he'd said. 'Something to occupy yourself.' The piano that he'd arranged to have moved from her parents' house into his, a week before the wedding.

But the big house was without charm, the fancy dining room used only on the mercilessly few occasions when Michael decided they needed to entertain his business associates, whose wives made small talk with Maria and criticised her choice of furniture with perfectly made-up eyes.

And the little bookshop was a tax break, bought as much for him as for her, even though it was in her name. Not that she didn't enjoy it, even if it barely ticked over, even if she just about managed to pay Oliver every week. Like music, it was her refuge every day, her escape from a life she hadn't seen coming.

But more than everything else, the piano was her salvation. The small back room that housed it, which Michael had used as a store room before his marriage, got little daylight and looked out on the least interesting part of the garden, but it was where she and Pat spent most of their free time, leaving the sitting room with its television and coal effect gas fire and curved bay window to Michael.

She'd bought a beanbag for Pat, and when he refused to have any of his bedroom toys moved, she'd assembled an identical collection in what she privately called the music room. There the two of them would go every day, after she'd collected him from her parents' house and wheeled him home in his buggy, and Maria would play Chopin and Beethoven until it was time to make dinner, and Pat would lie on his beanbag and run a hand over the spiky, rubbery hair of his Bart Simpson doll, or roll the wheels on his red car.

Michael hated her using the buggy 'He's four, he's well able to walk. Everyone is laughing at you.'

But on this, Maria was uncharacteristically adamant. 'It's well over a mile, too long a walk for him. He'd be exhausted.'

'It's ridiculous, going to school and still in a buggy.'

64

Why do you care? she wanted to say. *He's nothing to you. You disowned him the day you found out he wasn't perfect. What does it matter to you whether he sits in a buggy or walks?*

It was the way Pat didn't look at you that she'd noticed first, when he was still a baby and she'd say his name softly and he'd never turn his head towards the sound, never respond like all the other babies in her La Leche group.

'I think there's something wrong with Pat,' she'd told Michael.

'What, is he sick?' he'd asked. 'Has he a temperature?'

'No, but I just feel he's not right.'

'Is he eating?'

'Well, yes, but–'

'He's grand. Stop fussing.'

When nothing had changed by the time he was one, she thought he might be deaf. Without saying anything to Michael, she'd brought him to the paediatrician, but he'd passed the hearing test.

'It might be nothing. They all develop at different rates,' the doctor had told her.

'He never points at things,' Maria had said. 'He never babbles or smiles. He doesn't respond to his name.'

The doctor had nodded. 'It's still very early. We need to–'

'Isn't there another test you can do?' She hadn't cared about interrupting him; manners hadn't come into it. 'Can't you check for ... anything else?'

Autism, she'd wanted to say. According to the websites she'd looked at, Pat had all the early warning signs, but she hadn't been able to say it.

'Unfortunately, the systems aren't yet in place to test someone as young as Pat,' the doctor had told her gently. 'I can see you're worried–'

'We can go privately. We can pay whatever it costs.'

'It's not a matter of money, I'm afraid.' The doctor had paused. 'Look, I'll write to the HSE, put your case forward. That's really all I can do, but try not to get your hopes up.'

While she'd waited to hear what the Health Board would say, Maria had watched Pat. She'd watched him lying in his cot, staring at nothing on the ceiling. She'd seen him sitting on the floor by the wall, running his finger along a tiny crack in the plaster, up and down, up and down, over and over. He'd do it for hours, if he was left there.

She'd watched him lining up his toy cars on the dressing table, pushing and poking them until they were exactly the way he wanted. Always the red one in front, the green always at the end.

She'd tried introducing him to new foods, but he'd refused everything except cream crackers and smooth peanut butter – shrieking loudly when she tried to substitute crunchy – mashed potato occasionally, and now and again a banana with perfect yellow skin.

She'd felt how he pulled away when she picked him up, how he turned his head when she tried to kiss him.

'Don't you see?' she'd asked Michael. 'He's not right. Something is wrong, I know it is.'

Michael had shrugged. 'He's quiet alright and he's a bloody fussy eater, you give in to him too much there – but I can't see anything to worry about. He's an only child; maybe if he had a brother or sister.'

He turned to her in bed and lifted her night-dress about twice a week, and she opened her legs and let him climb on top of her, listening for Pat, who was a poor sleeper. Michael's hand on her breast didn't arouse her, or the feel of him as he pushed his way into her. She assumed she wasn't highly sexed, and accepted it like she had accepted his proposal.

She'd rung the doctor once a week, and when he still hadn't heard back from the HSE after six weeks she'd rung them directly, and was eventually told that Pat's case was pending, and that her GP would be notified in due course. Three months later, Pat's case was still pending.

By the time Pat was two, he still hadn't spoken one word, and Michael had begun to avoid spending time with him. The day after his birthday, Maria had taken him in a taxi to the HSE offices.

She'd walked up to the reception desk and said, 'My name is Maria Talty. I'd like to get my child tested for autism.' She'd gone beyond being afraid of the word. Now she was more afraid of not knowing.

The receptionist had run a finger along a page in front of her. 'Do you have an appointment?'

'No.'

'I'm sorry, you need to go through your GP. If you–'

'I went through my GP a year ago, he wrote to you and phoned you and nothing happened. I want my child tested for autism.'

The receptionist had heard the stone in her voice and had reached for the phone on her desk. 'If you'd just take a seat in the waiting room, Mrs ... Talty, I'll see if someone can see you.'

Maria had stood where she was. 'I'm not going to be fobbed off. I'm not leaving here today until I get a date for my child to be tested.'

A tiny frown had appeared between the receptionist's over-plucked eyebrows. 'All I can do is get someone to talk to you. Please take a seat and I'll see who's available.'

Maria hadn't moved. 'I'd rather wait here.' Pat's hand, as always, had been flaccid in hers.

The receptionist's expression hadn't changed. She'd pressed three buttons on the phone and after a minute she'd said, 'I've got a lady here who needs to talk to someone.' She'd listened. 'It's difficult to explain—'

Maria had said loudly, 'Tell them I want my child tested for autism.' Beside her Pat had squirmed and Maria had loosened her grip slightly on his hand.

The receptionist had listened again, said, 'Right,' and hung up. 'Someone will be with you soon,' she'd told Maria. 'Why don't you sit down now?'

'Thank you,' Maria had said. She'd turned and walked with Pat into the empty little room off the lobby and had sat there pretending to read *Hello* until a woman in a navy suit had appeared in the doorway.

'Mrs Talty?'

Two months later, what the HSE called a multi-disciplinary team had begun testing Pat. Over the following several weeks, he'd been seen by a clinical psychologist, a speech and language therapist and an occupational therapist. Maria had attended, and had often contributed to, each diagnostic session, but Michael had not.

'You'd no right going behind my back,' he'd raged at her. 'I'm not having them putting a label on him, that'll go against him everywhere.'

'We have to know what's wrong with him,' she'd insisted. 'We have to find out so he can get the help he needs.'

But Michael had refused to have anything to do with the process. By then he was barely speaking to Pat, and he'd begun to withdraw from her too.

Except in bed, where he still silently claimed her body every few nights, and she lay beneath him, eyes closed.

Eventually, when Pat was almost three – and still not talking, apart from calling Maria 'Mah' and grunting a little – he'd been diagnosed as falling within the autism spectrum.

'It's not a mental illness, it's a communication disorder,' they'd told her. 'It wasn't caused by anything you did, or neglected to do. It's nobody's fault – and it's not the end of the world. It just means that Pat isn't the child you expected him to be. He's physically and mentally healthy,' they'd said, 'but he has difficulty relating to the world around him in a way that is considered normal.'

'What can I do?' she'd asked. I, not we. By then she'd known she was on her own.

'You can send him to a school with an autism unit,' they'd said. 'There are two in the city. Or he can attend a mainstream school and they can apply to get him a Special Needs Assistant who'll work with him in the classroom.'

And so far, Pat was coping well in the unit she'd managed to get him into the previous September. He was with one other child his own age and a few slightly older ones. Each child had his own brightly painted cubicle, and there was a central area where they sometimes worked together.

The four teachers seemed perfectly at ease handling their young charges, and the head teacher had assured Maria when she'd made enquiries that everything possible would be done to help Pat.

'It's great that you got him diagnosed so young,' she'd told Maria. 'That doesn't happen a lot – most children don't come to us until they're six or seven.'

'I had to do a bit of persuading.'

After the first week, when Maria had taken Pat by taxi every morning and helped him to settle in, she'd asked Michael to drive him.

'You pass it going to work,' she'd pointed out. 'You wouldn't have to go out of your way.'

They might bond if there was a daily routine. He might talk to Pat, try and get closer to him.

'It's daft me getting a taxi when you're passing the door,' she'd said. 'It might be hard to explain,' she'd said, 'if any of your colleagues ever saw me.'

And of course he'd agreed then, as she'd known he would, anxious to keep up the façade of the perfect family man. So every morning he drove Pat to school, and Maria waited for a change in the father–son relationship, but nothing happened.

Her parents collected Pat from the unit every afternoon and brought him to their house, just a few streets away, and looked after him until Maria picked him up when she left the shop at four. One of the perks of being the boss was that she could set her own working hours, so Oliver opened the bookshop at half nine and closed at half five, and Maria arrived at ten and left at four.

She checked her watch now as a tousle-headed man cycled past, jacket tails flying out behind him, and then she hurried back inside to wash the breakfast dishes.

Harry Buckley

'You never emptied the cart.'

Harry was halfway out of his jacket. 'Pardon?'

'The cart,' Linda said impatiently. 'You were last out yesterday and you should have emptied it. Last out always empties the cart.'

'I know that.' He hung up his jacket. 'I was in a bit of a rush, I must have forgotten. Sorry.'

Linda said nothing as he pulled off his bicycle clips.

'It's no big deal,' Harry said. 'I'll do it now.'

'Don't bother – it's done.' She swept past him with a bundle of magazines. 'I did it when I got in.'

Harry watched her arranging the magazines on the rotating display stand beside the desk. So what if he hadn't emptied the damn cart? It was the last job of the evening, just before they closed

71

up. Did she think someone was going to break into the library in the middle of the night and look for a book that couldn't be found because it was still sitting on the cart?

It had probably taken her ten minutes to put them back on the shelves when she'd come in. The twelve-hour delay wouldn't have put in or out on anyone. It was the first time Harry had forgotten to do it, but she had to make a big deal out of it, had to make it sound like yet another disaster caused by her imbecile co-worker.

He imagined her face if he told her he'd got a part in a play the night before.

'I'm going to be a gardener,' he'd say, and she'd look blankly at him because they never chatted, never exchanged any kind of personal information, and she wouldn't know what to do with it.

He stowed the bicycle clips in his jacket pocket, logged on to the computer and began checking e-mails.

The graze had darkened overnight, there was a tenderness in his palm and a slight ache in his hip when he walked, but otherwise his tumble from the bike hadn't done damage.

People came up to the desk as he worked and he stamped books and located authors, added names to the waiting list and took bookings for the computers and language lab.

Linda came and went from the desk area. Harry could smell her lavender perfume as she moved around. He used to like the smell of lavender; he remembered pulling sprigs from the bush at the back of the house as a child and crushing them between his fingers, and holding his hands up to his face. Now it made him feel slightly queasy, in the same way as eating a whole packet of Jaffa cakes would.

At eleven o'clock he stood up and stretched. 'I'm putting on the kettle,' he said to Linda, at the children's shelves. 'Do you want a cup?'

'Yes please.'

She made tea for herself at least twice a day and never once asked Harry if he'd like a cup. He always offered if he was making it, and she always said yes. But life was too short to let that kind of thing upset you.

In the kitchen he put two tea bags into the pot and folded his arms as he waited for the kettle to boil. Tomorrow was Saturday; he must remember the grapes on the way home. Purple, Ma didn't care for the green ones. And make sure to get seedless this time.

He thought back to his conversation with Babs a few nights ago. As soon as he'd mentioned his idea, she'd thrown cold water on it.

'Harry, she's in no fit state to be taken out, not even to a private house, and certainly not to a restaurant. Look, I can't possibly make the day itself, in the middle of the week, but I'll be up the Sunday after and I'll bring a cake, and well have a bit of a party in the nursing home, the three of us. Wouldn't that be much more practical?'

And when Harry hadn't backed down, the rising anger in her voice. 'Have you any idea how ridiculous you're being, are you mad?'

Harry had stuck to his guns. 'She'll be seventy-five – I want to mark it.'

'Well, of *course* we'll mark it, there's no *question*

of that, but your idea is just plain crazy – no way would Ma be able for it.'

She must have been in touch with Charlie that same night. She must have got one of her boys to e-mail him in Hong Kong, because the following morning, when Harry had logged on, there'd been a message waiting for him.

Harry, you've really upset Babs, Charlie had written. *I know you mean well, but you must see that it's out of the question, Babs says Ma wouldn't be able at all for an outing like that. Bring her a nice present instead, what about fancy chocolates? Or maybe a few books on tape, you'd be able to find good ones through the library, wouldn't you?*

Charlie would send Ma a nice present from Hong Kong. Perfume that she'd never wear, or jewellery that would sit on top of her locker till somebody took a shine to it, knowing that Ma would never look for it, that she'd have forgotten it had ever arrived.

Four years she'd been living in that nursing home, sleeping in the same narrow bed in the room she shared with Pauline now. Before Pauline it was Christine, who'd died of pneumonia, and before that – who? The woman with the shakes, who never closed the door when she went out – that used to drive Ma mad.

Harry was twenty-five when Ma was put in the home. By then, Da had been gone fourteen years, dropping like a stone one afternoon in the sitting room when Harry was eleven. Dead before he hit the ground, the doctor had said. After that it was just Harry and Ma, Babs and Charlie having both left home years before.

Babs was thirty-three when Da died, married to Tony and living in Mayo with their two children. Charlie was thirty-one, working in an Italian bank in Dublin. Before Da's funeral, he hadn't been home since Harry's eighth birthday.

Harry didn't recognise the man in the grey suit who'd put a hand on his shoulder in the hushed kitchen and said, 'Hey, bro, you OK?' The woman who'd arrived with Charlie was tall with a navy coat and shiny shoes with long, pointy toes. She'd ruffled Harry's hair and called him hon. Harry had met her just once before, when Charlie had married her in Dublin. He couldn't remember her name.

Ma was forty-six when Harry was born, Da fifty-two. There was a twenty-year gap between the births of their first and second sons.

'You were our surprise,' Ma told Harry. 'You surprised the life out of us. Charlie and Babs didn't know what to make of you.'

The kettle began to sing and Harry bent to take the carton of milk from the fridge. He didn't think it was mad to want to take our mother out for a birthday meal. Even if she was a bit scattered, even if she got things a bit muddled sometimes She was nearly seventy-five – of course she'd get confused, naturally she would.

Babs hadn't called Harry back since their last phone conversation. She probably assumed the e-mail from Charlie would have made him see sense. Charlie hadn't sent a follow-up mail, even though Harry had ignored the first one. He'd have assumed that Harry would take his advice, he'd probably phoned Babs and told her it was all sorted. They'd have joked a bit, maybe, about how clueless their baby brother was. So sure, both of them, that Harry's plan was outlandish, that it hadn't a hope of working. So convinced that Ma wouldn't be able for a treat.

But what if it really perked her up? What if she smiled at Harry across the restaurant table and called him by his right name, and said this was a wonderful idea? What if that was all she needed, a bit of a change, a decent meal instead of that nursing home food?

And a cake. He was going to get the restaurant to bring out a cake after dinner, a lemon sponge like the ones she used to bake for his birthdays. He'd get a pack of candles for them to put on top. They might sing happy birthday. Other people, at other tables, might join in. Ma would love that, a bit of a fuss made.

The water in the kettle bubbled, and Harry filled the teapot and carried the tray out to the reception desk.

Linda looked up and said, 'You haven't sent out the rest of the reminder postcards yet.'

Ellen Greene

Her toothbrush was wet. She hated when they used her toothbrush.

But at least he hadn't made a fuss when she'd shaken him awake at eight – he'd been out the door by twenty past, after a quick repeat

76

performance of the night before, which most of them looked for. She hadn't offered breakfast – that wasn't part of the deal – and he hadn't asked for a phone number, which saved her having to make one up.

Although he'd been quite sweet, compared to some of them.

She rinsed the toothbrush in scalding water and cleaned her teeth and tongue. She pulled off the socks she always wore when she shared her bed, and tucked her hair into a flowery plastic cap. She stood under the shower and spread gel onto an exfoliating glove and scrubbed all over, until every inch of her tingled. She patted herself dry and applied moisturiser and body lotion. Then she sat in front of her dressing table mirror and made herself up, very slowly and carefully.

She had to look nice for Danny.

She ate breakfast in her dressing gown, the usual half a grapefruit and two crispbreads with a tomato sliced on top. As she ate, standing by the window, she watched a thrush hopping along the old stone wall at the end of the garden.

Afterwards she threw the clothes from last night into the laundry basket and dressed in her grey trouser suit and black pumps, and pulled her hair into a pale green slide and sprayed perfume on her wrists and cleavage.

On her way downstairs she passed Mrs Carmody coming up.

'Morning,' Ellen said, knowing there wouldn't be an answer. Mrs Carmody hadn't spoken a word to her since she'd knocked on Ellen's door one day, a couple of months after Ellen had moved into the building, and asked her if she was planning to make a habit of bringing home strange men, because they weren't living in that kind of place. Ellen had told her to mind her own bloody business and slammed the door in her face.

Mr Carmody was much nicer. He didn't seem to mind how many men Ellen brought home – although he didn't look at her if he was with his wife, which Ellen understood.

The sky was cloudy. She should have brought her umbrella. In the flower shop she asked for a single white rose, and when she walked out the rain had begun. She stood in the doorway and decided to give it five minutes to go away again.

A woman swept past, head bowed, and turned into the charity shop two doors up. She wore red shoes and one of her hands was clamped to the bright green scarf wrapped around her head. What Ellen could see of her looked vaguely familiar.

Derek hadn't questioned her dental appointment. He hadn't questioned her doctor's appointment last year, nor whatever excuse she'd given him the year before that. Ellen was certain he didn't notice that she always had a reason for not going to work on the morning of the twenty-fifth of April.

'I'll be in by twelve,' she'd told him yesterday and he'd just nodded.

She always went in the morning because she didn't want to risk meeting Danny's parents, couldn't face his mother's forced small talk, his father's silence. And evenings wouldn't do because the cemetery closed at five from October till May.

She visited Danny at other times, of course. She went regularly in the summer, when the graves were bright with potted plants and vases of flowers and the cemetery hummed pleasantly with bees, even if the sun didn't shine all that much.

She went in winter too, with the frost silvering the granite slabs and the grass crunching under her boots, but not as often. It was much lonelier in winter, he felt further from her.

The rain eased and she set off, walking briskly up the hill and beyond the city council offices, down to the river and past the hospital, round the corner to where the road forked, with the big grey church in the angle of the fork and the cemetery stretching out behind it.

She pushed the white iron gate and it moved in stiff jerks, scattering water onto her shoes, reluctantly allowing her in. She made her way along the gravel paths until she came to where Danny lay.

She squatted and put the rose in front of his gravestone. She ran a finger over the raised letters, knowing the terrible words by heart. She closed her eyes and remembered. She didn't want to remember, but she had to.

The twenty-fifth of April, six days before his twenty-third birthday. An unexpectedly warm Saturday, only the wispiest clouds scattered across the pale blue sky. She was home from college for the weekend, and they decided to spend the day on the beach, forty miles away.

She had a new bikini, blue and white stripes. Her mother warned her not to stay in the water. 'It's only April, even if it feels warm.'

Her father reminded her to wear her helmet,

although they knew she always did, although they trusted Danny not to go mad on the bike.

They stopped on the way and bought rolls and sliced ham and a giant bag of tortilla chips and a litre of water. They'd gone another ten miles or so when it happened.

A van coming towards them veered suddenly onto the wrong side of the road, too late for Danny to react. Danny shouting something she couldn't make out – the heartbreak, the heartbreak of that afterwards, of never knowing what his last words to her had been.

Ellen clutching him tighter, pushing her face into his leather jacket, not wanting to see as the van headed straight for them–

And after that, nothing. No memory of what came next – had she been conscious, had he died in her arms? – until she woke in an unfamiliar bed with clean white sheets, her parents and Maria standing around her, looking exhausted.

'Where's Danny?' Cracked, hoarse words. Her mother's face collapsing, her father squeezing her hand. 'Where?'

In the end, in tears, Maria had told her, the only one of them able to say it. Ellen pushing her away, shaking her head in horror, calling her sister a liar, trying to scream, trying to get up–

The driver of the van died that day too. No heart attack, no alcohol or drugs in his system, so they could only suppose that he'd fallen asleep at the wheel. Thirty-seven, with five children. Not that Ellen cared in the least. Not that it mattered who else had died.

No, that wasn't true. She hated him. Her hatred flooded through her, scalded her. She was glad he was dead.

She was lucky. Everyone told her how lucky she was. A deep wound high on her outer thigh that left a rippled kidney-shaped scar, even after the skin graft. A wide ribbon of cuts and grazes along her right side. Two toes on her right foot amputated, too badly crushed by the impact to survive. Learning to walk again, to find her balance with a mutilated foot. No more sandals for her, no more barefoot runs on the beach.

But she was lucky.

Her grief was immense. She spent a month in hospital staring at the ceiling, picking at food that tasted of nothing, just to silence the coaxing voices of the nurses. Nights were desperate struggles to stay awake, because sleep brought her back to the horror of that sunny country road, to the parts her conscious mind refused to remember.

And from the hospital, she was taken straight to the other place. Profound depression, her doctor called it. A danger to herself, he told her parents. So she sat in an armchair for another three months, with a book open in her lap to keep away the other road accident victims and the cancer survivors and the transplant patients who thought the silent young woman might like some company.

She took the pills the nurses gave her in little paper cups, she told the psychiatrist what he wanted to hear. She ate what she could – the food was slightly more tolerable, but still she was never hungry for it. She put one foot in front of another whenever they asked her to. She kept her nighttime devils away with more pills.

And then one day, almost four months after the

accident, she was deemed well enough to leave, and her father arrived to take her home. Her mother and Maria were standing at the front door when the car turned into the driveway, roast chicken came out of the oven for Ellen.

Her room was just as she remembered it, when she used to live there a million light years ago. When she was happy.

It was awful. They were all horribly, falsely bright, like she was someone with dementia who had to be humoured, like they were afraid she was going to go off and slit her wrists unless they kept up the incessant, inane conversation.

Danny wasn't mentioned, which made her feel both relieved and enraged. She couldn't have borne them talking about him, but she hated that he seemed scrubbed out of their collective memories.

Living under the same roof, they may as well have been on a different planet to her. She could never let them see the extent of her grief, the endless, bottomless pit of it. She knew they didn't understand that life hadn't just stopped for Danny on that country road.

The first time she visited his grave, the day after she came home, she insisted on going alone. Her parents tried hard to change her mind, but Ellen was determined.

'I'll go,' Maria said. 'I'll wait at the gate.'

'No.' How could she explain? She hardly understood it herself, the urge she had to do this by herself. 'I'll be fine,' she said. 'It's OK, really.'

Her mother opened her mouth to argue again, and then thought better of it. Ellen limped into a taxi and told the driver to take her to the cemetery.

She'd missed the funeral, which she regarded now as a mixed blessing. She should have been there – but how could she have survived that last goodbye to him, the sight of his coffin on the grass, the thought of him lying inside, waiting to be put into the ground?

His grave was marked with a small temporary cross that just gave his name and the date of his death. She knew where to look, beside the grandparents whose plot she'd visited with him every Christmas.

She stood there, numb, until a man crunched across the gravel towards her and told her gently that he had to lock up. Back home she couldn't talk to them, couldn't eat. She lay on her bed and wondered despairingly how long this hell would last.

Maria tried, sometimes, to get through.

'Do you feel like going to see a film?' she'd ask, or 'Want to come shopping? The sales are on,' and while Ellen appreciated her efforts, she couldn't respond, couldn't pull herself out of the place she lived in now, where the past was all that mattered.

At night she lay in her single bed and remembered the first time she'd met Danny. They were both thirteen. He went to the Christian Brothers, down the road from her convent school. She knew one of his friends slightly, a twin brother of a girl in her class. She'd noticed Danny before they ever spoke. She liked his dark hair and the fact that he was a head taller than most of his friends (but that wasn't to last much past fifteen). She liked his grin, the cockiness of it.

They met through the twins, whose parents had organised an outing to the local bowling alley for their joint birthday. Danny's team played in the adjoining lane to Ellen's. She watched surreptitiously as time after time he rolled the ball and knocked little or nothing, as his friends yelled in mock rage, one jumping on his back.

Danny pushed him off, laughing, not at all put out. Ellen caught his eye once and he shrugged in a what-can-I-do gesture. She looked away immediately, suddenly shy, but as they queued for chips and burgers afterwards, she felt a tap on her shoulder.

'So what did you think of my bowling?'

She didn't know what to say. He could be joking, but his expression was serious. He might be embarrassed, but why draw attention to it then?

'I think you stink,' she said. His face split into a grin – and her stomach, out of the blue, somersaulted.

Their first date, several weeks later, was to the cinema. Ellen looked at the screen all the way through, but when they came out, she hadn't a clue what the film had been about. His arm had been slung across the back of her seat, his hand resting lightly on her shoulder, and she'd felt the warmth of it through her T-shirt, and she'd sat like a coiled spring, wanting more, and terrified of more.

Nothing happened until two dates later, when he bent and brushed her lips as they said goodnight, and she took forever to fall asleep afterwards, so full of a new, delightful excitement.

'I hear you have a boyfriend,' Maria said eventually.

'He's more of a friend really,' Ellen answered quickly, because Maria was nearly sixteen and not showing any signs of getting her own boyfriend. 'We just hang around together.'

But the weeks turned into months, and by Christmas, when they'd both turned fourteen, everyone knew they were a couple. Danny met her after school and walked her home. They went to the cinema, they walked Brutus, Danny's golden Labrador, they hung around with the rest of their friends in parks and outside chippers. They drank cider and tried pot, and decided against cigarettes.

They never went bowling.

They kissed in doorways and held onto each other. The first time he mentioned love was eight months after their first date. Her hands were in his, down deep in his coat pockets, trying to get warm, and her head was pressed to his chest, and she knew they'd get married and live together for the rest of their lives.

Her parents were against the relationship at first.

'You're too young to tie yourself down,' her mother told Ellen. 'You'll meet lots of boys before you're ready for this. You don't believe me now, but you will. Your father feels the same way. Danny's a nice boy, but you're just too young, darling.'

That was when Ellen started to draw away, knowing they were wrong and knowing, too, that there was no way to make them understand how things were between her and Danny.

So she made sure to be seen with plenty of others anytime they went out together. And when she and Danny drifted off alone afterwards, it only added to the thrill. Ellen felt like Juliet, sneaking away with her one true love, battling against the odds to be together.

And as time passed, her parents gradually came to accept that Danny wasn't going away, and they stopped encouraging Ellen to look in other directions.

She and Danny broke up once, when he was seventeen and she was three weeks off it, over some ridiculous argument that neither of them could remember a year later. Ellen felt like someone had torn her arm off, or ripped some vital organ out. She couldn't understand how she was still functioning, so desolate she felt without him.

And after a week that seemed like a lifetime, there he was, waiting outside her school gate, looking nervous.

'Sorry,' he said the minute she was near enough, even though several of her friends were within earshot too.

Ellen was terrified she'd start crying, so she grabbed his hand and practically ran down the road, dragging him after her. Waiting until they were out of sight of the others before she stopped and hugged him tightly and thumped his chest and kissed him and punched his arm, not knowing what she wanted, all the time half laughing, half crying.

'Do you think you're going to marry him?' Maria asked her once. 'Is this it?' Twining Ellen's hair into a French plait for Danny's surprise eighteenth party.

'Maybe,' Ellen answered, because Maria was twenty then, almost twenty-one, and still waiting for her first boyfriend. She worked in an office, typing up documents for a team of architects. Despite there only being the two of them, the sisters had never been confidantes, never sat up chatting at night, never exchanged secrets – but Ellen was quite sure Maria had never been asked on a date, never been kissed in a dark doorway.

'You should come out with us sometime,' she said, but Maria wasn't one for crowded cinemas or noisy cafés. She went to concerts and art exhibitions and occasionally the theatre with one or other of the girls she'd gone through school with. Ellen wondered sometimes if Maria was gay, but wouldn't have dreamed of asking.

When Danny got the motorbike, Ellen's parents were horrified.

'It's only a hundred cc,' Ellen said. 'It can't go very fast. And Danny's very careful.'

'Still, I really would much rather you didn't get up on it,' her mother said.

'You hear of awful motorbike crashes,' her father said. 'We wouldn't sleep a wink.'

'What about all the motorbike journeys that don't end in crashes?' Ellen asked. 'What about all the people who've been driving them safely for years? We need some kind of transport,' she said, 'and he can't afford a car.' They were both nineteen at this stage and Ellen was in first year in college, almost a hundred miles away.

'Look,' she said. 'Danny won't drink and drive, I'll make sure of that. And I'll always wear a helmet. We'll be as careful as possible, honest.'

And less than three years after that, a van had crashed into them on a sunny country road in April and Danny had been taken away from her forever.

She didn't return to college. She missed her final exams, and by the time she could bear the thought of facing people again, the repeats had already taken place.

'You can always go back later,' her father said. 'What's a year at your age?' But Ellen had lost interest in her college course; the idea of being a food scientist meant nothing anymore.

On the first anniversary of Danny's death, her parents went with her to the cemetery. They met his parents by the graveside and spoke in low voices, and murmured a decade of the rosary together as the sun slid from behind a cloud and made the raindrops on his brand new headstone sparkle. And Ellen stood stiffly beside them and wished them all a million miles away. She couldn't share him – he was hers, not theirs. It was her life that had been shattered.

Eventually her father found her a job in the office of a business associate's construction company. Ellen didn't take to Michael Talty, with his bitten fingernails and grubby white shirts, and breath that always smelled of coffee. She didn't care for the way his eyes slid down to her chest when he talked to her, didn't like his habit of putting a hand on her arm as he spoke. She said no immediately when he asked her to go for a drink after work one day.

And then, before you knew it, he was taking her

sister Maria, who'd dropped by the office one day, out to dinner. Calling around to the house where they both still lived with their parents, laughing and joking with their father while Maria tried on skirts and sprayed perfume upstairs.

And what could Ellen say? All the years growing up, she'd been the one with the boyfriend. Maria had never given the smallest indication that she minded, but Ellen had always felt guilty that she had Danny and Maria had no one.

Ellen couldn't tell her that Michael Talty was too old, that he gave her the creeps every day in the office, that the thought of having any physical contact with him, let alone sex, made her want to throw up. All she could do was watch while he wooed her sister, congratulate them when Maria came home one evening with a diamond ring, stand beside her at the altar in a lilac dress while Maria promised to love, honour and obey him for as long as they both should live.

And Ellen? Heart shattered, body broken, unable to imagine another man in Danny's place. She was a wreck, a walking ghost who forced her way through each day until she could go to bed and cry herself to sleep.

It took her two years to be able to go out again in the evenings, to make small talk in the pubs, to smile. To try and convince herself that that was where she wanted to be, because what else was she to do for the rest of her life? She was exhausted from grief, weary of heartbreak.

The small talk made her want to scream, the banality of it irritated her beyond belief. She couldn't care less about the new Colin Farrell film that everyone raved about, she didn't give a damn how Ireland did in the Eurovision or whether some famous singer got married in County Mayo. But there she stood, weekend after weekend, smiling through tightly gritted teeth, willing the time to pass until she could yawn and say she was tired, she'd been up early and would they mind terribly if she slipped away?

Until one night, standing at a crowded bar counter, she was pushed up against a man wearing a leather jacket. She inhaled the heavy animal smell of it, felt the hard warmth of his body against hers for an instant before she managed to pull back.

'Sorry, someone shoved me.'

He had dark hair and white, slightly too large teeth. 'No problem – feel free to come closer anytime.'

The scent of the leather came to her in wafts. She drank it in, she couldn't help it.

He noticed. 'Either you like my deodorant or you're doing deep breathing to survive in this place.'

He was younger than her, no more than twenty. He had dark hair like Danny. His jacket smelled like Danny's. Ellen felt something stir inside her.

She moved closer. 'Have you got somewhere we can go?' she said into his ear.

It was awful. It was sordid and sad and awful. She cried as he thrust himself into her, quietly so he wouldn't hear. She left her socks on. As she came she called him Danny, holding him close, moaning, sobbing. She left straight afterwards, tears still streaming as she pulled on her jeans, as she buttoned her shirt. He didn't ask why she was crying or if he could see her again.

The next time it happened he was blonde, with an earring through his right eyebrow. He told her he was twenty-four, but she guessed younger. He pushed her down onto the back seat of his Honda in a warehouse car park. There was a rip in the seat that scratched against her buttocks. The car smelled of cabbage.

He was rough and his hands were cold, but she closed her eyes and imagined Danny's hands, Danny's mouth. The soles of her socked feet beat a muffled rhythm against the car window as he panted his way in and out of her. She arched against him, pulling him deeper inside, craving the release that left her feeling emptier.

As he was zipping up his jeans she said she'd walk home, and he didn't try to change her mind.

When she moved into the apartment she began to take them there, wanting the comfort of her own bed, wanting to fall asleep with a man's arms around her, despite the exquisite pain of realising, as she awoke, that he wasn't Danny.

They were all young, all happy to be chosen. None of them objected to being sent home early in the morning. Hardly any of them asked to see her again, and those who did were sent off with a non-existent phone number. She was fairly sure they wouldn't use it – or if they did, they wouldn't be too upset when she wasn't on the end of the line. They were still at the game-playing age, and she was just another player. It was exactly what she wanted.

She wasn't being unfaithful; she was keeping

Danny alive. She wasn't having sex with strange men, she was making love to the memory of Danny. She was using them, of course – but so far, none of them had objected.

Nobody knew. Her parents, who she visited once a week for Sunday lunch, hadn't the smallest idea. They were glad she was moving on at last, relieved that she'd finally got over the accident and its aftermath.

And Maria, married now, with her own house, her own life, didn't know either. Maria wouldn't understand about the men, and Ellen wouldn't expect her to. Like everything else that surrounded the events of April the twenty-fifth, nineteen ninety-nine, it was something she kept to herself, the private, unspoken part of her life. She was hurting no one. It was nobody else's business.

The sisters still saw each other regularly. Maria and Michael came to Sunday lunch too, and now and again on her day off Ellen dropped into Maria's bookshop. They talked about their parents, and Ellen told Maria about films she'd seen and Maria told her what new books to look out for. Maria went with Ellen to a house contents auction when Ellen was furnishing her apartment, and Ellen was the first to hear when Maria discovered she was pregnant with Pat.

They didn't talk about Maria's marriage. Ellen never asked her sister how she and Michael were getting on. And Danny was never mentioned, by either of them. But they got on fine for all that.

Ellen stood up slowly, easing out her cramped legs, pulling the creases from the damp fabric. Time to move, time go home and change out of her good clothes and take the ashes from last night's fire and set today's, ready for when she got home from work.

She touched Danny's headstone. 'Bye, my darling,' she said.

She turned and walked back along the gravel path that led to the cemetery gate, clenching her hands, shivering in the chilly air.

Judith O'Sullivan

She closed the bathroom cabinet and studied the face that slid in front of her. Eyes you couldn't put a colour on, hovering somewhere between watery blue and faded grey. Lines fanning out from the corners that she hardly noticed any more, they'd been there so long. New creases in the last few years, running along under her lower lids before curving downwards to cup her cheeks. A ridiculous tilt at the end of her nose that she'd learned, finally, to live with. Lips too thin for all but the palest lipstick to be comfortable with. A deepening groove running from each side of her nose to the edges of her mouth, and a horrible accordion of lines above her top lip that popped out every time she spoke. A recent slight flabbiness in the skin of her cheeks – how they creased when she pinched them now. Hair that had held onto its light brown colour – no sign of grey there yet, and her mother practically white at Judith's age.

Not that fifty-four was old; far from it. She

could go on till she was eighty-one like Mam had, or longer even. Middle-aged, that's all she was, in the middle of her ages.

She was right, wasn't she, to take early retirement? Life was too precious to spend it with bored teenagers, trying to interest them in art and history and failing miserably most of the time. The thought of no more struggles in the classroom, no more trying to be heard above the constant muttering buzz, was wonderful.

She brushed her teeth and put the toothpaste back in the cabinet. Good that she could take her time on Friday, hadn't to be in school until eleven, and then the double art period in the afternoon with the third years, the least challenging of her classes. Quite a nice bunch in comparison with her sixth years – she'd be glad to see the back of them in another few weeks. Not a single one showing any interest, not a sign of any artistic talent there. They'd be lucky to pass the Leaving – and guess who'd be blamed if they didn't?

She dotted foundation on her cheeks and blended it in with her fingertips, covering the broken veins, softening the shadows under her eyes. She didn't believe that Hollywood make-up artists used the same brand – surely they could rise to a little more than twelve euro a tube? But it did her well enough, hid the worst of the damage.

Downstairs she took the *Irish Times* from the doormat – her Friday treat, having it delivered – and opened it straight to the crossword page as she walked into the kitchen. She switched on the kettle and put porridge, raisins and water into the microwave and filled in three answers as the bowl rotated slowly. Not her best, but sometimes she got none at all before the ping.

She took paper, porridge and teapot to the table by the window. The roses were slow in coming – she'd check for greenfly this evening. A few buds on the nearest clematis that always surprised her when she noticed them; she could never remember what flowered when in the garden.

Cup, milk, two spoons, one small, one big. No saucer when she was on her own. She sat at the table and looked at the crossword again. *The little dog would do wrong to be in such a row.* Seven letters, 'e' the second. She thought for a second and wrote *terrier.*

So lucky to have this little house, and her health to enjoy it. Her oasis after a day in the classroom. The garden just big enough not to be a chore, the neighbours smiling on the road but keeping to themselves otherwise, which suited Judith just fine.

Yes, she was lucky that things had turned out well.

Eventually.

She added milk to her tea and stirred it. She blew on a spoonful of porridge. In the hall there was a faint, familiar sound. Judith didn't react, except to pause briefly as she wrote the next answer.

Leave it a while. Probably nothing, probably a bill. The ESB was due.

She ate her porridge slowly, shifting her spoon now and again to the other hand so she could fill in more of the crossword. Drank her tea, refilled her cup. At last she got up and brought her bowl to the sink, and walked out into the hall and picked up the single envelope that lay on the carpet.

And then she saw that it wasn't an envelope at all, but a postcard with her name and address typed onto it. She turned it over and read that the new Anne Enright she'd requested from the library was now ready for collection.

Not a birthday card at all. Of course not a card. Foolish to be expecting one when none had arrived last year, when no mention of her birthday had been made in the phone call that had come two weeks later.

No matter. She wasn't into birthdays. What were they when you grew beyond the excitement of candles on a cake and brightly wrapped presents, only regular reminders that you were that much older, that much nearer to the end, whatever end that turned out to be? Who needed reminding of that?

She took the postcard into the kitchen and propped it against the salt cellar and picked up her cup again. She leaned against the window sill and watched the black and white cat padding across the lawn, lifting its paws high with each step, stopping every now and again to sniff at the grass. She sipped her lukewarm tea, not tapping on the glass as she normally would.

And then, because her only child had forgotten her birthday again, because whatever small joy the day contained had already seeped away, she allowed herself the hollow consolation of memory.

She'd met Samuel on her twenty-eighth birthday, they'd got chatting in a queue at the bank. Judith was lodging the cheque her parents had sent in a card signed by her mother, who'd written *Keep an eye out for something nice.* She and Samuel had laughed about that later, how you could almost pretend that he'd been her birthday present from her parents.

'Just what you always wanted,' he'd teased and Judith had called him big-headed, but of course he was right. All her life, she'd wanted someone just like him.

She brought her cup over to the sink and sat it into the porridge bowl and filled them both with water. She picked up her basket and dropped the library card into it – she could call in on her way home from school. She took her jacket down from the hall stand and her keys from the hook on the back of the front door.

At least tomorrow was Saturday. At least there was that.

Robert McInerney

This is what he saw as Noah came racing towards the car: a flop of dark blond hair, a face pink with excitement, a too-big Manchester United top, a pair of scabbed little boy knees and two unnaturally white runners, before his son thumped into him, arms flung wide, smelling of grass and toothpaste.

'Dad, I got full marks in my spelling test.' Panting it out, hair damp with sweat, chest pumping.

'Remember, you promised me two euro–'

'Hey, steady on.' Robert crouched, putting his hands on Noah's shoulders. 'Have you any pants on under that top?'

'*Dad* – course I have.' Impatient, pulling up the top to show Robert a pair of football shorts. 'What about the two euro?'

'Hang on,' Robert said. 'The deal was if you got three full marks in a *row*, I'd give you two euro. This is the first, so well done, just two more to go.'

Noah's face fell immediately. 'Ah Dad, that's not *fair*, you said *one* week, or I mean you didn't say any week, just full marks, you *said*, I *heard* you, and so did Aidan.'

He was so earnest, so indignant, that Robert couldn't keep it up.

'OK, OK, kidding – that's brilliant, well done you.' He stood up and fished out a two euro coin from the jumble of coins in his pocket. 'Here, you've earned it. But now that you've done it once, I'll expect top marks every week, OK?'

Noah grinned, pocketing the money. 'Will you pay me every week if I do?'

Robert pretended to swipe Noah's behind. 'I'll give you this every week if you don't.'

Noah laughed and took Robert's hand as they walked to the front door. 'Aidan didn't get full marks.'

'Did he not?' The twins were in the same class, no other option possible in the small school Caroline had wanted them to attend.

'No, he got "accident" and "trouble" wrong.'

'Oh dear.'

'Yeah – he put "x" in "accident".' Noah looked up at his father. 'What's so funny?'

'You. You're so funny.' Robert ruffled Noah's hair. 'I think you'll be a clown when you grow up.'

'*Dad,* I will not.' Noah broke free and scooted in through the front door, and Robert heard his footsteps thumping up the stairs.

Ten years old and still living in a black and white, right and wrong world, not yet aware of the thousands of greys out there, all the maybes and should haves and if onlys. Robert prayed – surely every parent's prayer? – that his sons wouldn't grow up too soon.

'Morning.' Caroline met him at the door, wiping her hands on a little towel. 'Nice day for it.'

She wore shorts too, navy with a green pinstripe that stopped a couple of inches above her knees and a fitted, paler green top. Her hair was caught in a loose knot, through which she'd twined a thin rust-coloured ribbon. A delicate gold chain around her neck, tiny gold studs in her ears. She looked younger than thirty-two, and very clean.

'Come in,' she said. 'They're just about ready.' As she stood back to let Robert pass, a boy with Noah's face and darker hair appeared at the kitchen door.

'Hi Dad.'

Quieter, more thoughtful than Noah. Robert went over and hugged Aidan, breathing in his different, nuttier smell. 'Hey there. You all set?'

Aidan nodded. 'Will you come up and get my bag?' The enormous, almost black eyes, Caroline's eyes. The long lashes, the little mole to the side of the mouth, the mouth that took its time to smile.

'Course I will.'

At the top of the stairs Noah barged down between them, bumping his bag on every step. In the bedroom the boys shared, another two euro coin was quietly handed over, the promise looked for and given that Noah wouldn't find out. Robert could just hear Noah's outraged 'Not fair!' if he learned that two mistakes in the spelling test earned just as much as none.

Neither boy excelled at school – Noah because he couldn't be bothered, Aidan because he couldn't. From their first term at school, the boys were getting the same comments from teachers: Noah needed to put in more effort, Aidan needed to give himself a break. Funnily enough, their scores in tests were generally similar, with Aidan's slogging and Noah's scraping by putting them pretty much on a par.

Not fair indeed.

'Did you pack your toothbrushes?' Caroline asked as both boys buckled themselves into the back of Robert's car.

'Yeah.'

'Noah, have you got your inhaler?'

'Yeah.'

'Wellies? Raincoats?'

'Yeah.'

Robert rested his elbow on the window frame. 'Are you going to Tramore?'

She sometimes took the opportunity to visit her mother when the boys were away, but this time she shook her head.

'No, staying put. I've someone coming to dinner tonight.'

'Right.' Someone, rather than a name. He knew most of her friends, so it must be someone he didn't know.

None of his business. He pushed the key into the ignition. 'Have a good day, don't work too hard.' She was on duty in the salon later, liked to be around there when he wasn't. 'See you tomorrow.'

She blew kisses in the window at the boys. 'Be good, don't stay up too late, brush your teeth,' as the car reversed away from her, as Robert swung onto the road and straightened up.

The first twenty miles were full of the usual 'I Spy' and guessing the colour of the next car and windows up or down squabbles. Robert asked about school (boring), girlfriends (vomit noises), Manchester United (twenty minutes of players and match results and rival teams that meant little or nothing to him).

Ten miles outside Dingle he said, 'So, who's Mum cooking dinner for tonight?'

'Just some friend.' Noah, yawning.

'Sharon? Katy?' Her two closest girl friends, even though he was pretty sure it was neither of those.

'Dunno. Are we nearly there?'

'Nearly.'

It didn't matter in the least who she was cooking dinner for, and Robert had long since forfeited the right to ask. He was just curious, that was all.

Caroline had had boyfriends, naturally, in the

nine years since she and Robert had split up. A woman with her looks and intelligence – not to mention a partnership in a thriving hairdressing business – was as much in demand on the Portmaine social scene as Robert was.

But she was very discreet. Nobody ever came to collect her at the salon, he never met anyone at the house when he called to pick up the boys. Noah or Aidan might mention the odd male name occasionally, and a few times Robert had met her when they'd found themselves at the same play or in the same restaurant with their respective dates – inevitable when they lived in the same city – but he was pretty sure there had never been anyone long term for her since they'd split up.

Cheryl, a neighbour's teenage daughter, babysat the twins whenever Caroline went out. Robert wondered sometimes if Cheryl ever stayed overnight, if Caroline ever made up the bed in the spare room and told Cheryl she'd be back first thing in the morning.

He was pretty sure she didn't bring anyone home to spend the night in the house. The boys would surely have mentioned it to him – and anyway, Caroline was too careful a mother to want the boys to see a strange man coming out of her bedroom.

But now she was cooking dinner for someone, on a night when the boys were going to be away, when nobody would know if he – because it must be a he – stayed for more than just dinner.

Caroline was a good cook. He remembered the crab cakes she'd made the first night they'd spent together in the house, her goat's cheese and olive tarts, her smoked fish chowder. His mouth watered at the memories.

'That didn't say Dingle.' Aidan's voice pulled him back.

'What didn't?'

'That sign – it said "An" something.'

'It said *An Daingean*. Dingle is called that now.'

'Why?'

'Hey, look at the colour of that house – it's the same as my bike.'

'Where's our B&B, Dad? Can we go fishing when we visit the dolphin?'

'I'm *starving* – when are we having lunch, Dad?'

And Caroline – and what she might or might not be planning – was necessarily forgotten.

Theo DeCourcy

She bundled plates, glasses, cutlery and crumpled serviettes onto the tray. She picked up the two euro coins – two miserable euro – and slid them into the pocket of her white apron. As she was wiping the table top, the older of the two women said, 'I'll have the–'

'Could you give me one minute to get this out of the way, and I'll be right back?'

Without waiting for an answer, Theo picked up the tray and marched across the restaurant floor towards the swing doors that led to the kitchen.

A robot, that's what they thought you were. Switch you on and away you went, all bloody day long.

And she couldn't open her mouth to complain because that was all her sister needed.

'Serves you right for wearing those shoes. Didn't I say?' And as usual, Saint Hilary had been right. Older than Theo by six years and wiser by a lot more, and always, infuriatingly, right.

Theo pushed through the doors and dropped the loaded tray on the worktop beside the double sink, where Angie, sleeves rolled past her elbows, hands covered in bright yellow rubber, was washing glasses. Hilary insisted on glasses being done by hand. Of course.

'Jesus, I'm crippled.' Theo leaned against the worktop and shrugged each foot in turn out of its treacherous prison.

Angie smiled down at the purple shoes. 'They're beautiful though.'

'Aren't they? Unfortunately, where shoes are concerned, beauty usually equals pain. I don't know if I'm going to survive.'

The swing doors burst inwards and Hilary appeared behind a tray piled with plates.

'Theo, table seven is waiting to order.'

'On my way.' Theo pushed her feet back into the shoes and pulled her notebook from her pocket as she left the kitchen, trying not to limp.

The biggest problem with Hilary was that she was far too efficient. She never mixed up orders, she knew precisely when to remove starters, she could sense who was ready to get the bill and who wanted to be left alone for a little longer.

She refilled water jugs without being asked and had tables cleared almost before the last occupants had left the building.

And the second biggest problem with Hilary was that she expected everyone else to keep up with her.

One of the women at table seven asked if the vegetables were organic, and where the chicken in the stir-fry came from. The other wanted her béchamel sauce on the side, and no ice in the water and softer butter.

Theo lied about the vegetables, told them (truthfully) that the chicken was from a farm just outside the city, replaced their iced water, served the sauce in a little jug and softened their butter for four seconds in the microwave.

Her little toes pinched, her calves ached, her armpits were damp. Her scalp itched as usual under the wig.

She hobbled to another table and loaded up her tray with more used crockery, glancing at the clock on the restaurant wall. Ten to two, and she was working till ten. The house needed a good scrub, the freezer had never been so empty and Chrissy was on her last clean babygro. Christ.

And now there was that blasted play. She hadn't opened her script since Thursday night, and this was Monday. She tried to remember why she'd gone to the auditions, and couldn't.

She heard a rap on the nearby window and looked up to see Sean walking by with two friends, hand lifted in greeting. Off early each Friday so they could study for the Leaving Cert, only a few weeks away now.

Theo waved back, his broad, six-foot frame filling her, as usual, with pride. *Look what I made, everyone.*

Her son, almost a man now at seventeen. Over a year older than Theo had been when she'd discovered she was pregnant with him.

No one to blame but herself and Vinny. They'd known the risks and had taken them anyway. Of course Vinny should have used a condom, except that condoms weren't exactly thick on the ground eighteen years ago – no walking into Boots and picking up your favourite flavour. Theo remembered the furore when the Irish Family Planning Association was fined for selling condoms out of Dublin's Virgin Megastore – the mortification of being Irish then.

So she and Vinny had taken their chances, like everyone else – and Sean had arrived nine months later, long after Vinny had hightailed it to his cousins in Scotland.

And Theo DeCourcy had survived. She'd insisted on keeping Sean in the face of her parents' anger, despite her father's threats to throw them both out of the house (she knew he wouldn't, and she'd been right).

Of course it hadn't helped that while Theo and Vinny were doing what came naturally in the back of Vinny's Fiat 127, Hilary was meeting Francis at catering college and beginning an oh-so-respectable courtship. Francis came to dinner with a pot of irises for Hilary's mother, Francis took Hilary to the graduation ball, Francis proposed to Hilary in Paris, at the top of the bloody Eiffel Tower. He'd probably never had his tongue in Hilary's mouth before they were married, let alone his hand up her top. And he was never Frank; he was always Francis.

Although to be fair, Hils had been a real help when Theo's life had suddenly skittered off in the wrong direction. She'd helped with the night feeds any time she was home from college and kept Theo supplied with cast-offs from Francis's nephew. She'd even taken Theo and Sean up to her tiny flat in Ranelagh for a week when Sean's teething was driving everyone demented at home. And of course she was the perfect godmother, never forgetting a birthday, turning up for the communion and the confirmation, sending good luck cards before exams and fivers or tenners afterwards.

And three years ago, Hilary had persuaded Francis to replace her with a new manager in their small hotel on the outskirts of Portmaine, and she'd opened The Cow and the Moon restaurant in the city centre. Theo had handed in her notice at the supermarket and come to work for her sister, and by and large it had been a good move. Hils could undoubtedly be hard work sometimes, but Theo was quite sure she drove her sister cracked now and again too – fair exchange.

She leaned against the unattended reception desk and shifted her weight from one foot to the other, making circles with her ankles. She'd break the shoes in if it killed her.

The restaurant phone rang and Theo answered it and took a dinner booking for Wednesday week. Yes, he could have a quiet table, yes, he could drop a cake in beforehand and it would be brought to the table. Yes, he could bring candles too, that would be no problem.

His name rang a faint bell as Theo wrote it down. Wednesday the seventh, seven o'clock, see you then Mr Buckley. Wife's birthday probably, they always wanted a quiet table for that.

As she hung up she looked over at table seven, where the older woman had raised a hand. She pulled two dessert menus from the stack in front of her and started walking across the room on aching feet, deciding that whatever they looked for first was going to be just finished, so *terribly* sorry.

Edward Bull

They sat where they always sat in the Steak House, at the window table furthest from the door. More often than not, they had the whole restaurant to choose from. Who went out to eat at a quarter to six on a Tuesday, or on any day for that matter, apart from an eighty-six-year-old man who'd eaten his dinner at six o'clock on the dot for the fifty-seven years of his marriage and who saw no reason to change after his wife died, and his nephew who didn't care what time he ate, if at all?

Their usual waitress – fifties, built to last, perm, dangly earrings – approached the table with two menus tucked under her arm. She knew and they knew that the menus were surplus to requirements. Rory always had the eight-ounce sirloin, well done, extra gravy, and after that, apple tart and ice cream. Edward, not a big meat eater, always chose whatever fish option was on that evening and skipped dessert. But at Gerry's Steak House, tradition demanded they have a look.

'Good evening, gentlemen.' Her greeting as unchanging as the four starters, nine main courses and three desserts. Edward waited for her comment on the weather, and there it was. 'Bit chilly tonight.'

Rory said, 'Oh, it is, it's chilly alright.'

'Can I get ye something to drink?'

They didn't know her name – no badges in this establishment. Edward had decided on Shirley. It seemed to suit the earrings.

He turned to his uncle. 'Rory? What'll you have?'

And Rory answered, as he always did, 'I'll have a glass of Smithwicks so.'

Edward smiled up at Shirley. 'And a small brandy for me, thanks.'

She didn't return his smile, too busy writing in her pad. 'No problem.'

When she'd gone they duly opened their menus. Rory fiddled his glasses out of their cracked brown case and ran a swollen-knuckled finger down the list of starters, which they never touched.

'You might go for a steak tonight maybe.'

Every single solitary time he said it. One day Edward might actually order one, just to keep him happy. But not tonight.

'I'll see what the fish is first.' *And whatever it is, I'll have it.*

What a predictable life Edward lived now – not that his life up to this had been filled with excitement. He wondered sometimes what that would feel like, waking up in the morning, not knowing what the day was going to fling at you. Did anyone live like that though, or was everyone just filling in the hours each day until they could look at the clock and think 'time for bed'?

He and Sophie had lived pretty routinely. Both of them off to work every day, two weeks somewhere warm – but not too hot – every June, a week in the Italian Alps after Christmas. The fortnightly dinner parties at the home of one or other of their circle, the theatre every now and again. Once in a while a concert with friends.

The sex hadn't always been routine though.

He remembered Sophie walking out of the sea on that tiny beach they'd found in Greece a few years after they were married. Nobody else around, peeling the straps of her swimsuit off her shoulders as she walked towards him, stopping to roll it down slowly over her hips, stepping out of it.

Edward lowering his book to watch as she approached. Her unselfconscious stride, aware of the firmness of her body. Dropping to her knees beside him, her pale brown skin glittering with droplets. Her hands on the waistband of his togs, easing it down as she straddled him, her hair dripping onto his chest–

'Here we go, gentlemen.' Shirley with her tray, placing two fresh beer-mats in front of them. 'One glass of Smithwicks, one brandy.'

He doubted that Shirley had ever lain on top of

110

a man, ever rolled around on hot sand with him, ever washed the sand off in the same shower afterwards. Although she wore a gold band on the right finger, so who knew?

She'd have a job peeling off the togs, with those hips.

'What's the fish tonight?' Edward asked her.

'Cod,' she told him. 'In a beer batter, with mushy peas and fried onions.'

'I'll have that, without the onions.'

'Baked potato or chips?'

'Chips.'

'And yourself?'

'Eight-ounce sirloin steak,' Rory announced immediately. 'Medium to well done, extra gravy.'

'Carrots and broccoli?'

'Just the carrots.'

'And a baked potato, isn't it?'

'That's it.'

It was like a well-practised foxtrot, a she-steps-in, we-step-out-again kind of thing. Good old Shirley, never missed a beat.

When she'd gone, Edward picked up his glass and held it out to Rory. *'Sláinte.'*

Rory's hand shook badly. Beer slopped over Shirley's white cloth as the glass wobbled its way towards his already pursed mouth.

'You're keeping alright?' Edward asked when the glass had been set down again.

For someone who lived less than twenty yards away, he didn't see that much of Rory. The two men kept to themselves, passing each other the odd time in the garden, nodding through a window sometimes, but otherwise not coming into much contact apart from their two preordained dinner dates on Tuesdays and Fridays.

Rory wiped foam from his mouth. 'Not too bad, I suppose.'

'Sleeping alright?'

'Not great, but sure, it's a small thing, the sleep.'

They could talk about the play again, Edward could tell him about the auditions, but he doubted that Rory was interested – going to the theatre hadn't featured largely in his uncle's life. Still, it was something to say.

'I gave out a few parts for that play last week. Remember when I was putting the ad in the paper?'

'Oh yes?' Rory looked vaguely suspicious. 'And what's this the play is about again?'

Edward wondered if he thought they were all going to be dancing naked around a maypole, scandalising the good people of Portmaine. 'It's a whodunnit – a murder mystery. It takes place in a writer's house.'

'And which writer would that be?'

They should have stuck to the weather, or maybe Rory's arthritis.

'He's not a real one, just a made-up character. A murder takes place in his house – his housekeeper murders someone, actually.'

'His housekeeper.' Rory digested this as he took another wobbly drink. 'Never saw the point of them myself. Why couldn't the priests cook their own dinner like the rest of us?'

'Yes ... well, this one stabs her victim with a letter opener.'

Rory frowned. 'She kills the writer fellow?'

'No, a different character – a young girl who comes to stay in the house for a few days.'

'And you're in charge of this play.'

'I am. I'm directing it.'

Rory smoothed a bulge in the tablecloth. 'I suppose I'll go and see it when it's ready.'

Edward smiled. 'I suppose you will. I could get you a free ticket.'

They sat in silence for a minute or so. Outside, the path was full of workers finished for the day, heads bent, umbrellas shooting upwards against a sudden heavy shower. A line of cars crawled past the window, brakelights flashing and vanishing in sequence.

A woman walked quickly by, head covered in a woolly hat, pushing a child in a buggy that looked too small for him, his bent knees almost touching his chin.

'Raining again.'

Rory's eyes were almost silver, the blue long since rinsed out of them. The pouches of skin underneath were rimmed with red, making him look as if he were about to burst into tears, or had just finished.

Edward had never seen his uncle cry, not even when Nuala had died five years earlier. Rory had sat stoically in the funeral parlour, his black suit smelling of must, offering his hand to be shaken by the small procession of mourners. Blowing his nose loudly now and again, but no tears that Edward, seated next to him, could see.

He pointed to Rory's glass as Shirley elbowed the kitchen door open, carrying two plates. 'Will you have another?'

And Rory, as always, looked at the remaining inch of beer and said doubtfully, 'I suppose I could.'

First Rehearsal Night: Thursday, 1 May

McMillan's Pub

'If I could have your attention.' Edward waited for silence. 'Well, thank you for all being here on time. Tonight we're going to have a look at the first half of act one.' He indicated the space in front of where he sat. 'This will have to do for our stage. It's a lot smaller than the one you'll perform on, but that can't be helped. Remember to speak your lines clearly, never turn your back fully to the audience and don't block anyone.' He consulted his script. 'Betty, you're on first.'

Judith got up. 'Whereabouts should I stand?'

'Wait offstage until I give the command, then walk on slowly and come all the way forward, keeping to the side,' Edward told her. 'You'll be speaking directly to the audience. And Dorothy,' he turned to Ellen, seated on his left, 'you're lying on the ground back there.'

Ellen looked down at the carpet. 'You expect me to lie on that?'

Edward frowned. 'What's wrong with it?'

'It's filthy. Can't you just pretend I'm lying there, and I'll bring a towel next week?'

Edward looked at her impatiently. 'It's only for a minute.'

Ellen didn't move. 'I'm dead, I have no lines – what difference will it make whether I'm there or not?'

He stood his ground. 'Betty needs something to focus on. I really can't see what the problem is.'

'The problem,' Ellen told him evenly, 'is that

117

it's filthy. God knows what I could pick up from it. I'm sorry, but I'm not lying on that carpet until I have something between it and me.'

She was determined, Edward could see that. Not five minutes into the first rehearsal and his authority was being questioned.

'It's alright,' Judith said tentatively. 'I don't mind, I'm sure I can manage.'

That's not the point, he wanted to say. But there was little to be gained from further argument. Edward glared at Ellen and turned back to Judith.

'You're going to have to assume that the body of Dorothy Williams is lying on the study floor. Take your time with this. Don't be afraid to pause.'

Had he made a mistake with Ellen Greene? Was it too late to find another Dorothy? Was there a danger he'd lose the sister too if he sent the first one packing? He stifled his annoyance. Too soon to be making enemies. He'd look past it this one time.

'And ... let's go.'

(BETTY the housekeeper enters and walks downstage.)
BETTY: Such a tragedy *(pause)*. A young girl, all her life ahead of her, stabbed through the heart with Mr McCarthy's letter opener. A murder committed right there *(turns to look upstage)* in Mr McCarthy's study. Who could have guessed what was ahead when she arrived at the house just five days ago?
(Exits slowly.)

'Well done. Next scene. Betty and Dorothy, take your positions please.' Edward turned to Ellen. 'That is, of course, if you can bring yourself to walk on the carpet.'

Theo laughed.

Ellen got up. 'Very funny. Where do I come on?'

'Over there.' He was reminded of the limp as she walked to the far side of the stage and he thought of the conversation they'd have to have later. He turned and addressed the others.

'Five out of the six of you are in this scene. I expect you to pick up your own cues and come on as necessary. Right?' Without waiting for an answer, he swung back to face the stage.

'And ... let's go.'

(DOROTHY approaches the front door of the large, ivy-covered house and sets down her small suitcase before pressing the brass bell. As she waits, she glances around, taking in the long French windows and the stone tubs overflowing with lobelia, nasturtium and begonia. The door opens and DOROTHY turns to face BETTY.)

'Hold that pause,' Edward said quickly, and both women froze, eyes locked. 'Betty, stop smiling.' He counted slowly to three. 'Right, on you go.'

BETTY: Yes? *(Regards DOROTHY coolly.)* Can I help you?

DOROTHY: Good afternoon. My name is Dorothy Williams, I'm a freelance journalist, and I'm here to interview Mr McCarthy. I'm doing a piece on him for **Writers' World** magazine.

BETTY: Oh, yes. He's been expecting you. *(Makes no attempt to take the suitcase.)* Follow me, please.

(They enter a spacious hall, from which a wide staircase sweeps upward in an elegant curve.)

BETTY: Wait here.

(BETTY exits through a door to the left of the hall: DOROTHY sets her case on the tiled floor and wanders past the intricately carved hallstand–)

'What are you doing?'

Ellen turned to Edward. 'I'm picking up a book. She needs something to do while she's waiting.'

'A book?' His voice rose in exasperation. 'Who said there are books in the hall? There's no mention of a book in the script.'

'Well, he's a writer, of course there'd be–'

'A writer would keep his books in a bookcase, not thrown around the hall.' He was determined not to lose this battle. 'Please stick to what you're given – all it tells you to do is wander around the hall. Let's not make it up as we go along, alright?'

She glared. 'Alright. No books in the writer's hall.'

Edward looked down at the pages on his lap. 'Let's take it from Betty's last line – "wait here".'

BETTY: Wait here.

(BETTY exits through a door to the left of the hall: DOROTHY sets her case on the

tiled floor and wanders past the intricately carved hallstand, observing, but not touching, the various pieces of furniture, the collected ornaments, the gilt-edged mirror.)

'Tom,' Edward said sharply.

No movement from the others.

'Tom!' Edward barked, and Harry jumped to his feet.

'Sorry.'

'You're on. Get over there – now!'

'Sorry–' Harry darted to the far side of the stage.

(A door opens from the rear of the house and TOM the gardener appears. He spots DOROTHY and immediately pulls off his green woollen hat.)

TOM: Oh ... beg pardon. I was looking for Betty.

DOROTHY: Is she the unfriendly woman in a grey dress who looks like a housekeeper?

TOM: *(smiles shyly)* She *is* the housekeeper.

DOROTHY: She's gone to find Mr McCarthy ... do you work here too?

TOM: Yes, I do the gardens... I'm Tom.

Robert got up and joined Judith at the side of the stage.

DOROTHY: *(moves towards TOM, hand outstretched)* I'm Dorothy. I'll be staying for a few days...

Ellen trailed off, hand still extended, and Harry darted a look back at Robert.

'Come on, McCarthy – come in sooner!' Edward snapped. 'You should be in before she finishes talking!'

'Sorry–' Robert stepped forward. 'Wasn't sure when my cue–'

Edward sighed. 'Halfway through that sentence ... it's in the script: They're interrupted by the arrival of a blah blah–' Was he going to have to hold their hands all the way through? What had possessed him to do this? He took another deep breath. It was the first rehearsal. Things could only get better. 'Back to your last line, Tom – "I do the gardens".'

TOM: I do the gardens... I'm Tom.
DOROTHY: *(moves forward, hand out-stretched)* I'm Dorothy. I'll be staying for–
(JACK emerges from the front room with BETTY.)
JACK: Miss Williams, welcome. I'm Jack Mc-Carthy, and I'm delighted to meet you.

Maria got up quietly and tiptoed to the far side of the stage.

DOROTHY: *(shakes JACK's hand as TOM and BETTY exit)* Thank you, Mr McCarthy.
JACK: Please – call me Jack. We're going to have to get to know each other if you want to write about me.
DOROTHY: *(laughs nervously)* Well, in that case, I'm Dorothy.
(They both turn at a sound, and watch as PENELOPE walks downstairs.)

JACK: Penelope, this is Miss Dorothy Williams, the reporter I told you was coming. *(Turns to DOROTHY)* Allow me to present my sister, Penelope McCarthy.

DOROTHY: *(extends her hand)* Please call me Dorothy.

PENELOPE: *(coolly)* How do you do. Will you be staying with us long?

JACK: *(frowns)* Penelope, that's hardly necessary.

PENELOPE: *(looks unconcerned)* I'm merely wondering what to tell Betty about housekeeping arrangements. Miss Williams doesn't mind the question, I'm sure.

DOROTHY: Not at all. I thought five or six days, a week at the very most.

PENELOPE: I see. *(She moves towards the back of the house.)* If you wait here, I'll ask Betty to show you to your room. *(Exits through kitchen door.)*

JACK: Don't take any notice of her – she loves to throw her weight around, act like the lady of the manor *(sweeps a hand to indicate the hall)*. So how do you like my little house?

DOROTHY: It's beautiful; I can see–

Ellen stopped abruptly, frowning.

DOROTHY: Er, now I can see–

Ellen stopped again.

'Now I can see where you get your inspiration! Learn the lines!'

Ellen whirled towards Edward. 'Give us a

123

chance, for Christ's sake – it's the first bloody rehearsal and I have *loads* of lines.'

A second of dead silence, all eyes on Edward.

After a moment he said calmly, 'You're quite right – I do apologise.' And as he had hoped, that shut her up.

He checked his watch. 'Why don't we break for ten minutes after this scene?'

'Thank God,' Theo said. 'I thought I was going to be part of the furniture for the night.'

The pink hair, he'd have to have a word about that too. He turned back to Robert and Ellen.

'From McCarthy's last line, please – "So how do you like my little house?"'

JACK: *(sweeps a hand to indicate the hall)* So how do you like my little house?
DOROTHY: It's beautiful; I can see where you get your inspiration. I'm going to enjoy staying here. Thank you so much for having me.
(BETTY and PENELOPE reappear.)
PENELOPE: *(to DOROTHY)* Betty'll show you to your room. We eat dinner at seven. Please let Betty know if you have any dietary requirements.
DOROTHY: *(meekly)* Thank you *(follows BETTY upstairs)*.
PENELOPE: *(to JACK)* I suppose I have to be on my best behaviour.
JACK: *(smiles)* I'd appreciate that. It's only for a few days.
PENELOPE: I should hope so. *(Walks back upstairs as JACK goes into his study.)*

'Right.' Edward stood. 'Ten minutes please.'

124

'Anyone for a jar?' Robert was already halfway to the door.

Theo got to her feet. 'I'd love one.'

'Me too.' Ellen was rummaging in her bag. 'Maria, have you money?'

In the end, they all went downstairs except Edward. 'I need to make some notes,' he told them. Which was an out and out lie – he'd been making all the notes he needed as they'd played the scene. He had no intention of becoming friendly with his cast.

'You have nine and a half minutes left,' he told them sternly as they walked out, and he pretended not to hear Ellen's snort.

This early, the pub was quiet. They chose a round table near the bottom of the stairs, and after an initial confusion over who was buying what, they eventually paired off – Maria and Ellen, Robert and Harry, Theo and Judith – and got themselves sorted with drinks.

'What is he like?' Theo twisted the cap on her little bottle of red wine and it cracked open. 'If he's this bad on day one, can you imagine him nearer the time?' She looked at Ellen. 'You two are going to come to blows.'

Ellen shrugged. 'He doesn't scare me. There was no way I was lying on that filthy carpet.'

'Ah, he's not too bad.' Robert watched his pint settle. 'Just takes it all very seriously, which we probably need.'

'I'm enjoying it though,' Judith said.

'Me too.' Maria sipped her coffee. 'Anyone done this before, or are you all complete amateurs like me and Ellen?'

Judith, it turned out, was the only experienced one. 'But just in college, years ago.'

'You've got the best part,' Theo said. 'Mine is rubbish. I wish I got to kill someone.'

'I've seen you somewhere,' Robert said to Maria. 'Do you work locally?' She told him about the bookshop. 'That must be it – I've been in there a few times. Nice little place.'

'And you? Are you working in the city?'

He mentioned the salon name and Maria nodded. The swanky one, all darkened windows and leggy blondes. She might have known. He looked the part.

'I didn't realise that was you, at the auditions,' Judith said to Harry. 'You looked familiar, but I couldn't think where I'd seen you. Isn't that silly, and me in and out of the library all the time?'

'I recognised you,' Harry said. 'I'm good with faces, it's the names that get me.'

'Of course it's a wig,' Theo told Ellen. 'I've worn it since I went bald.'

'What?' Ellen stared.

'Well, pretty much. I've a bit left, but nothing you'd want to be seen out in public with. Female alopecia, part genetic and part hormonal, apparently.' She sipped her wine. 'Could be worse, couldn't it? Doesn't really bother me any more.'

'Good for you,' Ellen said faintly, lifting her gin and tonic, wondering if the nine and a half minutes were up.

Edward spoke above the chatter. 'Settle down everyone, please. Places for the post office scene. Ursula and Betty into position. And ... let's go.'

(The door of the village post office opens and BETTY walks in. URSULA, standing behind the counter, looks up from the bundle of forms in front of her.)
URSULA: Morning, Betty. How are things up at the Big House?
BETTY: *(drops her shopping bag onto the floor and leans against the counter)* We have a visitor.
URSULA: Oh yes? *(Pushes the forms aside.)* Do tell.
BETTY: She's a–

'Hang on a minute. Sorry, but I really don't like that line.' Theo looked at Edward. *'Do tell* sounds a bit ... Enid Blyton.'

Edward took off his glasses. 'A bit Enid Blyton?'

'Oh, you know what I mean – a bit jolly hockey sticks. Not something an Irish person would say.' She looked around at the others. 'Would anyone here say *do tell?*'

Edward watched as they all shook their heads. Wonderful. Now they were rewriting the play.

'And what,' he enquired, 'would Ursula rather say?'

Theo didn't notice or chose to ignore the sarcasm. 'What about *tell me more?*' she asked. 'That sounds much more natural.'

127

Edward considered, and decided it wasn't worth arguing about. 'Right, but that's the only change we're making, understood? You're an actor, not a writer.'

Theo smiled happily. 'I'm an actor.'

'And do try,' Edward told her sternly, 'to stay in character throughout a scene – keep the questions for later, right?'

'Right.'

'From your last line please, Betty – "We have a visitor".'

BETTY: *(drops her shopping bag onto the floor and leans against the counter)* We have a visitor.

URSULA: Oh yes? *(She pushes the forms aside.)* Tell me more.

BETTY: She's a journalist *(BETTY rolls her eyes)* and she's writing an article on Mr McCarthy for some fancy magazine.

URSULA: *(smile fades)* What age woman would she be?

BETTY: Oh, young, definitely still in her twenties. And good-looking. *(She glances slyly at URSULA.)* Young and good-looking.

URSULA: And she's staying for a while, is she?

BETTY: Four or five days at least, Miss McCarthy says. And causing all sorts of ructions already.

URSULA: What sort of ructions?

BETTY: *(leans further across the counter)* Well, she has Tom all up in a heap, for one.

URSULA: *(looks surprised)* Tom? You mean Tom Drury, the lad who does the gardens?

What's he got to do with anything?

BETTY: Well, she wasn't there five minutes when she was flirting away with him in the hall *(sniffs)*. Probably doing the same with Mr McCarthy, while they're holed up in his study all day.

URSULA: *(frowns)* Surely not. She's there to work, it's just a job.

BETTY: *(smirks)* I wouldn't be too sure about that – isn't Mr McCarthy a rich widower, isn't he the most eligible man for miles around? Why wouldn't a young one throw her cap at him?

URSULA: *(sharply)* Don't be ridiculous.

BETTY: Oh, I wouldn't say it's ridiculous. I'm sure there are plenty of lonely women in the neighbourhood who wouldn't object to becoming the next Mrs McCarthy.

URSULA: *(pulls the forms back in front of her)* Did you want to buy something? I'm really too busy to gossip.

BETTY: *(enjoying her discomfiture)* I'll take two stamps please. *(The transaction is conducted in silence.)*

BETTY: Thank you, Ursula *(attaches the stamps to envelopes she takes from her bag, and hands the envelopes to URSULA)*. I'll leave these with you.

(URSULA takes the letters silently.)

BETTY: Goodbye now.

URSULA: *(sourly)* Good day.

(BETTY exits, looking extremely pleased with herself)

'Right.' Edward stood, pulling off his glasses.

129

'Let's take it from the start again. Betty, if you please.'

'Good,' he said eventually. 'That'll do for tonight, thanks everyone. Same time next week, and please try to be on time. We'll be going back over what we did tonight and moving on further. Please start having a look at the lines of act two – the sooner you learn them, the better.'

As they shuffled into coats and gathered bags, he said, 'Ellen?'

She looked over, one arm into her lemon jacket. 'Yes?' Defensive.

'A quick word, if you don't mind.'

She stood in front of him, bag dangling from one hand. 'What is it?'

'I was just wondering about something.' Edward indicated a chair. 'Won't you sit for a minute?'

He waited, and then said, as quietly as he could, 'It's about your limp.'

She stiffened but said nothing. She looked directly at him.

He ploughed on. 'I'm sorry to have to ask you, but I'm concerned that it's something that'll have to be explained to the audience. They'll expect a reason for it, you see. Why is Dorothy limping? What happened to cause it?'

'I don't think it's that noticeable.'

He'd hit a nerve. It had to be sorted. 'I'm sorry,' he said again, 'but I noticed it, remember, as soon as you walked in last week?' An image of her hair arcing across her face flashed in his mind's eye.

'So what do you suggest?' Voice taut as a pulled-back catapult. Fingers tight on the strap of the bag in her lap.

She wasn't giving anything away. Edward picked his words carefully. 'Well, I was thinking that she would have been injured in the accident that killed her sister and mother, and that that injury might have caused the limp.'

Her expression froze, the colour draining from her face.

'Are you alright?' Edward asked. She looked as if she might be about to faint.

She stood up abruptly, slinging her bag onto her shoulder. 'I – I can't talk about this now, I'm sorry. I have to go.'

'You might have a think about it before next week?' It had to be cleared up, whatever the sensitivities.

He got no response. Ellen walked quickly, unevenly, across the room and said something in a low voice as she reached Maria, who threw a glance at Edward before hurrying after Ellen through the doorway.

That hadn't exactly gone well. Edward wondered if either of them would turn up for the next rehearsal. It wasn't too late, was it, to find two replacements? He still had the list.

He picked up his briefcase and walked wearily downstairs, and after a quick glance around the pub – no sign of Robert, no sign of any of them – he ordered a large brandy from the young girl behind the counter and brought it to the quietest corner he could find.

He pulled out his notebook and wrote *First half*

of act one gone through. Lines generally well learned. Cues need to be worked on. Lack of focus at times. Voice projection.

He sipped his brandy and wrote *Ursula's hair colour.* He'd forgotten to address the problem of the pink hair. He wondered how Theo DeCourcy, not exactly a shrinking violet, would take being asked to tame it down.

And Ellen Greene. He wrote *Dorothy's limp.* Ellen was going to be a handful, no doubt about it. That's if she was still in the play, of course.

He sighed. The thought of backing out of the whole thing was terribly tempting. He was too long out of it; he should never have let William Crosby talk him into it. It had been fun in their twenties when they were both full of energy, but now directing a play seemed like some enormous task that he had no appetite for any more.

But he couldn't back out now, he couldn't admit defeat. He'd never given up on anything in his life.

Apart from your marriage, a voice reminded him. *Gave up on that quickly enough, didn't you? Couldn't wait to be rid of that, could you, Edward?*

He closed the notebook and finished his drink in one long, burning swallow. He picked up his briefcase and left the pub and drove home.

In her bed Ellen wept, the hot tears dampening her pillow. He would have been thirty-two today. They'd have gone out to dinner maybe, a baby-sitter – her mother – at home with the children. Ellen would have given him his present, they'd have ordered a nice bottle of wine, or even

132

champagne. They'd have gone home and he'd have put her mother in a taxi and then taken Ellen to bed, and they'd still have had years and years ahead of them. Nights and nights ahead of them.

She turned her pillow over and laid her hot, wet face against its cottony coolness.

Robert

'I have a picture.'

As the woman in the mirror reached into her handbag, Robert prayed she wasn't going to take out Jennifer Aniston. He dealt in haircuts, not miracles.

'Here.' She unfolded a magazine page and held it up to him. Not Jennifer Aniston, but his heart sank anyway. He studied the impossibly shiny, beautifully layered style, the rich colour, the shimmering highlights, the unlined, twenty-something face underneath it, already searching for the most tactful way to say that his customer would never in a million years have a head that looked remotely like that.

'This is a difficult style to carry off – that asymmetrical cut can be very unforgiving.' *It's thirty years too young for you.*

'But it's lovely, isn't it?' Smiling hopefully at him.

Robert lifted a handful of the ruined hair, frizzy, rusty orange creeping towards flat, greying

133

roots. 'You see, your hair is a good deal finer than this model's. *You've permed it to within an inch of its life and destroyed it with chemical dyes.*

'Yes.' Same polite smile. Still hoping.

'Also, your bone structure is very different.' Bone structure, the hairdresser's friend.

Her smile began to fade. Robert kept going, determined not to send her out looking like something from *Star Trek.* 'That kind of style really wouldn't flatter the shape of your face.'

'Oh.' She held out her hand and he gave her back the picture. 'But I really like it.'

Her children had treated her to a voucher for her birthday, she'd told him, no doubt realising that mother's hair was in dire need of serious attention.

He tried again. 'I can give you a very nice short cut, with a conditioning treatment to bring back the–'

'But I want this one.' She smoothed out the picture in her lap, not meeting his eye now. 'And I'd like some colour too.'

'Colour?' His heart sank deeper. Let her mean a well-behaved chestnut, with perhaps a touch of subtle lowlights.

'Yes,' she said firmly. 'That lovely strong red, I love red hair. The brighter, the better.'

'Right.' Her mind was made up, no point trying to change it. 'You're the boss. We'll go for that cut and some nice strong colour.' *And it won't do a thing for you, but hopefully you'll be happy.*

At least it was Friday, the day he left the salon at four to pick up the boys from their after-school hurling club, and kept them till bedtime. Some-

134

times he brought them to the gym, and they swam in the pool while Robert lifted weights and did his circuit. Occasionally they went bowling or to the cinema. If the weather obliged he brought them to the park, where they kicked a football around for an hour.

And every now and again he took them shopping, indulging them with the latest designer trainers or new football jerseys, knowing that Caroline would be annoyed at his extravagance and knowing too that he was compensating, pitifully hungry for their beams of pleasure, their quick, delighted hugs.

But today was a different Friday. Today there was to be no bowling, no shopping. Today they were going to the city library, where Noah was being presented with a prize for his entry in the Write a Story competition that Carran Computers sponsored each year as part of its contribution to the local community.

Noah's story was called 'The Monster Who Was Afraid of Boys', and it had taken him three weeks to write and illustrate, and in his father's completely unbiased opinion, it was wonderful. Aidan had opted out of the competition, and neither Caroline nor Robert had tried to change his mind.

Noah had won a book token for fifty euro, the third place prize in his age group. Today he was being presented with his token by William Crosby, the managing director of Carran Computers, whose thick, dark brown hair Robert trimmed every six weeks.

But in the meantime, there was his customer

135

and her birthday voucher. 'Now,' he said, 'let's get you sorted.'

And as he'd suspected, the cut didn't work. It perched uneasily on her head, like a wig she'd pulled on for a laugh, and the red shade they'd finally settled on only added to the cartoonish effect. Robert braced himself for her reaction as she inspected the result.

'I love it,' she said. 'It's exactly what I wanted. You won't miss me now in a crowd.'

'Indeed you won't,' he said, whipping off the nylon cape and brushing the stray hairs from her V-neck jumper. 'I'm glad you like it.'

'Wasn't I right?' she asked, turning her head this way and that, beaming. 'I knew it would suit me.'

'You were right,' Robert agreed. 'It's a good job I listened to you.'

He passed Caroline on his way out. She wore a black and grey patterned dress and snipped at the head of an attractive blonde woman who smiled at Robert.

'Nice work on your last client,' Caroline said under her breath. 'You must be very proud.'

'Funny,' Robert replied. 'I'm off now – don't be late.'

'See you.'

She was meeting them at the library. Unlike Robert, Caroline worked a full day on Friday, but she was taking an hour off to be there when Noah collected his prize.

The boys were coming out of the clubhouse when he pulled up fifteen minutes later. Noah broke into a jog when he spotted the car, leaving

Aidan walking steadily behind him.

'All set?' Robert dragged Noah's hair into some semblance of a style with his fingers. 'Did you have a shower?'

'Yeah.' They piled into the back, hurleys clattering, filling the car with their young boy energy.

'Shove *over*.'

'Move your gear – Dad, tell him to move his gear, it's sticking in my side.'

'No it's not – you've *loads* of room.'

Robert wished he could make time stand still. Could any age beat this magical, squabbling, innocent one? In a heartbeat they'd be teenagers, and remembering all the angst and mood swings of his own youth, Robert dreaded it. So many possibilities for disaster during those awkward, uncertain years.

'There's plenty of space for two back there. Come on, sort yourselves out.' And of course they did, because he was still Dad, who had to be obeyed – most of the time.

The library was hot and full of neatly dressed children, scrabbling for seats among the rows of collapsible chairs that had been assembled in the pathetically small space in front of a narrow wooden podium.

Robert eventually found a chair for Noah. 'Aidan and I will stand at the back,' he told him. 'Good luck – and tuck in your shirt.'

He spotted William Crosby to the left of the podium, talking to a low-sized woman with bright red cheeks. A harried-looking man appeared carrying a stack of folded chairs, and Robert remembered Harry mentioning that he worked in the library.

Caroline arrived a few minutes later, threading her way through the crowd till she found them. 'I thought I was late.'

'You are, but so are they. Hang on.' He walked over to Harry, who was jerking the chairs open rapidly and creating new rows in an area to the side of the podium. 'Hello there.'

Harry glanced up. 'Oh – hi.' He unfolded another chair. 'You're here for the Write a Story?'

'One of my boys came third. Here–' Robert took a chair from the bundle and pulled it open.

'Oh, thanks very much, just beside those ones.' Harry's round face was pink with exertion. 'I'm afraid we're a bit disorganised.'

'You should have someone to help you,' Robert said.

'She's busy,' Harry answered, jerking his head towards the woman who was smiling and nodding at William Crosby. A few minutes later she approached the podium, taking no notice at all of Harry and his labours.

She pulled the microphone towards her and said loudly, 'Good afternoon everyone.' Her face was shiny and very red. The string of blue heads around her plump neck looked uncomfortably tight. She stood waiting, a forced smile on her red face as the chatter gradually died away.

'Thanks,' whispered Harry. 'I think we'd better leave it at that.' The new chairs were already occupied, claimed as soon as they were put in place by waiting children.

'See you Thursday.' Robert moved back to where Caroline and Aidan stood.

'Do you know Harry?' Caroline asked.

'He's the gardener in the play. I forgot he works here.'

'He's lovely to the boys when I bring them in. That woman at the mike is a pain, giving everyone dirty looks if they open their mouths.'

From his chair, Noah turned and waved at his parents, grinning. Caroline waved back and pulled a tissue from her bag.

'Good afternoon,' the woman at the podium said again. 'My name is Linda Delahunty and on behalf of Portmaine Library I'm delighted to welcome you all here for what has become one of the highlights...'

Robert let his eyes wander around the room as her voice washed over him. The children's heads in front of him bobbed constantly, a barely dampened excitement stirring through them. William Crosby waited beside the podium, grey suited, a rolled-up page in his hand.

Robert turned to Caroline. 'Sure you won't come and eat with us?' He was bringing the boys to the little pizzeria near the salon that Noah, as guest of honour, had chosen. 'We can easily while away a couple of hours till you finish.'

But Caroline shook her head. 'No thanks, I've things to catch up on.' There was a sudden burst of applause as William Crosby stepped up to the podium. 'Actually, we're going out to dinner again on Wednesday.'

Robert turned to look at her. 'You are?'

'Mmm.' She watched the podium, her face in profile.

For the next few minutes, Robert listened to

William Crosby telling them all how much he enjoyed sponsoring the Write a Story initiative, how pleased he was that so many boys and girls had taken part, how difficult it had been to choose the winners, the standard was so high.

And then, when the youngest children began to be presented with their prizes, when it was clear that Caroline wasn't giving any more information away, Robert murmured, 'What's the occasion?'

'Hmm?'

'Why are you eating out next week?'

A little girl in red curls and a blue dress took her medal. William Crosby bent and shook her hand solemnly and everyone clapped again.

'Robert,' Caroline said softly, 'I've met someone.'

'You have?' Robert watched a boy in a wheelchair being pushed towards the podium.

'He wants to meet the boys and I thought it might be best if it happened on neutral ground, so I suggested he take us out.'

'I see.'

She'd cooked dinner for him last weekend. He'd probably spent the night, and now she was letting him meet the boys.

'He's French,' she said. 'He's here on business for six months. He works–'

'It's nearly Noah's turn,' Robert said. Out of the corner of his eye he saw her head tilt towards him, but he didn't look away from the podium. She fell silent.

Noah's name was eventually called. They clapped as he was handed his prize and Robert gave him a thumbs-up sign as he walked back to

140

his seat, face flushed, grinning.

'By the way,' Caroline murmured, 'I haven't said it to the boys yet about ... the meal out, so keep it to yourself, will you?'

'Right.'

He was only in Ireland for six months. Presumably he was going back to France then, so what was the point of the boys meeting him?

How had he and Caroline met? Had she cut his hair? Had he sat in Robert's salon, chatting up Robert's ex?

Robert imagined another man taking *his* sons out to dinner, another man joking with them, another man telling Noah not to eat so fast.

He wondered which restaurant they were going to. Prego Pizza House might be Noah's favourite, but it wasn't exactly the Ritz.

'Right, I've got to get back.' Caroline was slinging her bag over her shoulder. 'Have a nice time, see you later.' She bent and hugged Aidan. 'Tell Noah congratulations. Be good for Dad.'

She wove through the crowd, thinning now as parents claimed prizewinners and shepherded them out.

Noah appeared a few minutes later. 'Where's Mum?'

Robert took his hand and grabbed Aidan's with the other. 'She had to go back to work but she said you were great. C'mon, let's go and eat.'

'I want mushrooms and salami on my pizza,' Aidan said.

'I want pineapple and chicken, and pepperoni.'

'You're only allowed to have two toppings.'

'No way – can't I have more than two, Dad?'

'Absolutely.'

'And ice cream after?'

'No problem.'

If they asked for the moon on a gold plate tonight, he'd make damn sure to get it for them. They left the library and Robert pulled out his car keys and shepherded his sons – *his* sons – across the road.

Ellen

The green Land Rover sat in the driveway, dwarfing their father's Toyota behind it. Ellen left her car on the street in front of the house and checked that the faint red circle just above her breast was hidden by her top. A love bite at thirty-one – that's what you got for bringing big boys home with you.

She walked up the path and let herself in, and the aroma of roasting meat swept forward to meet her.

Her mother came out from the kitchen, pulling off her apron. 'Hello, love. You're late today, I was just going to give you a call.' She looked closely at Ellen. 'You look tired – are you alright?'

'I'm fine. I was doing a bit of tidying up and lost track of the time.' No need for the truth when it wouldn't be appreciated. She handed over the flowers and her mother said, as she always did, 'Oh now, there was no need for that.'

'Can I do anything to help?'

'Not at all, everything's done. Come in and say hello to the others.'

The Sunday lunch routine, the unchanging quality of it, the fence posts that anchored her weeks. The reminder that life trundled on, no matter how fervently you might wish it otherwise sometimes.

Her brother-in-law got up when she walked into the living room. The perfect gentleman, stepping towards her, smiling, arms outstretched. 'Here she is, the glamorous Ellen.'

'Hello Michael.' She hated him calling her that, hated the implicit insult to Maria, unnoticed by her parents. She endured his hands pressing into her back, his lips on her cheek, knowing he was relishing the contact.

She bent to kiss her father's velvety face. 'Hi Dad. Everything OK?'

'Fine,' her father answered. 'We were just wondering where you were.'

'Yeah, sorry about that, running a bit late today.'

She crossed to Maria and Pat, sitting side by side on the small wine-coloured couch. Pat held a small red toy car and ran his finger along the wheels.

'Hello soldier.' She ruffled his hair – the briefest, the lightest of touches – and sat on the arm of the couch. 'I've decided to stick with it,' she said in an undertone to Maria.

'Good.' Her sister held a small glass of sherry which her mother poured for her every Sunday, and which Maria never finished. 'I think you're right.'

'I'm still mad at him though.'

143

She watched her mother walk towards her with sherry. The shock she'd got when Edward had suggested that they make the accident in the play the cause of her limp.

She'd read the script, she knew that Dorothy had been involved in a car accident when she was young, and she hadn't taken too much notice of it. But when Edward had linked it to Dorothy's limp – to Ellen's limp – the horrible coincidence of it had brought her up short, had propelled her away from him before she could make a fool of herself or say something she might regret.

'I'm not going back,' she'd insisted to Maria on the way home. 'He can find another Dorothy bloody Williams.'

'Ah, Ellen, don't do that. Look, he obviously wants you for the part – he picked you from lots of others, so he's willing to make allowances–'

'*Allowances?* He has to make *allowances* for me, does he? Well, isn't he just *wonderful*–'

'El, watch the road, please.'

'How *dare* he–' She braked sharply as they came to the roundabout. 'The bloody *nerve* of him, invading my privacy like that.'

'He has to. If someone limps in a play you assume they're putting it on, and you're waiting to have it explained.'

Ellen said nothing to this, unwilling to allow the truth of it. The rest of the journey passed in silence.

When she pulled up outside Maria's house, her sister turned to her. 'Ellen, please don't leave. I won't do it without you.'

'Of course you will, don't be ridiculous. You

144

don't need me, you're well able to go on your own.'

'I'm not – I couldn't. It would be too awkward to get there. I'd have to get a taxi, and they could be late.'

'That's not fair, that's emotional blackmail.' But Ellen's anger was dampening already. Edward had no way of knowing how his suggestion had affected her. It wasn't fair to blame him, even if he was an obnoxious boor. 'Look, I'll think about it. I'll talk to you Sunday.'

And she did think about it, in turns furious with Edward for probing into what she considered to be none of his business, and grudgingly allowing that some mention of her limp would have to be made.

She should have known he'd bring it up again, she should have been waiting for it, but she'd forgotten because Thursday had been Danny's birthday, which was far more important than some stupid rehearsal – and because she rarely thought about the fact that she limped until some idiot mentioned it.

And now attention was going to be drawn to it. It was going to be written into the stupid play and she'd have to stand on a stage and talk about it in front of everyone. And worst of all, it was going to be linked to the fatal car crash.

Of course she could see that it made sense to have the limp as some kind of legacy of the accident, but could she bear art to imitate life so closely? Wasn't it going to be a constant reminder – not that she needed any reminding – of Danny's death?

On the other hand, it was just a play, and not a very good one at that. The accident – *her* accident – had happened nine years ago, she couldn't let it affect everything she did forevermore. But it would be painful; talking about accidents and death and injuries would certainly help to keep the horror alive.

Serve her right for ever getting involved in the stupid play – so much for trying to help Maria. Why couldn't Ellen have signed them up for an evening class instead? Wouldn't cookery or yoga or whatever have got Maria out of the house just as easily, without all this palaver?

It wouldn't be fair to back out of the play now, though. It would be too awkward for Maria, and awkward for everyone else too. But why did Edward Bull have to be such a disagreeable man? He might be a wonderful director – although Ellen had yet to be convinced of that – but he had little else going for him. He was rude and abrupt and probably well used to getting his own way.

She couldn't imagine him being married, hadn't bothered to check whether he wore a ring. His wife, if she existed, was to be pitied. Ellen had to acknowledge that he wasn't bad looking, which was probably the best you could say about him – not that she'd ever been into the brooding, hungry-looking types.

Her mother announced dinner then and they all trooped into the kitchen and ate roast beef, and the cauliflower cheese that was always served because it was Michael's favourite.

Pat had boiled potatoes, mashed with a little

146

milk and butter to a creamy purée with absolutely no lumps. They'd long since given up trying to introduce anything else to his plate.

They talked about the play.

'Isn't it exciting,' their mother said, 'both of our daughters on the stage. We'll all be dying for the opening night.'

'Hmmm,' Ellen said. 'We've got a long way to go yet.'

They discussed Michael's new contract for a housing estate outside the city.

'Work should be starting in September,' he told them. 'Fifty houses, a nice little job.'

'That'll keep you out of trouble,' their father said, and he and Michael laughed.

Somewhere around the apple sponge and custard, the subject of their mother's hip came up.

'It's at me again,' she said. 'We're thinking about a replacement.'

'Could make a new woman of you,' Michael said, winking at their father.

They talked about a neighbour's son going for the priesthood, and Michael's improved golf handicap and the rise in petrol prices. Pat spilled milk and got a replacement. Their mother went around the table with seconds, which everyone except Michael refused.

Ellen left soon afterwards. 'I promised Oliver I'd record a film on Sky Movies for him, and I forgot to set it.'

She was tired after an energetic night with practically no sleep. Not that she'd complained at the time – not that either of them had felt like sleeping – but now she was in dire need of a few hours alone under the duvet.

She kissed the top of Pat's head, as close as you could get to his little boy cheeks. 'Bye bye Patty-cake, be good.' A promise to call her parents during the week, a quick wave to Michael before he had a chance to get to his feet.

Back at the apartment, she stepped out of the navy trousers, unbuttoned the patterned top, dropped her underwear into the laundry basket. She tucked her hair into the plastic cap and stood under the hot shower, feeling the delicious tiredness in her bones, glad that she'd taken the time to change the sheets after he'd left, happy that she had a nice fresh bed waiting for her.

She poured gel into her palm and soaped her neck, her shoulders, her breasts, under her arms. As she massaged the sudsy gel, her fingers felt an unfamiliar swelling to the side of her left breast.

She ran the tips of her fingers to and fro, gauging the size of it. It was smooth, like a blister. She pressed it cautiously, felt its taut roundness. Like a lump.

A lump. She took her hands away and let the suds flow down her body until she was rinsed clean. She towelled herself dry and pulled the shower cap from her head and stood with her arm raised in front of the full-length mirror in her bedroom.

There was no sign of anything there, no swelling of the skin, it was probably nothing. Weren't most lumps just harmless cysts? Hadn't she read that somewhere?

She got into pyjamas and climbed in between

the fresh, cool sheets. Her hand crept towards it again, she felt the swelling through her pyjama top. If it was still there in a week's time she might get her doctor to take a look. But it would probably be gone by then.

She closed her eyes and waited for sleep.

Maria

She pushed open the door of the bookshop and the wonderful, clean smell of millions of bound pages rushed to meet her. She had tried once to define the scent of a new book, that delicious pungent-with-promise fragrance, and failed.

'Did you happen to see the moon last night?'

Maria smiled. 'Good morning, Oliver. Actually, I didn't – what did I miss?'

'She was magnificent,' he said, his hands in an opened box of books on the counter. 'Round and plump ... and serene, like a pregnant goddess.'

Maria knew better than to laugh. 'Really? I'm sorry I missed it – I mean her.' She began to unbutton her coat. 'Must remember to look out tonight.'

'Tonight,' Oliver said, 'she will be on the wane. Not the same at *all*.'

'Oh, dear, I've missed her then. Ah well.' Maria hung her coat behind the door that led to the kitchen and stowed the folded buggy underneath it. 'You'll have to let me know when she'll be back.'

Oliver Noble was the perfect assistant. Regular as the tides, opening up on the dot of half nine every morning, always beautifully dressed in suits that Maria guessed were custom made. Clearly, he wasn't dependant on the modest salary the bookshop paid him.

His caramel-coloured hair was fashionably cut, the tips subtly highlighted. He was taller than Maria, and slimmer. His skin gleamed. His age had never been mentioned, but Maria guessed not too far above thirty. She assumed he was unattached – in three years there'd been no mention of a partner.

He was, of course, blatantly gay. He lusted after Antonio Banderas and Jude Law. He was also impossibly generous, patient with the most awkward customers, never sick, and devoted to his cat, Skittles. He and Ellen traded DVDs and gossip magazines.

Maria blessed the day he'd answered her ad three years earlier, when the bookshop had suddenly taken second place to Pat and his problems, when part-time help was no longer enough. From his first week Oliver had proven his worth, and now she couldn't imagine running the shop without him. At times she felt like the assistant, which suited her perfectly.

'Where has that delivery come from?' she asked.

'This one,' he said, indicating the box in front of him, 'is from Books'N'Bobs, and that,' he pointed to another on the floor that Maria hadn't noticed, 'is from Maynard's, disgracefully late. I've had a stern word with Graham, and he's

150

giving us an extra five per cent off.'

'Good for you.' Maria looked around. 'It's quiet today, isn't it?'

'One purchase of a Collin's Atlas, two fiction purchases, one enquiry about the new Philip Roth in paperback,' Oliver replied.

'I see.' Again she hid a smile. 'Not too bad, I suppose, for the first half hour of a Monday morning.'

'As you say, not too bad.' He turned back to his box. 'I'll put on the kettle as soon as I've sorted these.' He drank countless cups of green tea a day.

Maria took her bag from the counter. 'I'll do it.'

'Right you are.' He lifted out books and laid them on the counter in neat piles. 'And if you have a little rummage,' he called after her, 'you'll find a few of auntie's almond cookies.'

'Oh, good.'

Oliver had a widowed aunt living on the other side of the city who he visited regularly, and who rewarded her nephew with home-baked treats: sticky gingerbread, crumbly golden shortbread, dainty florentines.

'And how,' Oliver asked as Maria returned, 'is that little scallywag of yours?'

Maybe the quality that most endeared her assistant to Maria was his affinity with Pat. Oliver treated the little boy exactly as he treated everyone else – with unfailing courtesy. He gave no sign of noticing that Pat was different, and Maria loved him for it.

'So tell me, young fellow,' he'd say as Pat rolled the wheel of his car, or sat unblinking on the chair Maria kept for him behind the counter, 'what do you think of this?' Holding up a picture book, pointing to the illustration. 'Isn't that a nice little blue van? I'd like one of those, would you?' Speaking half to himself, not looking at Pat, keeping his eyes on the book.

'Yes,' he'd say slowly, thoughtfully, 'if I had a little van like that I'd go to the seaside and have a picnic on the sand... And what, I wonder, would I eat? Let me see now...' not seeming to notice as Pat reached towards the book, as he touched the van with a small finger '...I think perhaps strawberries. I like strawberries, you see.'

His voice soft, almost sleepy, Pat watching the blue van, his hand stilled on his red car.

'And if you came too,' he'd say, not looking in Pat's direction, not taking his eyes off the book or altering his gentle, low tone, 'we would bring some crackers. You like crackers, don't you? And peanut butter, yes, lots of *yummy* peanut butter. And maybe a big' – pause – 'yellow' – pause – '*banana.*'

And so it would go, the man on his hunkers in his beautiful suit, book open on his lap, the little boy close by, the soft murmur of Oliver's voice, the occasional small guttural sound in response from Pat. It was wonderful for Maria to see.

She heard the faint click of the kettle powering itself off and set about making the drinks – one green tea, one coffee – but as she reached for the jar of instant coffee, she realised it wasn't what she wanted. Today she'd have green tea too, for a change.

She stirred both mugs, inhaling the light, grassy

152

scent. She found the cookies and put four of them on a yellow plate and carried everything out to the shop, where Oliver was dealing with a newly arrived customer. She put the plate of cookies on the shelf behind the counter, wondering why she didn't feel in the least like taking one.

And then out of nowhere a sensation in her abdomen, a cramp that caused her to draw her breath in, and bend slightly and press a palm there.

At the cash register Oliver turned and saw her white face. 'Go in the back,' he said quickly. 'Sit down, put your head between your knees. Deep breaths.'

In the kitchen, the cramps came in waves. Maria sat on the edge of a chair and leaned over, breathing through them. Her face was icily damp. As Oliver appeared the sensation changed, she felt a sudden surge and ran to the little toilet cubicle at the rear, just in time to throw up her breakfast cereal.

When her stomach was empty she rinsed her mouth and flushed the toilet and walked back out on shaky legs.

'Poor you.' Oliver was holding a glass of water. 'Could you manage a tiny sip?'

'I'm fine now. Just something I ate, probably.' She drank water and breathed deeply. 'Thanks. Sorry about that.'

'No apologies, please.' Oliver searched her face, frowning. 'Maybe you should go home and get yourself to bed.'

'Oh no – really, I'm fine now.' And she did feel

fine. Whatever it was had been purged. 'I'm better, honestly. Although,' she added, 'I might skip the cookies.'

'You certainly will,' Oliver agreed solemnly.

The day passed like Mondays generally did. In between customers, Maria told Oliver about the play. 'Of course I don't know them well yet, but they seem like a nice bunch. I wouldn't have gone at all, but Ellen needed me for moral support, and I actually found myself enjoying it. I think it'll be a good experience, as long as I can remember the lines.'

Oliver told her about his plans to redecorate his living room. 'I thought perhaps mink for the soft furnishings, such a peaceful shade, with splashes of sage and rust here and there, and ivory on the walls. What would you think?'

For lunch she cautiously nibbled a cheese sandwich, and it stayed down. At four she left the shop and wheeled the empty buggy to her parents', as usual, and collected Pat and brought him home.

She took in the washing and ran through her lines while Pat had his nap, and when he woke up she played the piano.

It wasn't until she was mashing his teatime banana that a tiny worm of possibility began to slither awake inside her. And by the time she was turning her husband's pork chop on the grill an hour later, and shaking frozen peas into boiling water, she was feeling terribly uneasy.

Harry

'You look nice.' Eve reached up and straightened Harry's one and only tie. 'Going somewhere interesting?'

'Out to dinner,' he told her. Eve was nosy, but not in a way that would annoy you.

'Really? Someone from the play?'

From the other side of the kitchen George said placidly, 'Mind your own business.'

'Be quiet and stir your soup,' Eve told him. She turned back to Harry. 'It's just that we need to know, you being our tenant and all. We need to make sure you're mixing with the right sort.'

Harry smiled. 'It's my mother's birthday. I'm taking her to a restaurant.'

'Oh, that's sweet. She'll like the change from the nursing home.' Eve turned back to George. 'When was the last time you took my mother out to dinner?'

George gave one of his sudden barks of laughter. 'Harry's taking his *own* mother out – it's slightly different.'

'Very convenient, considering your mother died years ago. How long till that soup is ready?'

Harry enjoyed living with George and Eve. It had been a good move, answering the ad they'd stuck onto the supermarket noticeboard. *One pelson wanted to share house,* it had read. *Own room. All mod cons. Rent reasonable.*

155

He wouldn't have put Ma away – he'd wanted to take care of her – but Babs and Charlie had insisted on the nursing home.

'It's too much of a responsibility for you. She could set the house on fire,' Babs had said. 'It's not fair on you, you have your own life to live.'

'What if something happened to her when you were at work?' Charlie had asked. 'You'd never forgive yourself.'

In the end, weary already from lying awake listening for her up in the night, Harry had given in. The house was sold and Ma was installed in the nursing home. In the meantime Harry had phoned a number on a postcard and found himself, a day later, sitting in Eve and George's front room answering questions.

They lived in a fairly new development, a mix of semi-detached and terraced houses with a green rectangle in the middle that had been claimed by the dozen or so young boys who set up their goalposts every fine night and played till bedtime. It was on the same side of the city as the library; had taken Harry just twenty minutes to cycle there from work.

'Why are you looking for a place?' Eve asked, direct as always, George silent beside her on the couch.

Harry told them about the family home being sold to cover the nursing home fees. 'Oh, shame.' Eve refilled Harry's cup from the big red teapot with black spots that reminded Harry of a ladybird. 'Your mother can't be that old.' George was beginning to look vaguely uncomfortable.

'Nearly seventy-one,' Harry told her. 'She was

156

well over forty when she had me.'

Eve offered him another mini Twix. 'And are you an only child, Harry?'

George cleared his throat. Eve glanced at him before turning back to Harry.

'No. I have a brother and sister, but they're much older than me. They'd both moved out by the time I was born.'

It didn't feel like an interrogation, more like a chat with friends. Harry didn't mind telling them all this. Who else was there to listen?

'I can't say I know them all that well, actually. They don't live around here – my sister's in Mayo and my brother's in Hong Kong – so I only meet them occasionally.'

'I see.' Eve pulled the wrapper off a Twix. 'Well, George and I would love you to move in, Harry – wouldn't we?' Turning to George, who'd barely opened his mouth throughout the conversation.

And George had given the only possible answer: 'Yes, of course.'

So four years ago Harry had taken possession of the medium-sized bedroom at the front of the house, filling it with his books and his CD collection and his box of swimming trophies. His bicycle shared space in the small wooden shed at the bottom of the garden with the lawnmower and the hedge clippers and the half full paint cans and Eve's broken teapots.

Eve and George were in their mid-thirties, both working in Carran Computers on the outskirts of Portmaine. They'd met there, Eve told Harry, seven years earlier.

They weren't married and there was no talk of

157

children, and not being blessed with Eve's curiosity, Harry didn't ask for details. Most of the time, landlords and tenant lived independently of each other – Harry ate dinner at six, as soon as he got home from work, with George and Eve normally turning up around half past, when Harry was washing up.

Sometimes he went swimming in the evenings, sometimes Eve and George went out. If they all stayed in, they accommodated each other easily. They never socialised together; nobody ever suggested a group outing. Harry paid a third of all the bills, along with two hundred euro a month, in return for having somewhere to sleep at night.

A car horn sounded outside. 'There's my taxi,' he said. 'I'll be off.'

Eve walked out to the hall with him. 'Tell her happy birthday. I'd have got a card if I'd known.'

He'd told Ma about Eve and George, he often mentioned them when he visited. He'd talked about the teapots Eve collected, about the ones she couldn't bear to part with even after they'd lost their lids or chipped their spouts.

'The shed is full of them,' he'd said, and Ma had looked past him. 'All colours, all different sizes. She has one with a sign painted on it that says, "If found, please return to the Mad Hatter".'

No smile from Ma. But she'd heard, he was sure she'd heard. And maybe she'd put the Mad Hatter teapot someplace in her head, and pulled it out again after he'd left, and had another look at it. And maybe it had made her smile then.

It took barely fifteen minutes to drive what took Harry nearly an hour on the bike every Sunday afternoon, but he preferred to cycle. The thought of owning a car had never interested him.

'I'll be right back,' he told the driver when they pulled up outside the nursing home. 'Just collecting someone.'

The glassed-in porch, where people often sat on wicker armchairs if they were waiting to be taken out, was empty. Harry pushed the bell and waited, and a minute later a woman in a white coat appeared and smiled at him through the glass as she turned the key.

'There you are, Harry – she's nearly ready. Come on in.'

'Thanks.'

He was never sure of their names, these women who looked after his mother. There was definitely a Marjorie and a Carmel and he thought there was an Ann, and hadn't one introduced herself as Lorraine, or Laura, a couple of weeks ago? Their names drifted around in his head and became disconnected from their faces, so Harry always played it safe and called them nothing.

The corridor smelled of bleach and frying meat. There was a faint clatter of cutlery coming from somewhere to the left of it, and a buzz of voices. Harry walked past half a dozen doors, all painted a darker green than the walls, before he reached Ma's room.

She sat on the side of her bed as another white-coated woman bent in front of her, tying her shoes. Ma looked at Harry as he walked in.

He smiled. 'Hello, Ma, happy birthday. How

159

are you?'

Her face showed no reaction. 'How are you.'

The woman at her feet said brightly, 'Hello, Harry. Look, Veronica, it's Harry, come to take you out to dinner for your birthday. Aren't you the lucky woman? I wish someone nice would come and take me out.' She spoke too loudly. 'And doesn't he look smart, all dressed up for you?'

Ma didn't respond. She wore the grey coat she'd bought for Harry's confirmation, and black shoes. Her hair, speckled beige and white, had been washed and brushed carefully. Someone had put pink lipstick on her. She looked at Harry blankly.

The other woman stood up, turning to Harry. 'Going somewhere nice?'

'The Cow and the Moon,' he told her. 'Thought I'd give it a try.'

'Oh, that's a lovely place.'

Harry hadn't had a clue where to bring Ma. He never ate out himself, had chosen the Cow and the Moon because there was a leaflet pinned to the noticeboard in the library. *Local produce*, it promised. *Varied menu. Friendly service. Recently refurbished.* He thought it sounded like it might suit Ma.

'Now Veronica, you have a lovely dinner and we'll see you later, alright?' The nurse handed Ma her black handbag and began to shepherd her towards the door, and Harry stepped backwards into the corridor.

'Sausages,' Ma said suddenly.

'Yes, dear, it's sausages here tonight, but you'll

160

have something much more interesting, I'm sure. You can tell us all about it when you get back.'

In the corridor, Harry tucked Ma's arm into his and the three of them moved slowly towards the front door. Ma kept her eyes down and took tiny shuffling steps, leaning against him, light as popcorn. He could smell the clean scent of her shampoo.

The nurse held the door open for them. 'Bye bye now, dear, have a lovely time. See you later.'

'Sausages,' Ma repeated, lifting a foot high over the threshold.

Harry led her down the three steps. The taxi driver got out and held the back door open as Ma was manoeuvred in. Harry buckled her seat belt.

'Where to?' the driver asked as he started the engine.

'The Cow and the Moon,' Harry told him, pulling his door closed. 'Over by the new bridge.'

'It's Wednesday,' Ma announced clearly from the back.

'That's right, love.' The taxi man's eyes flicked to the rear view mirror as he swung the car around. 'You're right there.'

'Where are we going?' she asked him. 'Where are you taking me?' A tiny, querulous edge to her voice.

Harry said quickly, 'We're just going out to dinner, Ma. I'm taking you out for your birthday, remember? I'll bring you straight back again.'

Ma said nothing. The taxi driver glanced at Harry and then said into the mirror, 'Happy birthday, love. Many more of them.'

Ma didn't answer.

161

'Eve says happy birthday,' Harry told her. 'You remember me telling you about Eve and George?'

No response.

The taxi driver began to whistle and a second later stopped abruptly. 'Not a bad day.'

'No.' Harry realised suddenly that he was clenching his fists. He opened them slowly and stretched his fingers. His tie felt too tight; he wriggled it looser and opened his top button. 'Hope we get a decent summer, after last year.'

'Now you said it.' The taxi driver pulled up at a red traffic light and tapped his fingers on the steering wheel. 'Could do with a bit of good weather is right.' He began to whistle again, something Harry recognised but couldn't name.

'We have sausages on Wednesday,' Ma said loudly. 'We don't have chops.'

Harry sat half turned towards her. 'That's right, Ma, sausages on Wednesday.' Her hair had been carefully parted on the left. He could see the pink of her scalp in the divide. 'What day do you have chops?'

'Thursday,' she said immediately. 'Chops on Thursday.' Her hands were in her lap, the fingers fluttering gently. She didn't look at him as she spoke, her gaze was off to his right.

'That's nice. You like a chop, don't you?' He supposed the food at the nursing home was no better or worse than in most institutions. Certainly Ma didn't look malnourished. She was thin, but she'd always been thin. She was rarely sick. 'You might like a change tonight – what about some chicken?'

She'd always roasted a chicken on Sunday, even

when it was just the two of them. They'd have what was left on Monday, with onion mash and white sauce. She'd always given Harry the two legs, although he secretly preferred the breast meat.

'A nice bit of roast chicken maybe?'

But she looked to his right and said nothing.

The restaurant was quiet. A man sat alone at one table, a newspaper propped open in front of him, and an older couple sat in a corner, eating silently. Two men were pushing back their chairs and reaching for jackets, one poking in his mouth with a toothpick.

A family group – dark-haired woman, blond man, two boys – were at a table by the window. The boys, certainly brothers, maybe twins, looked around the same age. Harry guessed ten or eleven. They both turned at the sound of the door opening, then looked away again.

Harry watched a blonde waitress walking towards them, wondering where he'd seen her before.

'Harry, isn't it? I should have recognised your name from the booking.'

'Yes.' He struggled to remember where they'd met.

'Theo,' she said quickly. 'I'm in the play. It's the hair that's putting you off. It was pink the last time you saw it.'

'Oh ... right, sorry. I just couldn't place–'

'Don't worry about it.' She turned to Ma and smiled. 'Hello there, you're very welcome.'

'My mother, Veronica,' Harry said, feeling an introduction was called for.

Ma peered at Theo. 'You're Yvonne.'

Theo showed no surprise. 'No dear, I'm not Yvonne, I'm Theo, I'm a friend of Harry's. Here,' she said, putting a hand under Ma's elbow, shepherding her across the room, 'come with me and I'll get you a nice table.'

Harry followed them. He wondered if he should mention the cake that he'd dropped in on his way home from work. Theo hadn't been around then. He'd had no idea she worked here. They'd hardly spoken at the rehearsal. He knew nothing about her, except that she wore unusual shoes, and apparently liked to change her hair colour.

'Now,' Theo said as they reached a table for two against the wall. 'Will this do?' Pulling out a chair. 'Is this alright for you, Veronica? Here, let me take that nice coat.'

The table with the two boys was closest, about six feet away. Ma looked around her as she sat. 'Where's Yvonne? Is she coming?'

Harry hung his jacket on the back of the opposite seat. 'It's OK, Ma, were just going to have some dinner now.' He didn't remember her mentioning an Yvonne before.

Theo placed menus in front of them. 'Yvonne is probably on the way. I'll just go and check.' She winked at Harry. 'Now, something to drink?'

'Just water,' Harry told her, and she walked away and disappeared through what he assumed was the kitchen door.

Ma looked at Harry, her menu ignored. 'It's not Sunday.'

'No, Ma, it's Wednesday. It's your birthday,

remember? We're going to have some dinner now, alright?'

Like a child, like humouring a small child. He opened his menu and turned to the main courses. 'Let's have a look here.' He scanned the dishes rapidly. 'Look, Ma, they have chicken casserole – you'd like that, wouldn't you?'

'I need the toilet,' Ma said loudly. She began to struggle out of her chair as the two boys' heads swung towards her.

Harry got up quickly, scanning the room for a sign. 'Hang on–'

By the time he found it, Ma was shuffling off in the wrong direction. 'No, Ma, it's this way.' He took her arm and turned her around and led her across the floor, conscious of heads following their progress. 'In here.'

He pushed open the door of the ladies' and Ma shuffled in. 'I'll wait for you out here,' he called after her. He stood beside the door, looking fixedly through the long window at the front of the restaurant.

He should have brought someone to help. He hadn't anticipated this, but he should have. Of course Ma would need the toilet at some stage, and now she was in there on her own, and maybe confused with the unfamiliar surroundings.

He felt people looking in his direction. His neck prickled and his face burned. He heard one of the boys at the other table saying loudly, 'I am *not*,' and someone shushing him.

The minutes ticked by. Harry kept his gaze on the flow of pedestrians outside, a couple stopping to read the menu by the door, a man rushing past pulling a little brown dog. Three girls in school uniforms walked by, arms linked, two of them laughing loudly.

Harry's shoulders ached. He forced himself to relax. Should she be taking this long? What if she'd locked herself into a cubicle? He looked at the closed toilet door. He was going to have to go in. He stepped towards it.

'Harry—' Theo was suddenly at his elbow. 'You sit down, I'll get her.'

'It's just that she's taking an awfully long time,' Harry explained, but Theo had already disappeared inside.

He walked back to his table. The two boys were eating dessert with great concentration, and ignored him as he passed. The woman looked up and smiled with what might have been pity. Harry forced an answering smile. The man didn't turn around.

Babs was wrong. This wasn't a bad idea, Ma just needed to get used to the different surroundings. It was going to be alright once she settled down.

There was a jug of iced water and a basket of bread rolls on the table. He scanned rapidly through the different dishes on the menu, saw pan-grilled steak, stuffed aubergines, fish cakes, roast duck, but the words made no sense to him.

He looked across at the still-closed toilet door. He parked his elbows on the table and lowered his head into his hands, pushing his palms against his closed eyes. Some birthday treat this was turning out to be.

No. Stop. He took deep, slow breaths, trying to

166

unclench his gut. He heard them coming back and lowered his hands, and got up to pull back Ma's chair.

'Now.' Theo held her arm as she sat. 'Alright, Veronica?'

'I think we'll order,' Harry said. 'Ma? You want the chicken?'

'Sausages,' said Ma, looking at Theo. 'Sausages on Wednesday. Tell Yvonne.'

Theo pulled a pad from her overall pocket. 'No problem, sausages it is. And you, Harry?' Giving him a look that was full of sympathy. 'What would you like?'

'Er, the—' he jabbed a finger at the menu '—the fish cakes, I'll have them please.'

'Good choice, they're yummy.' Theo wrote. 'And just the water to drink?' She bent to Ma. 'Would you like a glass of milk, dear, or a cup of tea maybe?'

She was wonderful. She didn't shout when she spoke to Ma, she didn't act as if there was anything at all different about this table. Harry slumped with relief. It was going to be alright.

'I think the water's OK,' he said when Ma didn't respond.

'Is Yvonne coming?'

'She is, Ma.' He watched Theo vanish again. 'She's on the way, any minute now.'

He assumed sausages featured somewhere on the menu – the children's section, maybe. He should have thought of that too, he should have realised that four years of sausages on Wednesday would have left its mark. Chops on Thursday, she'd said. Sausages on Wednesday.

167

He put a hand across the table and covered Ma's, sitting like a small animal on the white cloth, fingers curled into her palm. Her skin was cool, the bones heartbreakingly prominent beneath.

'Happy birthday, Ma,' he said. 'I hope you like the dinner.'

He hadn't thought to get her a present; hadn't thought beyond the meal. He remembered the cake. He imagined Theo sticking the candles in. Everyone would look when she brought it out, just like Harry had imagined. The boys would enjoy that. He'd offer them slices.

'Lorraine made me change my tights,' Ma said.

'Did she?'

He was sorry he hadn't ordered a glass of wine, he hardly ever drank, but he would have liked something now.

'Angela always left the door open,' Ma told him. 'I didn't like that.'

'No, you didn't.'

Angela – that was the name of the woman Ma had shared with when she moved into the nursing home. Angela who never closed the door when she went out. Angela who had a stroke after a few months and was taken somewhere else. Ma hadn't laid eyes on her in over three years.

She couldn't remember her son's name most of the time, but she remembered Angela.

'She's gone now, Ma. You have Pauline now. You like her, don't you?'

At the next table, the two boys were putting on their coats. They'd miss the cake. Ma's head drooped and Harry squeezed her hand gently.

168

'That's OK, Ma, everything is OK. We're having a nice time, aren't we?'

Ma looked up suddenly. 'Where's Pauline?' She looked around rapidly, her voice rising. 'Where's Yvonne? Why isn't she coming?'

Halfway to the door, the two boys turned back and stared. Their mother pushed them forwards, said something in a low voice. They moved on, still glancing back. The man had walked ahead of them and was holding the door open.

'Yvonne will be here any minute.' Harry tightened his grip on her hand. 'It's OK Ma, she's on the way. She's just a bit late, that's all.'

'Where's my sausages?' Louder still, struggling to her feet, pulling away from his hand. Harry pushed his chair back and came around to her as the door closed behind the family, as a recently arrived group lowered their menus and looked across at them.

Theo came out from the kitchen then and saw at a glance what was happening. She walked quickly towards the table, where Ma was half in and half out of her chair.

'Here we go now,' she said, putting plates in front of them. 'You'll need to sit down, dear.' She put a hand on Ma's arm and guided her back gently. 'We'll let Harry have his dinner, will we?'

Ma's plate had just two sausages on it. Harry got fish cakes sitting on a bed of mash and a little pyramid of mixed vegetables – peppers, onions, baby sweetcorn – that looked stir-fried.

Theo bent towards Ma again. 'Now Veronica, do you want mash or chips? I wasn't sure which you'd prefer.'

Ma began to shake her head. The fish cakes smelled good. Harry's stomach rumbled.

'What about a few chips,' Theo suggested, 'and maybe some carrots?'

'I don't like these sausages.' Ma looked up at Theo. 'They're not the *right* sausages. I want the right sausages.'

'Ma,' Harry said quickly, 'try those ones. I'm sure they're delicious.'

Ma's mouth trembled. She made no attempt to start eating. 'I don't like them,' she said.

Harry got up. 'It's OK, Ma,' he said. 'It's OK, you don't have to eat them.' He turned to Theo. 'I'm really sorry.'

'Don't be daft,' she said.

Ma began to struggle up again and Theo eased her chair back. 'Easy does it now, Veronica. Take your time.'

'If I could get the bill,' Harry said.

'We'll sort the bill out tomorrow night, at the rehearsal,' Theo told him, putting Ma into her coat. 'Have you a car?'

'No, we came by taxi.'

'I could phone you one, but you'd be quicker walking to the rank – it's just around the corner.'

'Thank you,' Harry said. It was too little, but it was all he had. 'Thank you very much.'

'No problem.' She walked with him as he guided Ma towards the door. 'Listen, don't beat yourself up about it – you were great to try and you haven't done any harm at all. She just wasn't able.'

She held the door open and waited till they reached the street. 'Now Veronica,' she said, 'be sure to go straight home, no stopping off at a nightclub.'

'Oh no,' said Ma.

'See you tomorrow night,' Theo told Harry. 'I still have to learn my lines.'

Harry sat beside Ma in the taxi. He kept his head turned away from the driver, who didn't try to talk.

'I'm hungry,' she said once, and Harry squeezed her hand and told her she'd get her dinner soon.

Back at the nursing home, he explained that she'd had nothing to eat and they promised her sausages and they looked at Harry pityingly.

'Bye, Ma,' he said, but she was shuffling towards the dining room and didn't look back.

He asked the taxi driver to let him off in town. He went into the first pub he saw and ordered a glass of red wine. When that was finished he walked across the road to Supermacs, and sat for an hour and ten minutes over a chicken wrap and large fries, and then he went home.

'How was it?' Eve asked as he walked into the sitting room.

'Good' he said. 'She enjoyed it.'

'What did you have?'

'I had fish cakes and she had chicken casserole.'

'Lovely.'

He sat and watched a documentary about Zimbabwe with them. Then he yawned and told them he was off to bed.

He was almost asleep, the hunger edging back, when he remembered the cake.

Judith

She wrote *Work not prepared* in red pen, added a C- in a circle and dropped the essay on top of the pile. She stretched her arms over her head and glanced at the clock on the classroom wall opposite. Half four, not too bad. With a run into Dunnes on the way she'd be home by half five, quarter to six.

Stir-fry tonight? No, she had the other half of last night's pasta, that would do with a bit of salad. Great that she didn't have to cook dinner for anyone else, that she could have exactly what she wanted, when she wanted it.

Of course, tonight she'd have to keep an eye on the clock, with rehearsal at half seven. Ten past she'd need to leave the house, to be sure of being there on time. She gathered her things together and left the classroom.

Walking to the car, she fell into step with Ben, also leaving.

'You're late today,' Judith said. He usually rushed off at half three to collect his baby daughter from the crèche.

'Change of routine,' he told her. 'My partner's got this new thing on Thursday evenings so she gets off work earlier. Leaves me a bit freer.'

She liked Ben, who taught chemistry and maths. Not that she knew him very well – with over seventy staff members in the comprehensive, there were some she'd hardly spoken to. But Judith taught art to Ben's older daughter, Gemima, so he was a parent as well as a colleague.

'See you tomorrow,' he said, getting into his green Peugeot.

In Dunnes, Judith bought toilet rolls and cod liver oil and tissues, and wholewheat pasta spirals and salad leaves, and a wedge of Brie and two tins of cat food. At the checkout, she added a Crunchie to her basket.

She saw the red-haired sister – Ellen, wasn't it? – two people ahead of her in the queue, bundling groceries into a small grey backpack before walking out of the supermarket. The limp wasn't terribly obvious, but it was there. What had happened? An accident? A legacy of some sickness? She didn't seem like the type who'd offer the information or thank anyone for asking.

Judith handed over her Value Club card to be swiped and stood while her purchases were scanned. They probably all had stories, all six of them. And Edward Bull too, he surely had a story.

As she packed her green Bag for Life, she imagined their faces if she went into tonight's rehearsal and started talking about Christopher. *Let me tell you about my son,* she'd say. She imagined the release of letting it all out, of handing it over to them. She could hear the words she'd use, like *drugs* and *gambling* and *stealing.* She could see their faces, she could taste their pity.

'He's in Greece now,' she'd say. 'He tells me he's teaching English, but I doubt it. I have no idea how he's making ends meet, and I think I'm

173

better off.'

Hannah's face flashed in her head, and was gone.

'Twenty-one ninety-four,' the checkout girl said. *Marilynn* was pinned to her overall. Her blonde hair had dark roots an inch long and she looked bored.

Judith handed her twenty-five euro. 'Thank you,' she said when she got her change, noticing, as she always did, the checkout girl's lack of manners.

As she lifted her bag, someone said, 'Mrs O'Sullivan,' and there in front of her was Hannah. The near-collision with her thoughts made Judith bring a hand halfway to her face.

'Hello, Hannah, how are you?'

'I'm alright.'

Hannah Riordan wasn't pretty, but her eyes were apple green and her skin was pale and clear, and her full lips gave her the appearance of being generous, which she was, and confident, which she was not.

She'd grown up two streets away from Judith and Christopher. She and Christopher had gone to school together, and to the usual discos as teenagers, and had hung around in the same general group. It was clear to anyone who had eyes to see that Hannah Riordan adored Christopher O'Sullivan, and equally, tragically clear that her adoration was unrequited.

And six years ago, when they were both sixteen and attending the comprehensive school where Judith taught, Hannah had knocked on Judith's door one evening when Christopher was out, and whispered that she was pregnant and begged her for help.

In the course of the conversation that followed, Judith learned three things: that Hannah had been drunk when she'd had sex with Christopher, that it had happened only once, and that she'd been a virgin before that.

Judith didn't question her story, didn't doubt a word. The truth was stamped painfully on the frightened pale face in front of her.

Hannah didn't say that Christopher – who stole from Judith's wallet, who regularly came home unable to string a sentence together – had made her do something she didn't want to. Nothing was said about advantage being taken; there was no mention of sweet-talking a drunk girl who he knew would do anything for him. Hannah didn't say a word against him and Judith didn't want to hear it.

'What are you going to do?' she asked Hannah when the girl's story had finally stuttered to a stop.

'I don't know.' Hannah's knuckles were white, her hands squeezed together in her lap. 'I can't tell my parents. They'd kill me.' She inhaled shakily, and then said in a trembling rush, 'But I'd keep it, if he … if Christopher would…'

She trailed off, and Judith could see the desperate hope she had of a white dress and a house and Christopher coming home to her every night. She reached out and covered Hannah's cold, clenched hands in hers. 'I don't think that will happen,' she said quietly, knowing there was no chance in the world that Christopher would stand by her, not the tiniest chance.

Judith watched the tears spilling down Hannah's plain, pinched face. She poured more tea and waited until they eased off, and then, feeling like the monster that she was, she said, 'It might be best if you thought about a termination.'

A fresh flood of tears then, with both of them realising the inevitability of it. Hannah had gone to London two weeks later with Judith's money in her suitcase, having told her parents that she was meeting up with a classmate who'd gone over on an earlier flight. She'd told them that they were staying with the friend's aunt in Twickenham, that she'd got them tickets for *Les Misérables,* which was on the Leaving Cert course. Knowing, as Judith knew, that Jim and Aoife Riordan would trust that their daughter was telling them the truth, like she always did, and wouldn't feel the need to check up on her story

Judith offered to go with her, but Hannah refused. 'I'll manage. You've done enough.' Her bleak, devastated face haunted Judith as she lay in bed, trying to push away the thought that she had paid for her grandchild's life to be ended before it had begun.

You've done enough.

She never spoke to Christopher about Hannah's visit. She had no idea if Hannah had told him about the pregnancy. She watched him eating his Weetabix every morning and she wondered how much destruction he had already caused unknown to her, and how much more he would be responsible for in the future.

The following week, Hannah walked into the art room with the rest of her classmates. She smiled at Judith like she did every time they met, but her smile was hollow, her eyes absent from it. She sat at her usual place and opened her notebook. Her face was pale, but then, it always was.

By then, Judith was appalled at the advice she'd given the girl. How could she have suggested it when the thought of abortion had always disgusted her, when the idea of ending an unborn life was abhorrent to her? But of course she knew why she'd done what she'd done. Like so many stupid mothers before her, she'd instinctively tried to protect a son who didn't deserve protecting – which only made her actions even more pathetic, more despicable.

Hannah left the art room immediately after the class, not meeting Judith's eye again. From then until the end of the school year four months later, the only time they came face to face was in a room with twenty-five others, when Hannah was just another sixth year.

There was never a sign of her in the group of teenagers who sat in the evenings on the low wall outside the local shop. Judith never picked her out among the girls who paraded, arms linked, through the shopping centres at the weekends.

When they spoke again, a week after school ended, it was as if their last conversation had never taken place. Judith walked into the library and there stood Hannah, her hand still reaching towards the door Judith had just pulled open.

Conversation was completely unavoidable.

'Hello, Hannah.' Judith's mouth was suddenly dry.

'Hi, Mrs O'Sullivan.' The same tense smile was there, but Hannah made no move to leave.

'I hope you're enjoying the holidays.' *I hope you don't hate me too much for what I encouraged you to do. For what I helped you to do.*

'Yes, thanks. I've got a job in Dublin, in my aunt's friend's shop. I'm going up tomorrow.'

She carried two books under her arm. She wore a yellow halter neck top that didn't flatter her complexion, and grey, calf-length leggings. She looked younger than she was.

'Oh ... that's good.' Judith nodded, searching for the words she wanted to say, but of course they couldn't be said. 'Tell your parents hello, won't you?'

'I will. Bye, Mrs O'Sullivan.' And she walked quickly through the door and was gone. She didn't come to the school on the day the Leaving Cert results came out, six weeks later. Judith met her mother in the autumn, who told her that Hannah had got a place in UCD to study arts.

'I'd prefer if she went to Galway, it's so much closer, or even Cork, but she's insisting on Dublin.'

Of course Hannah was insisting on Dublin – the further away from Portmaine, the better. She graduated three years later and got a job in the capital and only came home the odd weekend, and at Christmas.

'You look good,' Judith told her now, and she did. Her hair was cut into a short, feathery style that suited her small face and her jacket picked up the green of her eyes. 'Home for a while?'

'Just a few days, a long weekend. I took a day off for Dad's birthday.'

She didn't ask how Christopher was, of course. Judith assumed she'd heard he was in Greece now, from talk around the place. Her parents wouldn't have approved of Christopher, were probably relieved that nothing had come of their daughter's teenage crush.

Not many people who knew him envied Judith her son. There was probably a general feeling in the neighbourhood that she was better off without him.

'Well, I'd better go. It was nice to see you, Mrs O'Sullivan.'

'Mind yourself,' Judith said.

There was no blame – there never had been – when blame could so easily have been awarded. Mother and son had done wrong by her, and she had forgiven both of them.

Judith drove home, not looking forward now to the evening ahead, wanting only to sit in the bath with the CD player turned up loud, blotting our regrets and guilt. Or in front of the television maybe, letting gunshots or canned laugher or someone else's home improvements push everything else from her head. She dreaded the thought of having to spend a couple of hours in the company of people she didn't care about, and who didn't care about her.

She parked the car and carried her bag of groceries up the path. She turned her key in the front door – and as she pushed it open, the sound of voices reached her, and the smell of alcohol.

She stopped dead, letting the door swing fully open. There were people in the house, at least two people. She took a step backwards, heart thumping.

Just then, the sitting room door opened and a man walked out.

'I thought I heard you,' he said, carrying a glass of what looked like whiskey. He had a beard that needed trimming. He wore sandals and his feet were brown. 'I hope you don't mind,' he said, walking towards her. 'We opened the duty free.'

Judith dropped her shopping and put out her arms, smiling widely.

'Christopher,' she said as he bent to embrace her.

Second Rehearsal Night: Thursday, 8 May

McMillan's Pub

'Thanks very much.' Harry took the cardboard box. 'You didn't have to give it back, I wasn't expecting–'

'Why wouldn't I?' Theo asked. 'It's your cake, you paid for it, and it's only a day old. How's your mother?'

'Fine.' He smiled. 'Thanks for your help. It's just that she likes her routine.'

'Don't we all – although some routines I could do without.' Theo made a face. 'My future step-daughter visits every week; I have to be on my best behaviour.'

'Yes … and the bill, you must let me know what I owe.'

Theo shook her head. 'Forget about it. You ate nothing.'

'Oh no, I couldn't possibly–'

'Tell you what,' she said, 'you can buy me a drink at the break. How's that?'

As Harry searched for a response, Edward cleared his throat. 'We may as well all begin.'

'Judith isn't here yet,' Theo pointed out.

Edward looked pained. 'I'm aware of that, but we can't wait any longer. I'll read her lines until she turns up. Now, let's have a quick run through what we did last week, starting with Dorothy arriving at the house. Places everyone, please.'

Judith arrived ten minutes later. 'I'm awfully sorry,' she told Edward breathlessly. 'I had a … an unexpected visitor at the last minute.'

183

Edward studied her over his glasses. 'Please try to be on time,' he said coolly. 'Once a week isn't much of a commitment.'

'It won't happen again.'

He indicated the makeshift stage. 'We're just about to start your scene in the kitchen with Tom.'

Judith went to the edge of the stage and stood waiting for her cue. Ellen, sitting close by, whispered, 'Try not to have unexpected visitors again, OK?' Judith smothered a smile.

(BETTY enters the kitchen carrying a tray of glasses, and crosses to the sink as TOM opens the back door and enters.)

TOM: Morning, Betty *(shrugs his feet out of his boots, pulls off his cap and stuffs it into the pocket of his overalls).*

BETTY: Eleven o'clock already? Where's the time go? *(She takes the kettle from the stove and fills it.)* Well, don't just stand there – set the table. *(TOM begins to whistle as he takes two cups and a bowl of sugar from the dresser.)*

'What is that noise?'

Harry turned towards Edward, reddening, 'I'm not that good at whistling.'

Edward snorted. 'We'll have to change that. Can you hum?'

'Er, I think–'

'Right, we'll try humming. From your last line, Betty – "Well, don't just stand there".'

BETTY: Well, don't just stand there – set the table.

184

(TOM begins to hum as he takes two cups and a bowl of sugar from the dresser)
BETTY: You sound pleased with yourself this morning *(rinses the glasses)*.
(TOM breaks off immediately, looking embarrassed.)
BETTY: *(coaxingly)* Oh come on, you can tell me.
(TOM takes a biscuit jar from the shelf and sets it on the table.)
BETTY: *(drops teabags into the pot)* Not that you need to tell me anything – I've seen what there is to see.
TOM: *(sits at the table and opens the biscuit jar)* I don't know what you're talking about.
BETTY: It's that young reporter, isn't it? You've been mooning over her since she arrived.
(Tom eats a biscuit and ignores her.)
BETTY: *(brings the teapot to the table)* Well, let me tell you something. If you're interested, you'd want to make a move, because Mr McCarthy has his eye on her too.
(TOM stops chewing.)
BETTY: Thought that would make you sit up *(pours the tea into cups)*. He has his eye on her alright – clear as daylight, with the two of them laughing and joking in that study. You must have heard them from the garden.
TOM: *(shrugs)* What if I did? Some chance I have, against him.
BETTY: Now what kind of silly talk is that? You've got your youth, for a start – that man is old enough to be her father.
TOM: He's rich, though.

185

BETTY: So what? Money won't keep you warm in bed at night, will it?

TOM: *(looks glum)* He's good-looking too.

BETTY: Now you listen to me–

Judith stopped and stared at Tom for a second or two, and then she turned apologetically towards Edward.

'"You need to give her some kind of sign",' Edward said.

'Thank you.'

BETTY: Now you listen to me; you need to give her some kind of sign.

TOM: What kind of sign?

BETTY: *(impatiently)* A sign, a sign, some chocolates, or flowers – yes, that's it, of course. You're a gardener, for goodness sake; pick her a nice bunch of flowers and give them to her.'

TOM: *(looks alarmed)* I couldn't, I've never... I couldn't.

BETTY: Fine. *(Lifts her cup.)* Have it your own way.

(They drink in silence for a few minutes.)

TOM: I suppose I could give it a go.

BETTY: Of course you could, a fine strapping young man like yourself – wouldn't any girl be delighted to get a present from you? *(Gets up.)* Well, I have work to do, and so have you, I'm sure.

TOM: *(drains his cup and grabs another biscuit)* Thanks Betty. See you for lunch *(steps into his boots)*.

BETTY: Remember what I said. *(Turns back to the sink as TOM exits.)*

186

'Right,' Edward said. 'Let's break for ten minutes – and ten minutes does not mean fifteen minutes.' He looked pointedly at Theo.

She beamed back at him. 'Won't you join us, Edward? I hate to think of you all alone up here.'

'Actually,' he said, 'I've just remembered something. Would you mind hanging on here a minute? I'd like a quick word.' She was blonde tonight, which was a slight improvement on the pink, but he had to be sure she wouldn't go some other daft colour just before they put on the play. It needed to be said, and Edward warned to get it over with.

'Your hair,' he began, when the others had gone downstairs. 'It's just that I need to know which colour you're planning for Ursula – for the week you're onstage, I mean.'

He braced himself for her reaction – she really seemed quite unpredictable – but to his relief, she laughed.

'Oh, poor Edward,' she said. 'Is that what's bothering you? Ursula can have any colour hair you want – it's up to you, really. Although,' she added, 'I think I'd have to draw the line at green – it clashes horribly with my eyes.'

Edward had no idea what she was talking about. Was she joking?

'You mean ... you'll dye it whatever colour I want?'

Theo looked at him in surprise, her face softening. 'Oh Lord, you think this is real?' She reached up and pulled off her wig, and Edward stared at the layer of prickly brown hair that

187

barely covered her skull.

'Sorry, I should have warned you,' she said quickly 'Don't be embarrassed, it doesn't bother me in the least. I have alopecia, got it a while back. I keep it shaved now because it's so thin, and cover it up with a wig mostly.'

Edward couldn't speak. He was mortified, there were no words.

'Bless you for not noticing,' Theo said, wriggling the blonde hair back into place as she stood up. 'And of course we can agree on a nice safe colour for Ursula – I'm sure my hairdresser can help out with a loan of something for the week. Now,' she said, clip-clopping on her ridiculous shoes towards the door, her almond scent still in his nostrils, 'the postmistress needs a little drink. Sure you won't join us?'

'No thanks,' Edward managed.

She turned at the doorway. 'And since you delayed me, I may be a teeny bit late back.'

She thumped down the stairs, leaving Edward to gather his scattered wits together.

Of course it wasn't real, no real hair could go that pink without falling out – or go from shocking pink to blonde, just like that. How had he not realised? God, when she'd pulled it off he hadn't known where to look. He'd certainly picked himself an interesting cast for this wretched play. He sat back slowly, wondering uneasily what other surprises they were waiting to spring on him.

'You mentioned visitors,' Harry said.

Judith smiled. 'Yes, my son and his girlfriend arrived unexpectedly from Greece. He's been

188

teaching English over there.'

'I was wondering if you could use a cake.'

'A cake?'

'Yes. I bought it for my ... for an occasion, and it never got used.'

'Oh, well–'

'It's a long story,' Harry said quickly. 'Something came up and it wasn't eaten, and I'd hate to see it go to waste, so I thought, with your visitors...'

'That's awfully generous of you,' Judith said. 'I'm sure I could use it. Thank you very much.'

'It's upstairs,' Harry said. 'I didn't bring it with me, Theo brought it to give back to me, because it got left behind in the restaurant.'

'Oh, I understand,' said Judith, not understanding at all. Too much drink; maybe that was what had him so embarrassed. Maybe he'd drunk too much at some celebratory dinner and forgotten about the cake. Funny, Judith wouldn't have taken him for a drinker. Wasn't that orange or lemonade he was having now? Maybe he was one of those people who only drank on occasion, and invariably overdid it then. 'Well, thanks again. I'm sure it'll come in handy.'

'Excuse me,' he said, pushing his chair back abruptly. 'I need to get Theo a drink.'

Maria studied her sister. 'Are you alright?' You seem quiet.'

'I'm fine, just tired. I slept badly.' She couldn't say anything. Maria had enough on her own plate. And anyway, it was probably nothing. 'You're quiet yourself.'

'I'm always quiet,' Maria said, smiling. 'I'm the quiet one, remember?'

'You're a hairdresser,' Theo said to Robert. 'I recognise you from the salon. I go to Caroline.'

'Ah yes, I knew the face was familiar,' he lied.

'You've realised I'm wearing a wig, right?'

'Yes,' he said. 'But not because I'm a hairdresser.'

'Because they look so false?'

'No, because otherwise your hair would have to have grown about two inches in the past week.'

'Oh, right.' She smiled her thanks as Harry put a little bottle of wine in front of her. 'That would be a bit of a giveaway, I suppose.' She told Robert about her conversation with Edward. 'He hadn't a clue. He was mortified when I whipped it off.'

'I'm surprised to hear it,' Robert said. 'I would have thought our director was sharper than that.'

'Oh he's sharp alright.' Ellen, on Theo's other side, overheard. 'He doesn't miss much.'

Theo turned to her. 'Why did he ask you to stay back last week? Was it to give out for being cheeky when you wouldn't lie on the carpet?'

Ellen made a face. 'He wanted to know why I limp.'

'I was wondering the same thing myself,' Theo said. 'What happened, was it an accident or something?'

Ellen raised her glass and didn't answer.

'Sorry,' Theo said. 'None of my business. Tell me to shut up.'

'Shut up,' Ellen said calmly.

They were getting to know each other.

(PENELOPE enters the village post office. URSULA is behind the counter.)
PENELOPE: Good afternoon, Ursula. I'd like a book of stamps please.
URSULA: Ah, Miss McCarthy. And how is everything with you and your brother?
PENELOPE: *(opens her handbag)* Everything is fine, thank you. A book of stamps, if you don't mind.
URSULA: I hear that you have a visitor.
PENELOPE: *(icily)* I would imagine that you hear quite a lot.
URSULA: *(holds out the stamps)* Oh yes; working in a post office you get to hear all the gossip.
PENELOPE: (snatches the stamps and rummaging in her purse) How much is that?
URSULA: Eight euro twenty, if you please *(takes the money).* I believe that she's writing a piece on Mr McCarthy.
PENELOPE: And I believe that you should stick to what you're paid to do – sell stamps. Good day. *(exits)*
URSULA: Stuck up old cow; I'll put her in her place.
(She reaches under the counter and pulls out a writing pad. After a few seconds' thought she begins to write, smiling.)

'Good.' Edward turned to the others. 'Right, final scene in act one – Tom and Dorothy in the garden, please.'

He watched Ellen get up and walk to the stage.

191

She hadn't looked in his direction all evening – probably still stewing over their conversation last week. But at least she'd turned up.

'Quiet, please. And ... let's go.'

(DOROTHY sits on a garden bench to the right of the stage, reading. TOM walks on-stage and stands uncertainly some distance away. One hand is behind his back, the other pulls his woolly hat off his head. Eventually he coughs and DOROTHY looks up.)

DOROTHY: Tom – hello there. Isn't it a beautiful day? *(Sets aside her book and stretches her arms above her head.)* It's good to be alive, isn't it?

TOM: It is that. *(He produces the bouquet and thrusts it clumsily at her.)* Here ... I picked these for you.

DOROTHY: Did you really? How sweet. *(Buries her face in the flowers.)* They're lovely, thank you Tom *(indicates the bench)*. Why don't you sit for a minute, if you're not too busy?

(TOM hesitates, then perches on the opposite end, leaving a space between them.)

DOROTHY: *(scans the garden)* You're a wonderful gardener, Tom. This place is really beautiful. Where did you learn it all?

TOM: *(shrugs)* My grandfather used to be gardener here, when Mr McCarthy's parents were alive.

DOROTHY: Really? How nice. So when did you start working here?

TOM: A few years ago; I don't remember exactly when.

192

DOROTHY: I see.

(They sit in silence for a few seconds.)

TOM: *(clears his throat.)* Er, I was wondering...

DOROTHY: *(speaks at the same time)* So, did you–

(They both break off)

TOM: Sorry – go on.

DOROTHY: I was just wondering if you knew when Betty came to this house – when she started to work here, I mean.

TOM: *(sounds mildly surprised)* She was here before me. I don't know when she started, she never said.

DOROTHY: *(smiles)* Sorry Tom, I'm just being nosey. I don't often find myself staying in a house with its very own housekeeper or gardener.

(A voice OFFSTAGE calls for Tom, and he gets up abruptly.)

TOM: I have to go.

DOROTHY: OK – see you later. *(Calls after him.)* And thanks again for the flowers.

(She lifts the bouquet and buries her face in it. When she lowers it again her smile has disappeared.)

'Right.' Edward put down his pen. 'Back to the start for another run through. Dorothy and Betty, places please.'

They stopped at ten to ten. 'Well done, everyone. Let's leave it at that.' Edward closed his script and took his jacket from the chair beside him.

'Are you pleased with us?' Theo asked. 'Are we

193

shaping up?'

He eyed her sternly. 'In general I'm happy enough, but you've all got a long way to go.'

'But we're doing alright.'

'Yes,' he said evenly. 'So far.'

'So you're pleased. So far.'

He couldn't decide if she was trying to annoy him. He turned to the others before she had a chance to say any more. 'We'll be having a good look at act two next week, so make sure you know your lines.'

As the room emptied out, Ellen approached him. *Here we go,* he thought.

'You can go ahead,' she said coolly. Maria stood waiting by the doorway. 'Do what you suggested.'

Edward smelled the orange scent he had begun to associate with her. The contrast between her delicate hair colour and those dark brown eyes was striking. He hadn't noticed it.

'Right,' he said. 'Thank you.'

She turned away abruptly, her hair arching out, and he was reminded of the same movement in the first few minutes of their meeting.

'See you next week,' he said after her, not expecting, or receiving, a response. She left the room with Maria and Edward slowly gathered his things together.

Not a bad night, considering. The acting in general left something to be desired, of course, and all the movements needed more work. And he had to keep on at all of them, particularly Harry, about voice projection.

But the lines weren't bad – they were making the effort, he had to give them that. And next week they'd tackle act two.

Four weeks to go. He walked downstairs and caught the barmaid's eye, and pointed to the bottle of Courvoisier. 'Large,' he said. 'Please.'

As she placed the box with Harry's cake on the passenger seat, as she snapped her seat belt closed and turned the key in the ignition, Judith's thoughts rushed back to Christopher.

'Why didn't you tell me you were coming?'

'Wanted to surprise you – and there's another surprise.' He'd led her into the sitting room and the blonde woman had got out of the armchair, still holding her glass.

'Mum, this is Amanda.'

The woman had put out her hand. 'Pleased to meet you, Mrs O'Sullivan.'

She had an English accent. She was deeply tanned and several years older than Christopher; she had to be at least thirty. Judith assumed they were a couple.

'When did you arrive? How long have you been here?' she'd asked, still bewildered to see him standing in front of her.

'Couple of hours. Good job I hung onto my key.'

'Have you eaten anything? I was just about to make something for myself.'

Christopher had waved the whiskey bottle. 'Have a drink first, toast the prodigal son's home-coming.'

He'd forgotten she never drank spirits; forgotten how they upset her stomach. 'Maybe later.' She'd watched him refilling their glasses. 'Are you home for long? I mean, what are your plans?'

He'd scooped ice from Judith's mixing bowl. 'We're home for good, Mum.' He'd sat on the arm of Amanda's chair and she'd curled her hand around his arm. 'Greece is OK for a while, but we got sick of it.' He'd grinned. 'Too full of bloody Greeks.' Amanda had laughed.

'So you're moving back to Ireland? You've given up your job?'

Christopher had glanced at Amanda. 'Like I said, Mum, we're back for good.'

'We'll be looking for a place to rent,' Amanda had said. 'We'll start straight away.'

'Yeah, but in the meantime, we were thinking maybe you could put us up here? Just for a little while.'

'Of course,' Judith had said immediately. 'As long as you want.' All the times she'd wondered how he was getting on, she'd wished for more contact, and now here he was. 'This is your home.'

He'd smiled. 'Thanks, Mum.'

She'd walked towards the door. 'Now, I'm going to make us something quick to eat. I have to go out tonight, just for a couple of hours.'

'Oh yeah? Where to?'

She'd felt suddenly self-conscious. 'I'm in a play,' she'd told them. 'We're rehearsing it tonight.'

He'd looked at her, his mouth open. 'You? In a play?'

'It's just a bit of fun really.' She'd felt her face getting warm. 'Just something to do.'

'I think that's great,' Amanda had said. 'Well done. Do you do much acting?'

'Oh no,' Judith had laughed. 'No, no, I haven't been on a stage for years. I don't know what

196

possessed me, really.'

'I don't ever remember you on a stage,' Christopher had said.

'It was long before you were born,' she'd told him. 'While I was still in college.'

'Maybe we can come and see you in this one?' Amanda had turned to Christopher. 'Wouldn't that be nice, Chris?'

'Great,' he'd said, grinning. 'Can't wait to see that.'

They'd eaten pasta with salmon fillets that Judith had found in the freezer and poached.

'Delicious,' Amanda had said. 'Beats that Greek rubbish, eh Chris?'

They'd insisted on doing the washing up. 'Least we can do,' Amanda had said. 'Right, Chris?'

After the meal, Judith had left them washing up and had gone upstairs and changed the sheets on her double bed. Of course they slept together; she wouldn't even ask. She'd move to the spare room, it wasn't a big deal. Anyway it was quieter at the back of the house.

She'd taken her toiletries from the dressing table and run the hoover over the carpet. While she was putting sheets on the spare bed, Christopher had come upstairs.

'If that's for Amanda,' he'd said, 'don't bother – she can share my room.'

'I'm moving in here,' Judith had told him. 'You two can have my room, it's much bigger than yours.'

He'd frowned. 'We can't let you do that.'

'It's done,' she'd told him. 'I'm all moved out. I don't mind, honestly.'

He'd hugged her and he smelled the same as she remembered. She'd hugged him back, tightly. 'I'm glad you're home.'

'Me too.' He'd leaned in the doorway, watching her press the fasteners on the duvet cover together. 'Amanda thinks you're great.'

Judith had smiled. 'She seems nice. How long have you known her?'

He'd shrugged. 'Few months.'

'Oh.' He'd never once mentioned a girlfriend in his infrequent phone calls, and Judith hadn't asked, remembering Hannah. 'Well, I'd better make a move – our director is a stickler for time.'

'Right.'

Downstairs, she'd gathered her bag and script and jacket. 'There's plenty to eat if you get hungry again, cheese and fruit and stuff. I'm afraid there's only skimmed milk, but I'll get the other kind tomorrow. And you might find a nice film on telly.'

He'd yawned. 'You know, Mum, I think we'll probably go to bed – we've been travelling most of the day. What time are you up in the morning?'

'Friday's my late day,' she'd told him. 'I have a lie-in till about nine.'

'Right. We might not be up by then, so see you when you get home.'

She wondered how old Amanda was, and how they'd met, and whether they loved each other, and if he was happy. She hoped he was planning to shave off the beard.

He hadn't mentioned her birthday, just over a week ago.

She wondered how long it would take them to find jobs – they'd need money to pay rent. Maybe

198

Christopher was thinking of going back to the building sites, or maybe Amanda had a qualification of some sort. Maybe if Judith had a quiet word with her she might encourage Christopher to sit the Leaving Cert again – he was still only twenty-two, look at all the people much older than that who went back to school–

She stopped. Listen to her, trying to sort his life out like she'd always done. Asking around for summer jobs for him, phoning to make excuses when he slept it out. Paying his bail the time he'd been arrested for being found in possession of ecstasy tablets. Turning a blind eye to the fivers and tenners that had disappeared from her purse, ignoring the betting slips in his wastepaper basket. Giving him the price of the air-fare when he told her that a friend had got him a job teaching English in Greece, despite the fact that Christopher had never done a TEFL course. Despite the fact that his own English compositions, which Judith had often corrected, left a lot to be desired.

But he was a grown man now, and he had a girlfriend who seemed pleasant, even if she wasn't the one Judith would have chosen for him. It wasn't up to his mother any more what he did, or who he did it with.

The house was dark when she got home. She tiptoed into the hall. There was a strong smell of alcohol, but no sound. In the sitting room, she plumped cushions and collected glasses and put the almost-empty whiskey bottle into the press that held the port she kept for Christmas visitors, and the dusty half bottles of things she'd needed for long-ago cakes, like Drambuie and

Jamaica Rum.

The bathroom smelled of her bath oil, the towels slung over the side of the bath were damp. She'd forgotten to give them towels. She took a bundle of fresh ones from the hot press and hung them on the rail.

An open, bulging toilet bag sat on the bathroom shelf. Judith peered in and saw dental floss and lip balm and various tubes and bottles, and a foil card of tiny pills marked with the days of the week. At least they were taking precautions.

Judith's toothbrush had two companions in its glass, one in serious need of replacement. Her tube of toothpaste had been squeezed from the top and left uncapped.

She brushed her teeth and washed her face, thinking how relieved she was that he'd come home safe, and how nice it would be to have company in the house again. She undressed in the small bedroom, planning her shopping list for the next day.

Fish, definitely, for Amanda, who'd mentioned at dinner that she rarely ate red meat. Judith must find out what other foods she liked. And Weetabix for Christopher.

As she got into bed she remembered Harry's cake, still sitting in the car. Should she go down and get it? No – she'd bring it to school tomorrow instead; they were always delighted to get a cake in the staffroom.

She drifted off to sleep, happily aware that her child was sleeping less than twenty yards away. Safe and sound.

Theo

From Sean's bedroom window, a fretful Chrissy in her arms, Theo watched Ben's other daughter walking up the path.

Hair that framed her face in a perfect blonde curtain. Little navy pumps under the grey school uniform. A tan that had to be straight out of a spray can in this changeable weather. Lots of silver jewellery around her neck and up her arms and on her fingers. Probably to match the silver-coloured braces on her teeth that had cost Ben a small country's food budget.

It had been Ben's idea to have Gemima stay with them once a week, after Chrissy was born. 'She needs to get to know her sister,' he'd said.

'She can call and see Chrissy any time she wants,' Theo had felt obliged to point out. 'She only lives across town.'

'I know, but it would give me more time to spend with her too. I can hardly go and stay in Miep's, can I?'

Theo and Miep had never met, not formally, but Theo had studied Ben's ex from a distance, on the few occasions when both women found themselves in the same vicinity. Miep was tall and dark haired, and older than Theo by eight blessed years – forty-two to Ben's forty-one – and she was Dutch. She and Ben had met in their early twenties, on a camping holiday in Austria.

Their marriage had lasted four years, until Gemima was three.

Miep was a potter. She sold her work directly to a handful of Dutch galleries, where apparently there was big demand for it. Theo was privately impressed with the few elegant ornamental pieces that Ben had shown her.

When the marriage collapsed, Miep and Gemima had remained in the family home on the other side of Portmaine. Ben had signed a year's lease on an apartment in the centre of town, where he'd still been living when he'd met Theo, seven years later.

At the time, Gemima was spending alternate weekends in the apartment with her father, and Theo was careful not to overlap on those, but when Ben sold the apartment and moved into Theo's house, shortly after they discovered that Chrissy was on the way, Gemima opted out of the overnight visits, and she and Ben met during the day instead.

Theo occasionally felt guilty that she and Gemima were still practically strangers, despite the fact that Theo was as good as married to Gemima's father. But it took two to tango, and Gemima wasn't showing any signs of wanting to dance.

The first time they met was a few months after Theo and Ben had got together, and Ben had opted to drive Gemima to the Irish college she was attending for three weeks of the summer. He'd persuaded Theo to sit in for the two-hour drive.

'Come on, it'll give you a chance to meet and have a chat.'

It had been the longest two hours of Theo's life.

She'd insisted on Gemima taking the passenger seat, not wanting to suggest to the girl in any way that they were in competition for Ben's attention. She'd spent the entire journey perched uncomfortably in the centre of the back seat, leaning forwards through the gap, straining to hear Gemima's mumbled, monosyllabic replies to Theo's attempts at conversation.

'That went well,' she said as she and Ben turned for home. 'We got on like a house on fire.'

'Don't worry,' he told her, 'she's always shy at first. She'll be fine once she gets to know you.'

But on the odd occasions afterwards that the two females had met, the same tension was there, despite Theo's best efforts.

'She just doesn't like me.'

And Ben's answer didn't change. 'Give her time. She'll come round.'

They'd taken Gemima out to lunch shortly after Theo had discovered she was pregnant with Chrissy. Gemima had pushed her food around and looked off into the distance, again answering Theo's bright questions with as few words as possible. When the plates had been cleared away, Ben had told her about the baby.

Gemima had looked from him to Theo. 'Well ... congratulations.'

'You'll have a new brother or sister,' Ben had said. 'Isn't that exciting?'

'Yeah.'

And that was it. She'd refused dessert and sat, arms folded, while Theo and Ben had shared a mango and cranberry crumble. Theo was damned if a spoiled teenager was going to come between her and dessert.

They'd invited her to Chrissy's christening and she'd sat hunched in a pew at the church, jabbing surreptitiously at her mobile phone. She'd rushed off immediately afterwards, collected by Miep – who didn't get out of the car – for a French grind that Theo doubted existed.

Ben had wanted Gemima to be Chrissy's god-mother, but Theo was determined that her daughter wouldn't be saddled with a godmother who couldn't care less. 'I've already promised Steph,' she lied, praying that her friend would agree to take the job. 'She'd be so disappointed. Sorry, darling.'

When Ben made the suggestion, soon after the christening, of reinstating Gemima's overnight visits, Theo's heart had plummeted, but she couldn't very well refuse to let him see his daughter. And of course he was right – Gemima and Chrissy *should* get to know each other. And Gemima was Ben's firstborn child, so naturally he wanted to spend time with her.

So for the past seven months or so, Gemima had been arriving from school with Ben on Friday – she was a second year student at the compre-hensive where he taught – and staying till late Saturday afternoon, when Ben drove her home to Miep.

Theo tried her best. Sean was drafted in to help, with his mother threatening all sorts of dire consequences if he missed the evening meal. The freezer was stocked with Gemima's favourite strawberry Häagen-Dazs. Theo had rearranged her work shifts so she was off on Friday evenings, and she sacrificed her Saturday morning lie-in with Ben to get up and poach an egg for Gemima, who had a stage school class at ten.

And still, the distance between them remained as unbridgeable as ever. Gemima answered when spoken to. She never called Theo by name. She ate what was put in front of her but never touched the ice cream in the freezer, which Theo reminded her about every Friday. She remained remote and aloof, and gave no indication, ever, as to whether she was enjoying her visit or just enduring it.

It was the one subject Theo couldn't discuss with Ben. How could she admit that she dreaded his daughter's visits, that she counted the hours until he drove Gemima home again? Gemima was a child of thirteen, not some monster.

And still. And still.

Theo walked downstairs practising her smile, and opened the front door.

'Hi – come on in. Say hello to Gemima, Chrissy.'

'Hi,' Gemima said, glancing at the baby as she slung her school blazer over the banister.

'Dinner will be ready in about half an hour, OK?'

'Thanks,' Gemima said, walking towards the stairs with her overnight bag.

'Come down whenever you're ready,' Theo called after her, knowing she wouldn't reappear till dinner was on the table and her father went up to get her.

'Hey you.' Ben appeared at the door and dropped a kiss on Theo's cheek.

'Hey.' She handed Chrissy to him. 'Good day?'

He followed her into the kitchen. 'Fine. You?'

'Not bad.' Theo lit the oven and took a bottle of wine from the fridge and waved it at him.

He shook his head. 'I'm taking Gem to the shopping centre after dinner. She needs new shoes.'

Theo poured a glass for herself. She put Hilary's mushroom quiche on a baking tray and scattered frozen chips around it. She emptied salad leaves into a bowl and took the bottle of Thousand Island dressing from the fridge.

Ben laid Chrissy in her Moses basket. 'Where's the soother?'

'Sink.' He eased the green soother between Chrissy's lips, and she stopped whimpering and began to suck noisily. 'Great invention,' he said. He sat at the table, watching Theo as she moved around the room. Finally, he said, 'Are you going to tell me, or do I have to torture it out of you?'

Theo sipped her wine and pulled out the cutlery drawer. 'Tell you what?'

'Whatever's bugging you.'

Your daughter's bugging me, she wanted to say. *She robs us of our Friday nights and our precious Saturday mornings, she makes me feel guilty for no reason. She ignores every gesture of friendship I make. She's clearly determined to hate me, and there isn't a thing I can do about it.*

'Nothing's bugging me,' she said. 'I'm tired, that's all.'

She put the baking tray into the oven and lifted a stack of plates from the press. Ben took them from her and began setting the table.

'Maybe you shouldn't have taken on that play. Maybe you've enough on your plate, with the job and Chrissy.'

'Maybe.' Theo sipped the cold white wine. 'Too late now. I'd be lynched if I backed out.'

Chrissy opened her mouth to whimper again and the soother popped out. Theo put down her glass and bent to lift her out. 'Come on, lovey, I know what you need.'

The kitchen door opened and Sean walked in, his hair still damp from his hurling training.

'Hi. When's dinner?'

'Not long,' Ben told him. 'You've just got time to change Chrissy's nappy.'

Sean grinned. 'I'd love to, but I just remembered a pressing engagement upstairs.'

'Twenty minutes,' Theo told him.

'Gem's up there,' Ben called after him. 'No barging into the bathroom.'

They got on fine, Ben and Sean. They'd got on fine from day one. Sean was glad probably to have another male around the place, and Ben had the sense never to try and lay down the law. Not that he'd have needed to – unlike Ben's daughter, Theo's son was perfect.

'We won't be too long at the shopping centre,' Ben told her. 'We'll pick up a DVD on the way home.'

'Take your time,' Theo answered. 'It'll give me a chance to learn my lines for next week.'

Learning Ursula's lines was no problem – the postmistress didn't have that many scenes – but an hour or two without Gemima would be nice. Theo could watch Coronation Street without feeling the need to keep up some kind of running commentary, just to ease the tension created by

207

the girl sitting in the same room.

She took Chrissy upstairs and laid her on the changing mat in the bathroom. From Gemima's tiny bedroom, which always got fresh flowers on Friday, came the sound of a song Theo vaguely recognised.

'It's so incredibly hard to love you,' she sang to Chrissy, sliding off the sodden nappy and replacing it with a dry one, 'but I love you anyway.' She buried her face in Chrissy's plump belly and blew softly, making the baby gurgle delightedly. 'That's my girl,' she said, hoisting Chrissy into her arms again. 'Let's show our guest who the best daughter in this house is.'

Edward

General thoughts, he wrote at the top of the page.

1. Ursula hair problem sorted.

Theo DeCourcy made him nervous. Her exuberance unsettled him, the way you never knew what she was going to come out with next. But she was convincing enough as the gossipy postmistress, and at least Ursula wasn't going to look like the village comedian.

2. Spoke to J Crosby – Dorothy's limp to be incorporated into script, he wrote.

'Don't make much of it,' he'd said to Jonathan. 'It's a bit of a sensitive issue with the actor, so try not to draw a lot of attention to it. Make it almost an aside, if you can.'

He didn't have a lot of faith in Jonathan Crosby's ability to be subtle, but hopefully the inclusion wouldn't be too clumsily done.

3. Voice projection. Masking. Unnecessary moves.

He sighed. So many areas that needed work, so few rehearsals. On the other hand, in six weeks or so it would all be over, and he could put this whole frustrating business behind him. He thought beyond the play, to the weeks and months that stretched out in front of him. He thought of spending the rest of his days in Rory's little flat, and decided that maybe *Death by Dying* had its uses.

He checked his watch and shut the notebook. Rory would have the dinner on, the same dinner he cooked for Edward every Friday: scrambled eggs, baked beans and boiled potatoes – no meat on Friday for Rory. It wouldn't have been Edward's meal of choice, but washed down with a good Pinot Grigio, anything was palatable.

He took the wine and Rory's two cans of Smithwicks from the small fridge and let himself out, pulling the door closed but not locking it. Not much call for security in a place that had nothing worth stealing.

He opened Rory's back door and walked into the scullery that had smelled of rubber for as long as he could remember. Its wooden shelves held bundles of yellowed newspapers and empty glass jars that Edward kept forgetting to take to the recycling centre.

He walked into the kitchen. 'Hello? Rory?'

A covered saucepan sat on the hob. Edward lifted the lid and saw peeled potato chunks covered with cold water. Four brown eggs squatted in an opened grey cardboard carton on the kitchen table. The fridge door was slightly ajar. Edward pushed it closed and went through to the hall.

'Rory?'

The sitting room, where they always watched *Nationwide* after dinner, was empty. The ashes of the previous night's fire had been cleared, the fresh kindling and briquettes assembled but unlit. Rory always had the fire going by this time.

His glasses sat on the arm of the tweed sofa, on top of a folded *Irish Independent*. A half-empty bag of Liquorice Allsorts slumped on the coffee table, Rory's pipe beside it, a small scatter of blackened tobacco spilling from its bowl.

'Rory?' Edward took the stairs two at a time, pushed open doors on the landing.

Rory was behind the second.

He lay on his side on the bathroom floor, eyes half open, mouth slack, trousers and underpants bunched around his knees. One arm was pinned beneath him, the other stretched away from his body across the lino, fingers curling loosely into his palm.

Maria

There was no doubt about it now. She'd seen the proof, the damning blue stripe. Not that she'd needed proof, not since she'd thrown up in the shop.

With Pat, she'd never had to dash from the bed to the bathroom to throw up, like pregnant women in films. For her, morning sickness had struck later, maybe an hour or so after breakfast, and had been blessedly infrequent. And she hadn't been able to stomach coffee. She should have guessed – this was following exactly the same pattern.

She was on the Pill. Michael had no idea, he would have hit the roof. She'd started taking it a year after Pat was born, when her suspicions about him were growing stronger, and making her terrified of having any more children she couldn't understand. By the time he was diagnosed, of course, her reason for staying on the Pill, for not wanting more children, had changed.

But the Pill wasn't foolproof, and now she was pregnant again.

She couldn't bear it, this added tie to her husband. It was different with Pat – he felt like her child alone, not theirs. It didn't matter that technically Michael was his father – in reality, he was just the man who drove Maria's son to school.

But if she had a healthy second child, she and Michael would be pulled back together again. She knew Michael still wanted another child; he didn't have to say it. He wanted an heir who would follow in his footsteps, take over the business in time. Clearly, Pat was never going to do that, but the next one might. So he planted his seed in her regularly, and waited for it to take root.

She imagined him being a father to the new child, giving him all the attention he'd denied Pat. Sending him to private school, maybe, making sure he had the best of everything. Impressing her

211

parents with his generosity – not that they saw anything wrong with his treatment of Pat, because at the weekly Sunday lunches he was the perfect father.

Maria hadn't told him she was pregnant. She'd told nobody yet, not even Ellen, and certainly not her parents. She couldn't tell anyone, not when she was still trying to cope with the discovery herself, still trying to figure out how she was going to handle this bombshell.

A woman approached the bookshop counter.

'I'm looking for the new Colm Tóibín.'

Maria was glad of the shop, of the diversion it provided – especially today, when it got its share of the crowds who came into the city for the Saturday farmers' market and spilled into the surrounding shops. It kept her busy, kept the endless, fruitless worrying and questioning at bay for a while.

'Is this the only Paul Durcan collection you have? I was hoping for his earlier work.'

But she'd have to decide soon what she was going to do. She'd have to make up her mind, choose from the pitifully few possibilities – each of them, as far as she could see, equally awful.

'Is this book in the three for the price of two offer?'

She was tempted to confide in Oliver, who she instinctively knew would be wonderfully discreet, but maybe their relationship wasn't quite at that level.

'Do you have a Lonely Planet guide for the Czech Republic?'

She could tell Ellen. She was well aware what a

low opinion of Michael her sister had always had, how Ellen hadn't approved of the marriage from day one. Ellen would be sympathetic, but would it be fair to expect her to keep the knowledge secret from their parents? Because they couldn't possibly be told, not until Maria had decided what to do.

'Can I use this book token here?'

She was having lunch with Ellen. They didn't normally meet for lunch on Saturdays, the busiest day of the week for both of them, but Ellen had rung the night before and asked to meet her for a quick bite around two. Had she sensed something at the rehearsal on Thursday? Had she noticed how preoccupied Maria had been?

Maybe she'd tell Ellen at lunch. Maybe saying it out loud to someone would make it easier to see what needed to be done.

Ellen was waiting when she arrived at the café, ten minutes late.

'Sorry, we were busy. I couldn't leave Oliver until it quietened down.'

'Thanks for coming, I know it's a bad day to meet.' Ellen looked pale. She sipped from a pink mug. 'I ordered you a salad sandwich.'

'Thanks.'

The little café had emptied out, the main lunch rush over. The waitress arrived with the sandwiches, and Maria sent back the mug of coffee that had come with them and ordered green tea instead.

'Since when don't you drink coffee?'

Maria opened her mouth to explain the reason for her sudden aversion, but before she could say a word, Ellen spoke again.

213

'Maria – I've found a lump on my breast.'

Maria stared. 'What?'

'Well, beside it, really. I don't know what to do.' She looked anxiously at Maria. 'I wasn't that bothered when I found it, but the more I think about it, the more scared I'm getting.'

'When did you notice it?'

'Last Sunday, almost a week ago, and it's still there, it isn't going away. What should I do? Tell me what I should do.'

She looked so lost, her eyes full of fear. Maria spoke quietly, conscious of the waitress passing up and down. 'You'll go to the doctor. You need to get it checked out as soon as possible. I'll go with you if you want. It's probably nothing, most lumps are harmless cysts.'

'Yes, aren't they?' Ellen's eyes filled with tears. She pulled a paper napkin from the dispenser on the table and blew her nose. 'Thanks – I knew I could depend on you. You're always good in a crisis.'

Maria watched the waitress approaching with her green tea. She picked up her sandwich, throwing a lightning glance at her watch. 'That's what I'm here for,' she said.

She'd sort her own problem out by herself, like she usually did.

Harry

'See you later,' he said.

'Bye, Harry.'

He pulled the front door closed and walked around to the side of the house where his bike stood waiting, propped against the wall. He attached his kit bag to the carrier and tucked the ends of his jeans into his clips, and pedalled off in the direction of the municipal swimming pool, open till ten on Monday nights.

Ma had been her usual self the day before. He hadn't brought up the birthday outing, he doubted that she even remembered it. She'd called him Stephen at one stage – her father's name – and asked him if he'd got his hanky.

She'd talked about someone called Lucy – he hadn't heard that name before – and she'd complained that a doctor had given her the wrong pills and they'd upset her stomach.

She'd said she was being kept awake by a dog that barked all night, and she'd demanded that Harry talk to someone about getting it put down.

Exactly as usual.

Harry's sister Babs had arrived, as she'd promised, with a cake and a present wrapped in blue tissue paper. She'd kissed Ma's cheek.

'Happy birthday, Ma. Sorry the lads couldn't make it, and poor Tony is up to his eyes, but they all said to say happy birthday.'

She'd held out the present, and when Ma had made no move to take it, Babs had unfolded the tissue paper and lifted out the pink cardigan.

'It's a new cardigan, Ma – what do you think?'

Ma had looked at it expressionlessly as the woman who'd shown Babs in had said, 'Oh look, Veronica, it's beautiful. Aren't you lucky?'

'Could we possibly have a few plates for the cake, and a knife?' Babs had asked a little coolly, and the woman had gone off. Harry thought of the lemon cake he'd brought to the restaurant, that Judith had taken home from the rehearsal. Babs's cake was plainer, just a cream sponge with nothing written on top.

While they were waiting, as Ma had turned towards the window and ignored them, Harry had told Babs in a low voice about the trip to The Cow and the Moon. He figured it might come out at some stage, and it was probably better that she heard it from him.

As he'd expected, Babs had been furious.

'I don't believe it – after we *asked* you not to. After Charlie contacted you *specially*–'

'Look, I thought it was worth a try.' Harry had glanced at Ma. 'It didn't do her any harm. I just wanted to do something nice for her.'

'So bring her a bunch of flowers or a box of chocolates or something. How could you think for a minute that she'd enjoy going out like that? She's got *Alzheimer's*, for God's sake.'

They'd both looked at the Alzheimer's patient, who'd looked blankly back at them.

Harry was sick of it, tired of being the baby brother that Babs felt obliged to boss around.

'Look, I know you didn't want me to take her out – you made that quite clear. Well, I did take her out, and it didn't work, and you were right. Does that make you feel any better?'

'No, it doesn't. Who knows what you're going to come up with next? You'll probably want to bring her on a ... a *hot air balloon ride* or something.'

'Don't be ridiculous.' But the thought of Ma standing in a giant basket, hair flying in the wind, had made Harry smile. 'She's afraid of heights.'

'Oh, you can laugh. It's really funny when your sick mother is dragged out against her will.'

'It wasn't against her will.' How could it be, when Ma hardly knew what she wanted any more? 'She came out with me quite happily – she was just a little disorientated in the restaurant, that's all.'

Babs had sighed wearily. 'I know you're good to her, Harry. Don't think we don't appreciate it, because we do. It's good to know you see her every week. But I just wish you hadn't done it, that's all.'

The plates had arrived then, and they'd eaten cake and left it at that. Harry had tried, and Harry had failed, and Babs and Charlie had known better, as usual. End of story.

The smell of warm chlorine hit him as he opened the door of the building that housed the swimming pool. He inhaled deeply, relishing the sharp bite of it.

There were two men in the changing room, one of whom Harry knew vaguely to see, and they nodded at each other. The second man, pulling off his wet togs, didn't look in Harry's direction.

Harry changed quickly and bundled his clothes into his kit bag. He stood under a hot shower for a few seconds before paddling through the foot bath and stepping into the pool area.

He counted ten heads in the water, all moving purposefully through it – Monday night was for the serious swimmers. Harry moved to the deep end and stepped onto the low diving board, and stood there waiting until there was nobody too close.

And then big, ungainly Harry Buckley lifted his arms above his head and bent his knees and bounced once, lightly, before diving gracefully into the vivid blueness with scarcely a ripple.

He swam four lengths without a pause, moving swiftly through the water with a beautifully executed butterfly stroke. He switched to a crawl for the next four lengths, then turned onto his back and floated, panting deeply, the soft underwater murmur soothing in his ears.

He'd learned to swim when he was at school, surrounded by his six-year-old classmates in the shallow end of this very pool. He still remembered the thrill the first time he'd managed to propel himself through the water with a few clumsy breast strokes.

'Keep the feet up, keep the movement going,' the instructor had ordered him, and Harry had kicked and scissored and blown water bubbles and had stayed afloat for four wonderful seconds.

After that, it was down to practice. Harry had driven his father mad, begging for a drive to the pool whenever the poor man sat down with a fresh newspaper, or pulled on his old trousers for an hour in the garden to practise his golf swing.

Swimming had been the reason Harry had begged for a bicycle for his tenth birthday. With a bicycle, he could make his own way to the pool, he could go whenever he wanted – or at least whenever Ma deemed the weather good enough, or the homework sufficiently out of the way.

In the water, Harry was weightless and graceful, and he belonged. He was one of the swimmers, he was as good as any of them; better, in fact, than most. He started winning trophies when he was nine. By the time he was eleven he had a box of them, and there was talk of him trying out for the Irish swimming team.

But then Da had died, and he and Ma were left on their own, and the hours of training before and after school kept him out of the house for most of the day. It was worse when he started secondary school, an even longer day away from her.

Just before his thirteenth birthday, he'd gone to the coach and told him that he had too many other commitments, that he couldn't handle the swimming schedule any more.

He didn't regret it – in a way, it was a relief. Without the pressure to perform, to keep chipping away at his timings, he could relax and enjoy it. Now he swam twice a week at least, and he often took the bus to the coast on his day off and spent hours in and out of the water.

He swam another few lengths and then floated again, enjoying the blood surging through his body. The pool had emptied out a little, only about six others now. The good-looking lifeguard sat on duty, halfway between the shallow and deep ends.

He didn't look Irish. Olive skin, auburn hair cut short, eyes that looked dark brown from a distance. Muscular chest, flat stomach, strong, solid thighs. Girls often showed off in the pool when he was on duty, but Harry knew they were wasting their time.

Funny how you always recognised another gay man. He didn't have to speak to you; sometimes he didn't even have to move. There was just something, some signal communicated in the briefest of glances, that Harry assumed gay men recognised in him too.

He was pretty sure that George and Eve had no idea.

Thankfully, his sexuality was one of the few areas Eve hadn't covered in their initial chat. Maybe they wondered about him, but if they did, they kept it to themselves. It wasn't exactly something that came up in conversation, even with Eve.

The mortifying truth was Harry had never had a physical relationship, with a man or a woman. It had simply never happened – or rather, he hadn't allowed it to happen, hadn't put himself in the way of meeting anyone. He knew there were a couple of gay bars in the city, but he'd never been inside them. It was like a code he hadn't learned, a language he didn't understand. The thought of walking into a bar and striking up a conversation with a stranger, male or female, filled him with anxiety. How did anyone manage it? Harry would be sure to spill something, or knock something over, or make a comment so banal that whoever was listening would turn away, yawning.

How he'd summoned up the courage to go along to the auditions was still a mystery to him. Maybe knowing that everyone else was in the same boat had helped, maybe the thought of not having to be himself had done the trick. But in a bar, or in any other social situation, he'd be Harry Buckley.

He'd loved a man once, when he was fifteen and confused. Mr Fitzpatrick had been his English teacher, somewhere in his thirties, Harry guessed. He had sandy hair and a precisely trained beard, and he walked between the desks, hands clasped behind his back, and talked about the dilemma of Hamlet, or the poetry of Seamus Heaney.

Harry had no idea what Mr Fitzpatrick's first name was, or what he did when he left school every day, when he climbed into his silver Ford Escort and drove out of Harry's orbit for another sixteen hours. He presumed the thin gold ring on Mr Fitzpatrick's left hand meant that there was a Mrs Fitzpatrick, but he didn't think about her at all.

Harry wasn't top of the class in any of his subjects. He'd never been a natural student, preferring to spend time in a swimming pool than at his homework, but he slogged at English, and Mr Fitzpatrick rewarded him with B pluses, and occasionally A minuses, for his assignments.

Harry thought about him incessantly. Mr Fitzpatrick filled his head while he swam his lengths, while he ate the shepherd's pie Ma put in front of him, while he pretended to watch television. He imagined the two of them going on holidays to somewhere exotic, lying on a beach together,

221

swimming side by side in cool blue water.

He closed his eyes at night and there they were, doing everything Harry's fifteen-year-old body yearned to do. He heard the endearments Mr Fitzpatrick whispered to him, he felt Mr Fitzpatrick's hands on his trembling skin. He woke counting the minutes until his English class.

There was never a hint from Mr Fitzpatrick that he guessed where Harry's feelings lay, or that he returned them. He treated Harry exactly the same as the other students. His hand didn't linger on Harry's shoulder as he paraded between the desks, he asked Harry no more or fewer questions than anyone else.

Mr Fitzpatrick left the school at the end of the year. Harry didn't know he was going, didn't find out he'd left until a woman walked into the class in September and told them she was Mr Fitzpatrick's replacement. He mourned his old teacher quietly for a few months, still clinging to the daydreams, still filling his nights with thrilling encounters.

He searched for Mr Fitzpatrick in the city streets, but he never saw him again. Time passed and Mr Fitzpatrick's face began to blur in the daydreams, and gradually Harry moved on without him. He was no longer confused, he was sure now what he wanted, but he had no clue as to how to achieve it.

And here he was today, twenty-nine and never been kissed. Working with a woman he couldn't abide, living in someone else's home. Trying to act every Thursday evening when it was becoming increasingly plain to him – and no doubt to Edward – that he couldn't act to save his life.

He pulled himself out of the water and stood on the diving board again, squeezing the drops from his hair, feeling the slight sting of the cool air on his wet skin. He dived for a second time and glided underwater for half a length, then broke the surface and sliced through the water in perfect butterfly strokes till he reached the opposite end.

Strong. Graceful. Sure.

Robert

On Friday, he went to the cinema with a twenty-three-year-old blonde who worked in IT and dreamed of being a model. After the film he bought her two vodkas and told her, as she drank them, how sexy she was, how flattered he'd been when she'd agreed to go out him, and how certain he was that she'd make a wonderful model any day now.

And all through the evening, as he sat beside her on a red velvet seat and watched a film that he might have appreciated if he was fifteen years younger, as she squeezed his knee under the table in the bar afterwards, Robert was immeasurably, unutterably bored.

For once, the thought of taking her back to the apartment – where most of his dates ended up – didn't enter his head. He couldn't wait to drop her home afterwards, couldn't wait to get back to his own company.

Odd, not his usual style at all. He lay alone in

his four-poster and wondered.

The following day, Saturday, he rearranged his afternoon appointments and collected the boys from Caroline's mother and took them out. He drove them to a water park, where he watched them shooting from the giant slide to tumble into the pool, jumping the artificial waves and racing each other through the water. On the way home they stopped in a shopping centre, where he bought the Mario Striker Charged Football Wii game that Noah had been begging him for since it had come out.

In return, he learned that they'd gone out to dinner on Wednesday night with Alain the Frenchman, and that Alain had driven them home afterwards. They couldn't remember the name of the restaurant, but Mum knew the waitress who worked there, which was no help to Robert.

'Where is it?' They were eating pizza they'd picked up on the way back to Robert's apartment. 'Which street is it on? What's it near?'

'Dunno.' Two shrugs. 'Mum wanted to pay some of the bill, but Alain wouldn't let her.'

'I wouldn't let her either,' Robert felt obliged to point out. 'Who drove to the restaurant?'

'Alain. His steering wheel is on the wrong side.'

'I hope he didn't have any alcohol,' Robert said, adding his crust to the pile in the middle of the table. 'I wouldn't want him driving you home after drinking.'

'Nah,' Noah said. 'Mum had wine, but he didn't.'

'He did when we got back to the house,' Aidan said. 'Mum opened a bottle in the kitchen. I

224

heard it.'

'Did he stay long?' Robert asked. 'I just hope he didn't keep Mum up too late, with her going to work the next day.'

'Dunno – we were in bed when he went home.'

'He's funny,' Noah said. 'He does funny voices.'

'Yeah.' Aidan smiled. 'He's cool. He says Mum's name in French.'

'Really.' Robert chewed his pizza. 'But he's going back to France soon, isn't he?'

'Dunno.'

'He is, Mum told me,' Robert said. 'He's only here for a little while.'

He was well aware of how childish he was being, pumping his sons for information, making sure they knew that the wonderful Frenchman was soon leaving. But the thought of another man – any man – taking his place with his children, however temporary, was driving Robert towards all sorts of childish behaviour.

On Sunday, he went out to brunch on his own, and in the afternoon he sat by the bay window in his apartment and tried to learn his lines. In the evening, after a dinner of beans on toast, he lay in the bath imagining Alain the Frenchman being invited to Sunday lunch with Caroline and the boys, to thank him for the meal out. Arriving with a potted plant for Caroline, a bar of French chocolate each for Noah and Aidan. And some wine, of course. Some good, gutsy French wine to wash down Caroline's roast lamb.

On Monday Robert spoke to her, when they happened to grab a mid-morning coffee at the same time.

'The boys were telling me about their meal out on Wednesday.' He leaned against the sink, stirring sugar into his mug.

'It was nice – I like that restaurant. I know the owner's sister, she works there. Actually, you know her too, she was telling me she's got a part in the play – Theo DeCourcy.'

'Right.' He'd forgotten about Theo telling him she was one of Caroline's clients. Had she mentioned that she was a waitress too? He couldn't remember. He blew on his coffee. 'And what did your friend think of the boys?'

'He thinks they're great. He says they're very unaffected.' She shot him a mischievous look. 'He says they're a credit to me.'

'To you.' Robert knew she was teasing, and still his irritation rose. 'How *gallant* of him. I assume you made it clear that they have a hands-on father?'

She laughed. 'Stop getting jealous – they're not going to be snatched away from you.'

'I *know* that. I just don't want them getting too many treats.'

Caroline raised her eyebrows. 'Like you don't give them too many treats. Like you didn't spend Saturday afternoon treating them.'

'That's different, I'm their father.' He gulped the too-hot coffee, feeling it scalding him, making his eyes water. 'I'm entitled.'

'Robert,' she said, 'you've got nothing to worry about. They'll always be yours. I wouldn't have it any other way.'

'Better get back.'

He dropped his cup in the sink and walked out

226

of the kitchen before she could answer, annoyed at himself for sounding so insecure. Annoyed at her for humouring him.

That evening, he went for a drink alone to a little pub by the river and brought home a tipsy dark-haired woman who kept calling him John and who snored loudly as soon as she fell asleep. In the morning, watching her dressing hurriedly as he feigned sleep, he felt unaccountably depressed.

He was forty-two, still relatively young. He ran a successful business, he was financially viable. He had two sons he adored and he was on good terms with their mother. His social life was active, he was popular in his circle. So why did it all suddenly seem so horribly empty?

He pushed himself through Tuesday, doing his best with the customers, small-talking his way past the hours. He left work at four as usual to collect the boys from their after-school hurling, still trying to shake off this unfamiliar and inexplicable bleakness.

'Dad, guess what?' Noah said, clambering into the car. 'We might be going to live in France.'

Ellen

The doctor had told her not to worry. 'Four out of five lumps are benign,' she'd said. 'They're harmless cysts, or swellings caused by normal hormonal changes. Where are you in your menstrual cycle?'

227

'My period's due in a couple of days,' Ellen had answered, 'but I've never felt something like this before.'

'Any other changes? Any discharge from the nipple, any skin puckering or redness? Any nipple inversion?'

'No.'

'And when did you first notice the lump?'

'About a week ago, when I was showering.'

The doctor had nodded. 'It's good that you came so quickly The sooner we have a look at it, the better.'

Ellen had lain on the tissue-covered couch and looked at the ceiling while the doctor palpated both breasts gently. There was a thin, spidery crack meandering from the far corner to the centre, and a pale brown stain in the shape of Italy just above the chimney breast. A single long cobweb dangled from the light shade.

'Well,' the doctor had said when Ellen was pulling on her top, 'there is definitely something there, and we need to determine what's causing it.'

'What do you think it is?' Ellen had asked, watching her face.

The doctor had shaken her head. 'As I said, the chances are that it's a non-malignant cyst, a build-up of harmless fluid that can be drained. A lot of women have small cysts that they don't even know about – it's only if they swell that they become noticeable. But there's no way of knowing for sure what this is without further exploration.'

'Like what?' Ellen had felt clenched, her body tight within her clothes.

'Well, the first thing we have to do is notify the

breast clinic and you'll be called in for a mammogram or an ultrasound, or possibly both. They're
both quite straightforward, and over very quickly.'

'When will that happen?'

The doctor had scribbled on a form. 'I'll fax
this into them straight away, and you should get
an appointment within a week or so.'

'And how long will I be waiting for the results?'

'Not longer than a week, quite possibly less.'

'A week ... so two weeks from now, I should
have the results.'

'Yes, at the latest.'

Two weeks. Fourteen sleepless nights. Fourteen
days of worrying and imagining the worst. 'And
after that?'

'The next step, if it's revealed to be a cyst,
would be having it drained, where a thin, hollow
needle is inserted to extract the fluid.'

'And if it's not a cyst?'

'If there's still uncertainty you may need a
biopsy of some breast tissue.'

'Biopsy?'

'If there's any uncertainty at all,' the doctor
said. 'Just to be on the safe side.'

'Right.'

Four out of five were harmless. Ellen had four
out of five chances of walking away from this. But
what if she was the one in five who didn't walk
away?

Don't worry, they'd told her, the doctor and
Maria.

'Try not to think about it. Don't dwell on it,'
Maria had said. 'It's probably nothing.'

Easy for them to say. She should have asked the

doctor for a sleeping pill prescription while she was there.

She couldn't remember what eight hours of sleep felt like – if she got three these nights, she was doing well.

She thought of the days she'd gone to work exhausted after a night of little sleep with whoever she'd brought home the evening before. Now there was no one to keep her awake – the thought of sex hadn't entered her head since this had all begun – and still she tossed and turned till dawn.

And all the time it was with her. Breathing with her. Moving with her. Toying with her. She felt diseased, dirty, infected with some monstrous evil that was feeling its way around her body.

'I'll take two of the currant loaves and three custard slices.'

Ellen started. 'Sorry, I was miles away.' She reached for a paper bag behind the counter and began to fill it.

It'd been quiet all afternoon in the bakery, which didn't help. Only a couple of customers in the last half hour; nothing for her to do but think of the worst case scenario, and double it. She sighed.

'Might never happen, love.' The woman on the other side of the counter smiled as she handed over a tenner.

Ellen counted out her change. 'I sincerely hope not. Bye now.'

There wasn't breast cancer in the family, as far as she knew. An uncle had survived a brain tumour, a grandmother had died from lung cancer at forty. She suddenly remembered that one of her second cousins had recently been diagnosed with some kind of cancer. They'd been talking about it over Sunday lunch – skin, wasn't it?

The bakery door opened again and she looked up.

'Well,' she said.

Edward looked equally surprised. 'You work here?'

'No,' Ellen said. 'I just like standing behind the counter in a white coat.' He smiled. Not much of a smile, but there it was. 'So what can I get you?' she asked.

He'd never been into the bakery before. She would have remembered that craggy face, even before she knew him. He *was* quite attractive, damn it.

He studied the trays of chocolate éclairs and apple Danishes and fruit tartlets on the shelves beneath the glass counter. 'Have you got any plain buns?' he asked.

'Plain buns? You mean without icing?'

'I mean the kind of bun your mother probably made – you know, in a crinkly case. Just plain, no fancy stuff.'

'You mean a queen cake.'

'Do I? Maybe. Have you got them?'

'I did, but they're all gone.' She pointed to a tray on her left. 'I've got muffins though, which are kind of like big queen cakes. Cranberry and almond, chocolate chip or bran.'

Edward peered at them. 'Which is the least complicated one?'

'Least complicated.' Ellen lifted out a bran muffin. 'This one, probably. No fancy stuff. Full of fibre.'

Edward nodded. 'I'll take two of those then.'

Ellen put them into a white paper bag. 'A treat or a present?' she asked. A little small talk couldn't hurt, and he was being fairly civil this afternoon.

'Sorry?'

'Are you treating yourself or giving them as a present?'

'I'm bringing them to someone in hospital,' Edward replied a little stiffly.

'In that case—' Ellen reached under the counter again and pulled out a gingerbread man and added it to the bag '—here's a little extra, for the patient.'

'Oh.' Edward blinked. 'Thanks, that's nice of you.' He paid, and turned away. 'Well, goodbye.'

'See you at half seven,' Ellen said as he pulled the door open. 'Don't be late.'

He looked back blankly.

'At rehearsal,' she said. 'It's Thursday.'

'Oh ... yes, of course. Yes.' The door swished closed behind him. Had he forgotten? He'd seemed distracted. Imagine if they all turned up for rehearsal except Edward.

Maybe whoever was in hospital was someone close to him. Maybe it was his wife. Ellen should have asked. Mind you, whoever it was couldn't be too sick if they were able to eat muffins.

That green shirt suited him. He actually dressed quite well. She wondered who picked out his clothes.

She looked at her watch – twenty past five. She began to clear away the cakes that remained, realising that she hadn't thought about cancer for at least five minutes.

Third Rehearsal Night: Thursday, 15 May

McMillan's Pub

Judith hurried up the stairs, bracing herself for Edward's reaction. She was barely late – about three minutes – but he'd probably have something to say.

She walked through the doorway and saw everyone else. There was no sign of Edward.

'He's not here,' Theo said. 'He warns us not to be late, and he's late himself.'

'I was just saying,' Ellen added, 'that he might have been delayed at the hospital.'

'At the hospital? Is he sick?'

'No, he's got a friend there, or a wife or something. He came into my bakery and bought muffins for them.'

'Oh.' Judith unbuttoned her jacket and sat next to Harry. 'Well, I hope it's not bad news.'

'Which bakery do you own?' Theo asked Ellen.

'I don't own it, I just work there. Baker's Dozen, near the hospital.'

'Thanks for that cake,' Judith said to Harry. 'It was delicious.'

It had given her a right land. She could see the funny side now, but not then, not when she'd opened the box in front of everyone in the staff-room and seen *Happy Birthday Ma* in yellow letters staring up at her.

She'd stared back.

'Oh, is it your birthday, Judith?' they'd asked. 'You never said.'

'And your son got you the cake – isn't he sweet.'

235

Judith had gone along with it and let everyone think the cake had come from Christopher, because how else was she to explain it?

But why would Harry give her a cake that was obviously meant for his own mother? The only conclusion Judith could come to was that they'd quarrelled after he'd got the cake and he couldn't bring himself to hand it over. How sad, if that was the case.

Pity he hadn't let Judith know about the message though. Imagine if she'd opened the box in front of Christopher, imagine how awkward that would have been. It would have looked like she was making a point, having a dig at him for forgetting her birthday.

They heard a step just then on the stairs, and everyone turned to see Edward hurrying through the doorway.

'I'm terribly sorry.' He looked flustered, far from his usual composed self. 'I was unavoidably delayed.'

'Unexpected visitors?' Theo asked.

'No problem,' Robert said. 'Could happen to a bishop.'

'How's the patient?' asked Ellen.

Edward ran a hand over his head. 'Not very well,' he answered shortly. 'He's ... pretty old.'

'A family member?' Judith enquired gently.

'Yes.' Edward opened his briefcase and pulled out his script. And then, because they all seemed to be waiting, he added shortly, 'My uncle.'

They murmured sympathetically.

'Yes ... well, we'd better get started.' Edward riffled the pages. 'I think, as we're a little late, we'll go straight into act two, with Jack and Dorothy in the study, if you please.'

Ellen got up and walked to the side of the stage. They were all slowly getting to know each other during the breaks. She knew that Robert had twin boys, and that Judith was a teacher, and that Harry worked in a library, and Theo was a bit of a pain, but none of them knew anything much about Edward. He kept his distance from them all.

'Right ... let's go.'

(JACK, sitting at his desk in the centre of the stage, smiles and puts down his pen as a tap is heard at his study door.)
JACK: Enter.
(DOROTHY enters carrying her notebook.)
DOROTHY: I hope I'm not disturbing you.
JACK: *(rises and approaches her)* Of course not, my dear. You always say that, and it's always a pleasure to see you. I enjoy our little chats – and anyway, you have your job to do *(motions her to sit)*. I trust you slept well?
DOROTHY: Yes ... thank you. My room is very comfortable. *(Looks around the study.)* I love this house.
JACK: (laughs) So do I, as it happens *(takes the armchair opposite her)*. It's been in my family for six generations.
DOROTHY: Really? *(Opens her notebook.)* You were born here?
JACK: Yes, in the room Penelope uses now. *(Winks.)* Thirty years ago.
DOROTHY: *(amused)* If you say so *(pause)*.

And ... Betty?

JACK: Betty? What about her? *(Smiles.)* She wasn't born here.

DOROTHY: *(quickly)* No, no, of course not. I was just wondering how long she'd been with you – she seems ... like part of the furniture.

JACK: Betty? Good lord, no. She's only been here for – let's see now, she came to help out when Mother got ill, and that would have been ... six or seven years ago.

DOROTHY: Oh, that recently? I see...

JACK: Yes, and Mother died a year after that–

DOROTHY: Oh. I'm sorry–

JACK: –but by then Betty had become something of a fixture, so she stayed.

DOROTHY: *(turns the pages of her notebook)* I wonder where she was before she came here.

JACK: *(mildly amused)* I'm beginning to think this is an interview about Betty instead of me.

DOROTHY: Sorry, my mind is wandering a bit today *(refers to her notebook)*. We were talking yesterday about your – about your–

'"Second novel",' Edward said.

DOROTHY: We were talking yesterday about your second novel being made into a film.

JACK: *(stands)* Tell you what – since it's such a beautiful day, why not do this in the garden?

DOROTHY: Lovely.

(They both exit.)

'Jack, you were wooden – loosen up. Put more

expression into those lines.'

'Right.'

'Dorothy, watch your voice projection – you need the audience to hear you.'

'OK,' Ellen said.

Edward consulted his script.

'Right, let's plough on – next scene is Jack and Penelope in the hall.'

Maria stood and took her place at the side of the stage. Edward watched Ellen slipping into the chair Maria had vacated.

'Quiet, please. And … let's go.'

(JACK comes out of his study and walks towards the front door as PENELOPE appears at the top of the stairs.)

PENELOPE: *(descends the stairs)* Jack, I need to talk to you.

JACK: *(glances at his watch)* Can't it wait? I want to get to the bank before it closes.

PENELOPE: This won't take long. *(Takes an envelope from her pocket and holds it out to him.)*

JACK: What's that?

PENELOPE: Read it.

(JACK extracts the single page and reads it silently, his expression darkening.)

JACK: Where did you get this?

PENELOPE: It came in today's post. *(pause)* Is it true?

JACK: *(in disbelief)* Penelope, this is an anonymous letter.

PENELOPE: And I'm asking if it's true.

JACK: *(angrily)* Of course it's not true – it's a

nasty lie. But even if it were—

PENELOPE: *(quickly)* Even if it were?

JACK: Penelope, you're being ridiculous. Whoever sent this was trying to rattle you, God knows why – and they're succeeding.

PENELOPE: I saw you, out in the garden with her this morning. The two of you looked very cosy.

JACK: *(coldly)* May I remind you that Dorothy is here to do an interview with me, which is what we were doing. I suggested that we work in the garden this morning because the weather was good.

PENELOPE: But you're attracted to her?

JACK: My God, you really believe this rubbish, don't you? Not that it's any of your business, but for Christ's sake, Dorothy is practically young enough to be my daughter—

PENELOPE: *(laughs harshly)* Since when did that ever stop a man?

JACK: *(thrusts the letter back at her)* I suggest you give this to the police, or burn it. Now if you'll excuse me—

(JACK exits through the front door. PENELOPE refolds the letter and slips it back into the envelope, and ascends the stairs slowly.)

'Right. Let's run through those two scenes again. Penelope, remember to straighten your shoulders. Jack, watch your positioning, turn more towards the audience.'

And, after a short pause: 'Dorothy, when you're quite ready.'

Ellen passed the white paper bag around the table. 'They were left over,' she told them, 'and they don't keep.' Everyone took a gingerbread man.

'Must be fun,' Theo said, 'working in a bakery.' Her hair was pink again tonight.

'Not bad. Except with a hangover, and then the smell makes you sick. My boss is nice, though. We get on well.'

'My boss is my sister – I work in her restaurant – and she's a right pain sometimes.' Theo turned to Harry on her other side. 'How's your mother doing?'

'OK, thanks. And, er, your family?' She'd mentioned a stepdaughter, hadn't she? And a baby, he thought.

Theo's face softened. 'I have the best son in the world,' she told Harry, 'and the cutest baby, and they're both well, thank goodness.'

'That's good.' No mention of the stepdaughter. Maybe Harry had imagined her.

'My son is staying with me at the moment,' Judith told Maria. 'He arrived home unexpectedly from Greece last week – for good, he says.'

'Really? Is he your only child?'

'Yes... He brought a girlfriend with him.'

'Oh? Had you met her before?'

'No. She's English, and quite a bit older than him, I think.' Judith hesitated. 'She's divorced, with two children.'

'Is she? Are they with her?'

'No, her parents are raising them in England.' Judith looked at Maria. 'They're ten and seven.

What kind of woman leaves two young children with their grandparents and goes to live in another country?' She hadn't meant to say it, but there it was.

'It does sound strange,' Maria agreed. 'And now she's in Ireland, with your son. Are they working?'

Judith shook her head. 'They say they're going to start looking, but there's no sign of that happening yet. Christopher says they're not sure where they want to live, so there's no point in finding jobs until they decide that.' She stopped. 'Sorry, listen to me. They're only here a week and already I'm fussing like a mother hen. But I can't help worrying... Do you have children?' she asked Maria.

'Yes,' Maria hesitated. 'I have one son as well, Pat. He's four, just started school.'

'Four – that's a lovely age.'

'Yes,' Maria said, 'it is. He's lovely.'

'They can't just up and leave,' Robert said to Ellen. 'They're in the middle of fourth class – how unsettling would that be, to move them to another country where they don't even speak the same language?'

'But they'll be finished fourth class in a few weeks, won't they?' Ellen said. 'You said they're not going till the holidays.'

'Yes, but–'

'So they'll have a few weeks to settle in and get acclimatised before the new school year starts. And think how great it would be for them to be fluent in French. I wish my family had done something like that when I was ten.'

242

Robert snapped the leg off his gingerbread man and crunched it crossly. 'Aidan is quiet – he takes a long time to make friends. I can't see him enjoying this at all.'

'He'll have his brother with him though – they'll support each other, won't they?'

Robert picked up his glass. 'I don't care for gingerbread,' he said. 'Sticks in my teeth.'

Ellen turned back to Theo. 'So what's the menu like at your sister's restaurant?'

'Break is ten minutes, not fifteen,' Edward said. 'Please try to remember that.'

'It takes five minutes for us all just to get served,' Theo pointed out. 'You should come and join us, and then you wouldn't notice an extra few minutes.'

Edward regarded her sternly but made no reply. 'Right, let's move on to Tom and Ursula's scene in the post office.'

Harry brushed gingerbread crumbs from his sweatshirt as he stood up. Theo gave her script a final quick glance before moving to the far side of the stage.

'Jack, standby,' Edward said. 'You'll be on shortly. Quiet everyone, please. And ... let's go.'

(The post office door opens and TOM enters.)
URSULA: Ah Tom, how are you?
TOM: Morning Ursula. I'd like to pay this bill please.
URSULA: No problem. *(Takes the bill, tapping at her computer.)* Any news from the

Big House?
TOM: Nothing much.
URSULA: Your visitor still there?
(TOM nods, looking uncomfortable.)
URSULA: Getting on alright, is she?
TOM: Far as I know. I don't see much of her.
(The door opens again and JACK enters.)
URSULA: *(brightens)* Good morning Jack –
haven't seen you around in a while. *(Passes
back TOM's bill without looking at him.)*
(TOM exits, nodding at JACK.)
JACK: Ursula, you're looking well.
URSULA: Go on, Jack McCarthy – you're such
a charmer. What can I do for you?
JACK: *(holds out an envelope)* Just a stamp
for this, if you please.
URSULA: *(opens a folder)* I hear you're
entertaining a young woman these days.
JACK: Word travels fast in a village. I assume you
also know that Miss Williams is a reporter writing
an article on me.
URSULA: Yes, I heard that bit too. *(Hands him
a stamp.)* But you know how people will talk.
JACK: I certainly do. I always think it's one of the
charms of village life – as long as the talk doesn't
turn nasty. *(Offers her a coin.)* Unfortunately,
you'll always find the few who love to cause
trouble, and see things that aren't there at all.
URSULA: *(fumbles for change, avoiding his
eye)* And your sister? Is she well?
JACK: Fine, never better. I'll tell her you were
asking for her, shall I?
URSULA: Please do.
JACK: *(takes his change)* Good day to you,

244

Ursula. *(Exits.)*

'OK, that was fine.' Edward waited until they were both seated. 'Now we come to the climax, the pivotal scene. Let's have full focus, everyone. Betty and Dorothy, please.'

Ellen approached the stage area, unfolding the towel which she brought to every rehearsal now. Edward didn't comment.

'And ... let's go.'

'Hang on,' Ellen said quickly. 'I just wanted to say ... I didn't get a lot of time this week to learn my lines, and this is a long scene, so I might need some prompting, OK?'

Edward studied her over the top of his glasses. 'Really.'

She returned his stare. 'I had ... a busy week.'

Edward started to say something, then seemed to think better of it. 'I'll bear that in mind. Let's go.'

(BETTY dusts the ornaments on the mantelpiece in JACK's study. DOROTHY enters silently and watches until BETTY senses her presence.)
BETTY: *(coolly)* Yes? Can I help you?
DOROTHY: *(approaches BETTY slowly)* You have no idea, have you?
BETTY: No idea about what?
DOROTHY: Why I'm here. *(Stops at the far end of the fireplace)* Why I came to this house.
BETTY: *(scornfully)* Don't be ridiculous. Of course I know why you're here – you're writing an article on Mr McCarthy.

DOROTHY: No, I'm not. In fact, I'm not a journalist at all. The press card I showed Mr McCarthy – Jack – belongs to my friend, Dorothy Williams.

BETTY: *(triumphantly)* I knew it — I knew you were here under false pretences *(sneers)*. One of his fans, are you? Thought you'd like to get closer to your hero, is that it?

DOROTHY: *(calmly)* Actually, I don't think much of his writing – far too commercial for my liking.

BETTY: How dare you, miss– *(tossing her duster aside)*. I'm going straight to Mr McCarthy–

DOROTHY: *(blocks her path)* No, you're not. You're not going to do anything *(pauses, then with great emphasis)* ... Marjorie.

BETTY: *(gasps)* What did you call me?

DOROTHY: Funny, isn't it? We're both using false names. You're really Marjorie Ellis, and I'm...

When the pause lengthened, Edward said, '"Caroline Jones".'

DOROTHY: You're really Marjorie Ellis, and I'm Caroline Jones.

(BETTY's hand flies to her chest.)

DOROTHY: Yes, I thought that name might ring a bell. You remember the Jones', don't you Marjorie?

BETTY: *(shakily)* Why – why are you here? What do you want?

DOROTHY: I want revenge, of course. I want to avenge the deaths of my mother and my sister, and I want to...

'"Make you pay for this limp",' Edward said.

DOROTHY: ...and I want to make you pay for this limp you left me with.
BETTY: I paid for what I did, you know I paid. Anyway, it was an accident–
DOROTHY: *(frowns)* An accident? You accidentally drank too much, did you, before you got behind the wheel of the car? You accidentally drove drunk with my mother and her two daughters in the back of that car?
BETTY: But I did my time, seventeen years I spent in that jail. It's all in the past now–
DOROTHY: *(angrily)* It's not in the past, it'll never be in the past! You killed my mother and my only sister, you ruined my father's life – till the day he died he mourned them – and I will never walk properly again!
BETTY: I'm sorry about all that, but I can't turn the clock back. I can't change–
DOROTHY: No, you can't – but I can have my revenge.
BETTY: *(fearfully)* You're not going to tell – you wouldn't do that.
DOROTHY: That's exactly what I'm going to do. I'm going to go to your employer this instant and tell him who you really are, and what you did – I'll say this woman was my nanny, this is the woman ... this...

Edward said, '"This is the woman my father trusted."'

247

DOROTHY: I'll say this is the woman my father trusted with his family. This is the woman, I'll say, who, who…

'"Drove a car into a tree",' Edward said.

DOROTHY: This is the woman, I'll say, who drove a car into a tree after drinking heavily, who killed my mother and my three-year-old sister and left me, eleven months old, disfigured for life.
BETTY: No, no, you can't–
DOROTHY: Oh, but I can. I can tell your precious Mr McCarthy all about you – and there's nothing you can do to stop me.
(BETTY looks around in desperation and grabs the letter opener lying on the desk.)
BETTY: No! *(lunges at DOROTHY, who screams and collapses)*
(BETTY stands for a second, breathing raggedly, and then runs from the room.)

'Right, that's–' Edward broke off as Ellen leapt to her feet.
'I can still smell that bloody carpet.' She grabbed the towel and began bundling it into a plastic bag, her back to them all.
'You were really crying there,' Theo said. 'That was brilliant. I'd love to be able to cry on command.'
Maria said quickly, 'And Judith, well done – I was almost scared of you.'
Judith laughed. 'That's good, I suppose.'
'Yes, well done to you both,' Edward said.

Those tears had been real. That towel was taking a long time to get back into its bag. Not for the first time, he wondered what was buried inside her head.

'Right,' he said again. 'Let's have another look at a few of the earlier scenes.'

'It's beginning to take shape,' he told them at the end of the rehearsal. 'Next week we'll move on to the monologues, so please study those lines. Also, we need to start thinking about costumes, which is not my forte, so I'll be looking for ideas from you all. Have a think about what your character might wear, and we can discuss it next Thursday.'

'I have a suggestion,' Theo said.

Edward regarded her warily. 'Yes?'

'If people get a chance, they could have a trawl around the charity shops,' she said. 'I'm a great fan – you never know what you're going to find there.'

Edward eyed her orange and blue skirt, fuchsia top and green platform shoes. 'I suppose we could consider that. But,' he added quickly, 'please don't buy anything without discussing it with me first.' God alone knew what the postmistress might turn up in.

He turned to Judith. 'You mentioned painting backdrops at the auditions – maybe we can talk about that next week too.'

'Yes, I'd be happy to.'

'Right.' As he drank his brandy downstairs ten minutes later, Edward opened his notebook.

Discuss wardrobe and set budget with W.C.

They'd need money for clothes and some of the

props, and Judith would need to be given something for the painting. He had no idea whether her backdrops would be any good, but his instincts told him to take a chance with her. Money wouldn't be a problem with this production – he was pretty sure William Crosby would tell him to spend what he needed to. Still, no point in going mad.

Take measurements in Arts Centre and source canvas for backdrops. Paints, brushes etc? Check with Judith.

After a second he added, *Make props list. Circulate next Thursday.*

He stopped and had another sip. Things were gearing up. Characters were beginning to emerge, moving from descriptions on a page to living beings. There was still a journey to go, but they were on the way. And Edward was finally starting to enjoy it, starting to remember why he'd done so much of it when he was young.

He turned his thoughts to Ellen Greene. They'd definitely hit a nerve tonight, she wasn't that good an actor. She'd been subdued for the rest of the rehearsal and Edward hadn't pushed her.

Clearly the problem had something to do with her limp, but what could he do when Ellen had no intention of sharing any of that with him? It had been her choice to try out for a part, and her choice to accept the one he'd offered her. He didn't like to think of her upset, but what could he do?

He finished his drink and closed his notebook. Enough for one night.

When he got home he wandered through Rory's

house, pulling curtains closed, switching on the hall light, plumping cushions he'd plumped that morning.

In the kitchen, the door of the unplugged fridge stood ajar, having been emptied of its half pint of milk, its bottle of blackberry cordial, its tub of margarine, its jar of chocolate spread, its three wrinkled carrots.

The morning paper had been cancelled until further notice. A thin film of dust had already settled on the shelf of the ancient oak dresser.

Back in his own flat, Edward phoned the hospital, and heard again: *About the same, no change.*

'I'll be in tomorrow,' he said. 'Tell him, if he wakes up.'

If he wakes up.

He took the brandy from the press and had his second double of the night.

Theo stopped at the twenty-four-hour supermarket and bought a bottle of wine on the way home. Sean would be back from hurling practice and studying in his room, and with any luck Chrissy would be asleep, so Theo and Ben would have the downstairs to themselves. Time for a little chilling out.

Chrissy's wails met her as she opened the front door. She groaned softly as she left the bottle on the phone table and walked into the sitting room.

Gemima sat on the couch, jiggling a red-faced, yelling Chrissy on her lap.

Theo gaped. 'Gemima – why are you here? Where's Ben?'

She walked towards the couch and Chrissy

reached towards her, still wailing.

'At the hospital.' Gemima's normally iron-straight hair was tousled. There was a damp stain on her pale blue shoulder. 'He, like, said to tell you everything's OK.'

In the act of lifting Chrissy, Theo's heart stopped. 'Hospital? What are you talking about?'

'Sean was injured at training, but it's not–'

'Oh my God.' Theo thrust the screaming baby back at Gemima – *paralysed* – and pulled out her mobile phone – *brain damaged* – and jabbed at the buttons. 'Why the fuck didn't Ben call me?' *Dead.*

'He didn't want to, like, interrupt–'

Theo strode out of the room, ignoring her. Closing the door on Chrissy's freshly outraged cries. Digging the nails of her free hand into her palm as she waited.

'Hi, it's OK, he just broke an ankle.' Ben spoke in a rush. 'He got a whack of a hurley and–'

Theo closed her eyes. 'He's alright? You swear on the Bible?'

'He's fine, they're putting a cast on. We'll be home soon. Honestly, Theo, it's OK.'

'If you're lying,' she said evenly, 'I'll kill you. You should have rung me. Get him to call me as soon as he can.'

She hung up and walked shakily back into the sitting room, pushing her phone back into her pocket. Gemima was standing now, jiggling Chrissy on her shoulder. The baby was wailing frantically, her arms and legs pumping.

'Here, I'll take her.' Theo could see the wetness soaking Chrissy's yellow leggings practically down to the ankles. 'She needs changing.'

Gemima looked uncertain. 'Are you OK? I can hang onto her–'

Theo grabbed Chrissy, feeling a sharp stab of impatience. *'No.'*

Couldn't the girl see the baby was distressed? 'When did she eat last?'

Gemima looked blankly at Theo. 'I ... don't know.'

'How long have you been here?'

'About ... an hour.'

It was their longest conversation to date, and Theo was in no state to appreciate it.

'OK.' She carried the baby out of the room, not trusting herself to say any more. Ben must have phoned her when he'd got the news about Sean. He'd phoned his daughter and ignored Theo.

In the bathroom she changed Chrissy, who began to calm down. Her phone rang as she pressed the tabs of the new nappy together.

She pulled it from her pocket. 'Sean?'

'Ma – I'm fine, we're on the way home.' He sounded exactly the same. He didn't sound as if he was dying, or even in any pain. 'We'll be there in a few minutes.'

Still crouched over Chrissy, Theo started to sob, great heaves of relief that swept through her. 'You're OK? You puh-promise you're uh-OK?' She could hardly get the words out.

'Ma, I'm fine. Is that you or Chrissy making all that racket?'

'Both of us.' Theo tried to laugh and a completely idiotic sound – half grunt, half hiccup – came out. 'I have to fuh-feed her. You nuh-nearly gave me a heart attack, you buh-brat.'

Sean's laugh was wonderful. 'Sorry, Ma – I'll try not to do it again. Go on, I'll see you soon.'

She hung up and blew her nose and brought Chrissy downstairs, and mixed formula in the kitchen while the baby began to whimper again.

'Make all the noise you want,' Theo told her. 'See if I care.'

She sat at the table and lifted the warm bottle to Chrissy's mouth, and as the baby's lips found the nipple and closed over it, peace was instantly restored.

'You'll never want to play hurling, will you?' Theo asked her as she sucked loudly. 'You'll play the violin, or chess. Promise you'll never give me a heart attack.'

Chrissy gulped greedily, eyes fixed on Theo's face. Her cheeks were damp, and beautifully, heartbreakingly rosy. Theo's pulse gradually returned to normal. She rocked Chrissy gently as they sat at the table, and hummed a bit of a Boyzone tune that popped into her head.

Ten minutes later, the men came home. Theo heard the sitting room door opening, and Ben's voice, and remembered suddenly that Gemima was in the house. Sitting alone in the front room – typical. Probably had had enough bonding with her baby sister to last her a lifetime.

'In here,' Theo called, and a second later Sean shuffled in on crutches. He looked slightly paler than usual, but otherwise reassuringly whole.

'Hi, Ma. You OK?'

'Just about.' She looked at the cast. 'Is it bad?'

'No, clean enough. I'll be a few weeks out of action.'

Ben appeared. 'Everything alright here?' Theo nodded. 'I'm running Gemima home,' he said. 'I won't be long.'

Theo stood and walked past him, carrying the still-feeding Chrissy. Gemima stood in the hall, her jacket in her arms.

'Thanks,' Theo said. 'Thanks for coming to help.'

'OK,' Gemima mumbled, already turning towards the door.

'See you tomorrow,' Theo said.

Ben shot her a look she couldn't read, but he was gone before she could question it. When the front door had closed behind them, she turned to Sean.

'What a night.'

'Yeah.' He spotted the bottle of wine, still sitting where she'd left it. 'What's that doing there?'

Theo regarded it without appetite. She couldn't imagine why it had seemed like a good idea to buy it.

'Come on,' she said, fighting the sudden waves of weariness. 'Let's put this lady to bed and make pancakes.'

Robert

'So – what's new with you?'

Small talk, the grease that oiled the hairdresser's scissors.

'Well, my aunt has just announced that she's

going on a cruise to Alaska, if you don't mind.'

Robert smiled. 'Sounds like fun.' Snip, snip. Caroline caught his eye across the room and winked. Robert nodded stiffly back.

'And Skittles has developed this awful skin condition.'

'Oh dear.' Robert couldn't for the life of him remember whether Skittles was a dog or a cat. 'That's tough.'

'It's traumatic, that's what it is. I have to give him four tablets a day and apply this foul-smelling green ointment which poor Skittles detests...'

'When were you going to tell me?' Robert had demanded. 'Or were you planning to just disappear and say nothing?'

'...and nearly scratched my eye out – but of course he didn't mean it, the pet...'

'Don't be silly,' Caroline had said. 'Of course I was going to tell you. Noah just beat me to it, that's all. It's only for a year,' she'd said, as if that made it alright. 'They'll be back by next summer.'

'...and they're bright blue, of all colours, so even when I mash them up with his favourite tuna, he still spots them...'

'Think of what an opportunity for the boys this is,' she'd said. 'A new culture, a new language.'

'...a flea bite, the vet said, but I told him that it couldn't possibly have been a flea...'

'What about me?' Robert had asked. 'When do I get to see them?'

'...and he hasn't touched his toys all week, which is not like him at all...'

'You can visit,' Caroline had said, as if France

256

was a few bus stops away. 'Ryanair flies direct from Shannon to Nantes – and maybe they could come and see you at Halloween or sometime. Really, Robert,' she'd said, 'you're making a big fuss over nothing.'

'...and if all that wasn't enough, the vet's bill was ninety-eight euro, can you believe it?'

Was Robert making a big fuss over nothing? Did she really expect him to roll over and wag his tail, or whatever, when a Frenchman they knew nothing about decided he liked the look of Robert's children?

'...and my boss is in a play, can you imagine?'

Robert elbowed the Frenchman away and paused in his snipping.

'A play?'

'Yes – I believe it's some kind of a whodunnit. She's poring over her lines at work, never did anything like this before. Of course, I shall go and support her.'

'Is it *Death by Dying?*'

'Pardon?'

'Is the play called *Death by Dying?*'

His client nodded slowly. 'I believe it is, yes.'

'Who's your boss?'

'Her name's Maria Talty – do you know her?'

'Yes. In fact, I'm in that play too,' Robert said.

'Are you now? In that case,' said Oliver, 'I shall certainly come and applaud loudly on opening night.'

Robert smiled. 'We're a long way from opening night – we haven't even run through the whole lot yet. And we're only starting to think about costumes.'

'Oh, I'd adore putting characters into costumes,' Oliver said immediately.

'Would you?' Of course he would; the man was made for putting people into costumes. 'Maybe you could help out.'

'Really? Do you think I could possibly be of any use? It would be such marvellous fun.'

'I think the director would be delighted to have some help – he said it wasn't his thing,' Robert told him. 'I'll give him a call if you like.'

'Oh, would you? Thanks so much.'

'Not at all – although I should warn you that it would probably be unpaid,' Robert said. 'We're strictly amateurs.'

'Oh, I wouldn't be looking for money,' Oliver assured him. 'Money would not be an issue in the least.'

Caroline appeared at Robert's elbow. 'I'm leaving now – see you at seven.'

Robert's heart plummeted as he remembered what lay ahead. In a moment of inexplicable weakness, he'd agreed to have dinner with the Frenchman.

'You really should get to know each other,' Caroline had said. 'If nothing else, it might put your mind at rest.'

'I'd rather not,' Robert had answered. 'Thanks all the same.' Put his mind at rest indeed.

'Come on,' she'd urged. 'The boys would love it, to see you both getting on. They're not too happy about leaving you, you know.'

'Well then don't take them.' But even as he'd said it, Robert knew he was wasting his time. Caroline's mind was made up.

So he'd eventually agreed, and tonight he was going to sit opposite the Frenchman at Caroline's table and attempt to eat whatever she put in front of him. And he was looking forward to it with about as much enthusiasm as he would to a root canal treatment.

The Frenchman's sister-in-law, it turned out, was a hairdresser too – how bloody serendipitous. She'd suggested to Caroline, through the French-man, that they do a job exchange for a year, because guess what? She wanted to improve her bloody English.

Robert thought the idea was ludicrous. 'You want me to take in a new stylist for a year, knowing nothing about her? What if she's crap? What if she drives the customers away?'

Caroline had pointed out that the French salon would be taking precisely the same risk with her. 'And anyway, she's been cutting hair for a lot longer than me – I'm sure she knows what she's doing.'

'And if I refuse?'

'If *you* refuse?' Caroline's expression had hardened. 'Robert, in case you've forgotten, we're partners – which means I have a say in this.'

'Yes, but we both have to agree.'

She'd sighed heavily. 'Look, my mind is made up. If you refuse I'll be disappointed, but I'm determined to do this and you can't stop me. We'll just have to work out some kind of compromise.'

Much as he hated to admit it, Robert suspected the boys would benefit enormously from a year in another country.

'The last thing I want is to fall out with you,'

Caroline had said. 'Imagine what that would do to the boys. But I think this is too good an opportunity to miss.'

Robert had no idea how she felt about the Frenchman, and he wanted to know, badly. Not because he was jealous – far from it – but if this was serious, it could well mean a permanent move to France for her and the boys.

'You are coming back, aren't you?' he asked. 'It is just for a year, isn't it?'

When she didn't answer immediately he added quickly, 'Caroline, you must see how hard it will be for me to live apart from the boys. I'll miss them desperately.'

'I know,' she said quickly, 'and they'll miss you too, you know they will. Look, at the moment it's just for a year. Let's not think beyond that, OK? Let's take it as it comes.'

So he'd left it at that, not at all satisfied.

In the apartment, he showered and shaved and brushed his teeth three times, he splashed on aftershave and sprayed on deodorant and dressed in the black shirt that Yolanda on reception said was amazing on him, and the grey Paul Smith suit he'd picked up for almost nothing on his last trip to the US.

A silver French-registered Peugeot was parked outside the house. Caroline answered the door. She wore a skirt he hadn't seen before, in a shade somewhere between peach and pink, and a blue top splashed with small white flowers. Her cheeks were faintly flushed from cooking, and she looked nervous.

'Hi – come in.' She took his arm and led him

through the hall. 'The boys are upstairs, they'll be down in a minute.' The hall smelled of spices.

Caroline opened the sitting room door and said, 'Alain, this is the boys' father, Robert McInerney. Robert, Alain Defois.'

The man who was intent on stealing Robert's children and ruining Robert's happiness got to his feet and put out his hand, smiling pleasantly.

'Delighted to meet you,' he said. '*Enchanté.*'

Ellen

A mammogram has been arranged for you as well as an outpatient appointment, the letter said, giving her a time and a date for both.

The accompanying leaflet read, *Mammography is the X-ray examination of the breasts. Over 90 percent of these examinations are normal.*

But she'd already found a lump, so the result couldn't be normal. Right away she was in the other 10 per cent.

You will be asked to undress to the waist and put on a gown. The radiographer will take a short history prior to the start of the examination.

A short history

Nine years ago, she would say, I lost my lover and my best friend. The End.

Would that be short enough?

Judith

She opened the fridge to see what needed replacing. She lifted the lid of the bread bin. She shook the box of Weetabix. She checked the fruit bowl.

On her list she wrote *milk, eggs, cheese, sausages, Weetabix, brown bread, oranges, fish.* After thinking for a minute, she added *toothpaste, bath oil, loo rolls.* Amazing what a difference two extra people made in a house.

Amanda was perfectly pleasant. It was Mrs O'Sullivan this and Mrs O'Sullivan that whenever they met.

Just a few things for the wash, if Mrs O'Sullivan didn't mind her putting them into the laundry basket. She was about to put on the kettle, would Mrs O'Sullivan fancy a brew? Weather not the best, but tomorrow was another day, eh Mrs O'Sullivan?

The divorce had been mentioned casually, over a suppertime cup of tea, a few days after they'd arrived. Judith had told Christopher that a cousin of his had got married in Rome a couple of months before.

'I got married in Rome too,' Amanda had said, stirring sugar into her tea. She'd laughed. 'Didn't make it last any longer, though.'

Judith had looked at her in surprise. It hadn't occurred to her that Amanda might have been married. 'Oh, I'm sorry.'

'Don't be – he was a right scumbag, we were better off without him. Never saw a penny of child support.'

'You have children?'

Amanda had nodded. 'Two – boy and girl, ten and seven.'

'Oh.'

If she expected child support, surely that meant the father wasn't bringing them up. So where were they?

Before Judith could ask, the question had been answered. 'I imagine you're wondering what I've done with them, but don't worry, they're quite safe. My folks are looking after them, in Surrey.'

'Oh, I see.'

But Judith hadn't seen at all. Christopher's girlfriend had abandoned her children, and it didn't seem to bother her – or Christopher – in the slightest.

'Do you see much of them?'

'Oh yes – I was over at Christmas, and I'm planning to go back in September for a week or two.'

Christmas, nearly six months ago. Her young children hadn't seen their mother in six months. And they wouldn't see her for another three because she was too busy swanning around with a man years younger than her.

After several days of close proximity, Judith had revised her opinion of Amanda's age – the woman was closer to forty than thirty. What was Christopher doing with her? Couldn't he find a woman his own age?

That apart, she wished they'd come to some decision, settle on where they wanted to live or what they planned to do, but she couldn't bring it up in case it sounded like she was trying to get rid of them. They seemed content to let the time slide away from them, spending the first half of most days in bed and the second half not doing very much of anything.

The furthest they'd gone since they'd arrived was to the nearest pub, two or three times. They'd invited Judith along – well, Amanda had – but Judith had found an excuse each time and they didn't persist.

Amanda did get the bus into the city once, and came back with a tin of biscuits for Judith.

'Least we could do,' she'd said, and Judith had thought, *Yes, it is the least you could do after eating my food and sleeping in my bed for almost two weeks.*

They must have money if they could afford to go to the pub. Judith wondered how long it was going to last – and what then, when it was all gone? But none of her tentative questions to Christopher got her anywhere.

'We're fine, Mum, OK? We saved a bit and we're fine for now.'

'Look, Mum, we're just having a bit of a break. We need to chill for a while, take it handy.'

'Mum, just back off, OK? We'll get to it.' Impatience creeping into his voice.

So Judith had backed off, not knowing what else to do.

She listened in the hall now – nothing. There'd been no sound since she'd got home from school, and now it was almost five o'clock. Could they still be in bed, at this hour? Should she leave a note, tell them to get their own dinner if she wasn't home?

She took her jacket from its hook. They'd eat if they were hungry. She drove to the shopping centre and made her way to the supermarket.

The day was chilly for the middle of May. People wore heavy coats and jackets. One woman had a scarf wound around the bottom half of her face. Judith wished, like she often did, that she'd been born into a warmer climate.

Imagine knowing every year that the sun was going to shine for five months solid or more, instead of this awful cold one day, sun the next, showers whenever. Imagine waking up to the sun every morning.

Greece would be like that, good weather most of the year. She'd never been to Greece, but in any photo, on any TV programme, the skies were blue and the sun shone, and the flowers were vivid pinks and reds and purples – wonderful to have that without fail each year. You'd have to be happy living in constant sunshine, wouldn't you?

She wondered if Christopher had been happy in Greece. He certainly hadn't been happy leaving Ireland. She remembered the evening he'd told her over dinner that he was going.

'What about your work?' He'd been with a furniture removals firm for a few months, the latest in a long line of short-lived positions.

'I've given it up,' he'd told her, helping himself to a third potato, not meeting her eye. 'I've been offered a job teaching English. A friend – well, a friend of a friend – is out there doing that, and he says they'll take me on.'

'Teaching? But you've no–'

'They'll train me up,' he'd said, cutting butter into his potatoes. 'Few weeks, no problem.'

Judith had been full of questions. She'd picked one. 'But why do you have to go so suddenly? Couldn't you–'

'They need me to go now, otherwise they'll give the job to someone else.'

'But surely you could get another one? There must be lots of–'

'Mum, would you leave it?' Stabbing a piece of meat with his fork. 'What's the point in waiting around? It's not as if I've anything going for me here. I've had nothing but crap jobs, I hated them all. I want to make a change, alright?'

She'd been tempted to point out that he could make a change without going to Greece, that he could stay in Ireland and repeat the Leaving Cert he'd made no effort to pass first time round. That he could get a better job with some qualifications.

But she'd said nothing. His mind was clearly made up.

'What about somewhere to live?'

He'd shrugged: 'Your man says there's lots of cheap places. Costs nothing to live in Greece.'

She couldn't imagine him teaching anything. He'd never mentioned it as a possible career, never shown the slightest interest in becoming a teacher.

'Mum, can you lend us some money?' Watching her face to see what she'd say. 'I had to get a loan to buy my plane ticket.'

He'd already bought a plane ticket. He'd known he was going and he'd said nothing to Judith. He'd planned all this, and told her nothing.

'How much?'

'Two hundred euro – I'll send it to you when I get paid.'

After dinner, she'd driven to an ATM and taken out three hundred euro. 'I don't want it back. Just give me a ring to let me know you're settling in.'

She hadn't heard from him for two weeks. Every time the phone rang, she knew it had to be him, and it wasn't. Finally, late one night, it was.

'Mam? It's me.' There'd been music behind his voice. 'Just to let you know I'm OK. I've got a job, I started today.'

'Teaching English?'

'Yeah, it's cool.'

'And you have a place to stay?'

'Yeah, everything's OK. Look, I'm going to be cut off in a minute, so–'

She'd said quickly, 'Have you a number, or an address or something?' She'd tried a few times to ring his mobile, but she kept being told that it was powered off and to try again later.

But his voice and the music had stopped abruptly, and she'd waited almost a month to hear from him again.

She walked along the cereal aisle, searching for the biggest box of Weetabix. Not much point in getting anything smaller, with no sign of him moving out in the near future. She went down through her list, filling her trolley with food and toiletries for three, and then she headed to the checkout.

As she stepped through the automatic doors of the centre a few minutes later, she felt a cool mist on her face. She stopped and pulled her umbrella from her bag, and a woman standing to one side of the doors caught her eye.

'Maria?'

The woman turned. 'Oh, hello. Miserable weather, isn't it?' A boy sat hunched in a buggy beside her.

Judith pushed her umbrella up and smiled down at him. 'Hello, there. What's your name?'

He took no notice of her, just kept rolling the wheels of a little red car he held, his mouth pursed.

'That's Pat,' Maria said quickly. 'He's ... a little shy.'

'Not to worry.' Judith held the umbrella over the three of them. 'Have you a car?'

Maria shook her head. 'I don't drive. I'm waiting for a taxi, they're always pulling up here.'

'I'll run you home,' Judith said. 'It's no trouble, I'm not rushing.'

'Oh, I couldn't.'

'Please – I'd like to.' And it was true, she realised abruptly – she would like an excuse to stay out of her own house. 'Honestly, I don't mind.'

They folded up the buggy and buckled Pat into a seat belt. He seemed unusually quiet, unnaturally preoccupied with his little car. He never once looked at Judith, didn't engage in any way with his mother. It was none of Judith's business.

As they drove off, she said, 'So how are the lines coming along?'

Maria made a face. 'I'd forgotten how tedious it

is trying to learn something by rote. It takes me ages to get them into my head. The week seems to fly too – I usually end up trying to learn them all on the Wednesday night.'

'You said you have a bookshop.'

'Yes, along by the river. And you're in the comprehensive?'

'I am, but not for long. I'm taking early retirement in a few weeks.'

Maria turned to her. 'Are you really? That's a big step.'

'Yes.' Judith laughed lightly 'I haven't quite decided what to do next...'

She trailed off, struck for the first time by the notion of Christopher and Amanda living with her through the summer and beyond, sharing the life she thought she'd be spending alone.

'And your visitors? Are they still with you?'

The tracking of her thoughts startled Judith, making her feel oddly guilty. 'Yes ... but it's fine, really. I'm just used to having the place to myself, that's all.'

'Left at the next lights,' Maria said. 'Thanks very much.'

'Not at all. I just wish Christopher would settle on something, you know? Put down some kind of roots somewhere. I know he's still young–'

'How old is he?'

'Twenty-two – but he's never had a proper job. He failed the Leaving Cert and just got casual jobs after that, and even those–' She stopped abruptly. 'Sorry, I shouldn't be– Is it straight through this roundabout?'

'Yes, thanks ... forgive me, but ... is his father in

the picture?'

Judith shook her head quickly. 'Not for years. He left when Christopher was four.' Still the bitter taste, still the echo of pain when she thought about Samuel. 'He met someone else.'

'I'm sorry.'

There was silence for a few minutes. Judith glanced in the rear view mirror and saw Pat, head bent towards the little red car. She could hear the tiny plasticky whirr of its wheels going round.

Maria said abruptly, 'Pat is autistic. His father doesn't want to know.'

Judith said, 'I'm so sorry.' No reaction from the boy in the mirror.

Judith had never come into direct contact with autism. There'd been a boy in the comprehensive with Asperger's a few years previously, but he hadn't been in any of her classes. She'd see him in the corridor occasionally, or he'd pass her in the yard when it was her turn to supervise.

Always the same neutral expression on his pale face, usually in the company of one or other of the unfortunate few deemed to be different by the rest of the students. His voice had an odd robotic quality about it, the words clipped, with no trace of an accent. She'd never seen him smile.

'Is he your only child?' Judith asked.

'Yes.' Maria's hands sat loosely in her lap. Her nails were bitten.

She wore a diamond and a plain gold ring on her wedding finger.

Judith said, 'I would have liked more children.'

Maria turned her head and looked out the

window, away from Judith.

'I'm the next right,' she said.

'OK.'

Judith had been thrilled to find out she was pregnant after four years of trying not to worry when another month went by and another egg leaked out of her. Samuel had been happy with the news too. He was still three years away from switching jobs – and meeting his new secretary.

She turned right, into an estate of detached red brick houses, and drove slowly up the wide avenue, waiting for more directions.

Still looking out the window, Maria said, 'I'm pregnant.' Her face when she turned back to Judith, registered no emotion. She could have been commenting on the weather.

'Oh, that's–' Judith stopped. Clearly it wasn't wonderful news that the man who'd washed his hands of his autistic son was going to be a father again.

Maria looked down at her hands. 'I'm sorry,' she said. 'I wasn't going to say anything, I don't know why I did. I'm just up here,' she said, 'on the left. Number fourteen.'

Judith stopped the car and turned off the engine, and waited.

'We should never have got married,' Maria said quietly. 'He was the first man to ask me out. He's a lot older than me. He knew my father before he knew me.'

She was in her thirties, Judith guessed. At least mid-thirties. She'd married the first man who'd shown an interest. Grateful, maybe, that he'd come along, maybe convincing herself that she could be happy with him.

'We hardly talk now, except when we have to.' Her mouth twisted. 'But we still share a bed – obviously.'

Her engagement diamond was large. He had money. That may have helped to move things along.

'My parents have no idea – he's always the perfect husband and father when they're around. Even Ellen doesn't really know. I mean, she knows we're not – but...'

Samuel had stayed with Judith for a year after meeting Claudia. Judith wondered afterwards – when it was still a torture to think about him, but when she couldn't *not* think about him – how long he'd been sleeping with both of them.

'I can't face the thought of having another of his children. I was on the Pill, but it didn't work.'

Judith had never used contraception. She'd longed for a second child with Samuel.

'I hate the thought of not having it, but I can't think what else to do. I feel I have no choice.'

It was nothing to do with Judith; they hardly knew each other. Maria wasn't looking for advice, she just needed someone to listen. She'd come to her own decision, sort it out herself.

Maria reached for her bag on the floor of the car. 'I'm sorry for dumping all that on you. I'm sure you're delighted you offered us a lift now.'

Judith smiled, opening her door. 'Don't be silly.'

'It's just that I have nobody else to tell.' She got out and opened the back door and unbuckled Pat's seat belt, and he climbed out and stood on the path while they unloaded Maria's shopping and the buggy.

Placid. Removed from them.

'See you on Thursday,' Judith said, getting back into the car.

'Thanks,' Maria said again, wheeling the buggy towards the front door, the shopping piled into it, Pat's hand in her free one as he walked beside her. 'See you.'

Judith drove back through town, easing her way through the heavy teatime traffic. She'd thought the sisters were close, the way they came to the rehearsals together. Not that close, obviously, when Maria didn't feel able to confide in Ellen.

She turned her thoughts to home as she drove back through the streets. Fish for dinner, unless they'd eaten already, in which case she'd have an egg.

Edward

On Tuesday evening he brought a box of jellies. He put them on top of the locker, beside Monday's Maltesers. The liquorice Allsorts of Sunday were underneath, next to Saturday's two chocolate brownies, which were beginning to curl at the edges.

One of the nurses had told him, after he'd arrived with the bran muffins on Thursday, that there wasn't much point in bringing any food in for Rory.

'Not the way he is at the moment,' she'd said. 'You're just wasting your money.'

Edward had looked coldly at her. 'How I choose to spend my money is none of your business,' he'd answered, and she'd kept quiet after that.

Rory had suffered a massive stroke. 'There was a lack of blood flow to the brain,' the doctor told Edward. 'A clot lodged in an artery and cut off the supply. It was most likely caused by a combination of his age, his high blood pressure and his smoking.'

'Will he recover?' Edward had asked.

'Hard to say,' the doctor said. 'At eighty-six, his recuperative powers aren't what they used to be. If he rallies a little, we can certainly try some physical and speech therapies, but I wouldn't be optimistic that he'll ever get back to where he was before.'

Rory lay immobile in the hospital bed. His face was pulled down on one side, the left eyelid drooping, the mouth skewed. His breathing was slow and harsh, his eyes unfocused. A tube dripped into the back of each hand.

'He may be able to hear you,' the doctor had said. 'Feel free to talk to him, but you won't get a response.'

So every day, Edward sat in the chair beside Rory's bed and talked.

He told him about the play.

'It's coming along. We're into the final act now and it's shaping up. Three weeks till opening night. The actors are amateurs, of course, so the standard isn't too high, but all things considered, they're not doing badly...'

'One of them wears a wig. I had no idea until she whipped it off one night to show me. I was mortified. I forget what she said caused it. She's promised to get a brown one for the show, which is a relief. She usually wears a bright pink one, if you can believe it...'

'Another one limps in real life, so we had to make some mention of it in the play. She's the one who works in the bakery where I got the bran muffins last week, remember? She's playing Dorothy, the murder victim. I'm not sure what to make of her, to be honest. She doesn't make it easy...'

'I got a call from one of the others today – it seems he has someone who wants to help out with costumes. I told him to bring them along to the rehearsal. The more help we have, the better...'

Sometimes he talked about other things.

'I went fishing with Tim Farrelly on Monday, remember Tim? He called round once when you were there, you met him, works in the City Hall. We went for a drink after. He was telling me about his son getting engaged, you wouldn't know him...'

'Another murder last night, a young woman found dead in her house. Husband was out of the country, so it couldn't have been him, but I suppose he could have paid someone...'

'Raining for the past four days, you're as well off in here. No sign of summer yet, although it's not as cold, and you'd notice a bit of a stretch in the evenings...'

And sometimes he wandered back through their shared memories.

'My mother used to call soup spoons Rory spoons, because that was the only time we used them, when you came to visit – did she ever tell you that? She used to make celery soup when you were coming. We hated it, but she said it was your favourite...'

'I remember your Bing Crosby records. You used to play them when we came to visit, you and Nuala used to dance to them. Nuala tried to teach me once, but I hadn't a clue...'

'You gave me ten shillings for my confirmation, I bought my first fishing rod out of it...'

'You took us to Ballybunion on holidays one year, to that caravan, when our mother was having the hysterectomy. I must have been eight or nine, and I got so sunburnt one day Nuala had to take me to a doctor, and I threw up all over his waiting room. He wasn't happy...'

Sometimes he ran out of words and just sat there, his hand resting lightly on Rory's, listening to the slow, laboured breathing and watching the hollowed-out chest rising and falling under the new blue pyjama top.

He was dispirited tonight, not in the mood for talking. The room was uncomfortably over-heated, even without his jacket. He leaned back in his chair and closed his eyes, and thought about his life.

Forty-four years old, living alone, an after-thought at the bottom of his uncle's garden. Broken marriage, no job, no children, few friends. One brother he rarely met, through mutual disin-terest. His only purpose in life these days to direct a group of amateur actors in a mediocre play.

'Hello, Edward.'

He opened his eyes and turned towards the voice, and saw his wife standing in the doorway.

'Hello.'

He'd sent her a brief note to tell her about Rory, feeling that she should probably know. He thought that maybe she'd show up sometime, but still the sight of her took him by surprise.

She walked into the room and stood at the end of Rory's bed. She wore a deep plum jacket with a grey and lavender scarf knotted at her throat. Some jewel or other sparkled in each of her ear lobes, and her jasmine scent crept through the room until it reached him.

Her dark hair, shimmering under the bright hospital lights, was swept upwards – he had often watched her dipping her head so the hair fell forward, gathering it into her hands and twisting it, straightening up to capture it on the top of her head with an ornament of some sort.

Women and their hair. The undoing of him.

'What a terrible thing to happen,' she said softly, one hand reaching towards the twin bumps of Rory's feet.

She and Edward had visited Rory and Nuala every year on Christmas morning, and Rory would pour Baileys, which Edward couldn't stand, for both of them. After Nuala died, Rory had come to them instead and stayed for Christmas dinner, and spent the night with them. Rory and Sophie had met occasionally in between, for funerals, birthdays and other family-related occasions.

'Was it very sudden?' She still wore her wed-

277

ding and engagement rings. The diamond glittered when she moved her hand. 'You must have got an awful shock.'

Edward hadn't seen her since he'd left the house over a year ago. It had taken quite a few months before he'd stopped searching every street he walked for her, scanned every restaurant window, every cinema queue for her. Despising himself, struggling to resist the impulse, but seeking her out all the same.

And now here she was, standing less than three feet from him, talking to him as if they'd parted a few hours ago.

He'd forgotten – he'd forced himself to forget – how attractive she was. He found himself unable to return her tentative smile.

'How are you?' she asked him.

'Fine,' he told her. 'Keeping busy. You?'

She tilted her head, a tiny movement that he remembered. 'Getting on with things.'

'And your father?'

He'd had no contact with Cathal, there was never a mention of him in conversations with mutual friends.

'He's fine. Missing his righthand man, of course.' Her hand stroking Rory's leg through the sheet, running up his calf until she reached the raised mound of his knee, and back down again.

Edward pulled himself up from the armchair and lifted his jacket from the floor, where he'd thrown it.

'Well, I'll be off. Thank you for coming, I'm sure he'd appreciate it.'

Sophie picked up her bag and umbrella. 'I'll

walk down with you, if I may.'

The stairs were wide enough for them to leave a respectable distance between them. 'Thank you for coming,' Edward said again. He felt the need to say something, and that seemed all he could think of.

Sophie gave him a look he couldn't read. 'Did you think I wouldn't?' At the front door, she turned to him. 'Are you rushing away, or have you time for a drink?'

When he hesitated she said quickly, 'Edward, I'm not asking you to come back, I'm just looking for a vodka.'

He gave a tight smile. 'Sorry. Yes, let's go for a drink. There's a pub just across the way.'

At the side of the road he took her elbow without thinking about it, and they walked across together. Like they'd always done.

Ellen

The breast clinic was on the top floor of Portmaine's busy hospital, over-looking the river. From the tall windows that surrounded the waiting area, you could see quite a bit of the city, if you were in any mood to look out.

Ellen turned the pages of a two-month-old magazine, glancing at celebrities she didn't care about posing in the magnificent homes that their last film or tour or album had paid for. What did it matter how many bathrooms you had, or how close to the perfect beach your balcony was, or whether your curtains matched the designer valance around your queen-sized bed? What did any of that matter?

She closed the magazine and dropped it onto the seat next to her. There were eight other women in the waiting area, and seven of them were strangers to her.

She turned to Maria. 'Thanks for coming. I hate dragging you away from the shop.'

'Not at all – Oliver loves having it to himself. Did I tell you, by the way, he wants to help out with our play?'

'Oliver? Doing what?'

'Costumes. Don't you think he'd be perfect?'

Ellen shrugged. 'I suppose so. When did this come about?'

'Well, it turns out Robert cuts his hair, and Oliver was there this week, and it just came up in conversation. Oliver's very excited.'

Ellen gave a faint smile. 'Robert was probably bragging about being in a play.'

'Well, however it happened, Robert phoned Edward, and Oliver is to come along to the rehearsal on Thursday.'

'Right.' Ellen sighed and rubbed her face. 'They could dress me in a black bin bag for all I care right now. God, I wish this was all over.'

'I know.' Maria squeezed her hand. 'It soon will be.'

Ellen leaned back and looked at the ceiling. 'Did I thank you for coming?'

'Yes, several times.'

The door opened and a woman about Ellen's

age appeared, wearing wine-coloured scrubs.

'Ellen Greene, please.'

'Do you want me to come in with you?' Maria asked quietly.

'No – thanks.'

Ellen followed the woman down a short corridor and was shown into a small cubicle off a larger room. She caught a glimpse of a big machine in the room as she stepped into the cubicle.

'Please undress to the waist,' the woman said, 'put your top layer back on and come out.'

She closed the door and Ellen was left alone. There was a bench attached to the far wall of the cubicle. She undid the buttons of her cardigan and took it off. She pulled her T-shirt over her head and laid it on the bench. She undid the hooks of her bra and slipped it off and tucked it under the T-shirt. She put her cardigan on again and walked out into the room.

'My name is Olive,' the woman said, indicating a chair. 'I just need to check a few details.' She held a clipboard.

She asked Ellen for her date of birth, and her address, and whether there was a history of breast cancer in the family.

'OK,' she said, putting the clipboard on a shelf. 'Now you can take off your top and stand over here.' She wrapped an apron that felt heavy around Ellen's waist. 'This won't take long.'

The mammogram was uncomfortable and awkward rather than painful. The plates between which Ellen's breasts were compressed, one at a time, were hard and cold, and squeezed tightly. It took less than five minutes, and then the woman, whose name Ellen had forgotten, disappeared to develop the X-ray. Ellen sat on the chair and looked at the cream wall, her arms wrapped around her bare chest.

After a few minutes the woman reappeared and untied the heavy apron. 'That's fine, Ellen, you can put your top layer back on and I'll bring you for your ultrasound now.'

'There was no mention of an ultrasound on the letter,' Ellen said. 'Just a mammogram.'

'It's nothing to be alarmed about,' the woman told her, 'we usually do both procedures on the same day. Bring your clothes and follow me.'

Ellen walked after her down another corridor and was shown into a second cubicle.

'You can take the cardigan off again,' she was told, 'and put on a gown, open to the front. Someone will be along in a minute. Good luck.'

Ellen listened to her footsteps going back along the corridor. Why had she wished her good luck? Was there something she'd seen on the mammogram that made her think Ellen would need luck?

The cubicle was identical to the first one. She saw a bundle of what looked like giant dark blue tissues on the bench. She lifted the top one and shook it out, and discovered it to be a shapeless top with long sleeves and no buttons or fasteners of any kind.

She took off her cardigan and slipped on the top, which swamped her. Should she hold it closed when she went out, or let it float open? What did dignity matter now?

After what seemed like a long time, the cubicle

door was opened and she was shown into another room in which there was a bed, and beside it a machine that Ellen recognised from TV programmes where pregnant woman got scans.

The man standing by the side of the bed shook hands with her. His skin was warm. 'Miss Greene, how do you do? Fintan Moloney.'

He was around sixty. His cropped hair was silver and he had a double chin and the skin on his face was scattered with pale brown circles the size of one-cent pieces. He smelled of soap, and he looked to Ellen like someone's kindly uncle.

'Ellen,' she said. 'Call me Ellen.'

He smiled politely and indicated the bed. 'Up here, please.'

Ellen sat on the side of the bed, holding the gown closed. A little dignity wouldn't hurt.

'Now Ellen, as you have detected the presence of a mass, or lump, on your left breast, I'm going to perform a breast ultrasound today to see what I can discover about the properties of the mass. The ultrasound will involve coating the breast with a harmless water-soluble gel and passing a transducer over it, which will direct sound waves to the breast tissue and allow us to see a picture of it on the screen here. The procedure is completely painless, and takes about one minute.'

His voice was deep and reassuring. Ellen clung to it.

'So if I could ask you to lie down, please.' She lay down. She closed her eyes and inhaled his soapy scent. 'Please take your left arm out of the gown.'

She slipped out her arm and the gown fell open.

'Now raise your arm above your head, please.' His fingers touched her breast. 'Is it just here?'

She nodded and tried to think about something else, anything else. The next rehearsal, in two days – that would do.

Edward would probably want to go back over the murder scene with Betty in the study. The tears had surprised Ellen; she hadn't felt them coming. She supposed they suited the scene, but they were Ellen's tears, not Dorothy's. She'd be ready next time, make sure it didn't happen again.

She'd been hoping none of the others would comment, and then Theo had blurted it out – typical. Loved the sound of her own voice, that one.

But Edward must have realised that Ellen was genuinely upset. He'd gone easy on her when she'd forgotten a few lines. She'd been surprised at that, and grateful. He wasn't entirely bad.

'And now I'll apply some gel – you may find it a little cool.'

It was shockingly cold after the warmth of his hand. Ellen felt her nipple tightening as he spread it around the area.

She pictured Edward watching them carefully as they said their lines. What did he think as he sat there every Thursday? Was he wishing he'd never got involved, or did he enjoy it? He was so hard to read, so removed from them all.

'I'm going to use the transducer now.'

It pushed gently, painlessly, against her skin. She opened her eyes and watched the alarmingly huge black circle on the screen, watched as

Fintan Moloney marked its dimensions.

Eventually he pressed a switch on the machine and the screen went blank. 'There we go, all done.' He turned to Ellen.

'I can't get an accurate reading, which needn't alarm you. Some are simply clearer to read than others, it's no indication of anything sinister at all. It just means there'll be a follow-up procedure, a fine needle aspiration, which will give us a more accurate result.'

'Right.' Her doctor hadn't mentioned anything about a follow-up procedure. 'Is that the same as a biopsy?'

'No, no,' he said, 'this is just a little extra check before anything like that needs to be done. When you're ready, you can sit up.'

Ellen sat up. No indication of anything sinister at all. She had to believe him.

He pulled a length of blue tissue from a roll and handed it to her. 'You'll want to wipe off the gel before you get dressed.'

'Thank you.'

'Try not to worry,' he told her. 'Try to keep busy.' He checked her chart. 'I believe your next appointment is on Friday.'

'Yes,' she said miserably.

'Fine, we'll do it then.'

Back in the cubicle, she pulled on her clothes. She let herself out and retraced her steps to the waiting area. Nobody paid her any attention on the way.

'What's next?' Maria asked as they walked downstairs.

'Fine needle aspiration on Friday. Just another

check, they tell me.'

The weather was warmer today, short sleeves on the braver pedestrians. Two boys ran past them, both wearing Man United shirts, the slower of the two calling, 'Noah, *wait!*' to the speedier one, who ignored him.

'Will you come in?' Maria asked outside the bookshop.

'Better keep going – I said I'd only be an hour.' Ellen hugged her, something they rarely did. 'Thanks again. See you tomorrow night.'

Try to keep busy, he'd said. As if anything could take her mind off it. But maybe the play would help. Better have another look at those blasted lines tonight.

She reached the bakery and pushed the door open.

Fourth Rehearsal Night: Thursday, 22 May

McMillan's Pub

Edward walked slowly up the stairs, his hand gripping the rough wood of the banisters. His limbs felt heavy, but his head was filled with skittering-about thoughts that made him restless and impatient. He could do without this rehearsal.

There was a very real possibility that Rory would never come home. Unless some miracle occurred, the furthest he'd get from the hospital would be a nursing home of some kind, which left the question of what to do with his house.

Allowing it to stand idle and empty made little sense – and of course, if Rory did end up in a nursing home, the house would need to be sold to cover the expense – but the notion of selling it, or even letting it to strangers, wasn't something Edward could bring himself to think about.

He still visited it every morning. There was nothing to be done – he'd taken the ashes from the grate, he'd made Rory's bed with clean sheets, he'd swept the floors and stopped the paper delivery – but he opened each door and walked around the silent rooms. Rory's smell was still faintly there, a mix of pipe tobacco and the hair cream he'd combed in each day.

In the bathroom cabinet there were pills for high blood pressure and half a tube of ancient indigestion tablets, a box of hot lemon drinks with one sachet inside and a bottle of liquid denture cleaner. On the shelf below there were two wrapped bars of Palmolive soap and an unopened packet of five disposable razors and a bottle of shampoo for dry hair.

There were so many things Edward didn't know about his uncle. Had Rory made a will? Did he even have a solicitor? Anyone Edward might have asked was gone: his mother, who'd been Rory's only sister, Rory's wife Nuala, Rory's brother Joseph – all dead. What was Edward to do?

He'd slid open drawers and gone through presses in Rory's house, feeling like a thief. He'd found Rory's pension book, and a passport thirty-seven years out of date, a three-year driving licence that was good for another year and a statement from the credit union telling Rory that he had one hundred and eighty nine euro and forty cents in his account.

And as if one momentous problem in Edward's life wasn't enough, there was Sophie.

They'd been married for over twenty years. They'd met shortly after twenty-three-year-old Edward Bull had gone to work for Sophie's father, Cathal. The boss's daughter had been pretty and charming, and it hadn't taken Edward long to ask her out.

The marriage hadn't been perfect; far from it. There'd been plenty of times when Edward was tempted to walk away – and probably Sophie too, if he was honest – but they'd weathered the shaky periods and stayed together.

There hadn't been children. They'd both been examined and there was no sign of a problem with either of them. Edward's sperm count was healthy, Sophie's womb produced an egg each month – but for whatever reason, children didn't happen. Edward would have considered adoption, but Sophie didn't want to know. And their life together went on, until a man had come to landscape the garden.

And shortly after his arrival, Edward had walked into the shed one morning to collect his fishing rod, and there they were.

In a second he had seen it all: Sophie pressed up against the back wall, eyes closed, mouth open, bare legs wrapped around the man's waist, hands clutching his black, tousled hair. His jeans and underwear around his ankles, his hands cradling her hips. Her skirt bunched up around her waist, his naked buttocks clenching and unclenching as he pounded against her, panting–

For months afterwards, Edward saw Sophie's eyes snapping open, widening with shock, starting to say his name as he turned and strode away, as he blundered up the path and into the house, slamming the back door behind him to keep them out. To keep her out.

Then her tears, her protestations, her apologies, her pleas. And after that, the long, stunned silence. After he'd walked away from their marriage, away from his job and his life up till then. After he'd turned up on Rory's doorstep, and his uncle had taken him in.

He missed Sophie, of course. He missed her company. He hated living alone, and especially eating alone. He wanted to look across the table and watch someone cutting into a steak, or lifting a glass to drink. He wanted to hear the clatter of someone else's cutlery. He wanted to talk about someone else's day, or tell them about his.

He felt her loss when he shopped for groceries, trailing through the aisles with his basket, hunting for black pepper and milk and frozen peas, never remembering where to find eggs or anchovies.

He missed her in bed, missed being able to reach out and touch another person, to feel the warmth of someone else's skin. He wanted to hear her voice, to smell her. To taste her.

And now, after the long separation, she'd re-appeared.

Their conversation in the pub had been careful. He'd asked about her charity work, about her sister who had multiple sclerosis, about the neighbours he hadn't seen since he'd left. He'd mentioned the play.

She'd enquired about his hay fever, and how his back had been behaving. She'd told him about the neighbours' extension, and a trip to the Canaries with a couple of friends at Easter.

She hadn't brought up the cheques he sent each month, with no covering note, that remained uncashed.

Edward hadn't asked how the garden looked now.

Neither of them had talked about their first Christmas apart, or what they'd done on their birthdays.

And then, just as they were about to leave, as Edward was shrugging into his jacket, Sophie had said, 'So you're not coming back to me? You're never coming home?'

Her tone had been light. She might have been asking him if he'd brushed his teeth that morning.

Edward had buttoned his jacket slowly and hadn't answered, because he didn't know how.

Sophie had walked out of the pub ahead of him. He'd asked if she had the car with her and she'd said yes, in the same casual voice.

In the car park, he'd put out his hand and she'd looked at it for a few seconds before taking it.

'Look after yourself,' he'd said, and she'd dropped his hand and slid the key into the door of her blue Astra.

Since then, Edward had been tortured with indecision.

She'd made it plain that she wanted him back, but could he swallow his pride? Could he find a way to forget, or at least forgive, what had happened? Did he want to? Could it ever be the same between them?

He imagined returning to the house he'd vowed never to set foot in again. He thought about the comfort of it, the tastefully decorated rooms, the space and light of it. The bed where he and Sophie had lain side by side for twenty years.

It was tempting; of course he was tempted. But then he'd think of the garden that was now presumably beautifully landscaped by whoever had finished off the job, and he'd remember walking into the shed, and the fury and the hurt would come flooding back.

He had no rest. Her question had thrown him into confusion. It haunted him, it kept him from sleep.

At least he'd have to concentrate on the rehearsal for the next couple of hours or so. He took a deep breath and walked through the doorway at the top of the stairs.

Ellen sat alone in an oversized armchair. She wore loose-fitting jeans and a top in a tiny pink and white check. Her feet were tucked under her.

'Maria's on the way,' she said as soon as she saw Edward. 'She's helping Oliver find a parking space. I've no idea where everyone else is.'

'I see.' As Edward wondered who Oliver was, the thump of footsteps sounded on the stairs and Robert and Judith appeared.

'Sorry Edward, I was ages finding a place to park,' Judith said. 'I think there's something on in the art gallery next door.'

'We're not late, are we?' Robert asked. 'My watch is two minutes to half past.'

'Not late, no.' Edward opened his briefcase and took out his script and notebook. Focus, he told himself. Forget about everything else.

'Is Maria not coming?' Judith asked Ellen.

'On the way,' Ellen answered, and immediately they heard more footsteps. 'This'll be her now.'

But it was Theo, clattering through the doorway with Harry.

'–and I told him if he ever picks up a hurley again, I'll clatter him with it.' She wore a lime green top under a purple knee-length tunic, and the hideous purple shoes that Edward remembered from the audition night. This evening the pink hair was topped with a blue and green striped beret.

He wondered if she ever looked in a mirror. Or maybe she was colour blind.

'Hello everyone,' she said. 'Who's missing?'

Ellen uncurled her legs and stretched them out.

'Maria – she's parking.'

'Any gingerbread men?' Theo asked her. 'I'm starving.'

'Sorry, not tonight.'

Edward cleared his throat. 'Good evening, everyone,' he said. 'We may as well get started.'

Hurried footsteps on the stairs just then, and Maria appeared with a man Edward didn't recognise.

'Sorry,' she said, crossing the room. 'The car park's full, we had to go down the street. This is Oliver – Robert phoned you about him, he wants to help with costumes. Edward Bull, our director,' she told Oliver.

The elegantly dressed man put out his hand. 'Delighted,' he said fervently. 'Thanks so much for allowing me to be involved.'

His hair was too long, he smelled like a boudoir. He cradled Edward's hand in both of his and squeezed it gently.

Edward had completely forgotten Robert's phone call.

'I'm so looking forward to this,' Oliver said. 'Costumes are such a *vital* part of any production, aren't they?'

'Er, yes. You'll need a script,' Edward began, but Oliver wasn't listening. 'We've met somewhere, haven't we? I'm *sure* of it.' Studying Edward, frowning.

Edward shook his head. 'I don't think–'

'I have it.' Oliver exclaimed. 'You buried poor Uncle Henry two years ago. Such a wonderfully dignified send-off you gave him. And now you're directing a murder mystery – how appropriate.'

295

'You're a *gravedigger?*' Theo asked.

Edward felt the situation slipping away from him. 'An undertaker – used to be,' he said curtly. He turned to his briefcase. 'I may not have a spare script on me this–'

'Ah, but we don't need one,' Oliver told him. 'I took the liberty of photocopying Maria's – I do hope that was acceptable?'

'Oh.' Edward couldn't fault his enthusiasm. 'Right, well ... have you had a chance to read it?'

'Twice,' Oliver said immediately. 'Once quite hurriedly to satisfy my curiosity, and the second time at my leisure,' he paused, 'in the bath.'

A delighted ripple of amusement from the others.

'A charming little melodrama,' Oliver continued, seeming not to notice the smiles. 'Reminiscent of an Agatha Christie tale, I thought. One could just imagine–'

'Indeed,' Edward said hastily. 'Well ... we must sit down at some stage and, er, discuss ideas.' One feather boa and he was out.

'Most certainly,' Oliver said promptly. 'I am at your disposal, Edward, and I hope you shall find me a worthy wardrobe mistress.'

A snort from Theo, which she quickly turned into a cough as Edward glanced in her direction.

Oliver pulled a wallet from his breast pocket and slid out a small cream card. 'My contact details, for future reference.'

'Thank you.' Edward shoved the card quickly into his briefcase. 'Now, I presume you're happy to sit and watch the rehearsal?'

'Delighted,' Oliver answered. 'Honoured. I

could prompt, if you like?'

'Thank you, that won't be necessary,' Edward assured him. He turned to the cast before Oliver had time to offer his services in any other capacity.

'Right everyone, let's begin. During this rehearsal we're going to have a look at each character's monologues. You are all now suspects in Dorothy's murder, and one by one you must present your version of events, in the manner of a person being questioned by the police.'

He paused, glancing in Ellen's direction. 'If time permits, I should also like to have another look at the murder scene.'

A slight inclination of her head.

'Right. Tom, you're up first.'

'OK.' Harry took up his position at the side of the stage.

'Beg pardon,' said Oliver, 'but where should one sit?'

Edward shot him an impatient look. 'Wherever you like.' Was the man going to interrupt all evening?

He turned back to Harry. 'Now, you have to imagine a detective standing in front of you, listening to your version of events. Take your time with it. Don't rush it.'

'Right.'

'Quiet please, everyone. And ... let's go.'

(TOM enters and faces the audience.)
TOM: My name–

'No – don't talk straight away,' Edward said

quickly. 'Count to five slowly in your head. Go out and come in again.'

'Right.'

'And ... let's go.'

(TOM enters and faces the audience. He is silent for a few seconds.)

TOM: My name is Tom Drury—

'Sorry,' said Edward quickly. 'We need a chair, you need to be sitting. Can we have a chair, someone?'

Oliver leapt up. 'Allow me.' He grabbed a chair and carried it onstage and placed it behind Harry, who smiled his thanks.

'Right,' said Edward. He waited till Oliver had taken his seat again. 'Carry on, Tom.'

(TOM enters and sits facing the audience. He is silent for a few seconds.)

TOM: My name is Tom Drury and I work for Jack McCarthy as his gardener.

'Louder,' ordered Edward. 'Sit up straight.'

Harry blinked.

TOM: My name is Tom Drury, and I work for Jack McCarthy as his gardener. I first met Miss Dorothy Williams shortly after she arrived at the house—

'Slower, stop racing through it. Start again.'

'Sorry.'

'Don't apologise. Stay in character. Begin.'

TOM: My name is Tom Drury, and I – er – work for Jack McCarthy as his gardener. I first met Miss Dorothy Williams shortly after she arrived at the house five days ago. She told me she was doing some research for an article she was writing on Mr McCarthy. I met Miss Williams on a few occasions, sometimes in the house, sometimes in the garden. On the morning of Miss Williams' death, I was working as usual in the garden. I overheard a scream and ... er, I ... er...

Harry stopped, looking apologetically at Edward.
Edward sighed loudly. '"And I went to see what had caused it".'

TOM: I overheard a scream and I went to see what had caused it. It seemed to have come from the study, so I walked over to the window and looked in. At first I saw nothing, and then I looked down and I noticed ... somebody's arm. I couldn't see any more because Mr McCarthy's desk was in the way. I ran around to the back door and entered the house, and I found the housekeeper, and told her what I had seen. She said to wait in the kitchen ... and she went to the study and found ... Miss Williams ... and she was dead. *(Bows his head)*

'Stay there. Count to ten and then leave. Well done.'
As Harry walked off, there was a burst of clapping behind Edward. He swung around, and

Oliver stopped immediately.

'Sorry – is it not done?'

'No,' Edward said evenly. 'It is not.'

'Righto. Not another squeak.'

Edward gritted his teeth and turned to Maria. 'Penelope, your turn.'

Maria made her way to the side of the stage.

'Right everybody, and ... let's go.'

(PENELOPE enters and sits, looking defiantly at the audience.)

'Count to five again.'

PENELOPE: My name, as you well know, is Penelope McCarthy, and I live with my brother Jack in the house where we both grew up. I make no secret of the fact that I objected to this ... person's arrival, as I resented the intrusion into our privacy.

'Pause. Take your time. More haughtiness.'

PENELOPE: I also got the distinct impression that Miss Williams had designs on my brother. This impression was formed from my own observations ... and from the anonymous letter which I received two days ago, and which I have already submitted to you.'

'Count to five.'

PENELOPE: At the time of the ... incident, I was upstairs in my room, which is at the front of the house, away from the study. I heard nothing until the housekeeper knocked on my door in an extremely distraught condition, and told me what she'd discovered in my brother's study. I went downstairs and saw for myself that the person was clearly dead. That is all I have to say on the matter, except to repeat that I had nothing whatsoever to do with Miss Williams' death.

Maria made as if to stand and Edward said quickly, 'Stop – count to five before you get up.'

(PENELOPE sits for a moment, looking straight at the audience, and then stands and exits slowly.)
'Bravo!'
Edward swung around and glared, and Oliver said hurriedly, 'I'm terribly sorry, it just slipped out.'
'Jack,' Edward barked. 'Your turn.'
Robert took up his position.
'Remember the pauses,' Edward told him. 'Take your time. Don't be afraid of the silences. Speak slowly and clearly.'
Robert nodded.
'Quiet everybody. And ... let's go.'

(JACK walks slowly to the chair and sits. He looks at the audience steadily for several seconds without speaking.)
JACK: I'm Jack McCarthy, author of fourteen novels and two biographies. From time to time, I receive enquiries from journalists who want to interview me, and on occasion I agree. This was

one of those occasions *(pause)*. The reason I agreed to Dorothy's – Miss Williams' – request was that the publication she claimed to represent was a well-respected one, which I have read myself on several occasions. *(Sighs deeply.)* Miss Williams seemed to be settling in very well. We usually spent a few hours each morning in my study, where she would question me about my work. I became ... quite fond of her – but there was never a suggestion of ... impropriety, despite what my sister might tell you *(pause).*

'Sorry,' Robert said eventually. 'I've forgotten.'
'"At the time of her death".'

JACK: At the time of her death, I was absent from the house. I'd gone for a walk alone, as I do regularly. When I returned to the house, the police – you – had arrived, and ... well, you know the rest. *(Shakes his head.)*

Edward watched as Robert stood unhurriedly and left the stage.
'Good. Well done everyone, so far so good.' He checked his script. 'Ursula, your turn.'
Theo approached the side of the stage.
'You're trying to be defiant,' Edward told her, 'but you're also nervous.'
She nodded.
'Take your time with this. And ... let's go.'

(URSULA walks to the chair and sits, her hands gripping each other in her lap.)
URSULA: My name is Ursula Fitzpatrick. I've

been the local postmistress for twenty-two years, and this is the first time anything like this has happened *(pause).* I never met Miss Williams. She never came to the post office, but I knew she was staying with the McCarthys. In a village our size news travels fast – especially when there's a gossip like Betty O'Donnell spreading it.

'Change your tone now,' Edward ordered.

URSULA: *(scowls)* I wish you wouldn't keep going on about that letter. The only reason I sent it was to put the wind up Penelope McCarthy *(sneers)* with her airs and graces, acting Lady of the Manor whenever she deigns to honour the post office with her presence.

'Good,' Edward said quietly.

URSULA: Who did she think she was, talking down to me? Acting like I wasn't good enough for – *(pulls herself up abruptly)* – acting like I wasn't good enough *(pause).* At the time the murder was committed, I was having my break, like I do at the same time every day. I was in the Post Office but the door was locked, like it always is at that time *(pause).* I had nothing to do with Miss Williams' death. That is all I have to say. *(After another short pause, URSULA gets up and leaves the stage.)*

'Well done,' Edward said. He turned to Judith. 'Ready?'
  She stood. 'I hope so.'

No direction, she didn't need it. 'Right. And ... let's go.'

(BETTY walks slowly to the chair, her hands loose, her face expressionless. She sits and regards the audience calmly, hands resting in her lap.)

Edward waited. The room was silent.

BETTY: My name is Betty O'Donnell. I have worked in this house for the past six years *(pause)*. I came originally to help out after old Mrs McCarthy took to her bed. I'm not a trained nurse, but I was able to carry trays and ... give her a wash, that sort of thing. After she died, Mr McCarthy asked me to stay on as his housekeeper, which I agreed to do *(pause)*. I notice things, see. I keep quiet and I notice. Soon after the young lady came to the house, I noticed that the gardener, young Tom Drury, was interested in her. I encouraged this, thinking she'd suit him well. I told him he should ask her out. So he took my advice and approached her, but he told me she turned him down, and he was most upset about it – almost angry, you might say. Not that Tom would be capable of anything – no, I'm sure not. No, you mustn't for a minute think poor Tom had anything to do with this shocking business *(long pause)*. And he wasn't the only one to be attracted; I also noticed that Mr McCarthy himself was quite taken with the young lady. In fact, I happened to overhear a conversation in the garden between them, just a few days ago, where

he confessed his attraction. Oh yes. *(Sighs.)* But it was just the same with him – the young lady as much as laughed in his face, told him she was flattered, but he was too old. No man likes to hear that from a pretty lady... But of course Mr McCarthy would be the last person in the world capable of violence, dear me, no. *(Shakes her head slowly.)* And then there was Miss McCarthy. Oh, she didn't take to the young lady at all, not at all. If you ask me, she was terrified that Mr McCarthy might take up with her and move her in permanently – and then where would Miss McCarthy be? *(Another shake of her head.)* No, she wouldn't want that at all. What woman would like another moving into her home, taking over? Now, *(leans slightly forward)* far be it from me to spread gossip – but you need to know all the facts, don't you? You've met the postmistress. Ursula Fitzpatrick? Well, it's no secret that she has her sights set on Mr McCarthy – not that he has the slightest interest in her, why would he? But you can see why she wouldn't have liked the notion of him taking up with the young lady either, can't you? In fact, *(thoughtfully)* in the few short days she was here, that unfortunate young Miss Williams seems to have made a lot of enemies. I'm not saying that any of them murdered her, of course – but when you think about it, they all had some kind of a motive, didn't they?
(BETTY sits silently for a few more seconds, and then gets up and exits slowly.)

Edward closed his script. 'Good work everyone,

and well done on the lines. I suggest we take a ten-minute break now.' He emphasised the 'ten' slightly – they were still slow in coming back. He needed to keep the pressure on.

There was a general shuffle as everyone began to stand.

'We go downstairs to the bar,' Maria told Oliver.

'Lovely.' As he walked to the doorway with the others, Oliver noticed that Edward wasn't moving. 'Aren't you joining us, Edward?'

'No,' Edward answered. 'I prefer to stay up here.' He hoped fervently that his new wardrobe mistress wouldn't feel compelled to keep him company. 'I like to be alone for a few minutes, to gather my thoughts.'

'Righto – I'll grab a tiny G&T and be right back.'

'Take your time,' Edward told him.

'I must say,' Oliver declared, 'I think every one is *terribly* good. I'm looking forward to hearing more.'

'You won't hear much from me,' Ellen told him. 'I've been stabbed through the heart.'

'Oh, yes – poor, tragic Dorothy-stroke-Caroline.'

'So how's everything with you?' she asked him. 'Haven't met you for a while.'

Oliver sighed. 'Can't complain, Ellen dear, and even if I did, who would listen?'

Ellen smiled. 'Any boyfriend?'

'None; I'm as tragic as Dorothy.'

Or as Ellen. She pushed the thought away, determined not to dwell on it tonight, and looked

306

across the table at Harry, in conversation with Robert. Were her suspicions right about him? There was nothing she could put her finger on, but in his company there was none of the barely discernible sexual tension that normally seemed to manifest itself between a man and a woman, regardless of attraction.

She'd felt it from Edward Bull, for goodness' sake – not that he'd admit it in a million years. But there it was between them, simply because they were programmed to mate with each other's gender.

She turned back to Oliver. 'Harry is perfect as Tom the gardener, isn't he? Maybe because he's like that in real life, all shy and awkward. Quite sweet, really.'

Oliver regarded Harry. 'How adorably shaggy he is – like a giant retriever puppy.'

Ellen laughed. 'He works in the library. You should talk books with him.'

'Indeed,' said Oliver thoughtfully. 'Does he indeed.'

'How have you been?' Judith asked Maria.

Maria glanced quickly towards Ellen, safely out of earshot. 'Alright, thanks. Sorry about the other day.'

'Don't be silly. I'm glad I was there to listen.'

'And you? Are your visitors still with you?'

'Yes. No sign of any change there.'

'Surely they'll run out of money eventually?'

Not if they keep stealing mine. 'Yes, I suppose that'll happen at some stage.'

She wouldn't mention the missing notes. That

307

was the last thing Maria needed to hear. They sipped their drinks silently, each lost in her own uncertainties.

'Two boys, twins. Ten years old.' Robert pulled the photo from his wallet and passed it to Harry. 'Noah and Aidan. The fairer one is Noah.'

'They look nice.' Harry never knew what to say when people showed him their children.

'They don't live with me, they're with their mother. I see them a lot though.'

'Right.'

'But she's just announced that they're going to live in France for a year,' Robert said grimly. 'I'm not too happy about it.'

'France?' Theo said on his other side. 'Sorry for butting in, but did you say Caroline's moving to France? So it's serious with her and that French guy?'

Robert looked coolly at her. 'I have no idea,' he said.

So Caroline was telling people about the Frenchman. Which of course meant nothing at all – women told each other everything, however trivial.

'Wow,' Theo said. 'It must be serious if she's moving over there.'

'Only for a year,' Robert replied, willing her to go away, or shut up, or both.

'Which part of France are they going to?' she asked. 'I love France, it's my favourite country – well, next to Spain. I *adore* Spain.'

'Near Nantes,' Robert said shortly.

'Oh, I've been there – do you know exactly

where they're going?' She was unstoppable.

'Saint-Nazaire.' What would it take to shut her up?

'I know it,' she said excitedly. 'Ben and I drove through it last year. He surprised me with the trip, just after I found out I was pregnant with Chrissy.'

'Delightful,' Robert said.

'It was, it was really romantic. Saint-Nazaire is a port, lovely atmospheric place. We had dinner there on ... the second night, I think it was – what was the name of the restaurant again? I can't remember, something about a mariner I think – or was it Neptune? Of course I steered clear of the shellfish, but Ben raved about it, and I had the most *divine* duck, and then the desserts...'

Robert snuck a look at his watch, wondering why ten minutes had always seemed too short for the break.

'Right,' said Edward. 'Before we move on, could I have everyone's attention for a minute please?' The chatter stopped. 'Let me remind you all of the timeframe. Today is the twenty-second of May, and our production is scheduled to begin on Monday the ninth of June, which is just over two weeks away.'

Indrawn breaths, expressions of alarm. He saw Theo's mouth opening and hurried on.

'The play will run for six nights, from Monday the ninth to Saturday the fourteenth, at eight p.m. nightly. Between now and then we have two Thursday rehearsals and one dress rehearsal on Sunday the eighth, and I'd also like to schedule

in one extra rehearsal during the last week –
possibly Tuesday the third, if that suits everyone.
That gives us four more rehearsals in total after
tonight.' He paused. 'Any questions?'

'The *ninth?*'

'Two and a half *weeks?*'

'Only *four* more rehearsals?'

'But we haven't even–'

'I had no idea it was so–'

'There's no way we'll–'

'I'll never remember–'

'Two and a half weeks?'

Edward held up his hand, and gradually the
voices died away. 'It may seem like a daunting
prospect right now – after all, we haven't even
run through the entire play yet. But if we work
hard for the next two weeks, I have every confidence that you will all be ready by opening
night. Alright?'

Six sceptical faces looked back at him. He
couldn't blame them. The chances of them being
as ready as he would like by opening night were
slim, to put it mildly.

He picked up his script. 'Right, let's move on.
We can settle on a day for the extra rehearsal next
week, once you've all checked your schedules.'
He riffled the pages. 'Now, I was thinking about
the monologues during the break, and I think
they might work better if everyone is onstage
together, seated in a row, and each character
delivers his or her speech in a spotlight. Let's try
it that way and see how it works.'

He turned to Oliver. 'May I have five chairs in
a row on the stage please?'

May as well make him feel useful.

'That'll do for this evening, except,' he paused, looking at Judith and Ellen, 'as I said earlier, I'd like to revisit the murder scene.' Ellen groaned quietly. Edward pretended not to hear. 'There's no need for everyone to stay, I only need Betty and Dorothy. The rest of you, please go back over your lines for the entire play – we'll be having a complete run through next week.'

'But I'm getting a lift home with Oliver,' Ellen said. 'He drove us in.'

'We can wait for you, can't we?' he asked, turning to Maria, who nodded.

'I'll drive her home,' Edward said quickly. He'd had quite enough of Oliver for one night. He looked at Ellen. 'If that's OK with you.'

'You don't know where I live,' she said. 'It might be miles out of your way.'

'North or south?' he asked mildly. Charming, how reluctant she was to spend any more time with him than was necessary.

'North.'

'Me too,' he lied. 'No problem.'

'Fine,' she said glumly. 'Whatever.'

'You'll be in touch, Edward?' Oliver asked.

'Yes,' Edward replied, his spirits sinking at the prospect of an undiluted helping of Oliver.

While the others were leaving, Edward wrote *costumes* in his notebook. He pulled Oliver's card from his briefcase and read Oliver Noble, Bookseller, followed by a mobile phone number and e-mail address, and underneath, in a small, ornate script: *The meeting of two personalities is like the*

311

contact of two chemical substances: if there is any reaction, both are transformed. – Carl Jung.

Good grief. He slipped the card back and turned to Ellen and Judith. 'Right,' he said. 'Let's take it from–'

'I forgot my towel,' Ellen said.

'Your towel?'

'For when I fall on the floor.'

'You're only there for a second, can't you put up with it just once?' He was conscious of treading carefully with her, but surely she wasn't going to insist on the damn towel?

'I need something, it makes me feel sick.'

He looked around and grabbed his jacket. 'Here, use this.'

'You'll have to get it dry-cleaned after.'

'Fine.'

Get it dry-cleaned, my foot. He watched her place it on the floor.

'Betty, take your time noticing Dorothy coming in. Let her walk halfway towards you before you realise she's there.'

'And try and stab me over the jacket,' Ellen said, and Judith smiled.

'Let's have some focus please,' Edward said coolly. 'This scene is vital – I need both of you totally in character.'

Judith was a natural, finding her way confidently into Betty O'Donnell's personality. Her interpretation of the murderous housekeeper, if not flawless, was certainly impressive.

And Edward had to admit to a certain pleasure as he watched Ellen's performance. Her anger, as she raged at the housekeeper, was convincing.

312

The tears didn't feature this time; he suspected her determination was all that kept them at bay.

Afterwards, the three of them walked downstairs together.

'I'm picking up the canvas for the backdrops during the week,' Edward told Judith. 'Can I leave the painting materials to you? Any expense will, of course, be reimbursed.'

'Fine,' she said. 'Let me know when you're ready for me to start.' In the emptied out car park she said goodbye to them and walked towards a maroon Ford.

Ellen looked at Edward. 'Where are we?'

We. Talk about the odd couple. 'This way.'

In the car, her perfume was stronger. 'You smell of oranges,' Edward said without thinking.

She glanced at him as she clicked her seatbelt closed. 'Grapefruit, actually. Grapefruit shampoo.'

'Right.'

He started the engine and she added, 'And your jacket smells of that manky carpet.' She searched the surface of the door. 'How do you open this window?'

Edward reached across and pressed the button, and the window slid open. His jacket lay on the back seat. He picked it up and sniffed. 'I can't smell anything,' he told her. 'You're imagining it.'

'I am not – it's disgusting.' She stuck her head out the window and inhaled deeply.

'Where are we going?' he asked.

'Right, then left at the roundabout.'

They travelled in silence through the darkening streets, Ellen's window still wide open, the wind whipping her hair around wildly. Once or twice it flicked against Edward's face. Ellen didn't seem to notice.

They passed the hospital and she turned to him. 'How's your uncle? I forgot to ask earlier.' Her cheeks were pink from the wind. She pushed her hair away from her face.

'He had a stroke,' Edward answered. 'He's old, he won't get better.'

'Oh. That's too bad. I'm sorry.' He didn't respond. 'Left after this pub.'

A group of smokers were clustered around the pub door. Edward thought about brandy. 'Can I ask you something?' He knew he was taking a chance.

'What?'

'Does the scene in the study upset you?'

She looked out the window and her hair flew up. She said something, but the wind whipped it away.

'Pardon?'

She turned back. 'It's just acting,' she said.

'OK.'

'I'm over here.' She pointed towards an apartment block on the right. Edward pulled up and stopped.

Ellen got out quickly. 'Thanks for the lift. See you next week.'

'See you.' He waited until she'd opened the front door and disappeared. Then he turned the car around and drove all the way back through the dark city streets, past McMillan's pub again.

And as he drove, he told himself that he'd imagined the infinitesimal flicker, the tiny static-spark, as his arm had brushed briefly against her body, his face inches from hers, when he'd leaned across to open her window.

Pure imagination. His mind, weary from too little sleep and too many questions, was playing tricks on him. Her window was still open, the night air sweeping in. He pressed the button and the glass rushed upwards.

Back home he held his jacket to his face, and smelled only grapefruit.

'Harry?'

'Yes?' He pulled his key out, and a second later Eve appeared.

'Your sister phoned twice. She said to ring her as soon as you got in.'

'Thanks.'

Babs needing him to do something, which was the only time she phoned. Or maybe to complain about something he'd done, or had forgotten to do.

He pulled his mobile phone from his pocket – Edward insisted on them all being silenced during rehearsals – and saw he had three missed calls, all from Babs. He checked his voicemail, but there was no message.

He phoned, and his brother-in-law answered on the second ring. 'Harry, there you are. Hang on, I'll get Babs.'

A whispered conversation just out of earshot, and then Babs's voice. 'Oh, Harry–'

Crying. Something wrong. One of the children, an accident–

'It's Ma, Harry, she–' A burst of sobbing, and a rustle, and then Tony again.

'Harry, I'm very sorry.'

Harry gripped the phone tightly.

'It's your mother, Harry. She died.'

Harry closed his eyes and leaned forward until his forehead touched the wall.

'She's dead, Harry.'

Nothing. He could say nothing. There were no words.

'Harry? Are you there?'

Maria stood in the doorway of Pat's room and watched him breathe. He always seemed to do it too fast. It made her feel panicky, made her own breath quicken, to see his small chest rising and falling so rapidly.

Slow down, take your time.

He clutched his red car, as usual. She'd given up trying to figure out why he rejected all his soft toys in favour of its cold metal hardness each night.

She pulled his door out softly, leaving it ajar so the light from the landing would comfort him if he woke. She walked the few steps to her own bedroom door and opened it.

The smell of her husband's sleeping body curled around her as she undressed silently. She pulled on her nightdress and slid between the sheets as noiselessly as she could. She turned on her side away from him and lay unmoving, willing him not to wake.

He stirred, his breathing changed. A second later, she heard a rustle and felt his hot hand on her bare calf. She stiffened.

'You're home.'

She said nothing, closed her eyes as he found the hem of her nightdress, as his hand slid up her leg, up her thigh, as he fumbled with his pyjama bottoms and kicked them off and pulled her around, onto her back.

'Come on.'

His breath was stale. He yanked her nightdress above her breasts and put his face down and searched with his tongue until he found a nipple. He took it in his mouth and sucked loudly. She winced as he pressed a knee between her legs, forcing them apart.

'Mah.' Faint. Barely audible.

She opened her eyes. 'It's Pat – he's awake.'

Michael's hand slid underneath her and cupped her buttocks, his groin pressed into hers.

'Mah.'

Maria struggled, trying to push him away. 'Please, I have to.'

He lifted his head, easily strong enough to keep her trapped beneath him. 'No rush,' he breathed. 'He'll be fine, he can wait a while.' Pushing roughly, painfully into her, making himself comfortable on top of her. 'Now, that's it ... ah, that's it now ... ah, that's it.'

She closed her eyes again, feeling the wet heat of tears on her face. She lay silently as he pounded into her, as her body was forced into his rhythm, trying to blot out the moist, sucking clamminess of his skin on hers, the feel of his fingers clenching her buttocks. She endured his quickening moans, his animal heaving, the grunt of his release before he finally pulled himself out and rolled away from her, panting heavily.

She leapt out of bed and ran towards Pat's room, pulling down her nightdress. He was sitting up, hair spiky from sleep.

'Mah,' he said.

'Drink?' she asked, feeling the warm semen trickling down her thigh. 'Do you want a drink, love?' She lifted the beaker from his locker and held it out to him, and he took it and gulped the water.

'Do you need the toilet?'

But he was already lying back, his eyes closing again, his fingers curling around the red car and pulling it in against him.

Maria sat on the edge of his bed, watching him fall asleep.

Soon. She had to do it soon.

Robert

'You know you're spoiling them. They don't need all this.'

'All what? I'm their father, and I want to take them out – what's wrong with that?'

'What's wrong is that it's too much. Tonight it's out to dinner, Wednesday it was the cinema, Monday–'

'Well, in a few weeks you're taking them off to France–'

'Ah, Robert, not this again.'

'–and I'll see them once or twice a term, if even that. Is it any wonder I'm spending as much time as I can with them now?'

Caroline sighed. 'No, I suppose not.'

'Anyway, it's their birthday in September. Can't this be their birthday treat?'

She smiled faintly. 'Robert, September is nearly four months away.'

'Exactly – and they'll be in France, and I'll be here. So I have to treat them now.' He knew he was being stubborn, and he didn't care.

An ad was going into the following week's paper, looking for tenants for the house. The boys' headmaster had been informed of the move and had agreed to keep places for them in sixth class, which they'd be ready for when they returned in a year's time.

If they returned.

Robert couldn't shake the fear that they'd never come back to live in Ireland. If Caroline remained with the Frenchman, if things worked out between them, if Caroline's job went well and they boys settled, what possible reason would they have for coming back to Ireland? Robert's presence wouldn't be enough in itself, he knew that, not when it was so commonplace now to hop on a plane.

He imagined the long years between now and when the twins were eighteen, and free to live wherever they chose. What were the chances that they'd want to come back to Ireland after so long? What hope did Robert have of tempting them back here, with him becoming more of a stranger to them as each year went by?

He hadn't a word of French, beyond *bonjour* and *au revoir*. They'd be fluent in a few months.

How soon before the Frenchman became Papa, in name at least?

Caroline had got Peter, one of the other stylists, to cut her hair. It was a good six inches shorter now, stopping just above her shoulders and layered around her face, with deep red lowlights and a long fringe that brushed against her eyelashes. A new look for her new man.

Robert looked at his watch. 'Are they ready?'

She turned and called up the stairs. 'Come on you two, Dad's waiting.'

No sign of the Frenchman since the meal last week, although Robert presumed Caroline was still seeing plenty of him. Thank God for the boys, who'd argued and chattered through that dinner as usual.

They'd seemed at ease with the visitor – Robert could not bring himself to use the man's name – and thankfully the Frenchman had directed most of his conversation to them and Caroline, no doubt sensing Robert's reluctance to chat.

His English was heavily accented, but quite fluent. He was younger than Robert by at least half a dozen years, but he was also heavier and a couple of inches shorter, and Robert rejoiced to see that his hair was thinning on top quite noticeably.

His cologne or aftershave or whatever it was smelled expensive. His nails were buffed and well cut, and his suit had cost a bit – probably a bit more than Robert's cut-price Paul Smith.

'Please, call me Alain,' he'd said, and Robert had taken great care to call him nothing at all, and hadn't offered in turn to answer to Robert.

Call me Alain, indeed.

His thoughts were interrupted by the boys pounding downstairs. Caroline looked sharply at them.

'Have you both washed your hands?'

'Yes,' they chorused, Noah's hands disappearing immediately into his pockets. Robert grinned.

'We'll be back by eight,' he told Caroline as they scrambled onto the back seat of his car. 'Don't wait up.'

'Very funny.'

'Come with us,' he said suddenly, without knowing he was going to say it. 'Why not?'

Caroline shook her head. 'Thanks, but I don't think so.'

'Why not?' he repeated, and immediately, but too late, he wished the question unasked.

'I have plans,' she said.

The Frenchman was calling around for a bit of how's your Papa.

'OK,' Robert said. 'Just a thought.'

He didn't wave as they moved off, didn't look for her in the rear view mirror.

'Guess where we're going?' he said to the boys. 'Somewhere really great.'

'Supermacs,' they both said immediately.

'No, nicer.'

'Prego Pizza?'

'No, nicer than that too.'

They looked blankly at him.

Robert sighed. 'We're going to a really cool restaurant called The Cow and the Moon,' he told them. 'Bet you've never been there before.'

'Yes we have,' Aidan said immediately. 'They've wicked desserts.'

'You couldn't finish yours,' Noah said.

'Shut up, I could so.'

'You've been there before?' Robert asked innocently.

'Yeah, Alain brang us.'

'Brought,' he said automatically.

It had been easy to find out the name of the restaurant the Frenchman had taken them to, once he'd discovered it was where Theo worked. And who said he couldn't bring his boys to the same place? All Robert was trying to do was replace one memory with another, to wipe out their first visit to the Cow and the Moon and replace it with this evening's one. Nothing wrong with that, was there?

He pulled up outside the restaurant and turned to the boys. 'Let's have a great night,' he said. 'Even better than the last time you were here.' This early in the evening, the place was still fairly empty.

'Hello there,' said Theo. 'I remember these boys – two of our best customers.'

'Except Aidan couldn't finish his dessert,' Noah told her.

'Noah,' Robert said warningly.

Theo laughed. 'Well, let's see if he can manage it tonight. The secret,' she told Aidan, 'is to leave a little bit of dinner behind, to make more room.'

'You had blonde hair before,' Noah told her.

'I sure did,' she said. 'You've got a good memory. Now follow me.' She wore turquoise shoes with green heels.

It suddenly occurred to Robert that Theo might begin telling the boys how lucky they were to be going to live in France – she was definitely the kind who spoke first and thought later. He determined to cut her off immediately if the subject looked like coming up.

She led them to a table by the window. 'You're in luck tonight,' she said, pulling out chairs. 'The King of Romania's table is free.'

'It's the exact same as the table we had last time,' Noah said, 'over there.'

'Well, this is the only one the king will sit at when he comes to dinner here.' She passed menus around. 'I keep it for special people.'

'Why did she change her hair to pink?' Noah asked when she'd gone. 'It looks weird.'

'I suppose she likes it,' Robert said.

'Her shoes are funny.'

'Are they?'

'Do you know her?' Aidan asked.

'I do – she's in the play too. She's the lady who works in the post office.'

'Does she get murdered?'

'No.'

'Is she the killer?'

'No, but she does get to write a nasty letter.'

Theo didn't mention France. She took their orders for cheeseburger and chicken kebab and fillet steak, medium to well done, and by the time she'd delivered the plates the restaurant had begun to fill up, and she and the other waitresses were kept busy.

The boys had Mississippi Mud Pies for dessert, with ice cream on the side.

'You don't have to finish it all,' Robert told Aidan. 'I don't want you getting sick.'

Aidan put down his spoon. 'Dad?' he said.

'Yes?'

'Why can't you come to France with us?'

Robert looked at his son and felt a wave of emotion that threatened to undo him. He put down his coffee cup.

'Someone has to stay and mind the salon,' he said, resisting the impulse to gather Aidan – to gather them both – into his arms. 'But I'll really miss you guys.'

'Yeah.' Aidan picked up his spoon and dug it into the chocolatey mess.

'But Mum says you'll come and visit us,' Noah said.

Robert smiled. 'Of course I will, every chance I get.'

'Will you come at Christmas?'

'If I can.'

'If you can't come,' Noah told him, 'you've got to post our presents.'

Robert pretended to be offended. 'Hey, I thought it was me you wanted, not the presents.'

Noah grinned. 'Well ... maybe we could have the two.'

Robert would miss them. He'd miss them desperately. A year seemed like an eternity. He couldn't contemplate any longer than that. The bill arrived and he handed Theo his credit card. 'Thanks.'

'You're welcome.' She slid the card into the machine and pressed buttons, and waited for him to input his PIN. 'This place belongs to my sister.

You can spread the word in the salon.'

'Will do,' he promised. 'See you Thursday.'

The boys were quiet on the way home. For once there was no arguing about who sat where, or how much space they took up.

The silver Peugeot stood outside the house. As Robert pulled up, the door opened and Caroline appeared.

'Coming in for a coffee?' she asked him as the boys raced inside.

'Better not – meeting someone in a while,' he lied. 'See you tomorrow.'

With great restraint, he avoided putting a dent in the Peugeot as he drove off.

Judith

The fifty euro note was missing. She'd got a hundred euro cashback in the supermarket, she'd paid thirty for petrol on the way home and now there were two tens in her purse and nothing else, which meant the fifty was gone.

She had to say something. She had to face him, and say – what? She shrank from the confrontation. She couldn't accuse him. He was stealing from her, and there was no earthly way that she could bring herself to say anything. How could she, when it might ruin everything between them, when she might lose him altogether?

She'd coped badly when it had happened before. When he was a teenager and not making much money of his own, Judith had tried for a while to convince herself that she could survive the loss of the odd fiver and tenner, that every lad his age did it. When it began to stop her from sleeping, she'd taken to keeping as little cash as possible in her purse, knowing it was wrong to say nothing, despising herself for taking the coward's way out.

It's your fault, she'd told Samuel in her head. *You left him, and look how he turned out. You caused this.* But Samuel wasn't there to answer; nobody was listening. So Judith had continued to suffer the loss of the occasional fiver – no more tenners now – and she'd waited for it to stop, and eventually, when he'd begun working himself, it had.

Only now it looked like it was happening all over again, when Christopher was old enough to know better, and Judith was just as hopeless at dealing with it.

She could hardly remember what it felt like to have the house to herself. The bathroom was always a mess, with sodden towels strewn on the floor – how much energy did it take to hang the damn things up, or put them into the laundry basket? Long hairs clogging the bath plughole, powder scattered in the sink, unfamiliar cosmetics that had gradually found their way out of the toilet bag and were now taking up every spare inch of shelf space.

Apart from one time when Amanda had made rubbery omelettes and opened a can of beans, nobody cooked dinner except Judith. The rest of the time they ate what was put in front of them or helped themselves to whatever was in the fridge, never replacing what they took.

The washing up was occasionally done, but neither of them had looked for the hoover or swept a floor since they'd arrived. Judith dreaded to think what state her bedroom was in. She was torn between offering clean sheets and waiting to see how long it would be before they looked for them.

She'd stopped waiting for them to talk about finding work or a place to live. Maybe that had been the plan all along, to move in here and just stay put. Maybe this was it, the three of them under one roof until one of them – Judith, probably – died.

'No way will she throw us out,' Christopher would have said. 'She's soft, she wouldn't do that. We'll be able to stay as long as we like, rent free.'

The school was closing for the summer holidays next week, the rest of her life about to begin – only now it was all different. She imagined she'd be spending a lot of time in her studio, which was really the shed at the bottom of the garden with an easel in it. If the weather was fine she'd pack up the car and take day trips. She wouldn't think about winter; she'd sort that out when it came.

At least the backdrops for the play would keep her busy once the holidays started – she guessed they'd take up most of the following week. She was glad she'd offered now, glad she had something to take her mind off the situation at home.

But in the meantime, she was down fifty euro.

She walked into the sitting room. Amanda was

on the couch, reading one of the books she'd brought home from the library last week on Judith's ticket.

'Hello there. Good day so far?'

Always so breezy, always in such good humour. Did she never get upset about not seeing her children? Did she even think about them? Was there no twinge of guilt about moving into a stranger's house and treating it like a hotel?

'Fine, thanks.'

The niceties always observed, when what you really wanted to say was *Get a job, get a boyfriend your own age, go home and look after your children. Get out of my house.*

'Where's Christopher?'

Amanda shrugged. 'In our room, I should think. He said something about a lie-down.'

Our room.

'I seem to have lost fifty euro,' Judith said evenly. 'You wouldn't have seen it lying around, would you?'

No hint of guilt in the eyes that widened, no sign of an uneasy conscience. 'Oh, you haven't, have you? I hate to lose something, me – especially money.' She got up. 'Here, I'll help you look. Where's the last place you remember having it?'

In my purse. Judith shook her head. 'No, it's alright, I thought it might have fallen out of ... don't worry, it'll probably turn up.'

Amanda might not be aware of what Christopher was doing. She could be as innocent as she looked.

'I'll tell Chris to keep an eye out, shall I?'

'Do that.'

No harm in letting him know that Judith had missed it, that she'd mentioned it to his girlfriend.

She had to get out – but where? She'd already done the shopping, cleaned the kitchen, hoovered the downstairs. The rest of Saturday stretched ahead of her, and it was still only half twelve.

Maria. She'd call into the bookshop and maybe they could go to lunch or have a coffee or something. Anywhere would be better than hanging around here.

She turned towards the hall. 'I'm going out for a while. See you later.'

'Have fun.'

Maria was behind the counter, serving a customer. There was no sign of Oliver. Judith walked slowly along the aisles, running a hand along the spines of the books, pulling out the odd one that caught her eye.

'Hello – I thought it was you.'

Judith smiled. 'I was passing and I wondered if you'd had lunch yet.'

Maria checked her watch. 'Actually I haven't, and I'd love to. Oliver should be back any minute, if you can hang on–'

'Perfect.'

'–and if you fancy eating outside, I was planning to get a sandwich and go to the park just down the road. The weather's so fine, I hate to waste it indoors.'

'Sounds good.' Judith looked around the shop. 'I was just thinking how nice it must be to work in a quiet place like this. Compared to the mayhem of the classroom, I mean.'

Maria smiled. 'It's not always this quiet, especially on Saturdays. I should be worried, but to be honest this is more of a hobby for me than a livelihood.' She paused. 'My husband bought this place as a tax write-off.'

Her face, when she mentioned him. The smile gone.

Judith searched for a safer topic. 'Oliver is sweet, isn't he?'

'Very sweet – and invaluable here. I don't know what I'd do without him.' She turned as the door opened. 'Oh good, here he is.'

Oliver strode in, unwinding a narrow scarf in the palest shade of blue. 'You were talking about me, I can sense it.' He recognised Judith. 'Why, hello there. Isn't that strange, I've just been talking with Edward, and now here you are.'

'You met Edward?' Maria asked.

'Not yet – he phoned to arrange a little rendezvous. I told him I'd meet him at three for half an hour, if that's alright with you.'

'That's fine.'

Judith smiled. 'I can't wait to see what costume you pick out for me.'

'In that case,' Oliver told her, 'I should warn you that I intend you to look extremely murderous indeed – very Whatever Happened to Baby Jane. We may have to talk about hair in a bun.'

Maria laughed. 'I wonder if poor Edward will have any say?'

Oliver draped his scarf on the counter. 'Indeed he will not – but of course I shall make sure the poor man thinks he's *completely* in control. And now I presume you're going to go to lunch with this wicked housekeeper, and leave me to my own devices?'

'I certainly am. I'll be about forty-five minutes, OK?'

'Lovely. *Bon apetit.*'

In the park, they found a bench and unwrapped the sandwiches they'd bought on the way. Maria twisted the top off her bottle of water.

'I normally get tomatoes in a ham sandwich, but when I'm pregnant I can't abide them. Tomatoes and coffee.'

Judith sipped her apple juice. 'I don't remember going off anything when I was expecting Christopher, but I got a craving for oranges – couldn't get enough of them.'

They sat without speaking for a few minutes. The park was small – you could see all around it from wherever you were. To their left there was a children's play area where two small girls poked around in a sandpit, and a teenage girl sat nearby flicking through a magazine, her jaws working rapidly.

'I've thought about an abortion,' Maria said, watching the children.

Judith, about to take a bite, lowered her sandwich.

'But I've decided I can't go through with it.'

One of the little girls burst into tears suddenly and ran to the teenager, who took her onto her lap. The other little girl scooped sand and flung it into the air and the teenager spoke sharply to her.

'Are you sure about this?'

Maria nodded slowly. 'My mind is made up.' Her face was in profile, still turned towards the girls. 'I'm going to have the baby. I thought I should tell you. I thought ... you might be wondering.'

'I was. I'm glad,' Judith said quickly. 'I was so afraid you were going to do it.'

Maria turned to her then. 'You're against abortion.'

'Yes.' Judith held the edges of her sandwich, she pressed the bread together. 'But I once advised someone to have an abortion. I gave her the money, I made it easy.'

The three girls left, the teenager holding the two little ones by the hand. Judith watched them blur as they walked away.

'My motives were purely selfish. I didn't think of her at all.' She looked down at the sandwich, at the cucumber circle poking out one side, and wiped at a tear that ran down her cheek. 'That was six years ago, and I've regretted it every day since. It would have been my grandchild.'

The sun went behind a cloud then, and the green of the grass in front of them darkened slightly. Judith put down her sandwich and pulled a tissue from her bag and blew her nose. 'So you'll have the baby.'

'Yes.'

'It might make things better.' But the doubt was there in her voice, and she knew Maria heard it. She raised the sandwich again and bit into it.

After a minute Maria said, 'So how are things at home?'

'Fine.' Why mention the missing money? What

good would it do?

'My visitors are still not showing any signs of moving on, but it's fine.'

So they ate and drank, and each kept her secret from the other, and the sun came and went.

Edward

He opened Rory's back door and stepped inside. The kitchen was cold, even though the weather had improved steadily over the past couple of days. He walked through to the hall and saw a white envelope just inside the front door.

Today was Saturday. There was no post on Saturdays. He'd been in the day before and had collected Friday's post.

He turned it over and his own name in Sophie's writing looked up at him. No stamp. She must have slipped it through the letterbox earlier – or last night.

He pulled the flap open and eased out the single page. She came straight to the point.

My dear Edward,

We need to sort things out. Either you find a way to forgive and forget, or we move on separately. I think we've spent long enough in limbo, don't you? I've made it clear that I deeply regret what happened, and I want you back. I still love you, and always will. Meeting you last week just brought it home to me how desperately I miss you.

Please get in touch so we can talk about it.

Your wife, Sophie
He read it through three times, carefully.
Your wife.
He refolded it and put it back in its envelope.
We move on separately.
He thought about divorcing her, about drawing a line under their marriage and beginning again. Or slashing a line through it, as if it had all been a terrible mistake.

But it hadn't. There had been no mistake, it had been exactly what he'd wanted. Edward Bull had loved Sophie Dunne; she was the only woman he could truly say he had loved. He remembered the joy of standing at the altar, watching her walk towards him on her father's arm. He remembered promising to love her until one of them died.

And he still loved her, didn't he?

Did he?

I still love you, and always will.

She'd promised to be faithful, and look how that had turned out. How could you love someone and do that to them?

Round and round, these endless maybes and what ifs and buts were driving him demented.

He walked through Rory's house, pulling back curtains, sliding windows open to let in the warmer air. He read his newspaper in Rory's sitting room, something he'd taken to doing lately.

He called to the hospital in the afternoon, on his way to meet Oliver. Rory was rallying, or trying to. Every day a little more recognition when Edward appeared, a grunting effort to speak, a slight upturn of the side of his mouth he had some control over.

He was still being fed intravenously, and Edward was still bringing the boxes of fudge and the bags of jellies. He'd given in and taken away the more perishable of the offerings – the muffins, the brownies – and now he only brought what would keep until Rory was eating normally again.

'I'm on my way to meet the man who's helping out with costumes for the play. I'm not too sure what to make of him – he's a bit … unorthodox. Hopefully he'll take instruction, and not try to run the show.'

'I got a letter from Sophie this morning. She was in to see you last week, remember? She was asking for you … and she wants me to go back. I don't know … I'll have to meet up with her, we'll have to decide on something.'

'I'm keeping an eye on the house, airing it out and that. The back lawn is looking well, that stuff we put down last month has improved it. The marigolds are coming up, you'll have a fine show this year. Mrs Wyatt was asking for you, I met her yesterday. All the neighbours are asking for you, they're all wondering when you'll be home again.'

'Weather's improving, and the forecast is good – looks like we might have a few fine weeks.'

And all the time, Rory watched Edward's face through his half-closed eyes, head moving in tiny bobs, mouth upturned lopsidedly, one hand twitching every now and again under Edward's.

'Aaah,' he said. 'Gnnnh. Ehhhh.'

'I brought a few jellies,' Edward said. 'You'll have them when you've more of an appetite.'

'I'll be off, so,' he said. 'Look after yourself, and

335

I'll be in again tomorrow.'

'Gnnnh.'

Butterball, the little café where Oliver had suggested they meet – 'Just around the corner from the bookshop, so we can have the full half hour' – was small and somewhat claustrophobic, thanks to the dark red paint on its carelessly plastered walls. It was not a place Edward would have chosen to meet anyone.

There was no sign of Oliver. Edward took a table by the wall and ordered a coffee. The waiter had a ring through his eyebrow, and the tips of his black spiky hair were blue. He wore a green T-shirt that said 'Up for it', and underneath was a line drawing of what looked suspiciously to Edward like an erect penis.

Oliver, when he arrived a few minutes later, was full of apology.

'I was ambushed by a dreadful woman who insisted that I go through every single cookery book in the place with her. In the end, she couldn't decide between Nigella and Jamie, so she bought neither.'

'Not to worry,' Edward told him. 'I've just got here.'

'At any rate, we have twenty-three minutes.' The blue-haired waiter returned with Edward's coffee, and Oliver ordered a green tea 'and one of your sinful peanut butter cookies, Joe.'

'Now,' he said, hands clasped, 'I have a few little ideas, Edward.'

Edward's heart sank. 'Have you.'

'Yes and I'm just dying to discuss them with you. I have a feeling that together we'll be a most

336

fruitful partnership.'

Edward reached into his briefcase, praying silently for the fortitude to survive the ensuing twenty-three minutes.

Maria

I'm pregnant.
'Is my blue shirt ironed?'
I was on the Pill, but it didn't work.
'Where did you put my grey tie?'
I don't want to be married to you any more.
'This tea is cold.'
I never loved you. I convinced myself I did – or tried to – but I didn't.
'Any more of that bread?'
I can't stand you touching me.
'Is that fellow ready yet? I'm going to be late.'
I hate living in your house. It's never felt like home.
'Jesus, would he ever get a move on?'
I hate you. I hate you.

Harry

The weather was wrong. They shouldn't have been saying goodbye to Ma under warm sunshine. It should have been raining, the sky should at least have been smudged with clouds.

Ma had tripped over a shoe on her bedroom floor and landed awkwardly, and broken her neck. It was a freak accident, and nobody's fault.

Harry's brother Charlie had arrived home early on Sunday morning, flying into Shannon, where he'd rented a car and driven the hour and a bit to Portmaine, straight to the hotel where he'd booked a room, and where he'd arranged to meet Harry for breakfast.

'Hey there.' He'd shaken Harry's hand, a near stranger in greying hair and a crumpled suit, paunchier than Harry remembered, and the glasses were new since they'd met. 'Poor old Ma.'

'How was your flight?' Harry had asked.

Charlie had grimaced. 'Flights – Hong Kong, Singapore, Paris – I've been on the go for twenty-something hours and it feels like a week.' He'd indicated the hotel brasserie. 'Come on, let's have a quick bite and then I'll hit the sack. What time tonight?'

'Leaving the funeral home at seven.'

'Right, that means we need to be there by six-thirty. Give me a call around six in case I'm still asleep. You expecting many?'

Harry had thought of Joan and Bridie, who'd gone with Ma for years to evening mass and bingo, and Mary, who'd taken the bus to Knock with Ma a couple of times a year, and Vivienne across the road who'd brought Ma and himself homemade apple tarts and loaves of banana bread after Ma had stopped baking.

They'd all visited her in the nursing home for the first few months, but gradually the visits had got further and further apart. You couldn't blame them, with Ma the way she was, and them trying to talk to a woman who no longer knew who they were, who forgot about them as soon as the visits were over.

'Not too many,' he'd said. 'I suppose a few from the nursing home might come – I mean the staff – and some of the old neighbours, maybe, if they saw it in the paper.'

Charlie had ordered the full Irish. Harry had gone for French toast, because it sounded like it mightn't be much.

'So,' Charlie had said as they'd waited for the food, 'any romance? Any lady on the scene for my little brother?'

I'm gay, Harry had answered, but only in his head. That wasn't what Charlie wanted to hear. 'Nobody special. How about yourself?'

Charlie's marriage to Fionnuala had lasted four years. Harry had no idea why they'd split up – he'd been thirteen at the time, and Da had been dead two years, and Ma had never talked about it. Charlie had moved to Hong Kong shortly after that and Harry had seen even less of him than before.

Charlie had rubbed his face. 'As it happens, there's been someone around for quite a while. Nadine. She's Swiss, works in the bank with me.'

'Oh ... that's good.' Babs probably knew all about Nadine.

The plates had arrived and Charlie had begun to eat rapidly. 'Jesus, I'm starving – that airline food isn't worth a curse.'

Harry's French toast had been golden and dense and had come with a doll-sized jug of maple syrup. He'd cut off a corner and chewed it and realised there was no way he could eat any more.

'I suppose Babs told you about me taking Ma out to dinner.'

Charlie had mopped his egg yolk with brown bread. 'She did, and I have to admit I was quite surprised, after us advising you against it. But it's all in the past now, no point in going into it.'

'I wanted to do something for her,' Harry had said. 'I didn't want to just bring a present, I wanted to do something that might ... get through to her.' He'd cut into the French toast again, just for something to do.

Charlie had chewed his bacon. 'And look how it turned out.' He'd drunk tea. 'Listen, I don't want to get into a row about it, OK? We were just surprised, that's all.'

Harry had watched him slicing into a sausage, and he'd realised that he had no feelings whatsoever for his brother, apart from a faint dislike.

He'd pushed back his chair. 'I have to get to work.'

Charlie had stared at him. 'You didn't take the day off?'

'I said I'd go in for a few hours,' Harry had lied. 'They're short staffed.'

'You hardly touched your breakfast.'

'I'm not hungry. Talk to you later.' He'd walked quickly from the brasserie before Charlie could say any more, and he'd been halfway home before he realised that he hadn't even offered to pay. No matter; Charlie could afford it.

The removal was quiet. A few of the old neighbours and two women he vaguely recognised from the nursing home filed past the coffin and shook his hand.

George and Eve came. Eve hugged Harry tightly and whispered, 'Poor darling. See you later.'

Beside Harry, Babs dabbed at her eyes with a damp tissue and whispered her thanks to the mourners. Charlie stood on her other side, and beyond him were Babs's sons – young adults now and almost unrecognisable to Harry – and her husband Tony in a grey suit and black tie.

Harry's colleague, Linda, arrived just before the coffin was closed. She wore a dark green coat and looked uncomfortable. She shook Harry's hand and told him she was sorry, and he thanked her for coming and introduced her to Babs and Charlie.

After the short prayers in the church, Babs drove home with Tony and the children and Charlie and Harry went to the bar in Charlie's hotel and tried to talk to one another for two hours. After the second glass of wine it got a little easier. After the third, Harry went home.

Eve had stuck a note to the front door, in black marker so Harry couldn't miss it.

Soup on the cooker – heat and eat. xx

He lifted the saucepan lid and smelled chicken and garlic – what Eve called George's Anti-Social Chicken Soup. He heated it and wolfed two bowls, and when it was finished he pushed the bowl away and laid his head on the table and cried as quietly as he could, given that he was more than half drunk and a big man, and thankfully nobody woke up – or if they did, they left him alone.

And in the morning the sun shone out of a deep blue sky, and they put Ma into a hole in the ground.

Theo

'Goodnight, my dumpling.' Theo kissed the top of Chrissy's head as the baby sucked her soother and regarded her mother solemnly. 'Please go to sleep soon for your big brother, and don't wake up till midday tomorrow.'

Sean laughed. 'That'll be the day.'

Theo put her arm around his waist and reached up to kiss his cheek. 'Well, we can only hope. Are you sure you can manage her?'

He was down to one crutch, which still meant he only had one arm to deal with a bad, bad baby.

'We'll be fine. She's practically asleep already.'

'We won't be more than a couple of hours, and Mrs O'Doherty is on standby.' Mrs O'Doherty lived two doors away. 'Her number–'

Sean pushed Theo gently towards the bedroom door. 'Ma, you've told me where her number is three times. See you later. Have a good night.'

Ben was standing in the hall.

'Ready?' Theo asked.

He nodded, lifting a hand to Sean at the top of

the stairs. 'See you.'

He hadn't joined Theo in the shower when she was getting ready. He hadn't commented on the top that for once wasn't second-hand. She'd given in and asked, 'Do I look OK?' and he'd glanced at her.

'You look fine.'

Fine. Almost as damning as nice.

It was a bad patch, that was all. He was cross with her. He'd get over it. In the meantime, she'd got the night off work to take him out to dinner for his birthday, and she was damned if he was going to sulk his way through it.

It was all about Gemima, of course.

'She doesn't want to stay with us any more,' Theo had told her sister at work.

Hilary had squeezed out her dishcloth. 'I thought you'd like that – you're always complaining about her taking up your Friday nights.'

'But she's Ben's daughter, he wants to see her.'

'Well, isn't she going to the comp? He can see her every day if he wants. And can't he take her out to places, like a lot of single dads do?'

'Mmm ... he's blaming me though. We haven't had sex since she stopped coming, nearly two weeks ago.'

'Sex? You're worried about not having sex? God, I wish I had your problems.' Hilary had wiped down the worktop. 'Grab that mop, would you?'

As far as Ben was concerned, it was entirely Theo's fault.

'You left her sitting in the front room on her own. She helped us out, and you ignored her.'

343

'I forgot she was there,' Theo insisted. 'I was frantic about Sean, and Chrissy was being very demanding. I wasn't ignoring her on purpose, honestly.'

'Well, it seemed like that to her.'

And for the past two weeks, Gemima hadn't appeared, and Ben had been cool with Theo.

In the car, she slid his Aerosmith CD into the drive. 'I love this song.' She turned up the volume, and 'Don't Wanna Miss a Thing' filled the car.

'I'm so looking forward to this evening. Do you know the last time we went out together was about three weeks ago, to that Italian place? We're turning into boring old farts, and we're not even married yet.' She put a hand on his knee. 'I'm too young to be a boring old fart.' Her hand inched up his thigh. 'Darling, let's be friends tonight. Let's enjoy your birthday, please.' She squeezed gently.

He glanced at her. 'Yeah ... sure.' He shifted gear and turned a corner. The Indian restaurant was two blocks away.

'I hope Sean's OK with Chrissy.'

'Why wouldn't he be OK?'

'Well, because he's on a crutch. She can be a right handful.'

Ben shot her a look and said nothing.

'I should have got Mrs O'Doherty altogether – she's so good with Chrissy.'

'Jesus, Theo, give it a rest, would you?' Ben said wearily, searching for a parking space on the street.

Theo looked at him in astonishment. 'Give

what a rest?'

'Oh come on – I get it. I should never have asked Gemima to stay with Chrissy.'

'I wasn't implying–'

'Like hell you weren't.' He pulled in and switched off the engine. 'Even though I've already told you that Mrs O'Doherty wasn't there that night, and even though I've told you that Gemima is well used to minding kids and babysits all the time for neighbours.'

'Ben, I didn't–'

'Chrissy is teething – you said yourself she's a handful. She would have been screaming with anyone that night.'

'I know, but–'

'And can I remind you that it was an emergency – I was rushing to help our son. I didn't have the luxury of picking and choosing someone to look after Chrissy. Gemima dropped everything and came right over.'

'I know.'

He never called Sean 'your son'. Theo reached across and grabbed his hand. 'I'm sorry. Will you tell Gemima I'm really sorry, and I'd love for her to come back?'

Some lies were excusable, surely. If they helped to patch things up between herself and Ben, they were perfectly allowable.

Ben was looking at her in disbelief. 'You'd love for her to come back?'

'Well, she's your daughter, and–'

He smiled, but there was no amusement in it. 'That's just it, isn't it? She's my daughter. Nothing to do with you at all.'

'Ben, that's not fair. I've tried my best to make her welcome. I've got her favourite ice cream–'

He made a noise that was somewhere between a snort and a grunt. 'It's not *ice cream* she needs.'

'Well, that's only–'

'Look,' he said, 'let's leave it, OK? Let's just enjoy this meal.'

Theo had never felt less like a lamb biryani. 'Will you please tell her I'm sorry?' she asked him. 'Will you try and coax her to come back?'

'OK, OK.' He eased his hand from hers and pulled the key out of the ignition. 'Come on, I'm starving.'

Theo pulled her wrap around her and braced herself for an hour or so of the smallest talk they could manage.

Ellen

The cemetery was between the breast clinic and the bakery, so she left work ten minutes early.

'Hopefully I won't be too long,' she said to Derek, her boss. She'd invented a tricky root canal treatment that required a few follow-up visits.

'Hopefully,' he said.

She knew he was beginning to doubt her stories, but what could she do? She was pretty sure he didn't want to hear about a lump on her breast, and she certainly didn't feel like sharing it with him.

There was a pot of pink begonias on Danny's

grave – his mother. Ellen put her three sun-
flowers beside it. There was a freshly dug grave
three spaces away, with two wreaths and a couple
of bouquets resting on the earth.

'I might be sick,' she told Danny. 'I might have
cancer.' The word caught in her mouth and she
had to force it out. 'I found a lump, and they're
investigating it. I'm on my way to have another
test now.' She'd forgotten what it was called –
something about a needle.

She pressed her hand against the hardness of
his headstone. 'I'm really scared,' she whispered.

She heard footsteps on the gravel behind her
and turned. 'Hello,' she said.

Harry looked surprised. 'Oh.' He was pale. He
came closer and glanced at Danny's name.

'Someone I used to know,' Ellen told him
quickly, before he could ask.

'Right. Sorry.'

He carried a small glass lantern with a fat
candle in it. He pointed towards the freshly dug
grave. 'My mother died on Thursday.'

'Oh Harry, I'm sorry.' Instinctively, Ellen put
her arms around him, and he returned the hug
briefly. He was solid, and several inches taller
than her.

He indicated the lantern, blinking rapidly. 'I
just dropped in to leave this. I meant to bring it
to the funeral, but I forgot.'

He looked lost, and too young for his big man's
body.

'Have you other family?' Ellen asked.

'Yes,' he said. 'My brother and sister. I'm
meeting them for lunch.'

'Good.' She glanced at her watch. 'Sorry, Harry, I have to go.' She squeezed his hand. 'Take care. See you Thursday – if you're up to it.'

'OK.'

His mournful expression was heartbreaking. She hoped he was close to his family.

She reached the hospital with a few minutes to spare. She stood outside the automatic doors and watched them sliding open as people entered and left.

In a few minutes she was going to have a needle pushed into her breast. She took a deep breath and stepped forward – and collided with a man coming through the doors.

'Sorry,' he said, putting out a hand to steady her, and then, 'Ellen.'

'Edward – hello.' She pushed her hair behind her shoulder. 'You're visiting your uncle?'

'Yes.'

'Er, any change?' She prayed he wouldn't ask what she was doing there.

'Not really.' He looked distracted. 'Thank you.'

'Right, well...' she began to edge past him. 'I'd better...'

'Yes,' he said quickly. 'Goodbye.'

'Oh,' she said, remembering, and immediately Edward swung back towards her.

'Yes?'

'I just met Harry. His mother died a few days ago. Just so you know.'

'Oh dear,' he said. 'Right, thank you for letting me know.'

'OK.' Ellen turned and walked through the doorway, her nervousness settling around her as

348

she climbed the stairs.

Maria was already in the waiting area. Ellen checked in at the desk, and then went to sit beside her sister.

'OK?' Maria closed the magazine on her lap.

'Yeah.' Ellen told her about meeting Harry in the cemetery.

'Oh, poor thing. Will he be at the rehearsal on Thursday?'

'He didn't say.' After a second she added, 'And I met Edward just now, downstairs. He was visiting his uncle.'

'Any change?'

'No.'

'He didn't ask what you...?'

'No.'

Fifteen minutes later, a young woman in a white coat appeared. 'Now, Ellen Greene, please.'

Ellen got up, legs suddenly shaky. 'I'm actually scared shitless. This is the last thing. They'll know after this.'

Maria squeezed her hand. 'You'll be fine. I'll be here when you come out.'

The consultant shook hands with her again. 'How have you been?' he asked her.

How do you think? 'A little worried,' Ellen said.

'Yes.' There was sympathy in his voice. 'Hopefully not for too much longer. Now, a fine needle aspiration, which we're going to do today, involves inserting a thin, hollow needle into the mass and extracting a sample of any fluid it may contain.'

'How long?' Ellen asked. 'How long before ... you know for sure?'

'Not long,' he assured her. 'A week at the very most, maybe sooner.'

'Go ahead,' she said, nails digging into her palms. 'Do what you have to do.'

The procedure was quick and almost painless. Ellen stripped to the waist again and lay down, eyes squeezed shut.

'Now Ellen, deep breath.'

She felt a slight pressure as he pushed a needle gently through her skin. She heard a tiny inhalation as he pulled the handle of the syringe towards him, and seconds later she felt the needle being removed. She let out a shuddering breath.

'Are you feeling faint or dizzy?' he asked.

'No. *Terrified out of my wits, but not faint or dizzy.*

'Very well.' He pressed a plaster to her skin. 'You can sit up slowly when you feel able and get dressed.'

As she was leaving, he took her hand to shake it, and held it a little longer.

'I can tell you, Ellen, that I'm optimistic. Try to keep your spirits up. We'll let you know as soon as we can.'

She smiled a ghost smile. 'I'll try.'

'He's optimistic,' she told Maria as they walked back to work. 'He wouldn't say that if he wasn't fairly sure, would he? I mean, he couldn't get my hopes up like that?'

'Hardly. Let's wait and see.'

Ellen squeezed her arm. 'I don't know what I'd do without you.'

'Don't be silly,' Maria said. 'You'd be fine. You're strong.'

Ellen looked at her in amazement. 'Strong?

Me? Everyone knows you're the strong one – I'm the mess.'

Maria didn't answer. At the door of the bookshop, Ellen stopped.

'Listen, is everything OK with you?'

'Fine. Why wouldn't it be?'

Because you're married to an obnoxious boor. Because your son is damaged. Because I'm leaning on you, and you never lean on anyone. And I can't remember when you looked truly happy.

'No reason. Just having peculiar thoughts today, that's all.' She waved. 'See you Thursday. Thanks again. Take care.'

And carrying on alone past the bookshop, Ellen Greene found herself having even more peculiar thoughts. She imagined dying, not being there any more. She pictured her empty apartment, still full of her things but without her. She pictured a fresh grave, like Harry's mother's grave, and tried to imagine how it might feel, lying beneath the crumbly brown earth. She thought about life ending, like it had ended for Danny. Like it had ended for her, too, the day she'd lost him.

But it hadn't ended. She was still alive.

And now, when there was a chance that she might die too, Ellen suddenly realised how badly she didn't want that to happen. She didn't want her life to end, she wanted it to go on.

Oh, God.

She stopped abruptly, causing a woman behind her to swerve quickly and glance at Ellen as she passed.

'Sorry,' Ellen murmured, too softly for the woman to hear.

I don't want to die, I want to live.

People brushed past her and she stood, hands clutching her bag, stock still in the middle of the path.

I want to live.

Fifth Rehearsal Night: Thursday, 29 May

McMillan's Pub

Theo walked through the doorway. 'Hello, everyone.' She sat next to Judith. 'Who's missing?'

'Harry's mother died,' Ellen said.

'Oh, Lord – when?'

'I think he said Thursday.'

'I met her,' Theo told them. 'He brought her
into the restaurant for dinner on her birthday, a
couple of weeks ago.'

'So she was OK then,' Ellen said.

'Well, not exactly – I mean, she might have been
healthy enough, but she was very dotty, didn't
really know what was going on. They left before
they got their meals, she just couldn't hack it, kept
calling me the wrong name. Not with it at all.'

Judith thought of the lemon cake, with its
cheery yellow *Happy Birthday Ma*.

Theo turned to Edward. 'Is he coming tonight?'

'I haven't heard otherwise,' Edward answered,
'so I assume he is.'

'And Robert?'

'He'll be a little late, he's delayed at work.' He
looked at his watch. 'Let's give them five minutes. In the meantime, I suggest you look over
the final scenes, which we'll be rehearsing first.'

Theo turned to Judith and whispered, 'What's
new with you?'

'Nothing, really.'

They'd never had a proper conversation. Theo
knew very little about Judith, apart from the fact
that she was a teacher somewhere.

'You're doing the scenery, aren't you?'

'Well, I'm painting the backdrops, if that's what you mean.'

Judith began turning the pages of her script, which Theo took as a polite hint to shut up.

Robert arrived a few minutes later, looking flustered.

'Sorry about that,' he said to Edward. 'Manic at work, couldn't get away.' He looked around. 'Who's missing?'

Harry appeared soon afterwards. He looked much the same, but there was no energy in the way he crossed the room. Edward stood as he approached and shook hands with him and spoke quietly, and the others murmured their sympathy. Harry smiled and nodded at them, and then sank into his usual armchair.

'Right then.' Edward cleared his throat. 'We've got to the final few scenes. We're starting with Ursula in the post office.'

Theo clattered to her feet. 'That's me.'

Edward waited while she took her position at the side of the stage. He counted slowly to five in his head, then quietly said, 'Right ... let's go.'

(URSULA enters the post office from the rear, carrying a small mailbag which she upends onto the counter. As she sorts the mail, one envelope attracts her attention. She takes a card from her handbag and lifts the phone on the counter and dials the number on the card.)

URSULA: Hello – is that Detective Murdoch?... Ursula Fitzpatrick here at the post office. I've

just come across something that might interest you ... yes, it relates to the murder you're investigating, it's a letter to the victim ... very well. I'll see you then. *(Turns the envelope over in her hands, studying the postmark and holding it up to the light.)*
URSULA: Well, let's see if you can tell us anything. *(Places it on a shelf behind the counter and returns to the rest of the mail.)*

'OK.' Edward watched her walk offstage and turned to Judith.

'Betty, the closing scene. Come as far upstage as you can, right to the edge, the same position as your opening scene. Pick a spot on the facing wall to focus on. Jack and Penelope, standby please.'

Robert and Maria got up and moved to the side of the stage.

'Right ... let's go.'

(BETTY enters and walks upstage, as in the opening scene.)
BETTY: *(calmly)* So it's all over. The letter did it, you see, the letter that came for her after she was dead. It ruined everything. It was from her boyfriend, wondering why he hadn't heard from her, wondering why he couldn't get through on her phone.
VOICE OFFSTAGE: Has anyone tried the garden?
BETTY: *(seems unaware of the voice)* The postmistress gave it to the detective, you see, who of course tracked him down, and got the whole

357

story out of him. How Miss Williams – *(checks herself)* – how Miss Jones had been obsessed with finding me ever since she'd discovered how her mother and sister had died ... she never knew, you see, nobody had ever told her what really happened ... and then her father died, and while she was going through his things she found the newspaper accounts of the crash, and the trial ... so she decided to hunt me down and take her revenge by telling everyone what I'd done.

VOICE OFFSTAGE: She's not in the kitchen.

BETTY: She hired a detective agency, can you believe it? And they found me, and she came here – and you know the rest, don't you?

VOICE OFFSTAGE: I'm going upstairs.

BETTY: You're probably wondering how I know all this. The police called a little while ago, you see, and spoke to Mr McCarthy, and I heard them, like I hear everything that goes on in this house *(sighs).* So now they're searching for me. They'll come up here eventually, up to the attic – I know that, I'm not a fool. *(Moves suddenly, dragging a chair across the attic floor to the window.)* But of course I won't be here. *(Steps onto the chair and opens the sash window.)* So I suppose you could say she got her revenge after all. *(Climbs onto the sill and disappears through the window as the attic door opens and JACK enters, followed by PENELOPE.)*

JACK: Not here. I didn't think we'd find her – she's probably miles away by now.

(PENELOPE notices the chair by the open window and walks towards it.)

JACK: *(unaware)* I still can't believe she killed

358

that poor girl. I mean, it was all in the past, ancient history. Who cares about what happened years ago?

(PENELOPE reaches the window and leans out as a shout is heard from the garden below.)

JACK: *(turning)* What was that?

(PENELOPE screams loudly.)

'And ... lights down,' Edward said quietly. 'It'll go completely dark at the end for a few seconds, and then the lights will come up again and you'll all come out to take a bow.'

'So what now?' Ellen asked.

'Now,' Edward said, 'we go back and start all over again.' He waited until the collective groan had died down and then looked at them over his glasses. 'What – you think you're all ready to go on stage now? You thought we'd have one run through and that would be it?'

'Well, we haven't exactly–' began Theo, and then, seeing Edward's expression, she stopped.

'We still have a long way to go,' he reminded them, 'and just three more rehearsals to performance.'

They were subdued tonight, there was none of the usual chatter. Harry, of course, he could understand, but the rest of them? Even Theo, who usually had plenty to say, was quieter than normal.

They were amateurs, of course. Whether he liked it or not, this was just a bit of fun for them – or at least, it was supposed to be.

He sighed. 'I suppose we could have an early break – and fifteen minutes at the very most.'

'How are you?' Ellen asked Harry.

'OK, thanks.' He didn't look OK, he looked empty. 'She had Alzheimer's, she didn't know us any more.' He wasn't having his usual shandy. He had no glass in front of him.

'She was still your mother, though.'

He rubbed a hand across his face. 'Yeah. She was still Ma.'

'Will you not have a drink?' she asked him. 'My treat – as strong as you like.'

He smiled gently. 'No, thanks all the same.'

'Any plans?' Maria asked Judith. 'For the summer, I mean.'

'Painting,' Judith answered immediately.

'Are you talking about the backdrops?'

'No, no, after the play, just my own dabbling. If the weather stays fine I'll do a few day trips, pack up the car and drive out the country, or go to the coast and set up my easel. If it's wet I'll stay at home and paint. I have a space in the shed I use.'

'Sounds good. I wasn't much of an artist at school, always preferred music.'

'You play?'

'The piano.'

'That's nice. Your little boy likes music?'

Maria smiled. 'Yes ... yes, he loves it. It seems to ... get through to him.'

'What age was she?' Robert asked Harry.

'Seventy-five, just gone.'

Robert shook his head. 'Not that old at all.'

'No.' The irony of that, when all through Harry's

growing-up years, Ma had seemed spectacularly older than his friends' mothers.

'Are you sure you won't have a drink?' Robert asked him. 'Might do you good.'

'I'm OK, thanks.'

'I don't believe it,' Judith said. 'You're Ben's partner.'

'I never knew you taught in the comp,' Theo answered. 'Small world. You don't teach my son. He's in Leaving Cert, Sean DeCourcy.'

'No, I don't know him, but I teach art to Gemima, Ben's daughter. She has a lot of talent.'

'Has she? I suppose she would, her mother's a potter – but you probably know that.'

'Yes, I've often met Miep. Nice lady.'

'Mmm.'

'She mentioned you,' Judith said.

Theo stared at her. 'Who, Miep?'

Judith smiled. 'No, Gemima. We were talking once about which colours go together, and Gemima said that her father's partner wore all sorts of crazy colours, but that it didn't matter because she always looked cool.'

'She said that?'

'Yes. And I thought it was very touching when she opted to paint her little sister.'

'What?' Theo pictured Gemima daubing bright blue paint onto Chrissy's face. 'When was this?'

Judith looked surprised. 'I assumed you knew. Oh dear, I hope Gemima wasn't planning a surprise for you.'

'I doubt it,' Theo said. 'Go ahead.'

'Well, when we were painting portraits just a

few weeks ago, I asked them to bring in a photo of someone they wanted to paint, and most of them brought in singers or film stars, but Gemima brought in a photo of your little daughter, whose name I'm afraid escapes me...'

'Chrissy,' Theo said faintly.

'Yes, of course – Chrissy. Gemima's so delighted to have a little sister. The portrait is excellent, she really did her best with it. I'm sure,' Judith added uncertainly, 'that she's going to show it to you.'

'Me too,' Theo said, lifting her glass and drinking deep.

'We need to revisit each scene,' Edward told them. 'We'll be looking at expression, movement, timing and voice projection.'

They sat quietly, listening.

'It's not as bad as it sounds. We should get through act one and part of act two tonight, tighten everything up. At our next rehearsal, which we've all agreed will be next Tuesday, we'll focus on the second half. During our final two rehearsals, Thursday and Sunday, we'll do two full runs-through. As I mentioned before, Sunday will also be a dress rehearsal, and it'll take place in the Arts Centre.'

'What's happening with costumes?' Theo asked. 'Are they sorted?'

Edward hesitated. 'I've had a meeting with Oliver and I have full confidence in his ability to handle the costumes. He'll be coming in on Tuesday to talk to you individually about his ideas and to show you whatever he has at that stage.'

After ten minutes in Oliver's company, Edward

had realised that he may as well resign himself to the fact that he would have no say whatsoever in what the characters wore. Oliver was a man on a mission, and he was taking his responsibilities very seriously indeed.

'I see Dorothy in pink when she arrives, to denote innocence – or at least the illusion of innocence.'

'You don't think pink will clash with her red hair?' It had sounded like a disastrous combination to Edward.

Oliver had smiled. 'Dear Edward, contrary to popular belief, redheads not only look good in red, orange or pink, they should be actively *encouraged* to wear them, and *fined* if they put on anything green,' he shuddered. 'And furthermore, Ellen's particular shade of red, which I should describe as soft strawberry, lends itself *wonderfully* well to all the warm colours.'

So Edward, never having heard of a colour with a temperature, had decided to give in and hope for the best.

'Now,' he said, 'if there are no more questions, let's go back to the beginning. Scene one – Betty and Ellen, if you please?'

Judith got home later than usual, having stayed behind to discuss the backdrops with Edward. They were meeting on Sunday morning and he was bringing her to the warehouse where they were being stored, and where she would paint them.

Tomorrow was her last day at work. They were all going out tomorrow evening for dinner, like they always did at the end of the school year, but Judith knew that at some stage someone would stand up and make a speech about how valuable a member of staff she'd been and how much she'd be missed, and they'd present her with some gift, a voucher maybe for one of the shops in town.

She didn't expect to miss the job, but she'd miss the company in the staffroom, the bits of gossip passed around, the banter between the men and the women.

She wondered again what the future held for her.

As she walked up the path, she heard music blaring from the sitting room, some song she didn't recognise. She turned the key and opened the front door and walked straight through the hall to the kitchen.

She filled the kettle and plugged it in and sat wearily at the table as she waited for it to boil. Summer on the way, hopefully with better weather than last year. She wondered if they'd ever have a proper heatwave again, with everyone getting sun-burned and peeling.

Maybe she should go on a holiday. Once upon a time she'd loved holidays, revelling in the slower pace of life, the silenced alarm clock on her bedside locker, the change from the normal routine.

Before she met Samuel she'd done all the usual things in summer with like-minded friends, from lying on a Spanish beach to visiting art galleries in Italy to drinking wine in France.

Some years she'd stayed in Ireland, packing up

her paints when the weather obliged and going wherever the mood had taken her. And once – just once – she'd gone alone on a disastrous singles holiday to Turkey, where the majority of the mostly female group were bitter divorcées or chronic nymphomaniacs.

And then Samuel had come along, and holidays had taken on a whole different flavour. They'd flown to Paris and Amsterdam and Berlin for long weekends, they'd climbed hills in Scotland, they'd rented cottages along Ireland's west coast.

Samuel had proposed on holidays, on top of a Scottish hill with the wind blowing Judith's hair across her face and reddening her cheeks, as he cupped his hands over his mouth and pressed them to her ear so she'd hear his question. Her joyful, 'Yes!' had echoed across the undulating green vastness, and he'd swung her around in a parody of a highland fling till she'd clung to him, caught between tears and laughter.

The holidays changed again after Christopher arrived. More cottages in the west, fewer flights to the Continent. Just three years of family holidays, because the year Christopher turned four, Samuel walked out on his wife and son.

The first cheque he'd sent her, six weeks after he'd left, she'd torn up, hardly able to see what she was doing, blinded by her angry tears, flinging the pieces into the bin. The second, a month later, she'd been ready for. She'd cut it into six pieces and sent it back to the address he'd written on the back of the envelope. She'd done the same with the third, fourth and fifth.

The sixth, when it didn't arrive, had led to a

depression that had stunned her in its intensity, that wrapped itself like a wet towel around her, that had clung on for weeks. She'd struggled through the days for Christopher's sake, saving the release of tears for the night.

Painting eventually became her therapy, her way of escaping the blackness of her thoughts. She began taking Christopher on the day trips of old, letting him play while she painted, for as long as he'd hold out. And for the next few years these little expeditions, once a week or so in the summer, were the only holidays they took. And then Christopher had grown older and the day trips had begun to bore him, so they'd stayed at home and Judith had painted in the garden or in the shed while he went out with his friends.

The kettle sang and she got up to make the tea. She could hear the music quite clearly through the closed kitchen door. She pushed down the pedal on the bin to drop in her tea bag, and as the lid swung open she saw pieces of broken glass sitting inside.

She bent and lifted one out, turning the crystal so it caught the light. Just then, the kitchen door opened and Christopher came in.

'Hi – thought I heard someone. What you doing out here all on your own?'

Even if he hadn't been slurring his words, she would have known by the looseness of his face that he'd had a lot to drink. Judith dropped the shard of crystal and straightened up.

'One of my good glasses is broken.'

'What? Oh yeah, sorry – I'll get you another one tomorrow.' He walked towards her unsteadily, a hand out. 'C'mon and have a drink – we're cele-brating.'

'Celebrating what?'

He grinned, grabbing her arm. 'I had a bit of good luck today. On the gee gees.'

Judith pulled away from him. 'Christopher, don't tell me you're gambling again.'

His grin faltered. 'C'mon, Mum, don't spoil it – come and have a drink. Amanda wants you to come in.' He reached for her arm again. 'C'mon.'

'No.' She moved away from him, putting the table between them. 'Where did you get the money to gamble?' Her voice wasn't quite steady, but he probably wouldn't notice.

The smile faded completely. He frowned. 'I got the dole, OK? I get it today. *Jesus.*' He began to turn away.

'I know what you're doing,' Judith said clearly. Her heart banged inside her.

Christopher looked back at her. 'What d'you mean? What you on about?' His face was hard.

She couldn't stop now, she had to say it. 'I know you've been taking money from me, from my purse.'

He turned abruptly and walked from the room, lurching against the door jamb on his way out.

'I would have given you a loan,' she called after him. 'You only had to ask,' as the sitting room door opened, music rushing out, and closed with a bang.

She poured milk and picked up her cup with trembling hands and sipped, standing at the sink looking out the window. After a few minutes the music was lowered. As Judith finished her tea she heard the sitting room door open again. She gripped her cup tightly and didn't look around as someone entered the kitchen.

'Judith,' Amanda said. Sometime over the past three weeks, Mrs O'Sullivan had become Judith. 'Let's not fall out, OK?'

Judith turned. Amanda had dressed up for the celebration, in a purple low-cut top Judith hadn't seen before. Her cleavage was very brown, the skin between her breasts creased. Her eye make-up was smudged. She held a lipstick-smeared crystal glass in her hand.

'Judith?' She swayed gently and leaned against the table. 'Chris is very upset. He says you think he took some money from you?'

Judith laid her empty cup in the sink. 'I really don't think it's any of your business.'

'Oh now, don't be like that.' Amanda put the glass on the table, dangerously near the edge. 'Chris wouldn't steal from his own mum, he'd never do that.' Her hands gripped the table. 'I know him, Judith, I know what he's like.'

Judith crossed to the table and moved the glass away from the edge. 'Please be careful with my glasses,' she said. 'You've already broken one, and they're expensive.' She moved towards the door. 'And please keep the music down – I'm going to bed.'

Her legs threatened to give out on her all the way up the stairs.

'I never knew you worked with Judith,' Theo said.

'Judith O'Sullivan?'

'Yes.'

Ben switched channels and some soccer match came on.

'She's in the play,' Theo said.

He looked at her. 'Is she?'

'Yes. She's got the biggest part.'

'Right. Good for her.' He went back to the screen.

'She teaches Gemima.'

'I know.'

'Did you know Gemima painted Chrissy?' Theo asked.

'Yeah – it's good.'

'Why didn't you tell me? Why didn't you show me?'

Ben shrugged. 'Didn't think you'd be interested.'

She stared at him while he watched the match. He didn't think she'd be interested.

'Did you tell Gemima I'm sorry?'

'Yes.'

'So is she going to come back?'

He glanced at her again. 'Dunno. They might be going to Holland for the holidays.'

'Oh.' Theo sat beside him for a few minutes, her eyes on the screen. Her thoughts miles away.

She stood. 'Right,' she said. She walked to the door. 'Right.'

Ben watched the match.

Harry

'Are you putting on the kettle?'

For a few days after the funeral, Linda had laid off him. No sniping if he dropped something – he dropped a lot of things when she was around – or forgot to do something. No sighing, no raising her eyes to heaven or snapping at his blunders. She'd even made tea for both of them on his first day back.

But now a week had passed, and whatever sympathy she'd felt obliged to display was obviously used up. Since Harry had arrived at work that morning, they were back to the bad old days.

'Will you *please* stop moving the paperclips?'

'I *asked* you not to leave that folder there, it's right in the way.'

'God, have you taken the biro from here again?'

So when he stood up at eleven o'clock and she asked, 'Are you putting on the kettle?' Harry decided to take a stand.

'No,' he said, 'I'm going to the toilet. But if you're putting it on, I'd love a cuppa.' He'd raced away before she had a chance to react. It was worth doing without the tea, just for the satisfaction of saying it.

When he returned to the desk she ignored him, and Harry felt a tiny stab of triumph. He'd last till lunchtime, no problem.

A few minutes after twelve, a shadow fell across

the book he was cataloguing and he looked up.

'Oh, hello,' he said.

'I've come,' said Oliver, 'to enquire as to your shoe size.'

Harry put down his pen. 'My shoe size.'

'Yes. I have found an interesting pair of brogues in the charity shop around the corner, and I feel they might suit the gardener. And for some reason, I neglected to take your shoe size at the rehearsal.'

'Oh, I see – I'm size eleven.'

'Size eleven.' Oliver scribbled in a small notebook. He stopped and looked up. 'And you are Harry…?'

'Yes,' said Harry. 'I mean Buckley. Harry Buckley.'

Oliver put out his hand. 'Oliver Noble. Delighted to meet you properly. I feel the rehearsal introductions were somewhat informal.'

His hand was cool and very smooth. There was a pleasantly woody scent about him.

'How did you know where I worked?' Harry asked.

'Maria told me,' Oliver said. 'Who, as you probably know, is my boss, and who has kindly given me some time off to source the costumes.'

'Oh, I see.'

'And please accept my condolences,' Oliver added, 'on the recent sad death of your mother.'

He was still holding Harry's hand, and now he released it.

'Thank you,' Harry said.

Oliver tucked his notebook and pen into an inside jacket pocket. 'And now I'm keeping you from your work, so I'll take myself off.'

'What size are the brogues?' Harry asked.

'Not eleven, I fear, but no matter – there are other brogues, and other charity shops.'

'I thought Wellingtons,' Harry said. 'Or maybe boots.'

'Perhaps, perhaps. I shall be patient, and hopefully my persistence will prevail.' Oliver lifted a hand. 'See you soon, Harry Buckley.'

'See you.' Harry watched as he pushed the library door open and disappeared through it.

Hopefully my persistence will prevail. Nobody talked like that – or nobody Harry had ever met.

Linda approached the desk just then, and he closed the book.

'Fancy that cup of tea now?' he asked.

Because some things just weren't that important.

Robert

'We're going to have a pool,' Noah said.

'In the back garden, our own private pool,' Aidan said.

'That's nothing. I have my own private pool here,' Robert told them. 'And it's got bubbles in it.'

'You do not have a pool. Where is it?'

'In the bathroom.'

Noah looked at him. 'Dad, you do not have a pool in the bathroom.'

'Yes, I do,' Robert said, 'but some people call it a bath.'

'*Dad.*'

Their looks of scorn would have been amusing if Robert was in any mood to be amused. Four weeks, give or take, before they flew away from him.

The closer their departure got, the more he dreaded it. He could think of little else. The idea of them being so far away – and in another man's company – was consuming him.

But now it was Saturday, and he'd invited Caroline and the boys over for pizza and a movie.

'Humour me,' he'd pleaded with her. 'I'm getting old and sentimental. I'm trying to give them good family memories, so they'll want to come back.'

She'd looked at him in disbelief. 'Good family memories? Robert, we haven't been a family since they were one.'

'I know, I know, but we *are* their parents, and we get on OK, don't we?'

'Well, most of the time, but–'

'And we've done family nights before. Remember just before they started school, and we all went out to dinner?'

She'd laughed. 'Robert, that wasn't a family night – that was a meeting for new parents. We collected the boys from the crèche afterwards and brought them to Supermacs on the way home because they were starving.'

'Well, what about when they made their communion? We went out then, remember? And after Aidan had his appendix out?'

Caroline had shaken her head, smiling. 'OK, OK, I give in. We're one big happy family. But you don't really need me there on Saturday night, do you?'

'We do need you,' he'd insisted. 'I want both of us to be there, because–'

Because what? What difference would it make to the boys, who saw her every day anyway?

'Look, I just want you there,' he'd said. 'Will you please come, for me?'

So the three of them came and Robert ordered pizza, and afterwards the boys watched some pirate film, and under cover of the shouts and splashes, Robert and Caroline talked.

'We've got tenants for the house,' she told him. 'A family from Limerick. He's just got a job here, and they're looking to buy.'

He liked her hair shorter, he liked the way it swung when she moved her head. It shimmered in the warm light of the sitting room. She wore a necklace he hadn't seen before, with deep red stones.

'I was thinking,' she said quietly, 'that you might like to pay the boys a surprise visit on their birthday.'

Robert nodded. 'I'd love to,' he said. 'Would that be OK?'

'Of course it would.' She picked a piece of cold cheese from the remains of her slice. 'You know you'll always be welcome.'

'Shhh,' said Noah from the couch. 'I can't hear.'

'Maybe you can find me a place to stay in the area,' Robert whispered.

'I'm sure I can.'

She'd eaten just one slice of pizza. Probably watching her figure for the Frenchman, not wanting to be shown up by all those skinny Frenchwomen.

'You are coming back, aren't you?' Robert asked suddenly.

Her eyes looked black in the light. 'Robert,' she said, 'you keep asking me that.'

'That's because I'm scared you'll stay there – you and the boys.'

She picked up her glass of water. 'All I can tell you – again – is that the plan is for one year.'

'But it might change? If the job goes well, or–' He broke off.

'Robert,' she said softly. 'Please.'

'OK, I'll stop.' He ran a finger along the rim of his glass. 'It's just that I'll miss you.'

She looked thoughtfully at him. 'Yes,' she said, 'and we'll miss you too.'

Their eyes held for a second before she looked away, towards the TV screen.

'Who's winning?' she asked.

'Shhh,' both boys said together, and she turned back to Robert and they exchanged a smile. Parent to parent.

He thought about her doing this in France, sitting with the boys watching some DVD. He thought about the Frenchman sitting beside her, maybe with an arm around her shoulders, maybe taking them all out for whatever the French equivalent for pizza was afterwards.

'So,' she said, 'how's your family night going?'

'Fine,' he said brightly. 'Thanks for coming.'

Four weeks, give or take, until they stepped on a plane and left him. He'd just have to live with the emptiness, he'd have to endure it until they came back.

Noah turned around. 'It's over.'

Robert got up. 'Right, hands up who wants ice cream?'

And it wasn't until much later, after he'd stood at the front door and waved them off after he'd thrown the pizza crusts into the bin and washed the glasses and swept the crumbs from the coffee table, that Robert McInerney finally saw what had been staring him in the face.

Judith

The warehouse stood on the quays, sandwiched between a large furniture store and Carran Computers. It was smaller than she'd been expecting – about twice the size of her sitting room at home – but the ceiling was high, which made it feel more roomy.

'It belongs to Carran Computers,' Edward told her. 'I understand it's usually used to store computers before shipment.'

One wall was full of windows, but too high for Judith to look out. No matter – she was here to paint, not to gaze at the scenery. Three lengths of material had been attached to two of the other walls. They were heavy, thick canvas – the kind, Judith imagined, that was used for awnings, and maybe circus tents.

At rehearsal, Edward had told her what was needed. One backdrop for Jack McCarthy's study and hall, one that would double for the post office and the McCarthy kitchen, and one for the garden scenes.

'Only three?' Judith had asked him. 'Are you sure that'll be enough? I can do more.'

It was a blessing, this job. A legitimate reason to leave the house. Something to eat away the hours until bedtime.

'I have plenty of time,' she'd said. 'Now that school is finished, I have all the time in the world. And I love to paint.'

'No, no,' Edward had assured her. 'Three will be plenty.'

And there they were, attached to the walls with what looked to her like carpet tacks.

'I hope they're at the right level,' Edward said. 'There's a stepladder there, to get to the top.'

'That's fine.' Judith looked around the space. 'This is great. I'm all set.'

'Warm enough? Should I get you a heater?'

'No, I'll be fine.'

'And you'll be alright on your own?'

'Absolutely.' Being on her own was the best part. Being on her own was bliss. 'It's not a problem, really.'

She turned towards the door. 'If you'll just give me a hand to unload the car, I'll get stuck in.'

'You're going to start now? Right away?'

'Why not?' she asked. 'I've nothing on today. I might as well.'

In the two days since she'd accused Christopher

of stealing from her, the house had filled with tension. He hardly spoke now when they met, just grunted at her as he opened the fridge door and lifted out the carton of orange juice, or passed her on the stairs.

Amanda had pulled back too. She still spoke to Judith – or rather, she responded if Judith asked her a question – but in a much more distant tone of voice. It was as if both of them had been mortally offended.

If they were in the sitting room when Judith walked in, they made no effort to include her in their conversation. They didn't offer to change the TV channel. Neither of them asked how her night out on Friday with the staff had gone. Amanda didn't offer Judith a cup if she was making tea.

It was ridiculous. Judith was a grown woman with an adult son for whom she was no longer responsible, yet she'd allowed him to install himself and his girlfriend for an indefinite amount of time in her house, to take over her bedroom and eat her food and use her facilities. And instead of being grateful and helping out around the house, Christopher had begun stealing from her. And when Judith had finally snapped and accused him, he'd chosen to ignore it.

It was intolerable, and it would have to stop. Judith would have to put a stop to it, and she cringed at the thought.

But not just yet. Now she had to paint the backdrops. They unloaded her things and she took the keys from Edward and watched him drive away, and then she walked back into the warehouse. Determined, for the next several hours, to think of nothing but paints and brushes and canvas.

Edward

He knew she'd be late. She'd never been on time for anything. He'd been sitting there now for twenty minutes, and there was still no sign of her. He ordered a refill and went back to the crossword he was pretending to do.

At twenty-five past eight his wife pushed the door open and walked in. Edward lifted his arm and waited until she saw him.

'Sorry – I was stuck in traffic.' She leaned across and touched his cheek briefly with hers. Her scent filled his nostrils. 'I'm glad you called.'

Edward signalled to the barman and ordered a vodka and orange juice. In twenty years it had never varied.

Sophie glanced around the bar. 'Can we go to a table? I don't fancy sitting at the counter.'

She wore a skirt he hadn't seen before, a colour somewhere between blue and purple, tight on her hips and ending just below her knees. Her top was the colour of lilacs, neckline cut low, sleeves just cupping the tops of her arms. The wrap slung across her shoulders was silver and looked very soft.

It occurred to Edward that she'd probably have made a good wardrobe mistress, with her sense

379

of how to put an outfit together.

They chose a table by the end wall, near enough to a window but too far from any of the scattered drinkers to overhear a conversation. It was early enough on a Sunday evening for the place to be fairly quiet. Edward sat facing the bar and Sophie took the chair next to him.

She lifted her glass. 'What should we drink to?'

And as Edward searched for a toast that could possibly be appropriate on this occasion, her mobile phone started to ring.

'Sorry – meant to switch it off.' She lowered her glass and rummaged in her bag and pulled out the phone. She glanced at the display and pushed back her chair. 'Won't be a sec.'

Edward watched her walk towards the door, phone against her ear, saw the glance she attracted from a man on the way. Sophie had never been short of male attention – maybe Edward shouldn't have been surprised that she'd finally succumbed to it.

Of course, that was assuming the landscape gardener had been her first act of betrayal. How was he to know about any earlier times? Who could say she'd never strayed before, just because Edward had no evidence?

And how was he ever to trust her again, having witnessed her unfaithfulness with his own eyes?

He sighed and glanced out the window. The earlier rain had cleared and given way to a watery sun that was only now beginning to sink. Summer on the way.

He turned from the window and looked up the room at the long bar counter and became aware of a redhaired woman sitting alone on the stool he'd so recently vacated. She must have just come in.

Her face was in profile, her hair screening most of it from him. She was hunched over the counter, looking down at a newspaper – the one he'd left behind?

Sophie reappeared, hurrying towards the table. 'Sorry, it's off now.' She sat and zipped the phone into her bag and picked up her drink. To Edward's relief, she didn't suggest another toast.

'So how's Rory?' She hadn't been back to see him again.

'He's improving, but slowly,' Edward told her. 'He seems to be aware of what's going on, but his speech is still very bad. It'll take a long time, apparently.'

At the counter, Ellen looked up as the barman put a glass in front of her and filled it from a bottle. Red wine.

'Poor thing.' Sophie sipped her drink. 'Will they keep him long in the hospital?'

Edward shrugged. 'They're not saying – it's still too early for him to be moved.'

Ellen wore something pale, cream it looked from where Edward sat. She played with her hair as she bent towards the newspaper again. Maybe she was finishing his crossword.

'And how's ... everything else?' Sophie asked.

Edward finished his brandy in one swallow. 'Fine.'

'The play?'

'Coming along, shaping up. We open the week after next.'

Sophie placed both hands on the table, on either side of her barely-touched vodka. 'Edward, we need to talk about this – about us.' Her nails were dark purple, almost black. Her diamond glistened.

'I know.' Edward stood up. 'I need another drink first. Will you have one?'

'No, thanks.'

He walked up to the bar, over to the corner where Ellen sat. 'Hello.'

She turned and gave him a small smile. 'Edward Bull.'

Not a newspaper in front of her after all but her script, which she pointed to.

'I'm doing my homework – and it's only Sunday. Aren't you impressed?'

He smiled. 'Very. Let me get you a drink as a reward.'

She indicated the almost full glass in front of her. 'Well, you could pay for this one if you like, thanks very much.'

She was different this evening, softer than she often came across to him. He signalled to the barman and asked for a brandy.

'Is this your local?'

She shook her head. 'I've never been here before. Wanted a bit of peace and quiet.'

His brandy arrived and he paid for both drinks and turned to go. 'Well, I'll let you get–'

'Don't go,' she said quickly. 'I didn't mean you. I wasn't hinting for you to get lost. I … I wouldn't mind some company.' She looked steadily at him. 'I mean, unless you want to be on your own. If you do, that's fine.'

Her lashes were dark, and very long. She pushed her hair behind her ear in a gesture that was becoming familiar to him. He smelled oranges – no, grapefruit.

He wanted, suddenly, shockingly, to stay with her. He wanted to take the stool next to hers and watch her lift her glass. He wanted to see her hair sliding down her back as she tilted her head, as the muscles in her throat contracted. He wanted to breathe her in as she sat there, to examine every detail of her, to memorise her.

He swallowed. 'I'm with someone,' he said. 'I have to go. Sorry.'

He turned abruptly and walked back to the table. Sophie put away her lipstick and mirror as he sat next to her, shifting his chair slightly so the bar wasn't directly in his sights any more.

He looked at his wife. His eyes flicked to her cleavage, to the diamond necklace he'd given her for her fortieth birthday, nestling between her breasts. He remembered her breasts, remembered the soft weight of them in his hands, the taste of them. He looked at her red mouth, at the carefully made-up eyes, at the dark, shining hair.

He reached for her hand. 'Look,' he said. He saw the years stretching ahead of him. He thought about spending them with her. 'Listen,' he said.

He began to talk.

And the next time he checked, less than twenty minutes later, the corner stool was empty.

Ellen

A benign cyst. Benign meaning kindly, caring, benevolent. No malice intended. She wasn't going to die – at least, not from cancer. Not now.

She lay smiling as the consultant drained it painlessly. She smiled as he stuck a fresh plaster on. She waited until he said, 'You can sit up when you feel ready,' and she sat up and got off the bed and hugged him, which probably wasn't the done thing. He smiled and pushed his glasses up on his nose.

She hugged the nurse, who laughed. 'Isn't that great now. Go off and enjoy yourself.'

In the waiting area, she hugged Maria. 'It's gone – it was nothing.'

'Thank God,' Maria breathed, hugging her back. 'Now you can relax.'

Ellen laughed as they walked downstairs. 'I don't feel like relaxing – I feel like celebrating.' She linked arms with Maria as they left the hospital.

'I met Edward last night,' she said.

'Did you?'

'Yes. I was having a glass of wine in a pub, trying to psyche myself up for today. I had actually brought my script with me, but it was really to discourage anyone from coming near me – I was only pretending to read it.'

'And Edward was there.'

'Mmm. He was with some woman, probably

his wife. I assume that's who she was.'

Casually, not as if she really cared one way or another. Nothing in her voice to suggest that the answer mattered in the least.

'Is Edward married?' Maria asked. 'I have no idea.'

'Me neither.'

But even if she wasn't his wife, he'd been with her. Ellen pushed him from her mind and went back to being delighted that she didn't have cancer. Wasn't that all that mattered? She gave a little skip and beamed at an elderly man coming towards them.

'Isn't it a beautiful morning?'

He smiled back at her. 'It certainly is,' he said.

They walked on in silence for a bit.

'Maria, are you OK?' Ellen asked as they approached the bookshop. 'I mean, are you really OK? You've been very quiet lately – I mean quieter than normal. I'm here for you if anything's wrong, you know that. I owe you a lot.'

'You don't owe me anything, and I'm fine,' Maria answered. 'Maybe a bit run down, that's all.'

'You should take a few days off work; I'm sure Oliver could manage.'

Maria hesitated. 'I might do that.' She nodded slowly. 'I ... might take Pat away for a few days.'

'Or leave Pat with Mam and Dad, and I'd help them out – give you a real break.'

'Mmm – maybe.'

Ellen studied her. 'And you'd tell me if something was wrong? Honestly?'

'Yes, I'd tell you.'

They reached the bookshop and Ellen refused

the offer of tea – 'I want *champagne,* not tea' – and kept going to the bakery, full of gratitude.

'There you are,' her boss said. 'All OK now?'

'Everything fine now,' Ellen answered, finding it impossible to take the smile off her face. 'All over, thank goodness. Sorry about all the time off.'

'That's OK.' He was so understanding. She was lucky to have such an understanding boss.

Probably best not to hug him though.

Local Production for Arts Centre

Next Monday sees the opening night of local playwright Jonathan Crosby's debut offering. *Death by Dying* is a murder mystery in the classic style, which uses a village setting complete with Big House, innocent young victim and plenty of suspects. Director Edward Bull has assembled a local cast who have been in rehearsal for the past several weeks. *Death by Dying* will run for one week, and booking is expected to be lively. Tickets available from the Arts Centre box office.

The Portmaine Herald, Arts Section, Monday, 2 June 2008

Maria

When she heard him coming downstairs, she crossed quickly to the cooker and spooned his egg out of the simmering water.

The door opened. He went to the radio and switched it on.

'Why is he not up yet?'

She dropped the egg into his blue eggcup and brought it to the table. 'He's got a temperature. I'm going to keep him at home today.' She knew Pat wouldn't appear and make a liar out of her.

Michael sat at the table. The thought of Pat being sick didn't seem to bother him. He probably couldn't care less if his son never went to school again.

The toaster popped and Maria lifted out the two slices and put them on a plate and brought them to the table.

Not a word of thanks, never a please or a thank you from him.

The kettle boiled and she made tea and sat opposite him. She filled her bowl with Special K and poured milk and began to eat, all the time keeping her eyes lowered so she wouldn't have to look at him picking off his eggshell.

Twenty minutes, she thought. He'll be gone by half eight and then we'll have an hour. I'll get Pat up and give him his breakfast, and the taxi will be here at half nine.

'Is the salt out?'

She checked the table. He could see the salt wasn't out, and still he asked. He could stand up and get it himself.

She dropped her spoon and walked to the spice rack and took down the salt cellar. No sound from upstairs. Someone was talking quietly about the Gaza Strip on the radio.

Michael shook salt onto his egg. He spooned egg onto his toast and folded the toast over and brought it to his mouth, he drank tea while his mouth was still full, sucking it in between his teeth. Maria ate her cereal and tried to block out his noises.

She'd never have to listen to him again, never have to clear the heap of eggshell from the table. Never have to lie under him trying not to feel anything, trying not to smell him. She and Pat would be free.

He pushed his chair back and stood up, still drinking the last of his tea. Not a word had passed between them except when he'd asked about Pat and looked for the salt. Maria waited until he left the room, until the toilet flushed a few minutes later, until the front door banged behind him.

She got up then and walked out to the sitting room. She watched from behind the net curtains as he backed down the driveway, turning the steering wheel with one hand, the other arm draped across the back of the passenger seat as he curved the Land Rover onto the road.

When he was out of sight, Maria walked upstairs and pushed open the door of Pat's room.

He lay in bed clutching the red car, a finger

absently rolling the wheels, his eyes on the ceiling above him.

'Hello, lovie.' Maria put a hand briefly on his arm and he turned. No expression on his smooth, pale face, his gaze falling somewhere beneath her eyes. 'Time to get up now.'

He slid out of bed and stood silently as she took off his pyjamas and dressed him in Postman Pat underpants and blue tracksuit bottoms.

'Lift up.' He raised his arms, yawning, and she pulled on his white vest and orange and blue sweatshirt. 'Good boy. You're the best, aren't you?'

His hair was matted at the back, but she didn't go near it. He yelled his way through the weekly wash, and she had to be satisfied with that.

'Now, shoes and socks. Down you go.'

He sat on the carpet while she slid his Postman Pat socks on. She reached under the bed for his canvas shoes. She pressed the Velcro fastenings closed, cradling his feet for an instant, her eyes full of sudden tears, before he pulled away from her.

In the kitchen, she tuned the radio to Lyric FM and turned it up, and Pat's head dipped and rose to the music as it filled the kitchen. She stood at the sink and watched him as he crunched his crackers and drank his milk, the red car in its usual position beside his plate. If he wondered why his father wasn't there with them, he gave no sign.

'Daddy is gone to work,' she said. 'You're coming with me today.'

He picked up another cracker from the plate,

yawning hugely. 'We're going on the bus,' she told him. 'A special bus. It'll be fun.'

She'd never learned to drive – had never felt any interest in it – and today was the first time she regretted it. If she could drive, they could go anywhere. They could hide anywhere.

Pat held his mug towards her and she went to the table and refilled it from the jug. 'Good boy.' She sat opposite him, yearning to reach across and stroke the velvety skin. 'You're my best boy, aren't you?'

He munched his cracker, one hand turning the wheels of the car, a foot banging gently against the leg of his chair.

'Mah,' he said.

'That's right,' she answered. It was lovely, just the two of them.

The remains of Michael's breakfast littered his end of the table. The mound of eggshell, the plate with toast crumbs, the butter-smeared knife, the cup. The empty, unused eggcup.

Maria crossed the room and tore a sheet of kitchen paper off the roll, and took a pen from the mug on the window sill and brought them back to the table.

She wrote, *Pat and I are leaving. We won't be back.* The pen tore through the soft paper. She signed her name and left the sheet sitting on top of the eggshell.

'Right, love,' she said to Pat. 'Time to go. Let's get our stuff.' As they left the kitchen, she turned the radio up louder.

Upstairs, she packed their night things and a few changes of clothes and the toiletries they'd need. She bundled Pat's cars and other toys into his schoolbag. As she buckled it closed, the taxi hooted outside.

'We're going to the shop first, OK?' she told Pat. 'I have to talk to Oliver for a minute.'

In the taxi, Pat examined the underside of the red car, lips pursed. Maria didn't look back as they drove away from the house. The rush-hour traffic was beginning to ease off, but it still took them twenty-five minutes to get to the bookshop.

'Please wait,' she asked the driver. 'We won't be long.'

Oliver was alone in the shop. He looked up as they came in. 'Ah,' he said, regarding Pat, 'I see we have a small visitor today.'

'Oliver,' Maria said, 'I'm terribly sorry, but I won't be in for a few days. Something's come up, and I need you to manage on your own.'

Oliver nodded calmly. 'Of course.'

'Close the shop for your lunch break, and ... call my parents if you need help. Their number is on the list behind the door. And you have my mobile, in case of ... any emergency. I'll be in touch soon.

'Right.' He paused. 'Am I to understand that you'll miss this evening's rehearsal?'

She'd forgotten about the extra rehearsal. Oliver was bringing in the costumes. All last week he'd been scouring the charity shops in his lunch hour, showing her what he'd found.

'I'm not sure,' she said quickly. 'I'll have to see about that.'

'Is there anything at all I can do?' he asked, 'other than hold the fort?'

393

For a split second she was tempted to tell him. She almost blurted it all out. But that wouldn't be fair, she couldn't do that to him.

'No,' she said, 'thank you.' She hesitated. 'Thank you for everything, Oliver, I'd never manage without you.'

'Of course you would,' he replied, 'but your thanks are appreciated nevertheless.' He crouched to Pat. 'And you, young man, have brought your car with you, I see – very sensible. One should always have a means of transport.'

The door opened and a customer walked in. Maria took Pat's hand as Oliver stood.

'We'll be off. Bye then.'

She couldn't say *see you soon*. She didn't want a lie to be the last thing she said to him.

The taxi took them to the bus station. Maria walked to the ticket booth and asked for two tickets to Ballyvaughan.

'One child,' she said.

'Single or return?'

'Single.'

'Change in Galway.'

She'd chosen Ballyvaughan because it was where they'd rented a house for two weeks one summer, when Maria was twelve or thirteen. For once the sun had shone most of the time, and they'd gone swimming at Bishopsquarter and Fanore, and walking in the Burren and along the Cliffs of Moher, and they'd hired bicycles and travelled the quiet country roads.

It probably wasn't half as idyllic as Maria remembered it, but it seemed to her like a good starting point. She'd booked a double room in a

394

local B&B for three nights. After that, something would turn up.

Pat hung back as they walked towards the bus.

'Look,' Maria said, holding on to his hand. 'A big bus, just for us.'

'*Mah.*' He pulled against her, dragging his feet. He'd never been on a bus, but what choice did she have?

'Come on, lovie,' she said. 'It'll be fun. Just for a little while. Come on, please.'

He hated change, hated any upset to his routine. How would he cope with a whole new life, with none of his familiar surroundings?

How would she?

She felt bad, running away like this. She'd have to phone Ellen first to make sure that she didn't turn up at the house to collect Maria for the rehearsal. How would Ellen react when she heard? She'd probably be mad that Maria was ruining the play, because it would have to be cancelled, wouldn't it? They'd never get someone else to play Penelope at this short notice.

Maria thought of Edward's rage when he heard. God, poor Ellen would have to tell him. She imagined that conversation.

And her parents, how would they take the news? She'd have to phone them as well, she couldn't expect Ellen to do that. They had no idea, not the smallest notion, of what Maria's life was really like, because she'd never let them see.

She was upsetting everything, leaving everyone behind, taking the coward's way out. But the thought of staying, even for one more week, had become unbearable.

395

The bookshop was hers, her only source of income now until she thought of something else. She'd have to phone Oliver later too, explain that she wasn't coming back and beg him to stay, to get someone else in to help, until she decided what to do with the shop.

She couldn't think ahead to the baby. There were too many questions to be answered about that. She wouldn't think about it now.

She carried Pat onto the bus, his feet thumping against her hips, his free hand pulling at her hair, pinching her face. He hated being carried.

'Stop, love, please stop.'

The driver helped with her bags. 'Someone got out of bed on the wrong side,' he said, smiling at Pat.

Maria struggled down the aisle, conscious of the curious glances of the few other passengers. Pat's flailing foot narrowly missed connecting with an elderly man's head.

'Sorry,' Maria said, clutching at the foot. The man glared at them both before raising his newspaper again.

She lowered Pat, who had begun to make a low, growling noise, onto a seat by the window, halfway down the bus. He lashed out at her with his red car and caught her a glancing blow on the side of her head. At the same instant, as she put up a hand to shield herself, her abdomen lurched.

God, not now. Please let it not happen now. 'Stop,' she begged Pat, 'don't–' She tried to sit beside him, tried to grab his hand, but he lashed out again as she doubled over, another cramp knifing through her, so the car caught her full in the face.

'Oh–' Her hands flew to her stinging nose. She could feel the trickle of warm liquid. She took her hands away and saw the red, and as she did, a final lurch brought her cereal up, all over her skirt and the floor of the bus.

The driver was very understanding. 'Could happen to a saint,' he told her. He gave her tissues from a box on the window sill beside his seat, and Maria cleaned herself up as best she could. Stumbling off the bus with a shrieking Pat, she could feel the antagonism of the others. Who could blame them?

The man whose taxi she hailed on the road looked doubtfully at them as they got in. Maria could smell the vomit from her clothes.

'Sorry – I got sick, but it won't happen again. I just need to get home.' She gave the address and sat back, one hand still holding Pat's. He'd calmed down a little after she'd told him they were going home, but his low growl continued throughout the journey, and his feet thumped hard against the back of the passenger seat.

The driver kept glancing at them in the rear view mirror, but made no attempt to speak to her.

In the house, Maria took off Pat's clothes and put him into the bath, which he loved. As he splashed, contented again, she slipped out of her skirt and top and washed her face at the sink. Her nose still throbbed but the bleeding had stopped, and the small pink mark on the side of her face, where the car had hit her, would be gone in a few days.

She got into her dressing gown and dried Pat and put him into pyjamas. They went downstairs and she played the piano until he fell asleep on his beanbag, clutching the red car that hadn't left his hand all morning.

She went into the kitchen and turned off the radio. She cleaned up the breakfast things and tore up the note and threw it into the bin.

She took lamb cutlets out of the freezer for their dinner.

Sixth Rehearsal Night: Tuesday, 3 June

McMillan's Pub

'Good lord.'

The room smelled strongly of mothballs. Garments were strewn over every available chair: stiff black skirts, something brown and furry, high-necked blouses with frills down their fronts, tweeds and corduroys, stripes and pastels and waistcoats and aprons and caps. Lined up on the floor, along by the wall, was a collection of footwear: wellingtons and high-heeled shoes and brogues and slippers and boots.

Piled in a corner were three large cardboard boxes.

Edward looked from the clothes to the shoes to the boxes to Oliver, standing by one of the windows.

'You've been busy.' How had he carted everything upstairs? 'You should have waited for help to unload it.'

'Good evening, Edward.' Oliver spread his arms wide. 'Welcome to my dressing room. It's been an interesting quest. It may not be over yet, but I feel that amongst my findings here, we possibly have the kernel of the wardrobe.'

'The kernel – yes.' Edward lifted a kind of furry scarf from one of the chairs. 'Penelope?'

'Exactly – when she visits the post office in act one.'

Edward fingered the fur, wondering how many costume changes Oliver had allowed for. 'Very good. Very appropriate.'

'I'm afraid I've rather commandeered your rehearsal space.'

'That's alright,' Edward said. He could hardly complain. He dropped the scarf and turned back to Oliver, hardly daring to ask how much had been spent.

He'd given Oliver two hundred euro, having been told by William Crosby to buy whatever the play called for. 'See how far you can make this go,' Edward had instructed. 'Let me know if you need a bit extra.'

Oliver had taken the money and tucked it into his wallet. 'I shall eke it out, Edward. I shall scour the charity shops for bargains. I shall be as tight-fisted as Scrooge himself.'

Now, looking at the array of clothing, Edward suspected that Oliver's idea of eking might differ slightly from his. There was no way this lot had come in under two hundred. 'Might I enquire as to how much all of this has cost?'

'Ah,' said Oliver, rummaging inside his jacket and pulling out a folded page. 'The reckoning, yes.'

Edward waited thinking, *If it's over five hundred he's taking some back.* He wondered if charity shops did refunds.

'The sum total,' Oliver announced, peering at the page, 'comes to exactly one hundred and seventy-three euro and forty-nine cent.' He looked up at Edward. 'With possibly a little more spending to be done.'

Edward looked at him. 'One hundred and seventy-three euro.'

'And forty-nine cent, yes.'

'For all this lot.' He swept an arm around the room. 'You got everything in this room for that money.'

Oliver nodded. 'Except for the fur wrap and that tweed coat, which both belong to my aunt. I acquired the loan of them in return for a pair of tickets to the opening night, which I hope you will agree is it fair exchange.'

'Well done,' Edward said, still unable to comprehend that what looked like enough clothes to dress a modest army could have cost so little. 'You've done very well indeed.'

Oliver beamed. 'Thank you. A refreshing alternative to selling books, much as I also enjoy that particular occupation.'

There were footsteps on the stairs, and they turned to see Theo appearing. She walked into the room and stopped dead.

'Oh. My. God.' She approached the clothes and began lifting and dropping them, bringing some to her face. 'Wow.' She held up a cream skirt, she wrapped a lace shawl around her and pulled a dark blue beret over her blonde hair. 'Gorgeous.'

She saw the collection of shoes and pounced, slipping off her orange ballet pumps to plunge her feet into a pair of red patent stilettos. 'Fabulous. Oliver, you're a genius.'

'This,' Oliver announced, holding up a wine-coloured skirt and grey jacket, 'is what I chose for Ursula's first outfit, and also that blouse, and those black patent court shoes.'

'I'll try them on.' Theo grabbed the clothes and disappeared behind one of the more generously proportioned armchairs.

Harry arrived, bicycle clips in hand, followed almost immediately by Judith and Robert. Oliver steered each of them towards their character's clothes and watched, lips pursed, as they slipped on shoes and pulled on jackets and hats.

Edward sat back, content to give them time to dress up. Amused to observe, as clothes were tried on, as Oliver adjusted and tutted and straightened and pinned, that the characters were slowly appearing before him.

There was Tom the gardener, in his baggy corduroy trousers held up with a pair of worn braces, his striped collarless shirt carelessly tucked into the waistband, his stout boots. When Harry pulled on the grey woollen hat Judith laughed, but Edward thought, *Yes, that's exactly right.*

There was Jack McCarthy in his beige tweed jacket, tailored shirt open casually at the neck, pressed trousers and leather brogues. A walking stick, Edward thought, and resolved to bring in Rory's blackthorn.

There was the postmistress in a tailored jacket and pleated skirt and shoes, ruffled blouse pinned at the throat with a cameo brooch – had Oliver overlooked anything?

Maria and Ellen arrived at a quarter to eight. Edward stayed where he was and watched as they came into the room. Maria made straight for Oliver and said something hurriedly. She looked pale.

Ellen wore a simple white V-neck shift dress that stopped just above her knees and flat white shoes with a strap across the instep. For the first time, she'd tied up her hair in a high ponytail. It made her look younger. She walked to where Edward sat.

'Sorry we're late,' she said. 'It was my fault, I was late leaving my house and got caught in traffic on the way to Maria's.'

'That's OK,' he said. 'Go and try on your costumes.'

She turned and walked back to the others. Her ponytail was caught in a blue clip and the back of her neck was pale. He watched her taking a bundle of clothes from Oliver and going behind the big armchair with Maria to try them on.

A good ten years younger than him, if not more.

He thought of her sitting alone at the bar. 'Don't go,' she'd said, looking lost. And the feeling he'd had then, that all he wanted to do was stay.

He'd thought about that afterwards. He'd pulled out the feeling and remembered how it had surprised him. He'd thought about having that feeling and then walking across the room to Sophie, and Ellen watching him.

He thought of Sophie and the decision finally made, and he knew it was the right one. He'd known, as he'd spoken to his wife, that it was the only choice he could make.

Everything was clear now, the bitterness of the past finally over. After a year of hating what Sophie had done, of wanting to punish her for hurting him, Edward had finally forgiven her, almost without noticing. How had that happened?

He saw Ellen come out from behind the chair.

She wore a soft pink suit, jacket and skirt and a fluffy cream beret. She'd had to let down her hair to get the beret on, and it fell over her shoulders.

'Well?' Edward heard her asking Oliver, 'will I do for Dorothy?'

'My dear,' Oliver answered, 'you *are* Dorothy.' He handed her a pair of lacy gloves. 'The finishing touch.'

She laughed. She looked happy tonight. And Edward had to admit that Oliver had been quite right; the pink shade worked beautifully with her hair colour.

He stood up and clapped his hands and heads swivelled towards him.

'We need to begin the rehearsal in the next few minutes,' he said. 'If you could each gather your own bits and pieces together, you'll be bringing them home this evening, and you'll be responsible for them from now on. If there's anything more you need to discuss with Oliver, I'd appreciate if you could keep it till the break. In the meantime, I'll take Ursula and Penelope please, for your scene in the post office, when you're ready. Thank you.'

He was glad something had made her happy.

'I'm still over the moon,' Ellen said, tearing open the pack of crisps. 'I can't keep the smile off my face.'

Maria shook her head as Ellen held out the bag. 'I know, it's wonderful.'

'Have you thought any more about what we talked about the other day?'

'What was that?' Maria reached across the table

for a beer mat.

'A holiday, a few days away on your own.'

'Yes, I'm thinking about it.' She began to peel off the beer mat's top layer.

'Good. A nice hotel in Galway maybe, pamper yourself.'

'When did you find time to get all those costumes?' Harry asked. 'Don't you work full time in the bookshop?'

'I snatched opportunities,' Oliver told him, 'from wherever they presented themselves. Where there's a will, Harry, I find there's generally a way.'

'I've never been into a charity shop,' Harry admitted.

Oliver smiled. 'Well, between you and me, neither had I. But I discovered them to be most enlightening, and by and large the assistants I met were very open to discounts for multiple purchases. What I particularly liked was the uncertainty you see – the not knowing what you might come upon on the next hanger or at the bottom of a basket – *that* was the thrill.'

'Yes.' Harry nodded. 'Yes, I see what you mean.'

'And you, Harry?' Oliver regarded him thoughtfully. 'What thrills you, I wonder? What makes your pulse race? What sends the blood galloping through your veins?'

Harry blushed. 'I like to swim,' he said. 'I'm not bad at it.'

'I've been an idiot,' Robert said.

'Me too,' Theo answered glumly.

Judith sat back and didn't talk to anyone. She was too busy talking to Christopher in her head.

You have to move out, she was saying. *I can't let you stay any more. I can't have you living off me like this, it's not fair. You need to find your own place. I'm sorry,* she was saying, *but there it is. I want my house back.*

She could hear the words in her head as clearly as if she'd stood up and spoken them aloud for the whole bar to hear. But try as she might, she couldn't for the life of her hear Christopher's answer.

The rehearsal ran late, but they managed to get to the end. The scenes ran smoothly, the lines more or less learned, the characters becoming more settled, more defined.

'I think we can call it a night,' Edward told them finally. 'I can see a big improvement this evening. It's really coming together now, and as long as we all stay focussed, we should be fine.'

He looked around at his cast. Theo was curled, legs tucked under her, in the big armchair that had served as their dressing screen earlier. Maria and Ellen were side by side on one of the window sills. Robert leaned against the wall next to them, legs crossed, hands in the pockets of his canvas jeans. Harry and Judith sat to Edward's left, Harry's long, solid legs stretched in front of him, one foot resting on the other's ankle. Oliver, who'd remained to observe the rest of the rehearsal, was perched on the edge of a spindly legged chair on the outskirts of the group, back straight, one hand cradling the other in his lap.

He might have been meditating.

'I think we can all agree that Oliver's done a fine job kitting you out.' Edward paused for a polite burst of applause while Oliver smiled and nodded. 'I presume you've discussed any outstanding wardrobe items with him, or exchanged contact details if you didn't get to try everything on.'

Nodding of heads.

'There remains,' Edward said, 'the matter of the various props. I have here' – holding up a bundle of pages – 'a props list which I've made out, and which I'm going to hand around. I'd like you to take a few minutes to run through it and let me know which props, if any, you can supply – or indeed, if you can think of anything I may have left out.'

He passed around the pages and they read in silence for a few minutes.

'I can bring the books,' Harry said. 'And I have access to lots of teapots.'

Edward scribbled on his list.

'I can bring the rest of the crockery and the biscuit jar.'

'I have a wheelbarrow and a garden seat.'

'I've got a letter opener.'

'I can get the kitchen table and chairs.'

'Good,' Edward said as one by one the various items were accounted for. 'Excellent. I can arrange collection of the bigger items if needs be – talk to me about that on Thursday.'

'What about the stairs?' Theo asked suddenly. 'We need stairs, don't we?'

Edward nodded. 'The playwright's father is getting some from a business contact. I don't think they'll be as elegant as I'd like, but we're lucky to get any at all.'

He checked his notebook. 'Oh yes, and one more thing. Judith has been working on the backdrops and they're coming along very well.'

They all looked at Judith, who smiled and went slightly pink.

'So,' Edward said, 'that's about all I have to say. Usual time on Thursday, everyone, for a full run-through.'

As they got to their feet, Oliver said, 'I wonder if I could possibly get someone to give me a hand with the boxes?'

'I'll do that,' Harry said.

'Maria.'

'Yes.'

'If I tell you something,' Ellen said, 'will you promise not to laugh?'

'Yes.'

Ellen changed gear and turned a corner. 'It's daft,' she said. 'You will laugh.'

Maria was silent.

'Actually,' Ellen said, 'I don't think I can tell you.'

She drove another half block, and then said, 'No, I have to.' She paused, and then said in a rush, 'I have feelings for Edward. Isn't that ridiculous?'

Maria looked at her in surprise.

Ellen grimaced. 'See how daft it sounds? The man annoys me. He's so bossy, everything has to be his way.' She turned another corner. 'And I can't stand how he's so finicky about time. That *really* bugs me, even if you're just a few minutes late.'

She pulled up at a red traffic light. 'And his sarcastic comments if anyone dares to argue – God, that really gets to me.' The light changed and she drove on. 'And then asking me why I limped, as if it's any of his *bloody* business.'

She reached Maria's estate and turned in. 'Can you believe it? The first man since ... Danny that I feel anything for, and it has to be bloody *Edward Bull.*'

Maria reached for her bag on the car floor.

'It's the last thing I wanted to happen – particularly as the man is probably *married.*' She sighed as she pulled up in front of number fourteen. 'As if it's not bad enough that I have these ridiculous feelings, they're also totally pointless.'

She turned off the engine and looked at Maria. 'You're speechless. I don't blame you.'

'Ellen,' Maria said.

'What?'

But Maria didn't answer. Her hands rested on the bag in her lap. Her face gave nothing away.

'What is it?' Ellen asked again. What's wrong?'

'I got on a bus with Pat,' Maria said slowly.

Ellen stared as her. 'You what? What are you talking about?'

'I got on a bus,' Maria said, then stopped, and pressed her lips together.

Ellen put a hand on her sister's arm. 'Maria.'

'I ... I went –' And her face seemed to collapse then, and she burst into loud sobs and lowered her head into her hands.

'God.' Ellen unbuckled her seat belt and leaned

towards her sister. 'Has something happened? What's wrong? Tell me.' She rested a hand on Maria's back, felt the shudders of her sister's distress. 'Please tell me what's wrong.'

But Maria shook her head, moaning. Ellen started the car and drove to the end of the avenue, and pulled in behind a dark coloured van. She yanked tissues from a box on the dashboard and pushed them into her sister's hands and Maria held them to her eyes.

'Tell me what's wrong,' Ellen begged again. 'Please Maria, you have to tell me.'

'I don't know how to.' Her voice was muffled, her face hidden behind the tissues.

'Just say it. Don't think about it, just talk.'

Maria took her hands away from her face. 'This morning I tried to leave Michael.' Her voice was thick with tears.

'Leave him? You mean – actually leave him? But why? I mean, why now?'

'Because I'm pregnant,' Maria said, her face crumpling again, 'and I couldn't bear the thought of bringing another child into that house.' Fresh tears pouring down her face, glistening orange in the light from the street. 'Living with him for the rest of my life, going to lunch at Mam and Dad's every Sunday and having him act like the perfect husband, the perfect father, sharing a bed with him, having him *force* himself on me whenever he felt like it–' her face screwed up now in disgust '–having my children grow up in a *sham* of a marriage, all that money and not *one* kind word spoken, not *one* generous act, no conversation between us except what had to be said, never a word from him to Pat–'

The tears overcame her then, and she stopped and covered her face again. Ellen pulled more tissues from the box.

'You're pregnant?' she asked softly.

Maria nodded. 'I was on the Pill, but it didn't work. I *hate* him,' she said, taking the fresh tissues, brushing angrily now at the tears that persisted. 'I can't *bear* being with him.'

'But why didn't you say something?' Ellen asked. 'Why didn't you tell anyone how bad it was?'

'Who could I tell?' Maria demanded, searching Ellen's face. 'Not Mam and Dad, you know how highly they think of him. And I couldn't tell you–' She broke off. Her ragged breaths sounded harsh in the silence.

'I know,' Ellen said softly. 'I was too wrapped up in myself. I'm sorry.'

'Don't be,' Maria said quickly. 'I'm not blaming you, it's just the way it was.'

They were silent again for some time, and then Ellen asked, 'So where did you go with Pat?'

Maria sighed and wiped a hand across her face. 'We got a taxi to the bus station and we got on the bus to Galway. We were going to Ballyvaughan.'

'Ballyvaughan?' Ellen stared. 'Who do you know there?'

'No one – but we went on holidays there once, years ago, and I liked it.'

'Did we? I don't remember. So you were going to leave without saying anything to anyone? What about the play? What about Mam and Dad?'

413

Maria's eyes welled again and she squeezed them shut. 'I know, I know – it was stupid, I hadn't thought it through. I should have known it wouldn't work. I was going to get in touch, honest, once we were settled. Anyway, Pat got very upset, I mean really distraught, and then I threw up on the bus.'

'God. How far had you got?'

Maria's mouth twisted. 'Nowhere – the bus hadn't left the station. We got off and went home, and I calmed Pat down and cleaned myself up.' She paused. 'I'd written a note for him. I tore it up.'

'God,' Ellen said again. 'How long have you been feeling this way?'

Maria shrugged. 'Ages. Since Pat was diagnosed. That's when ... Michael began to change, towards both of us.'

'When are you due?'

'January.'

Another short silence. 'You're not wearing your rings,' Ellen said suddenly.

Maria shook her head. 'I threw them into a bin at the bus station. He hasn't noticed – or if he has, he hasn't mentioned it.'

'So what now?'

Maria looked out the car window. 'I don't know. I still want to leave him, but I'll have to do it differently. I'll have to find a way that doesn't upset Pat.' She hesitated. 'And I *hate* having to tell Mam and Dad. That's really why I was running away – so I wouldn't have to face them when I told them. They'll be shocked. It'll kill them.'

'It will *not* kill them. They'll get over it. Don't

worry about them.' Ellen reached across and took her sister's hand. 'And I'll help, you know that – whatever you need me to do. And with the baby, of course.'

'Thanks.' Maria pulled fresh tissues from the box and blew her nose. 'Better go in. God, I must look a mess – not that he'll notice.'

Ellen turned the car around and pulled up outside number fourteen. 'You have to change this,' she said. 'You have to leave him.'

Maria nodded. 'I will. Soon.'

'Don't worry about Mam and Dad,' Ellen said again. 'Don't let that stop you.'

'No.'

All the way back to her apartment, she imagined Maria planning her departure, deciding what she'd need to pack. Leaving the house she'd shared with her husband, thinking she was never going to see it, or him, again.

And then, when everything went wrong, having to turn around and go back to the life she hated. Taking everything out of the suitcase again, putting their clothes back into the wardrobe, their toothbrushes back into the bathroom.

Terrible that she'd felt bad enough to take that drastic step. Even worse that none of her family, including her only sister, had had the slightest idea. Not the smallest inkling, apart from knowing that Maria's marriage wasn't exactly one of the made-in-heaven ones.

Ellen was deeply ashamed. Some sister she'd been, too wrapped up in her own miserable life to see her sister's pain. Too busy living with her memories. She cringed when she thought of all the pathetic, loveless one-night stands, and how she'd fooled herself into believing they were what she wanted, or needed.

But she was putting the past behind her at last. Danny would never be forgotten, but he belonged to a part of her life that was over now. And Maria was going to need her sister around, by the sound of it.

It wasn't until she was lying in bed over half an hour later that, much to her great annoyance, Edward Bull came nudging back into her head, filling her again with ridiculous, hopeless longing.

Theo

She wiped a smear off the stainless steel fridge with her sleeve. 'You know what you have to do,' she told the face that looked back at her. 'You just don't want to do it.'

She opened the fridge and took out a strawberry yoghurt.

'She's probably not even there,' she said, peeling off the lid. 'Or else she's still in bed. It's only eleven o'clock.'

She dipped a spoon in and swirled it through the pink gloop.

'Or her mother might come to the door, and what then?'

Ben walked in with Chrissy in his arms. 'Talking to yourself again?'

They were on cordial terms, like two office

416

workers might be, or patients in adjoining hospital beds. They hadn't had sex in over three weeks.

'Sort of,' Theo said. 'Will you manage if I go out for an hour?'

'I thought you were going to make chutney.'

'I was, but I forgot I need to talk to Caroline about a wig for the play.'

She was pretty sure she hadn't mentioned collecting the brown wig from Robert at last night's rehearsal.

'Fine by me,' Ben said. 'I'm taking Chrissy to the park.'

'Good idea. See you later.' She replaced the yoghurt in the fridge and grabbed her bag.

She knew where Miep lived. She'd found *Dollander, M* in the phone book and checked it out ages ago, curious to see what kind of house Ben had shared with his wife. She'd never mentioned it to him. He didn't need to know everything.

Number thirty-six Carlton Road was an ordinary-looking semi with a blue front door and a red brick porch. There was a small green car parked in the driveway.

Theo drove past it and pulled in outside number forty. She turned off the engine and sat. On a green further down, two men stood in conversation, their dogs circling each other. A marmalade cat leapt from a front garden onto a gatepost and sat hunched, watching the dogs intently. A woman came out from a nearby house, buttoning her grey coat as she hurried past the car, brown handbag tucked into the crook of her arm.

Theo looked back at number thirty-six. She tilted the rear view mirror to see her face.

'Well, you're here. Now what?'

She reapplied her lipstick and blotted it, and checked her teeth and tweaked her wig. She got out of the car and walked up the path and pressed the brass bell. She took a deep breath and pulled her stomach in.

The front door opened and Miep stood there.

'Hi,' Theo said brightly, her heart sinking. 'I'm Theo, as you probably know. I, em, I just wanted a word with Gemima, if she's around?'

Miep wore a stained dark blue man's shirt over a pair of baggy jeans. She carried what looked like a wooden spatula and she was barefoot. And instead of telling Theo exactly what she thought of her, she smiled.

'Ah yes,' she said. 'Won't you please come in?'

She held the door wide and Theo stepped past her into a hall with white walls and pale beige wooden floors, and an archway to the left.

'Please excuse my clothes,' Miep said, shutting the door. 'I am working.' Her English was slightly accented. She put a hand out to Theo. 'It's nice,' she said, 'to finally meet you.'

'Yes.' Theo shook her hand, a feeling of unreality beginning to steal over her. Of all the things she'd imagined she'd find here, a welcome wasn't one of them.

Miep indicated the archway – 'please' – and Theo walked ahead of her into a bright room with more white walls and two green couches with striped red and orange cushions. Lots of abstract paintings, and red curtains on the bay window and a big red rug on the wooden floor.

'I'm sorry to disturb you at work,' Theo told her. 'I really just came for a quick chat with Gemima. Not,' she added hastily, 'that I wouldn't want to talk to you too – I would – I mean, I wouldn't mind.'

She stopped. 'Sorry,' she said. 'I feel a little nervous. I'm not sure what you think of me.'

Miep frowned. 'But how could I think anything?' she asked. 'We have never met properly – I don't know why. All I hear is what Gemima tells me,' she shrugged, 'and of course she is still a child, with a child's opinions.'

While Theo was searching for a reply, Miep waved a hand at one of the couches. 'Please sit down,' she said. 'I'll get Gemima, she's in her room. Would you like some tea?'

'Yes, please.' Tea would be good. Tea would give her something to do with her hands. Wine would be so much better, but tea would be good. 'Thank you.'

Theo sat on one of the green couches and looked out the window, and counted to thirty-seven before Gemima walked through the archway.

'Hello,' Theo said. 'Bet you didn't expect to see me.'

'No,' Gemima said, walking to the other couch and sitting opposite Theo. She wore a short denim skirt over grey leggings and a black T-shirt that stopped a few inches above her tiny waist. A thin gold ring pierced the skin just above her bellybutton. 'I didn't believe it when Mutti told me you were here.'

Like her mother, she wore no shoes. Her toenails were dark blue.

'Gemima,' Theo said, 'I'm so sorry. I know it's
because of me that you've stopped coming over
to stay on Friday nights, and I'm really and truly
sorry.'

Gemima looked uncomfortable. One bare foot
beat a quick rhythm on the wooden floor.

'I know I'm not much of a future stepmother,'
Theo said. 'I'm brash and I'm in your face, and
I'm hopeless at knowing what thirteen-year-old
girls like, and you're probably mortified that I
wear a wig.'

Gemima's head was bent slightly, her eyes fixed
firmly on the coffee table between then. She
played with the ends of her hair, twirling a strand
between her fingers.

'I discovered something recently,' Theo said,
crossing and then uncrossing her legs. 'All along,
I'd been blaming you for us not ... getting on so
well when you came to stay. As far as I was
concerned, I was doing everything right, and you
were the one who was refusing to have anything
to do with me.'

Gemima pulled at the hem of her skirt.

'But then I began to think about it, and I
realised that I was jealous of you, because you
were Ben's first daughter and he's crazy about
you, and I was afraid he'd never feel the same way
about Chrissy.'

That sounded plausible, didn't it? And maybe,
on some level, it was even true.

Gemima lifted her head and regarded Theo in
astonishment.

'My dad loves Chrissy like anything,' she said. 'Anyone can see that.'

Theo made a face. 'Anyone except the blindest woman on the planet. All the time I was fooling myself into thinking I was being the perfect hostess by filling the freezer with ice cream and cooking the foods you liked, when in fact–'

She stopped – there was no kind way to say *I didn't want you in my house* – 'when in fact I was getting it all wrong,' she said instead. 'I just didn't know how to handle you.'

Gemima shrugged, a tiny movement of one shoulder that Theo took as agreement. She ploughed on.

'I mean, look what happened when you came to our rescue the other week, when Sean broke his ankle – I practically ignored you, I wasn't a bit nice to you, and then I actually forgot you were in the house.'

'That's OK,' Gemima muttered quickly.

'No, it's not OK, it was rude and appalling, and I apologise. I really did forget, but I shouldn't have.'

Gemima's fingers twined through each other. She cleared her throat, and Theo waited.

'I didn't know if you wanted me to come and stay,' Gemima said quietly. 'I thought maybe you didn't. My dad said of course you did, but I thought he was just trying to make everyone get along.'

She'd sensed Theo's feelings, she'd felt unwanted – which of course she had been. She was thirteen, still a child, and Theo had made her feel bad. She'd probably dreaded the visits as much as Theo had.

'Gemima,' Theo said quietly. 'I hate that you felt that way. I'm so ashamed. I wouldn't blame you if you never wanted to come back again.'

'But I miss Chrissy,' Gemima said quickly, then looked embarrassed. 'I mean–'

Theo smiled. 'It's fine – you're allowed not to miss me. At least Chrissy only screams at you, and she does that to everyone.'

'I don't mind when she screams,' Gemima said. 'That's what babies do.'

'You know, you're dead right – that's exactly what they do.' Theo suddenly remembered. 'I heard you painted her.'

Gemima shrugged again. 'It's not very good.'

'I'd love to see it. Could I, please?'

'It's upstairs.' Gemima got to her feet and left the room as Miep entered with a tray which held, among other things, a plate of what looked like homemade biscuits.

'You shouldn't have gone to all that trouble,' Theo said.

'Not at all,' Miep answered, pouring from a glass teapot. 'I would do it for any guest.'

Theo decided to take that comment at face value. 'Right.'

'I'm glad you're here,' Miep continued, offering Theo the biscuits. 'I gather there was a small ... misunderstanding, and I assume you've come to clear it up.'

'Yes.' Of course Gemima had told Miep what had happened. And Miep wasn't blaming Theo; she was trusting her to put things right. Theo took a biscuit. 'I hope I can.'

'And now,' Miep said, 'you will please excuse me – I'm quite busy with a new order and must return to my studio.'

'Of course.'

She put out her hand again, and Theo took it. 'Please call another time, if you would like,' Miep said.

'Thank you.'

She was nothing like Theo had imagined. She sipped Miep's delicately fragrant tea and nibbled Miep's cinnamon biscuits and adjusted her opinion of Ben's ex-wife.

Miep hadn't judged Theo, even though she must know how shaky the relationship between Theo and Gemima was. She'd been polite and welcoming, no hint of resentment for the woman who shared a home – and a child – with the man Miep had once married.

Gemima's feet pattered down the stairs just then, and Theo lowered her cup.

The painting wasn't a masterpiece – Chrissy's nose was too small and the proportions in general were slightly off – but it had been meticulously executed, down to the tiny pinpricks of white that Gemima had dotted into the blue irises, the tinge of rose in Chrissy's cheek and the barely there front tooth that was just beginning to push through the pink gums.

'It's wonderful.' Theo stared. 'I remember that tooth coming up – God, will I ever forget it.'

Gemima smiled.

Theo laid the painting on the coffee table. 'I didn't know you were good at art,' she said. 'There's so much I don't know about you.'

Gemima took it biscuit and broke off a tiny piece.

'I remember when I was your age,' Theo told her. 'God, I was a nightmare. I was only a few years older than you when I had Sean. If my parents had got divorced, I don't know what I would have done – gone even more off the rails, I suppose. Of course, it didn't help that I had the perfect older sister who never did anything wrong. Your mum's biscuits are yummy, by the way.'

Gemima glanced up. 'I made them.'

'You did? See, something else I don't know.' Theo lifted her cup, then put it down again. 'The thing is, Gemima, I'm not really looking for a step-daughter, and you certainly don't need another mother, or stepmother, or whatever you want to call it. But I could use a good babysitter now and again, and I know Sean thinks you're kind of cool, and he's never wrong.' Gemima smiled.

'Please come back,' Theo said. 'You can teach me how to bake biscuits, and we'll have strawberry ice cream for dinner every Friday and Chrissy will never cry again, I promise.'

Gemima gave a tiny laugh.

'OK, that last bit was a lie – and the others might only let us do the ice cream dinner once a month. But will you come back anyway?'

'OK.'

'Great – oh, and you are coming to the play, aren't you? I can get you a free ticket for opening night on Monday – and one for your mum, if she'd fancy it.'

'OK,' Gemima said again. 'Cool.'

Theo got up. 'I'm so glad I came,' she said. 'I

424

wasn't a bit sure that you'd want to talk to me. Please say thanks to your mum.'

They walked to the front door and Theo took a chance and hugged Gemima quickly, and if Gemima didn't hug her back, at least she didn't draw away.

'Bye. See you Friday.'

'Bye.'

The door closed as Theo walked down the path. In the car, she turned the radio up loud and sang along with it, gloriously out of tune, all the way home.

Maria

'If I say so myself,' Oliver declared. 'I feel I did rather well with the costumes. They seemed to find favour in general – although I did think Harry's jacket looked a little snug.'

Maria leaned against the counter, her gaze fixed on the shelf of books facing her.

Oliver glanced at her. 'Maria,' he began, 'far be it from me to pry, but one cannot help noticing that all does not appear well with you. You've hardly said a word all morning.'

Maria turned to face him. 'Sorry, Oliver, I'm afraid I'm ... going through a rough patch at the moment.' She hesitated, tracing the edge of the counter with a finger. 'Did I thank you for holding the fort yesterday?'

'As soon as you arrived at rehearsal last evening.'

'Oh ... good.' The old wood was smooth; her finger ran along it easily. 'Oliver, can I ask you something?'

'Of course.'

'If you were in a situation that was making you very unhappy, and if–' She broke off. Oliver said nothing. 'If the only way out,' she continued slowly, 'involved upsetting some people you cared about, what would you do?'

Oliver considered the question carefully. Maria watched his face.

'I assume the people I cared about would care about me too,' he said at last.

'Oh, yes.'

'In that case,' Oliver continued, 'they probably wouldn't want me to remain unhappy, would they?'

She thought. 'No, they wouldn't.'

'So if they thought that I could do something to make me happy again, surely they'd want that?' he asked gently. 'Even if it upset them a little?'

'It might upset them a lot,' Maria said.

'Oh, I don't know,' Oliver answered. 'I think if it were me, I'd be willing to take the risk.'

'I see.' She was silent for a few minutes, and then she said, 'Oliver, if for any reason I was to ... stop working in the shop for a while, do you think you'd be willing to take over as manager – with an adjusted salary, of course?'

Oliver showed little sign of being surprised. 'I should be delighted,' he said. 'I might, of course, need to engage the services of a part-time assistant.'

'Of course.'

'In that case, you can rest assured that I would step into the breach if required.'

Maria smiled. 'Thank you. Oh,' she added, 'by the way, I should probably mention that I'm pregnant.'

Oliver returned her smile. 'I had my suspicions. Hearty congratulations. A little sibling for our friend Pat.'

'Yes.' She looked at him in surprise. 'You know, that had never occurred to me.'

And for the first time, the idea of another child began to seem like it might not be a colossal disaster.

Judith

'I'm sorry,' she said, 'but you have to go. I can't afford to keep three people, not when I'll be on a pension soon. I want my house back, and you've stayed long enough. I'd like you to start looking for your own place.'

She hadn't counted on Amanda being there. She'd waited until after dinner, lingering at the warehouse until she knew they'd have eaten, rehearsing what she'd say to him. When she got home she'd heard them talking in the sitting room. She'd taken a deep breath – *get it over with* – and walked in.

'Hello there.'

Christopher had nodded, unsmiling. Amanda had said, 'Hello. Nice day?'

'Fine, thanks. Um, Christopher, I wonder if we could have a word,' – glancing apologetically at Amanda, 'in private?'

He'd looked coolly at her. 'You can say anything you want in front of Amanda.'

To give her credit, Amanda had looked a little uncomfortable. 'I'll go, Chris,' she said. 'Your mum would rather–'

'No, you stay,' Christopher had said, his eyes still on Judith. 'No need to go.'

So Judith stood in front of both of them as they sat on the couch and watched her, and she said what she'd been preparing to say for about a week. Her voice wobbled and her heart thumped, but she got it out.

There was silence when she stopped. Christopher kept staring at her. Amanda glanced at him, then looked down at the book in her lap.

Judith waited, forcing herself to hold his gaze. Feeling her pulse thumping through her. Finally she asked, 'Have you nothing to say?'

'What's there to say?' Christopher replied. 'You want us out, we'll go. End of story.' His voice was cold.

'Christopher,' she pleaded, 'try and see it from my point of view, please.'

He got to his feet. 'I said we'll go.' He walked past her and out the door.

She heard his footsteps on the stairs, her bedroom door banging closed. She looked at Amanda, still sitting on the couch. Amanda's head remained bent towards her book.

Judith was definitely Mrs O'Sullivan now. She left the room and went into the kitchen.

The neighbour's cat was sitting on her window sill. Judith took the carton of milk from the fridge and poured a little into a saucer and pulled the sliding door open.

'Here, puss.' She set the saucer on the patio and the cat leapt lightly down and began to lap softly. Judith stood in the garden breathing in the cool, damp air. She heard the rumble of traffic on the road outside the house, someone's television nearby, a rustle of leaves.

She went back inside and made herself a cheese and tomato sandwich and stood by the open door as she ate it. The cat finished the milk and began to wash itself.

'Puss,' she said. 'Good puss.'

Tomorrow, she'd spend most of the day in the warehouse again. The backdrops were difficult to work on, the material not stretched tightly enough for her to have as much control as she would have liked. But on that big scale, detail wasn't important, and she felt – she hoped – she was giving the right overall look to each one.

The air became chilly. She straightened and the cat slid away towards the darkness of the hedge. A rectangle of yellow light lay on the grass in front of her. She looked up at her bedroom window and wondered what they were saying about her.

The way he'd looked at her, so coldly. She shivered and moved towards the back door.

Robert

He was a fool. His ten-year-old sons were smarter than him. The truth was staring him in the face. It had been right in front of him for years, and he'd looked past it and refused to see it.

He loved Caroline. He'd fallen in love when they'd met and he loved her still. He'd been unfaithful – he'd given in to temptation and been monumentally stupid – and he'd been caught and he'd paid the price. And since then, he'd done a fine job of fooling himself into believing that he was happy, that he'd moved on – but he'd never for a second stopped loving her.

And it wasn't until it began to look like she might be about to leave Ireland forever that Robert was forced, finally, to admit the truth. It wasn't the idea of losing the boys that had scared him so much – he'd die before he'd allow that to happen – but the thought of never being near Caroline again was frighteningly real, and suddenly unbearable.

Of course it was too late now, with everything in place. Even if she still had those kinds of feelings for him – and given the Frenchman, that was highly unlikely – how could she ever trust Robert again? How on earth could he expect anyone to take him seriously, when at least half the single females in Portmaine had been on his arm – and in his bed – at some stage over the past decade?

He groaned. He put his hands in his hair and pulled, hard.

The kitchen door opened and Yolanda, the receptionist, looked in. 'Your three o'clock is here.'

'OK.'

'And your hair is messy.'

'Right.'

Robert poured his untouched coffee down the sink. Nothing to be done now; he'd burned any bridges that had ever been built. He smoothed down his hair and braced himself for at least half an hour of meaningless small talk.

In the salon, he walked past Caroline who was cutting the hair of a teenage girl. He stopped.

'Are you busy tomorrow night?' He hadn't planned it – the words were out before he knew he was going to say them.

Caroline looked at him.

'I need to talk to you. Maybe a drink somewhere?' The teenager was watching him in the mirror.

Caroline hesitated. 'I can't tomorrow night. What about tonight?'

'I have rehearsal tonight,' he told her, cursing Edward Bull.

'Oh yes – well, Saturday then?'

'Right,' he said. 'Saturday will be fine. Around eightish? I'll pick you up.'

'OK. I'll book Cheryl.'

He walked on, conscious of her looking after him. She had no idea; how could she? Probably thought it was something to do with the boys.

Saturday night. He couldn't think about Saturday night. He couldn't wait for Saturday night.

Maria

'Mam,' she said, 'maybe we could have a cup of tea.'

'Of course we could.' Her mother reached for the kettle. 'Sure, I'd given up asking you, you always seem to be rushing home to put on the dinner.'

'I am, usually,' Maria said, gathering Pat's things into her carrier bag. 'But today I wouldn't mind a bit of a chat for a few minutes. Is Dad around?'

'He's out the back.'

Her father was bent over one of the gooseberry bushes. Maria walked towards him and he straightened up when he heard her.

'Hello, love. You off?'

'Come in for a minute, Dad,' she said. 'There's something I want to talk to you and Mam about.'

Lying in bed, she'd thought about how to say it to them. She'd tried to make it sound reasonable and logical, tried to take the sting out of it. But whatever way she put it, whatever words she used, they were going to get the land of their lives. There was no way she could soften this blow.

Telling Ellen had been different – not that she'd planned on telling anyone. She hadn't been going to say a word, and then Ellen had started talking about something that had seemed so monstrously *trivial* – a crush, for God's sake, even if it

432

was on Edward Bull, of all people – and Maria's dam had finally burst and it had all come tumbling out.

She had to admit that telling Ellen had been an enormous relief – simply giving voice to it and having someone listen, just listen, had been wonderful.

But this was another story.

She looked at the two of them sitting across the table from her. Her mother looked faintly anxious, her father less so. On the floor by the sink, Pat arranged Tupperware containers in a row.

'The thing is...' she said, hands cradled around the cup that was waiting for tea. She looked up at mother's worried face and imagined how it would collapse when she heard what Maria was about to say.

She couldn't do it. She couldn't tell them, the words refused to come. 'The thing is, I've recently found out that I'm expecting another baby.' Her mother flying around the table to hug her. The relief, the delight on both their faces.

'Oh, lovie, that's marvellous news, you must be thrilled.'

Her father reached across to squeeze her shoulder. 'That's great news, love. Tell Michael we said congratulations!

Michael. She'd have to tell him before Sunday lunch. Her parents would turn it into a celebration.

'When are you due?' her mother asked.

'January, around the middle.' Maria stood up. 'I just thought ye should know,' she said. 'We'd better get going now.'

'What about the tea?' The kettle was singing.

'Sorry, Mam,' she said, 'I don't think I have the time after all. Come on, love,' she said to Pat, 'time to go home.'

Her mother looked at her. 'Are you feeling alright love? Is there anything you're not telling us?'

'No,' Maria said. 'I'm just a bit tired, that's all. Come on,' she said again to Pat. 'Let's go home.'

Home.

'We'll see you for lunch on Sunday,' she told them. 'As usual.'

They stood at the door as she pushed the buggy down the path ahead of her, eyes swimming with tears.

Seventh Rehearsal Night: Thursday, 5 June

Mcmillan's Pub

'No, no, you're *masking* him again.'

'*Project your voice,* I said – nobody will hear that. Bring your voice up from your abdomen, the way I showed you.'

'Don't move until you have a *reason* to move – unless you want something over there, stay where you are.'

'What's with the hands? You're a postmistress, not a conductor.'

'*Listen* when someone's talking to you – don't just wait for them to finish so you can talk.'

'A bit of *reaction* here would be good.'

'Good grief, if you don't know the lines by now–'

Edward was in fine form.

'He missed his vocation,' Theo muttered. 'He should have been a dictator.'

'Quiet offstage!' Edward barked, and they watched as Harry forgot his lines again, bringing Edward to the point of apoplexy and causing Oliver, who'd been given the job of prompter, to say hurriedly, 'Some chance I have against him.'

They were all nervous. Even Judith, who was normally line perfect, fluffed once or twice. In one of his scenes, Robert came in too early and had to backtrack rapidly as Edward flapped him away. Maria gave the wrong line to Ellen, who looked blankly at her until Edward shouted, 'Say *something,* for God's sake – don't just *stand* there!'

Ellen whirled towards him as Maria rushed in

with the right line. The moment passed and everyone breathed out again.

At the end of a particularly shaky scene, Edward closed his notebook with a thump.

'Take a break, take a break, come back with *focus,*' he told them irritably. 'Ten minutes, not a *second* longer. Have you all forgotten we open in four days? We need all the–'

They were gone. He was speaking to an empty room. He threw his notebook onto the chair beside him and ran both hands through his hair.

He shouldn't be taking it out on them. He was making them twice as rattled, ranting and raving at them. He wouldn't blame them if they didn't come back. They were amateurs. They'd worked hard, they didn't need this. He must calm down.

But his head was a mess. How could he calm down when he was tormented? How could he be reasonable with sleep an impossibility, with Ellen's face appearing whenever he tried to close his eyes? It was one thing knowing he'd made the right decision about his future – it was turning out to be quite another thing getting past that decision. Maybe it hadn't been the right one after all.

Edward sighed deeply. He stood and paced the floor of the long, narrow room. He was a mess. Maybe he was having a midlife crisis – at forty-four, he was probably the right age.

He'd never wanted a brandy more, but he'd be lynched if he ventured downstairs.

'I told Christopher to leave,' Judith said to Maria.

'Did you? How did he take it?'

'Not great. He hasn't spoken to me since.'

'But he's agreed to go?'

'Well, he said he would.'

'So you're just waiting now.'

'Yes ... and you? How are things?'

Maria swirled her water. 'Things are ... the way they are.'

'God, he's like a bear with a sore head,' Theo complained.

'If he says one more word to me, I'm going to let him have it,' Ellen promised.

'Ladies,' Oliver said, 'poor Edward is as jittery as the rest of us. True, he's not the most diplomatic of souls but–'

'He's making me forget my lines,' Harry said. 'He's giving me stage fright, and I'm not even on the stage yet.'

'I know, but a confrontation, however tempting, won't serve any purpose at this stage.'

'It would serve to make me feel good,' Ellen said. 'It would serve to put him in his place.'

Robert was silent. Nobody noticed Robert's silence.

'Right,' Edward said. He cleared his throat. 'I feel I have been a little harsh so far this evening. I would like to apologise, and assure you that I'll go easier from now on.' He paused, looking down at his script. 'Right, moving along. Next scene, Jack and Dorothy, if you please.'

Ellen stood at the side of the stage, waiting for the order to begin.

There were dark shadows under his eyes. He hadn't looked at her properly since she'd walked in. She'd been wrong about the night in the bar. It was wishful thinking to imagine he'd felt anything. It was probably a look of pity he'd given her, sitting up at the counter drinking by herself.

He wasn't wearing a ring, but she was pretty sure he was married. He had a wife, the woman in the bar had looked like a wife. Ellen would forget him and move on. After the play, they'd probably never meet again.

'When you're *quite* ready.' He was looking at her now, and it wasn't with desire. Ellen stepped forward and the scene began.

'*Don't* cross in front of him.'

'You're *fiddling* again – stop.'

'Don't stand until he suggests going out to the garden – you're not *psychic*.'

'Try to at least *look* as if you're listening.'

And she gritted her teeth and reminded herself that he had apologised, that he was trying to keep calm, but that he was probably as jittery as they were, like Oliver had said.

At the end of the scene, Ellen sat down next to Theo. 'He's asking for a slap.'

Theo grinned. 'Go for it.'

'Quiet back there.' Edward turned and glared at them, and Ellen stared back, resisting the impulse to stick out her tongue at him or make a different kind of rude gesture. Their eyes held for a few seconds before he turned away.

Ellen's mother had phoned earlier, when Ellen

was getting ready to go to the rehearsal.

'Did Maria tell you about the baby?' she'd asked.

'Yes.'

'Is there something else?' her mother had demanded. 'She didn't seem very happy about it. Is there anything we don't know?'

So Maria hadn't told them. She'd mentioned the baby and not the rest. Ellen had thought quickly.

'She might be worried because of Pat,' she'd told her mother. 'She might be afraid she'll have another autistic child.'

Another lie, or half-truth, or whatever you wanted to call it. They were full of them, herself and Maria.

At the end of the evening, Edward stood up. 'Well,' he said, 'one rehearsal to go. Needless to say, while I appreciate your efforts so far, I will be expecting a big improvement on Sunday afternoon. I accept that nerves are kicking in,' – pause – 'and I apologise again for being a bit hard on you tonight.'

He looked at his notebook. They waited.

'Please bring small props and costumes with you on Sunday. I've made arrangements for collection of large items on Sunday morning, and thanks to everyone for pitching in with that. Oh, and Robert has kindly offered to help with hairstyles, if any character feels the need.' He glanced at Harry and added, 'Not Tom – he needs to be, er, natural.'

Harry grinned. 'Righto.'

'The backdrops have almost been completed

and you'll see them hanging in the Arts Centre on Sunday. Thank you again, Judith, for your help with those.' Judith smiled. 'So – study those lines, get plenty of rest and let's make it work on Sunday. Three o'clock sharp, everyone, please. We'll need every minute.'

They got up and gathered bags and coats. Ellen folded her towel and pushed it into its bag, and turned to follow Maria out of the room.

Edward said quickly, 'Ellen?'

She turned back. 'Yes?'

'A word, if you don't mind.'

Edward waited until she walked over to him. The room was empty now, apart from Maria at the doorway.

'I was going to have a drink downstairs,' he said rapidly in a low voice. 'I thought, if you're not rushing away…'

An expression flashed across her face, too quick for him to read. 'I'm driving Maria home,' she said. 'Sorry.' She walked away, not giving him a chance to respond, and disappeared through the doorway.

Edward picked up his briefcase and crossed the room slowly, and made his way downstairs.

'What did he want?'

Ellen opened the car doors and got in, and leaned her head on the steering wheel. 'He asked me to go for a drink.'

'He what? Why didn't you go? I could have got a–'

Ellen raised her head and looked furiously at Maria. 'The man is *married*. He was out with his *wife* a few nights ago.' She started the car and drove jerkily towards the exit. 'How has he got the *nerve* to ask me to go for a drink? Who does he think I am?'

'You're overreacting – take it easy,' Maria said. 'Maybe he was just being friendly.'

'Friendly?' Ellen braked sharply. 'I've a good mind to–' She looked back towards the pub, then put the car in gear again. 'No – he's not worth it.'

'Ellen, don't you think you're being a small bit unreasonable here? The man just–'

'Oh my God,' Ellen said slowly. 'He saw me sitting on a barstool by myself.' She turned to Maria. 'What kind of woman sits on a barstool by herself?' She groaned. 'I asked him to join me.'

'Ellen, honestly, you need to calm down,' Maria said. 'Edward was wound up tonight and needed a drink, and didn't want to have it alone. He was just looking for company, that's all – I'm sure that's all. Edward isn't like that.'

'How do you know what he's not like? What do you know about him?'

'Well, not much, but–'

'I think we've established he's married – or at least with another woman. And now he's asking me out.'

They drove in silence for a few blocks, then Ellen said, 'Sorry, I'm doing it again. I'm going on about me when you're the one we should be concentrating on.'

'No, that's–'

'Mam rang earlier. She told me you'd been to see them. I didn't say anything on the way to rehearsal because I didn't want you going in upset, but Maria, honestly, I can't believe you didn't tell them you're leaving Michael. You told them about the baby and nothing else.'

Maria looked out the window.

'When are you planning to do it? Or do you want me to tell them altogether?'

'*No*,' Maria said immediately.

'No what? No you don't want me to do it, or—'

'I'm not telling them,' Maria said clearly, 'because I've decided not to leave.'

Ellen immediately pulled into the path and stopped. 'I don't believe this. What are you saying?'

Maria's face was calm. 'Look, El, I was over-wrought the other night, and stressed about the play, and my hormones are probably all mixed up with the pregnancy—'

Ellen looked at her. 'So what are you saying?' she asked again.

'I'm saying that I've decided to leave things as they are, and you need to accept that.'

'But you can't possibly—'

Maria put a hand on Ellen's arm. 'I appreciate you trying to help me, really I do, but there's nothing you can do now. It's ... easier to leave things as they are. It's just easier all round.'

'Easier?' Ellen stared at her sister. 'How is it easier to stay with a man you said you—'

'Ellen,' Maria said loudly, 'this is something *I* get to decide, not you – and what I've decided to do is work at my marriage. I'm sorry if you don't like that, but that's what I'm doing.'

'But—'

'I know how it looks. I know it looks like I'm just taking the coward's way out – and maybe I

444

am. But that's how it's going to be.' She stared straight ahead. 'Would you mind driving me home now please?'

Ellen started the car but made no move to get back into the traffic. 'I think you're making a big mistake.'

'I know you do,' Maria said calmly, 'and I appreciate your being there the other night. But you must let me live my life the way I choose.'

'OK,' Ellen said, swinging back onto the road. They didn't speak again until she drew up in front of the red brick house, five minutes later. Maria unbuckled her seatbelt. 'I know what I'm doing.'

'OK.'

'I need you to accept it.'

Ellen looked at her. 'OK. I do. I don't have to agree with it, do I?'

'No.' Maria opened the door. 'I'll see you Sunday.' They were meeting at their parents' and going straight to the dress rehearsal after lunch.

'See you Sunday,' Ellen answered She swung the car around, not waiting till Maria had gone indoors. How could she be so accepting of her awful situation? She'd told Ellen how she felt about Michael, and now here she was planning to stay with him for the rest of her life. How could anyone do that? How could anyone choose to live unhappily for years, and not go mad?

And all the way home, thoughts of Maria managed to keep all other thoughts at bay.

He hadn't known he was going to say it. He'd had no intention of saying anything. Why had he opened his damn mouth, when nothing had led him to believe she would say yes? Why had he opened his damn fool mouth?

She'd looked happy, that was it. Even when he'd snapped at her, even when she'd scowled back at him, there was a lightness there, some kind of bubbling happiness there that made him think she might just say yes.

But of course she'd said no. He'd known deep down she'd say no, and still he'd asked. He was an idiot.

He didn't order a drink in the bar, feeling the need to be home, even if home was a miserable two-room granny flat. He drove carefully through the streets and parked in his usual spot outside Rory's house. He let himself in and pulled Rory's curtains and switched on Rory's lights and put the security chain across Rory's front door.

And once all his responsibilities had been met, Edward left the house and walked down the path to his flat and opened the bottle.

Theo

The front door opened and she went out to the hall.

'Hi, stranger.' She smiled at Gemima.

'Hi,' Gemima said, a small, shy answering smile on her face. 'Is Chrissy in the kitchen?'

'Yes, she's just–' but Gemima had already vanished, just before a very large collection of flowers appeared at the front door – and underneath them, a pair of legs. 'What's all this?'

Ben's head appeared at one side. 'She just told me what you did. She was waiting with her bag packed when I called to see her. She said you really wanted her to come back.'

'I did,' Theo said. 'Now would you please put down those magnificent flowers and kiss your foolish wife-to-be and tell her you forgive her.'

'I forgive her,' he said, putting the flowers on the hall table and drawing her into his arms. 'I love her, even though she's extremely foolish.'

'Right,' Theo said five minutes later, patting her hair back into place. 'We'd better go in – the ice cream will be melted.'

Robert

'Why are you and Mum going out?' Noah asked.

'We have things to talk about,' Robert answered.

'Is it me and Aidan?'

He ruffled his son's hair. 'No – for once, it's not you and Aidan. It's...' he paused, 'grown-up stuff.'

'But why do you have to go out? Why can't you talk here?'

Robert smiled. 'Because we want a bit of privacy.'

'We could go upstairs.' Noah turned to Aidan. 'Couldn't we?'

'Yeah.'

'No,' Robert said firmly. 'For one thing, Cheryl is going to be here any minute. And for another–' He stopped. 'For another,' he repeated, 'I want your mum all to myself, just for a little while. OK?'

He'd avoided her all day in the salon, afraid that if she got the chance, she'd back out of their date, afraid she might have thought better of having a drink with her ex.

When he did see her across the floor, she seemed exactly as usual. She chatted with her clients like she always did and gave no sign that she was in the least bit preoccupied with the evening ahead.

She hadn't mentioned Alain since the night she'd had them both to dinner, and much to Robert's relief he never turned up at the salon, but thanks to the boys, Robert was well aware that the Frenchman was still very much on the scene.

'Alain says kids drink wine in France, but I bet Mum won't let us – she always says we'll see when we ask.'

'Alain's cousin plays for Toulouse – he was on the team when Munster beat them and won the Heineken Cup.'

'Alain bet us a fiver each that we won't eat a plate of snails. Aidan doesn't want to, but I *definitely* do.'

Robert was becoming allergic to the name. He felt helpless in the face of Alain's exoticism – what did he, Robert, have to offer that could possibly compete with snails and wine and a swimming pool in the back garden?

And what could he possibly offer Caroline, whose heart he'd broken, whose love he'd rejected?

No – he mustn't think like that.

'Just a private little chat,' he said to the boys. 'Sometimes grown-ups need that.'

The doorbell rang and Noah ran out to let Cheryl in. A few minutes later, while Robert was struggling to find common ground with a Leaving Cert student, Caroline appeared, dressed in a navy trouser suit that Robert had often seen her wearing. So she hadn't dressed up, not really. Probably thought a drink with her ex wasn't worth making much of an effort for.

'Hello, Cheryl – thanks so much for coming.' She turned to the boys. 'Be good for Cheryl, and be in bed by nine at the latest, OK? Don't forget to brush the teeth. I'll look in when I get home.'

'Will you look in too?' Aidan asked Robert.

Robert glanced at Caroline and said, 'If it's not too late. But you'll probably be asleep.'

He ached to touch her. He longed to put his arms around her and bury his face in her neck and feel the soft warmth of her.

He was going to tell her. He was going to lay his heart bare and tell her exactly how he felt. He had nothing to lose, it was lost already, and he was going to make one desperate attempt to win it back. He would throw himself on her mercy and beg her to give him another chance. He couldn't remember a time he'd been so afraid.

'Remember what your mother said,' he told the boys. 'Bed by nine. Show Cheryl where the fancy

449

biscuits are.'

They might have been an ordinary married couple, going out for the night with the baby-sitter on duty, getting home afterwards, checking on their sleeping children. It might have been like that for the past ten years, if he hadn't–

'Ready?' Caroline was slinging her bag on her shoulder. He smelled the scent she'd worn for as long as Robert had known her.

He rattled his car keys. 'Ready.' Now or never.

The twins stood at the front door as their parents drove off. Robert wondered if either boy had the slightest inkling of what their dad was planning. Weren't children supposed to be intuitive? It was better, of course, if they had no idea. Nothing to regret, no hopes to dash, if Caroline rejected him.

'So,' she said as he turned onto the road, 'what's all the big mystery about?'

'Let's wait till we get there.' He'd chosen a small, quiet pub about a mile from the house, frequented mainly by the elderly men of the vicinity and entirely lacking in televisions, pool tables and entertainment of any sort.

Caroline didn't push it. She knew something was up, she must suspect that Robert was about to surprise her in some way, but she said no more. It was one of the things he loved about her.

'Are you nervous about the play?' she asked. 'I know I'd be terrified.'

Robert shrugged. 'Not really.' The play was the least of his worries. He hadn't given much thought to tomorrow afternoon's dress rehearsal, hadn't even looked at his lines since Thursday.

'I've got tickets for you and the boys,' he told her. 'For opening night. And there's a reception backstage afterwards.'

'Lovely – they'll be delighted.'

By the time he walked onstage on Monday night, his future would have been decided. In the next half hour his future could well be decided. He indicated and pulled into the pub's tiny car park.

Caroline looked surprised. 'We're going here?'

'It's quiet,' he told her. 'We won't be disturbed.'

She didn't comment, didn't speak as they walked across the tarmacadam to the door, as she sat at a table and Robert went to the bar and nodded at the two men on stools, and ordered a dry white wine and a sparkling water.

As he'd expected, the place was quiet, with just the pair of them at the counter and three others at the far end of the room. Perfect.

'So,' Caroline said again as he sat.

'So,' Robert said. He drank some water and put down his glass. 'Caroline, there's something...'

She waited, her eyes on his face. He had no idea what she was thinking.

'Caroline, I need to tell you something,' he began again. 'I don't quite know how to.' He stopped and took a deep breath. 'I have discovered, no, I've *realised–*'

'Robert,' she said quickly, 'are you sick?'

He stared at her. 'Sick? No, I'm not sick.'

'Thank God,' she breathed. 'I was scared stiff you were going to tell me you only had a few months.'

'Why on earth would you think that?'

'Because you were being so mysterious. And because,' she said, 'you've been avoiding me all day. And you're acting like someone has given you bad news.'

'Am I?'

'Well, something is definitely up – and you don't look happy. So I need to know quickly what it is.'

'OK,' he said and searched again for the right words.

'Robert,' she ordered. 'Spit it out. I put on my favourite trouser suit for this.'

So he spat it out.

'I love you,' he said in a rush. 'I've always loved you, only I was too stupid to see it. I can't bear the thought of you going away. I thought it was the boys I was afraid of losing, but it's not – it's you. I know I can never lose them, but I'm terrified of losing you,' he said.

Caroline set down the glass she'd just lifted.

'You love me,' she said. Her voice was perfectly calm.

'I do,' Robert answered. 'I always have. There's never been anyone else – none of the others meant a thing.'

'And yet,' she said, 'you were happy to spend the past nine years with them.' Calm. Anger in the words, but not in the voice.

Robert felt something turn inside him. 'I've been stupid, I've been blind. It was there all the time, but I couldn't see it.'

'So what happened?' Her face was unreadable. She gave nothing away. 'What changed?'

'I don't know – maybe the thought of you

452

moving to France brought me to my senses. You must believe me,' he pleaded, resisting the impulse to reach out and take her hand. 'I love you, Caro, I truly do. I'm so ashamed–'

'Robert,' she said quietly, 'I know exactly what this is – it's a case of wanting what you can't have. Just when it looks like I'm going off with someone else, you decide you want me.'

Robert shook his head. 'No, it's not like that, it's not that, honestly–'

'You said yourself it was only when it looked like I was leaving that you decided you loved me.'

'Not decided – realised. I *do* love you,' he insisted. 'I've always loved you. It's not just because you're leaving.'

She tilted her glass, watched the wine climbing up the side.

'Have you–' He couldn't ask.

She lifted her head and looked at him. 'Have I what?'

He had to ask. 'Have you any feelings left – for me?'

Her eyes filled suddenly. 'Don't ask me that,' she said. 'You have no right to ask me that.' She blinked rapidly as she raised her glass and drank too quickly, as drops spattered onto her navy jacket.

'Sorry,' Robert said. 'I know I don't have any right. It's just that I can't bear the thought of you with anyone else. I just want to know, so badly. Please don't cry.'

She dabbed at her jacket. 'You broke my heart,' she said, her eyes glittering. 'You don't deserve me.'

It was true. He had no right to look for her forgiveness. It was insane to imagine that she would take him back, just like that. But as long as she sat across the table from him, Robert couldn't give up.

'Give me a chance to show you I'm serious,' he begged. 'Just one chance. I won't let you down, I swear. I'll never let you down again.'

She looked away from him, into the empty fireplace beside them. He dared to put a hand on hers. 'Please,' he said. 'Caro.'

She turned back to him and slid her hand from under his. 'You just don't get it, do you?' she asked, swiping at the tears that were running down her face now. 'My God, you can't see it.'

'Can't see what? What don't I get?' He reached again for her hand. 'Caro, don't cry, please. I'm sorry I upset you.'

She rummaged in her bag and Robert pulled out the hanky he'd folded carefully inside his breast pocket a million years ago, when he'd been getting ready to meet her. Out of the corner of his eye, he could see the men at the bar looking down.

Caroline dabbed at her eyes. 'You broke my heart,' she said again.

'I'm so–'

'You went to bed with someone else, you betrayed me, and I wanted to die, for so long,' she said, her voice clogged with tears. 'I wanted to die. But I couldn't die because I had the boys.'

She pressed his hanky to her eyes. Robert sat miserably beside her.

'And all the time I was trying to keep going,'

she said, reaching again for her drink, 'you were still around. It was unbearable to see you, but I managed.' The glass trembled as she put it to her lips. He heard the small sound of her swallow. 'And eventually,' she went on, 'I was over you enough to be able to talk to you without wanting to kill you, or wanting you to–' She broke off, his hanky a ball in her hands. Her eyes shone with tears, her mascara making two thin grey trails down her cheeks.

'I even went back to the salon,' she said, looking away from him again into the fireplace. 'God, that was hard. But I did it.' She turned and dropped his hanky on the table.

'Alain loves me,' she said slowly. 'He wants to marry me. Imagine that, after just three months.'

'And you?' Robert asked, dreading her answer.

Caroline looked towards the fireplace. 'We're going to France,' she said. 'We're going to live in France for a year.'

It wasn't an answer. It wasn't enough.

'Do you love him?'

She looked at Robert for what seemed like a very long time. He held her gaze steadily, his stomach tight.

And finally she whispered, 'No,' and looked away from Robert again.

He lifted his glass and drank slowly until the water was gone.

Caroline said again, 'We're going to France.'

'I know.'

'I won't change that now, it's all arranged.'

'No.'

But somewhere inside, a tiny hope flickered.

Dress Rehearsal Day: Sunday, 8 June

Judith

Something was different. Something had changed since earlier, but she couldn't think what. She walked slowly up the garden path – then stopped abruptly and turned back.

The car.

Her car was gone. She'd left it parked outside on the road like she always did. It had been there when she'd left for mass an hour earlier, she remembered looking in and thinking she must take her bag of paints out of it when she got home. And now it was gone.

She rushed back up the path and pushed her key into the lock. She'd ring the guards straight away – it couldn't have gone far. As she picked up the phone book, she glanced at the hook beside the door where she always hung the car keys, and saw that it was empty.

Her keys were gone.

She called 'Christopher?' twice, and nobody answered. She put down the phone book and walked into each of the downstairs rooms. No sign of a break-in, no window broken. The back door hadn't been kicked in. She went upstairs and saw her bedroom door ajar, and she pushed it open far enough to see that the room was empty.

Christopher must have taken the car; it hadn't been stolen at all. Judith felt a prickle of annoy-

459

ance. He hadn't even asked her, he hadn't left a note anywhere, he'd just taken it. He didn't care that she might need it for something, like a dress rehearsal this afternoon on the other side of town. If he wasn't back by twenty past two, she'd have to call a taxi.

She walked upstairs again and went back into the main bedroom. Rumpled bed, Amanda's musk perfume still hanging faintly in the air, a scatter of balled tissues on the floor by the dressing table.

She crossed to the wardrobe and opened it and saw empty hangers and a crumpled paper bag and nothing else. A squashed, lidless tube sat on top of the locker.

In the bathroom, they'd left empty bottles and more screwed-up tissues, and they'd taken her toothpaste and shampoo and shower gel. Long blonde hairs floated on the water in the toilet bowl. Judith flushed them away.

She went downstairs and had another look in the kitchen and sitting room and hall. Definitely no note, no message of any kind. She sat heavily on the couch.

They were gone. They'd moved out and they'd taken her car, because Christopher knew she wouldn't report the loss of it. They'd left without saying goodbye and they'd taken the car because they weren't planning to come back.

She breathed deeply, trying to keep calm. *It's a car,* she told herself. *It's a lump of metal and rubber, it doesn't mean anything. You can get another one, a cheap second-hand one.*

But of course it wasn't the car.

She stood and walked quickly into the kitchen, and then she couldn't think of anything she wanted in there. She'd been planning to have lunch before the rehearsal, but the thought of food held no appeal now. She unlocked the sliding patio door and pulled it open, and walked through to the garden.

Where had she gone wrong with him? She'd tried her best; she'd made every effort to be a good mother. She'd made allowances, maybe too many times. She'd been quick to forgive – should she have punished more and tolerated less? Was all of it her fault?

At a quarter past two, she gathered Betty's costumes together and phoned for a taxi.

Harry

He missed Ma. He felt scooped out. There was a hollowness inside him that hadn't been there before.

Sundays were the worst, his afternoons vacant now without the routine of the nursing home. Even though Ma hadn't known him a lot of the time, going to see her had anchored him, had connected him to his past. Now there was nothing.

Babs and Charlie were more strangers to him than a lot of his acquaintances. He'd never lived with them; they shared nothing except DNA. His nephews, Babs's children, were rare presences in his life, much, he supposed, as distant cousins would be in what he thought of as normal families, where brothers and sisters grew up together.

He was glad of the company of his housemates. Since Ma's death, Eve in particular had gathered him closer to her.

'Eating together in the evenings makes a lot more sense,' she insisted. 'I can't think why we didn't do it before.'

Now and again they rented DVDs Harry knew were more for him than for them – since when had either of them been fans of the Coen brothers? Eve asked out of the blue one evening why they'd given up playing Scrabble, and made Harry bring it downstairs again.

And on Sundays they made a special effort, with a roast beef lunch and enough newspapers to fill the rest of the afternoon for everyone.

There's no need, Harry felt he should say. *You don't have to look after me.* But their kindness touched him, so he allowed himself to enjoy it – and made sure not to win too many Scrabble games.

Today, as the three of them prepared the Sunday lunch together, Harry was jittery.

'Dress rehearsal, so exciting,' Eve said, tearing off a length of tinfoil.

'Are you terrified at the thought of opening night?'

'I am a bit,' Harry admitted, peeling the last potato and adding it to the strainer. 'Just hope I don't forget my lines – our director is a bit impatient.'

'All the best directors are fascists.' George

snipped rosemary and sliced garlic cloves. 'That's how they get results, by scaring the shit out of the actors.'

'Don't mind him,' Eve said, bending to put the beef fillet into the oven. 'You'll be brilliant. We'll be in the front row, cheering madly every time you appear.'

Harry laughed. 'God, don't do that – I'd definitely forget my lines.' He dried his hands. 'If that's all, I think I'll go for a quick cycle.'

Sitting around waiting for lunch would make him worse – no way could he concentrate on the papers, and he couldn't face another minute with his script.

'Be back by half one,' Eve ordered. 'You don't want to be rushing your meal before the dress rehearsal.'

'OK.'

He took his bike from the shed and pedalled off, and in less than ten minutes he was surrounded by green fields. He cycled fast, enjoying the rush of air as he sped along, filling his lungs and clearing his head. He allowed his thoughts to wander and they drifted back to the problem that had been nagging at him for quite some time – and lately, more insistently.

He would have to do something about his job. It was becoming increasingly difficult to put up with Linda's constant bickering. She put him down at every opportunity, making it impossible for him to enjoy the work he had once loved. Nothing was good enough for her, he'd never measure up – and Harry had finally had enough. He was going to look for a transfer, reluctant as he was to leave Portmaine, and if a transfer wasn't possible, he was simply going to quit.

He knew it was giving in. He knew he should stand up to her, he should tell her exactly what he thought of her, but it simply wasn't in him. He shrank from confrontation, he avoided arguments if he possibly could. He despised this cowardliness in him, but he didn't know how to change it.

He pedalled fast. Next week he'd do it, or the week after, when the play was over and things began to return to normal. He felt again the nervous lurch in his abdomen that happened every time he thought about walking out onto a stage in front of a crowd of strangers. The impulse that had led him to audition for the play seemed foolish now – he wondered where it had come from.

He remembered telling Ma about the play. It hadn't registered with her, she hadn't shown any kind of surprise or delight. He shouldn't have been disappointed – he'd known it was likely she wouldn't react – but he'd been in denial with Ma most of the time, he saw that now. Refusing to see what was obvious to everyone, convincing himself that he could pull her out of it, if only he could find a way through to her.

He rounded a bend, pulling out slightly to avoid an overhanging branch – causing a maroon car coming up at speed behind him to make brief contact with his rear wheel, the impact enough to knock bike and rider headlong into the ditch.

And as Harry crashed and tumbled through briars and hedges and bushes, the driver of the car changed gear, accelerated, and sped off.

Maria

When there was nothing more to come up, when the retching had finally stopped, she wiped her mouth and stood up and flushed the toilet.

She was lucky morning sickness struck so rarely. Only three times so far with this pregnancy, and by her calculations she was about seven weeks gone.

She rinsed her mouth and dabbed on lipstick, checking herself in the bathroom mirror. Slightly paler than normal, but otherwise there was nothing to suggest that she'd just lost her breakfast.

As she left the room she almost collided with Michael coming out of the bedroom next door.

'Sorry.' She walked around him, towards the stairs.

'Did I hear you getting sick?'

Her stomach lurched. She couldn't put it off any more. She put a hand on the banisters.

'I'm pregnant,' she said.

His right eye was slightly bloodshot. The pillow had drawn creases in his left cheek. His stubble was grey. Her hand ached from gripping the banister.

'How far gone are you?' No expression on his face.

'Seven weeks.' No point in lying now, nothing to be gained.

He nodded slowly. 'About time,' he said.

'I have to get back to Pat.' She turned away from him and began to walk downstairs.

'Let's hope this one isn't feeble-minded,' he said.

Maria closed her eyes briefly. How had she ever imagined she could stay with him? How in God's name had that ever seemed like a viable option? She stopped and opened her eyes and turned back to him.

'I'm leaving you,' she said. 'I'm taking Pat and leaving you.'

Michael regarded her for a few seconds. They faced each other across the slant of the stairs.

'You won't leave me. You've got everything here.'

'I've got nothing here,' she said. 'Nothing that matters. You've given me nothing.'

She turned and walked downstairs, stiff from expecting his hand on her shoulder, but the bathroom door had slammed before she reached the hall.

In the kitchen, she picked up her mobile phone and pressed Ellen's shortcut number. 'I need you to come around now,' she said. She hung up and allowed herself to sink slowly to the floor beside Pat and drop her head onto her knees.

Portmaine Arts Centre

The three canvas backdrops had been threaded onto rods and hung one behind the other at the back of the stage the day before by two art students on work experience at the Centre. The bottom of each backdrop had been tacked to a wooden strut to keep it flat. The struts were light enough to allow the canvases to be flipped over easily between scenes.

Edward stood in the centre of the auditorium, arms folded, and regarded the top one.

For Jack McCarthy's study, Judith had painted a wall that was cream above the high wooden picture rail and salmon pink below it. Two portraits – a man on a horse, a woman standing by a piano – hung from the rail. Flanking the portraits were two tall, narrow windows framed by heavy maroon curtains that were held back with thick gold-coloured ropes.

The illusion was startling. The curtains, folded and gathered, flaring out from their rope ties, looked three-dimensional, the windows behind them real enough to open, the pictures as if you could come along and lift them off their hooks. The room was there, waiting for Jack McCarthy to walk in.

It was precisely how Edward had pictured it. Judith had given him exactly what he'd asked for.

He turned to her. 'You've done a fine job with all three. Well done.'

Judith went pink. 'It'll be interesting to see

them with the props in place.'

'It certainly will.' He'd finally rounded up everything on the props list. The big pieces, collected that morning by a Carran Computers security guard driving a Carran Computers van, were all waiting backstage now to be put into position.

Jack's desk, a genuine antique, had been donated by Oliver. The garden bench and wheelbarrow had both come from Judith. Edward had borrowed a section of counter for the post office scenes from a tradesman who outfitted the local bars in return for an ad in the programme.

Harry had supplied a box of beautiful leather-bound books after Edward had promised not to reveal their source, and Robert had provided a bookcase and a kitchen table and chairs.

The two art students had offered to shift the props between scenes and to flip the backdrops.

William Crosby, father of the playwright, had come up with another employee – who Edward assumed was being rewarded for his efforts – to handle the lighting for the play. He'd been provided with a marked script and was coming along this afternoon, a John somebody or other.

Everything was falling into place – and in less than thirty hours, *Death by Dying* would officially open to the Portmaine public. As Edward glanced at his watch – two minutes to three – he heard footsteps. He turned to watch Robert and Theo walk up the aisle of the Arts Centre auditorium.

Three out of six, no lighting man or prompter, and two minutes to go. He willed himself to be patient.

'Hey, a proper stage,' Theo said, climbing up

the steps at the side. 'About time.' She scanned the auditorium. 'How many does this place hold?'

'Couple of hundred,' Edward told her, 'more or less.'

'Jesus – I'll be petrified.'

Robert inspected the backdrop. 'Did you do that?' he asked Judith. 'It's great.'

Edward indicated the backstage area. 'You three may as well go back and get changed. Dressing rooms are to the left – Robert, take the smaller one.'

'Righto.'

Fifteen minutes later, everything was ready. The props were in place for the first scene. John the lighting man had arrived and was checking out the Art Centre's facilities, Oliver was sitting in the wings with his script and the art students were chatting quietly on two front seats.

The three cast members were in costume – and the other three were still missing.

Edward paced the stage, having tried and failed to reach any of them. What was the point of giving him their phone numbers if they didn't answer their phones? Even if they arrived now they'd take another five minutes at least to change.

The play was an hour and forty minutes long – call it two with the inevitable interruptions. The Arts Centre was closing at six, by which time they'd have to have sorted out any glitches and changed out of costume, not to mention making sure that Lighting John knew what he was doing. How difficult was it to be on time?

At twenty past three, Harry arrived.

471

'What time do you call this?' Edward growled.

'Sorry,' Harry said, walking up the aisle towards him. 'I was in a bit of an accident.'

'Good God,' Edward said.

Harry's cheeks were crisscrossed with thin red cuts. His chin was grazed and there was a plaster on the bridge of his nose. His right eye was swollen and half-closed.

'Jesus,' Theo said. 'Were you beaten up?'

Oliver appeared from the wings and came quickly down the stairs. He looked at Harry's face.

'What happened?'

Harry tried to smile and then grimaced, putting a hand to his chin. He seemed embarrassed by the attention. 'I was knocked off my bike by a car into some bushes,' he said. 'I've been to casualty and there's nothing broken, just some cuts and bruises.'

He turned to Edward. 'My bike is wrecked. I had to hitch back into town, that's what delayed me.'

'The car didn't stop?' Theo asked.

'No, but I'm OK. I'm a bit sore, but it looks worse than it is. I'm sure I'll be fine for tomorrow night.'

'Let's hope so,' Edward said.

'I'll cover you up with make-up,' Theo promised.

Harry looked towards the stage. 'Where do I change?'

'I'll show you,' Robert said.

They all watched as Harry gingerly climbed the steps and disappeared into the wings.

'God,' Theo said. 'A hit and run – poor thing.

After his mother too.'

Nobody answered. Edward checked his watch again – almost twenty-five past. 'Does anyone have any information about the other two?'

'I could try phoning Maria,' Judith offered – and at that minute the auditorium door swung open and the two sisters came hurrying up the aisle.

Edward eyed them as they came towards him. No evidence of any injuries, no outward signs of calamity. No sign of an excuse. He could feel the tension rise within him.

'You're half an hour late.'

Ellen said quickly, 'Edward, we've had a–'

'This is the *dress rehearsal.*' His irritation and impatience got the better of him. 'Our last chance to go through the play before we open.' The anger burned through him. 'Our *only* chance to practise on this stage.' A tiny warning voice began to whisper in his head, but he ignored it. 'Harry managed to make it here, and he was in an accident.'

Maria looked pale. Ellen said, frowning, 'What?'

'I said,' Edward repeated evenly, 'Harry was in an accident, and he still managed to get here.' He glared at them. 'Neither of you looks to be injured.'

Theo, sitting nearby, said, 'Edward, maybe you should–'

Maria said, 'If you'd give–'

Oliver said, 'Let's just hear–'

Ellen broke in, silencing all of them. 'Listen,' she said, her voice tight, her gaze fixed on Edward, 'we have a *bloody* good reason for being late, and if you weren't so *pig-headed* we could tell you.'

Her eyes glittered. Her cheeks were flushed, her hair tousled. His frustrated desire for her only served to fuel Edward's anger. 'I'd be *terribly* interested in hearing it,' he replied icily.

Maria said quickly, 'Hang on, El–' putting a hand on her sister's arm.

Just then, Harry emerged from the side of the stage dressed in Tom's costume. 'I wonder if anyone would have a safety pin?' he asked. 'I think I've burst a seam.'

Nobody answered. All eyes were on Ellen, still glaring at Edward.

'You don't care, do you?' she asked him. 'As long as your damn play gets done, you don't give a shit about anything or anyone else.'

Edward was acutely aware of the others listening intently. 'For Christ's sake,' he said crisply, 'you were late for the dress rehearsal, and as director I'm entitled to question it. Get over yourself and let's hear this wonderful excuse of yours.'

There was a second or two of silence. Ellen's eyes bored into him.

'Fuck you,' she said calmly, pulling away from Maria. She turned and marched back swiftly, crookedly, through the auditorium.

Maria called, 'Ellen, please don't–'

As she burst through the swing doors, Edward started after her. 'Oh, for Heaven's sake–'

By the time he'd rushed through the lobby and out the main door of the Arts Centre, she'd disappeared. He scanned the street on either side, ignoring the curious looks of the woman behind the reception desk, and then he walked slowly back into the auditorium, mind racing.

'Oh, Edward–' Maria looked ready to burst into tears. 'I'm so sorry, it's all my fault–'

'I think you should get changed,' Edward told her curtly. 'We need to get started.'

'How can we do the play without Ellen?' Theo asked.

Edward barked, 'Oliver!' and instantly his head poked from the wings.

'Yes?'

'You'll be reading Dorothy's part today,' Edward said. He turned to the others, not waiting for Oliver's response.

'Right. You'll have to imagine Dorothy's presence whenever you share a scene. It's not ideal, but we have no choice. Oliver will give her lines and you will respond.'

He paused, trying to gather his scattered thoughts. 'We have a person working on the lights this afternoon. They'll be dimmed between scenes to allow changes to the set, so please be careful and watch your footing. Remember to project those voices – I'm going to be quite far from you, and I want to hear every word.'

He began backing away from them, down the aisle. 'Please take up your positions in the wings. Betty, stand by and wait for the command.'

He walked past the rows of seats, mind racing. She would turn up tomorrow night. He refused to consider the alternative. They'd manage without her today, and she'd be onstage tomorrow.

He chose a seat six rows from the back and sat. He couldn't imagine what had possessed her to walk out. He'd been his usual cranky self, but surely she was used to that by now? Surely to God she realised the importance of the dress rehearsal?

Maybe it was some real emergency that had delayed them. Edward should have been more patient, he should have controlled himself. But this was the *dress rehearsal,* she'd walked out of the goddamn dress rehearsal.

He thumped the arm of his seat loudly, and immediately Oliver's head shot from the wings.

'Are we starting? Is that the signal?'

Edward sighed. 'No, Oliver. The signal is when I say "let's go". That noise was me letting off some steam.'

'Oh – right. Terribly sorry.' He disappeared again.

Edward turned back towards the lighting box and raised his hand, and a single spotlight appeared to one side of the stage. Edward said loudly, 'Let's go. Walk slowly into the spotlight,' and after a second or two Betty the housekeeper stepped onto the stage.

'What happened?' he asked Maria. The others were in a huddle at the front of the stage, using the five-minute break he'd called to talk amongst themselves in whispers. He could guess what the topic was.

Maria sat in the seat next to him, her hands clasped in her lap. 'Edward,' she said softly, 'I left my husband earlier today. It happened ... quite suddenly, and I had to call Ellen to help me. That's why we were late.'

Edward looked at her, appalled. At last he said,

'I'm terribly sorry. Forgive me.'

She shook her head. 'No, no, you weren't to know. We should have contacted you, it was wrong not to let you know.' She bit her lip. 'It wasn't planned – at least, not like this.'

'You don't have to explain.' Edward was mortified. They'd been trying to tell him and he'd kept cutting them off.

'But I want to,' Maria insisted. 'With … everything that was happening, we never thought of getting in touch with you. And then we realised how late we were, but I couldn't find my phone, and Ellen said–'

'Really,' Edward said, 'you don't have to explain.'

'You had every right to be angry,' Maria said quickly. 'You weren't to know–'

'Will she come back?'

'Oh yes, I'm sure she will.' Maria hesitated. 'At least, I'm…' She didn't meet Edward's eye. 'She mightn't come back today,' she said uncertainly, 'but I'll talk to her afterwards, and I'm sure once she calms down…'

Edward groaned quietly, his head sinking to rest on the seat back in front of him. What if she didn't come back? The play would be finished, one of its main characters gone, and he'd have nobody to blame but himself. How in God's name would he explain to William Crosby?

'Edward – there's something else…'

He looked up.

'…but I'm not sure that Ellen would want me to say it.'

He waited.

Maria swallowed. 'Remember when you asked her to go for a drink the other night? After the rehearsal?'

His hand tightened on the seat back in front of him.

'Well, she thought you meant ... at least...' She frowned, then she looked him in the eye and said quickly, 'Edward, she was offended because she thinks you're probably married, and she thought you just wanted – you know.'

Edward's mouth dropped open.

Maria rushed on. 'You see, she mentioned meeting you with a woman in a bar the other night, and she thought when you saw her, I mean Ellen, having a drink alone, you might have ... gotten the wrong impression.'

Edward pictured her again, perched on the barstool with a glass of wine in front of her. Holding up the script to show him.

She'd seen Sophie, seen Edward with her. Taken them for man and wife, which indeed they were.

'Well,' Maria said, 'I can't be sure, but that might be part of the reason that she walked out today – I mean, the fact that she was already mad at you for presuming she was – you know, available like that.' Maria paused. 'I don't know, I just think it might be something to do with it.'

Ellen knew Edward was married; she'd assumed Sophie was his wife. She thought he'd just wanted a bit on the side when he'd invited her to go for a drink. He'd mortally offended her without realising it, and today he'd compounded the offence by barking at her, by being his usual hot-tempered self. No wonder she'd looked at him as if she hated him.

'I'll talk to her,' Maria said again. 'If you give me a phone I'll ring her now – she's probably cooled down.'

'Wait,' Edward said quickly. 'I'd like to talk to her. I need to explain something.'

'I don't know if she'd–'

'I'll risk it,' he said. 'I'll call around, after the rehearsal. I know where she lives.' He stopped. 'I'm not married, by the way,' he said. 'At least, I am still, technically, but it's over. We were ... sorting things out, the other night in the bar.'

'Oh.' Maria considered this. 'Oh, I see. And you're sure you want to call around?'

'Yes,' he said, 'I'm sure. Thank you.' He stood and clapped his hands, and heads swung towards him. 'Act two,' he said. 'Places, please.'

She'd shout, of course – that's if she didn't slam the door in his face. She might not want to listen, but he would give her no choice. That she felt nothing for him, that he annoyed and irritated her, he could live with, but the thought of her regarding him as some kind of dirty old man was reprehensible to him. He had to explain about Sophie, even if they never spoke again.

And of course there was the small matter of apologising for his lack of manners this afternoon and begging her, if he had to, not to desert the play.

He sighed. How ironic was it, after vowing never to look at another woman as long as he lived, that he was now utterly floored by someone who would cheerfully see him hanged, and dance afterwards on his grave?

He lifted a hand at the lighting box and turned to face the stage again. 'Right,' he said loudly, wearily. 'Let's go.'

The car was back. They hadn't stolen it, they'd just used it to move their luggage somewhere, and now it was back.

Judith got out of the taxi and peered through the window. Her painting box still on the back seat, nothing to show that they'd been in it at all. She turned to go indoors – and the jagged scratch cutting through the maroon paint on the side caught her eye. She ran a hand lightly over it, gauging its length – a foot and a half – and its depth, half an inch at its worst. Hopefully nothing that would cost too much to put right.

Christopher had scraped against something, a bollard maybe, or a parked car. But it was here, it was back. She let herself into the house and there were her keys, lying on the mat. She picked them up and hung them on their hook. She listened, and heard nothing.

'Hello?'

She dropped her costume bag on the phone table and walked upstairs. The bedroom was still empty; they hadn't changed their minds and moved back in. She gathered sheets and pillow-cases and towels together and brought the bundle downstairs and loaded the washing machine, her head full of questions.

Why wait until she'd gone out to take the car if Christopher had only wanted to borrow it? Why not just ask her, instead of sneaking off like that?

They'd definitely moved out, and presumably the car had been used to transport their luggage, so they must still be somewhere in the locality. But why not just tell her? Why all the secrecy? Was he punishing her for asking him to leave?

She closed the door of the washing machine and switched it on. Yes, she was being punished. He'd taken the car to give her a fright and then he'd brought it back later, just to keep her wondering and guessing. Serve her right for throwing them out, let her think what she liked.

Maybe he'd even scratched it on purpose.

Suddenly hungry – she'd had nothing to eat since morning, she hadn't felt like eating at lunchtime – she opened the fridge and noted, almost absently, its emptiness. She wouldn't have grudged them the food if they'd asked.

She looked at what they'd left her – a small wedge of hardening cheddar, a quarter-full mayonnaise jar, two onions, a dribble of milk in a carton – and closed the door again.

She'd go out and get a takeaway, and when she got back she'd change into pyjamas and eat it in front of the television. Tomorrow she'd do a big shop and clean out her bedroom and move back in.

And maybe in the autumn she'd take in a tenant. Some quiet girl from the country who went home every weekend and paid her rent on time and didn't spend hours in the bathroom.

She might join an amateur drama group too. She'd enjoyed the rehearsals for *Death by Dying,* she was pleased at how the backdrops had turned out and she was looking forward to the run.

She'd see what else was out there at the end of the summer.

And she'd give some more thought to a notion that had been festering inside her for months now. She'd take some time to investigate how exactly you went about giving private art lessons, to people who genuinely wanted to learn.

This was a good development, this was her life back again, her time her own once more. She picked up her bag and took the car keys from their hook again and let herself out, thinking about beef in black bean sauce.

No more soul-searching now, no point to that. She'd done her best with him, she needed to keep reminding herself of that whenever it got her down. Because of course it would get her down.

On the path, she knelt and examined the scrape on the car again. How had it been caused? Maybe he'd done damage to something else, another car, or–

Her hand stilled on the scratched maroon paint, as thoughts she didn't want came rushing in.

He'd brought the car back, after sneaking away with it. He'd damaged it and then he'd brought it back – because he didn't want to keep it any more. Because now it was a liability. Judith pressed a hand to her mouth and stood up, backing away from it. *Incriminating*, her head said. *Evidence*, it said.

Christopher had brought the car back so that whatever he'd done would be blamed on her. He wasn't still in the locality; he was as far away as he could get.

Dear God, let him not have killed someone, let her car not have been the instrument of someone's death or injury. And as she stood there feeling terribly cold, Harry flashed suddenly through Judith's head.

Harry, injured by a car this morning. What had he said? Pushed him into the ditch, or something. Hadn't the car stopped? Theo had asked, and Harry had said no.

No. No. Judith wheeled around and rushed back up the path, scrabbling at the door with her key, banging it closed and leaning against it, the fear uncurling within her.

It was Christopher, it had to have been. On his way to wherever they'd decided to go, colliding with a cyclist and driving on, not even stopping to see if he was still alive. And then checking the car later and seeing the scrape, and deciding that it was too risky to keep it–

But no, stop, she was jumping to conclusions. It might not have been Christopher at all who'd caused Harry's accident, it could have been anyone. It might just be a coincidence that he'd scratched the car. It might have been something very minor that had caused it, a scrape against a railing, something like that.

Maybe he had been planning to take the car, but he might have had a qualm of conscience about that, mightn't he, and brought it back? It could be something as simple as that.

But Judith didn't know. She'd probably never know if she didn't try to find out, and how could she go on living with that uncertainty? The thought of not knowing whether her son was a hit-

and-run driver, whether he'd knocked down a cyclist and left the scene, whether he'd brought back the car so his mother, if anyone, would be blamed – the thought of never knowing whether any of that was true might just be the undoing of her.

She opened the phone book and thumbed through its wafery pages, looking for Garda Síochána.

Edward pressed the bell beside *E. Greene* again and listened to the faint ringing inside. Maybe she wasn't home. Maybe Maria had called to warn her that he was coming and she'd fled. Or maybe she was inside, listening to the bell echoing in her apartment and waiting for him to leave.

The building wasn't a big one, just two stories high and four windows across, probably two apartments on each floor. He had no idea which one was Ellen's. She could be watching him from behind the net curtains of the windows directly above him or she could be just yards away, in one of the ground-floor apartments.

She wasn't there, or she wasn't going to talk to him. Edward turned to go – and then the door opened, and there she was.

She'd changed out of the grey trousers and jacket she'd worn to the Arts Centre and now she was dressed in jeans and a pale lilac top, and thick socks and no shoes. Her hair was pulled off her face into a knot. Her eyes were rimmed with pink, her face blotched, her lashes spiky. She looked fragile, and terribly beautiful to him.

'I'm sorry,' Edward said, his heart filling at the sight of her. 'I'm really sorry. Maria told me what happened. I was a pig.'

Ellen said nothing. She leaned against the door jamb and regarded him.

'I'm not married,' he said. 'I'm separated, and I'm going to get a divorce.' It felt like an offering, pouring out of him and sitting at her feet. 'My wife and I have been living apart for a year. It's over. We were just making it official in the pub the other night.'

We. He thought of Sophie's tears and pushed them away. Ellen blinked and rubbed a hand under her nose.

'I didn't want you to think badly of me,' Edward said. 'I didn't want you to think that all I wanted...' He couldn't finish it. His hands felt useless; he plunged them into his coat pockets.

She was a few inches shorter than him. She had no freckles. The neckline of her top was slightly frayed along its right side. There was a tiny blob of something black caught on one of her lower lashes.

'Please come back,' he said. 'I know you think the play is all I care about, but you're wrong.'

She bent her head and studied her stockinged feet, one resting on the instep of the other.

'I care very much about other things,' Edward said, 'and other people – but I am the director, and it's my responsibility, and sometimes I get carried away with that.'

'I shouldn't have walked out,' she said then, head bent, so softly that Edward barely heard. He leaned closer, his upper body swaying towards her.

'It was terrible, I shouldn't have done it.' She

raised her head quickly again, and he smelled her citrus scent. Her eyes had filled with fresh tears that she wiped away with her sleeve. Her distress was heartbreaking to him.

'It's alright,' he said, relief flooding through him. 'Don't upset yourself. I deserved it, I deserved every bit of it. If you can come in early tomorrow night we can go through a few things.'

She nodded. 'The reason I limp,' she said suddenly, 'is because I was in a road accident some years ago, and I had to have two toes amputated. And,' she added, wiping a sleeve across her eyes again, 'someone I loved very much died in the accident.'

It took Edward completely by surprise. He had no idea how to respond. At last he said, 'I'm so sorry. That scene in the study must be–'

'It's fine,' she said quickly, 'I've moved on. It just reminds me a bit, but it's OK. What time do you want me in tomorrow?'

He thought quickly. 'I'll be there at six,' he said. 'I've asked the others to be in by seven.'

She nodded again. 'I'll come straight from work; I'll be there soon after six.'

Edward smiled, relief flooding through him. 'Good,' he said. 'And if there's anyone you want to bring to the reception afterwards...'

'There isn't anybody,' she told him. 'Nobody at all.' Looking straight into his eyes, like she always did.

Nobody at all. Something fluttered gently inside Edward.

'I'll see you tomorrow night,' she said.

'Right.' He heard the door closing softly as he

turned away. He walked back to his car and got in and drove to the hospital.

Then he sat by Rory's bed and told him everything.

Harry lowered himself gingerly into the steaming, foamy water that smelled like pine trees.

'Sit in it for at least half an hour,' Eve had ordered, 'otherwise you'll be stiff and sore tomorrow. Keep topping up the water.'

He'd phoned them from the hospital earlier.

'Where are you?' she'd asked. 'Lunch is ready. Has something happened?'

Harry had told her.

'Oh my God – are you alright? Have you broken anything? Did you hit your head?'

'I'm fine,' he'd said. 'A bit scratched and bruised, but otherwise I'm OK. They've patched me up, and now I'm just waiting to get a tetanus shot.'

'But how did it happen? Where's your bike? How did you get to the hospital?'

She'd arrived twenty minutes later with warm beef sandwiches, just as Harry was being called in for his shot. She'd waited until he came out and got his painkiller prescription, and then she'd insisted on driving out to collect the bike from where he'd abandoned it.

'I can't believe they didn't stop – bastards.'

'Doesn't matter,' Harry had said, doing his best with the sandwich. 'Luckily I had a soft landing.'

'Not that soft,' she'd said. 'Your poor face. Long hot bath as soon as you get home.'

'I can't – I have the dress rehearsal.'

'Oh Harry, you can't go to that.'

'I have to,' he said earnestly. 'Edward would kill me.'

Eve grimaced. 'That man has a lot to answer for.'

The bike's back wheel was badly buckled. They'd pulled it free from the briars and bundled it into the boot. They'd stopped at a chemist and got Harry's tablets, and cream for his scratches. They'd driven home and collected Harry's costume, and then Eve had brought him to the Arts Centre and had offered to come and pick him up at six, but Harry told her he'd get a lift from one of the others.

He closed his eyes and inhaled the fragrant steam. The scratches on his face prickled. Already the skin around his eye was darkening – it would he interesting tomorrow, even with the arnica Eve had dabbed on. Hopefully Theo's make-up would disguise it.

His left side was bruised and he had grazes on both forearms. The nurse who'd given him the tetanus shot had warned him that he'd probably feel stiff in the morning.

He might have been killed. The driver hadn't stopped. What kind of person did that?

Oliver had driven him home. Oliver had wanted him to go to the guards.

'There's no point,' Harry had said. 'I've no idea what the car was like, it was gone before I had a chance to see it – and even if I did, it's probably miles away by now.'

'Don't you want to try?' Oliver had asked. His car was very clean and smelled expensive, and sounded powerful. 'Your poor ravaged face,' he'd said. 'Don't you have a desire to see justice done?'

Harry had leaned back against the headrest, his eyes closed. 'It isn't important. Really, it isn't.'

Oliver had driven confidently. Harry had felt safe.

'See you tomorrow,' Oliver had said, dropping him off. 'Goodbye, Harry, take good care of yourself.'

'Was that one of the other actors?' Eve had asked. 'He should have come in – we've plenty of leftovers.'

'Nice car,' George had said. 'I love those Aston Martins.'

The water was cooling and his skin was puckered. Harry pulled the plug out with his toes and got slowly to his feet and stepped out onto the mat. He patted himself dry, his limbs aching pleasantly. He put on his dressing gown and rubbed the steam off the mirror with his towel.

'Take good care of yourself,' he told the ravaged face, and it smiled gingerly back at him.

'Hi – me again.'
    'Did he call around?'
    'Yes, he's just left. We've sorted things out.'
    'Thank goodness.'
    'And Maria?'
    'Yes?'
    'He is married, but he's getting divorced.'
    'Yes, so he said.'
    'It's been a weird day, hasn't it?'
    'It certainly has.'

'Maria, are you alright?'

A pause. 'I will be.'

'No regrets?'

'Oh, plenty of those – but today I did the right thing.'

'Of course you did. And Mam and Dad?'

'Well, Mam has calmed down a bit now, she's up reading a story to Pat. But Dad is still in shock – he's going to talk to Michael tomorrow. I think he imagines he can make it all better.'

'God. I suppose we can't stop him.'

'No ... I should have said something sooner, so this wouldn't have come out of the blue for them today. Their faces when we turned up.'

'Don't worry about them, they're already getting over it. The worst is over now. Let's not look back, either of us.'

'Thanks, El. For being there today, I mean – couldn't have managed without you.'

'Well then, we're even. Oh, by the way, can you get Mam or Dad to run you in tomorrow night? I said I'd go in early, to make up for today.'

'Did you now.'

'Yes – Edward wants to go through a few things.'

'Does he really.'

'Shut up. See you tomorrow.'

Tomorrow she and Edward would be alone for almost an hour before the others arrived. Ellen found the thought ridiculously exciting.

She hung up and went into the kitchen to toast bread and make hot chocolate.

Or maybe she'd have a nice big gin and tonic instead.

Opening Night: Monday, 9 June

Portmaine Arts Centre

Death by Dying

A Play in Three Acts by Jonathan Crosby

Cast (in alphabetical order)

Tom Drury	Harry Buckley
Ursula Fitzpatrick	Theo DeCourcy
Dorothy Williams	Ellen Greene
Jack McCarthy	Robert McInerney
Betty O'Donnell	Judith O'Sullivan
Penelope McCarthy	Maria Talty

Directed by	Edward Bull
Wardrobe Manager	Oliver Noble
Backdrops	Judith O'Sullivan
Lighting	John Delamere
Backstage Assistants	Ger Ford & Len O'Keeffe

'I brought muffins,' she said holding up a large white bag, 'for afterwards. Cranberry and almond. None of your bran rubbish.'

'That stage looks huge,' she said. 'I'm pretty terrified.'

'You look very smart in a suit,' she said. 'What's the occasion?'

'Where's Oliver going to sit?' she asked. 'Where are the dressing rooms?'

'This place must hold at least a hundred,' she said. 'Were all tonight's tickets sold?'

'Our parents were going to come tonight,' she said, 'but they're going to wait till later in the week, and come on separate nights. They're looking after Pat, Maria's son. Maria and Pat will stay with them for a while.'

'What should I do?' she asked. 'Where should we start?'

'I suppose I could go through my scenes,' she said, 'if you read the other parts.'

'Are you alright?' she asked finally. 'Is something wrong?'

Edward shook his head. 'Nothing's wrong,' he said.

'Edward Bull,' Ellen said sternly, 'I nearly broke my neck getting here this early. We're here to work, and we've got forty-five minutes, so I suggest we get a move on.'

'Right,' Edward said, 'Let's go.'

'Harry? Could I have a word?'

Nobody had reported a hit and run, or any other driving incident, anytime yesterday morning in the area. Judith had left her details with the guard, who'd promised to be in touch if anything came in.

Harry's face was shiny with cream. The scratches had begun to heal, but were still very visible. His eye was dark purple.

Judith had to know.

'I was just wondering if you got a look at the car that ... hit you yesterday. You see, my son ... borrowed my car, and when it came back it had a scratch on it, and I'm afraid...' She trailed off, looking up at Harry with fright in her eyes.

Harry shook his head. 'It definitely wasn't your car,' he said. 'The one that hit me was yellow. I saw it driving off.'

Judith closed her eyes briefly. 'You're quite sure?'

'Absolutely,' he said. 'A yellow car.'

He watched the fear leaving her face. It wasn't important to him, not in the least. And Judith, who he'd seen getting into a maroon car after rehearsals, looked like she badly needed to know that it wasn't her son.

She smiled. 'Thank God.'

And who knew? Maybe it wasn't.

'Has anyone seen my grey skirt? It was here a second ago.'

'Jesus, look at that shiner – sit down and I'll put on my magic concealer.'

'I feel sick.'

'Can you keep your shoes in by the wall? That's

the second time I've tripped over them.'

'Who's got a script? Where's Oliver?'

'That stuff is great – it's completely hidden the bruise.'

'Did anyone have a look out? Are they letting them in yet?'

'Edward says it's a full house.'

'Anyone got a safety pin?'

'I've forgotten my first line.'

'Who took my comb? Should I put my hair back or forward?'

'I'd kill for a cup of tea right now.'

'Robert's just thrown up.'

'Right, everyone – two minutes. Take your places please, and try to stay focussed.'

'*Shit* – I mean, thanks Edward.'

'You'll be fine,' he told them all. 'I'm proud of you.'

The house lights went down, leaving the warm, crowded auditorium in complete darkness.

The audience hushed, and waited. Someone sneezed.

A single spotlight hit the stage.

A woman in a black dress and white apron walked slowly into the circle of light and stared out. After a few seconds, she began to speak. 'Such a tragedy,' she said.

The six actors stood in a line, hands clasped, and bowed as the applause continued. Ellen, on the far left, reached into the wings and pulled out Oliver, who smiled and bowed elegantly from the waist.

There were calls for Edward and Jonathan Crosby, who joined them on the stage.

Theo winked at Gemima, who smiled back.

Robert waved to the boys and tried to catch Caroline's eye, but she was looking in Theo's direction.

Oliver's aunt, minus her fur wrap, blew kisses at her nephew and knocked her neighbour's programme out of his hands.

The audience rose to its feet and clapped on.

'Jesus, I thought I would literally *DIE*.'

'Did you notice I nearly dropped the letter opener? My hands were shaking so much.'

'We got a standing ovation, can you believe it?'

'Who's got eye make-up remover?'

'I'll have to rinse out that blouse when I go home – I sweated *buckets*.'

'Jesus, when that mobile phone went off...'

'Did you hear it? I nearly got the giggles.'

'Was anyone looking at Edward at the end? Talk about the cat that got the cream – the man actually seemed happy.'

'Didn't he?' smiled Ellen.

Afterwards

'People think a book is soaked up by the reader, but in my opinion it works in a completely different way,' said Oliver, seeing a plate of muffins on a nearby stool. 'When you read a book, you impose your own values and insights and experiences onto every page, and your interpretation of what you read is informed by your personality. That's why one reader will love a book and another, equally literate and intelligent, will loathe it.'

'Interesting,' said Harry. 'When you think about it, it makes perfect sense.'

Technically, it wasn't a lie – he was sure it made perfect sense to Oliver.

'Your scratches are healing already,' Oliver said. 'You must have amazing powers of recuperation.'

'I think it's the cream,' said Harry.

Oliver took a muffin from the plate. 'Libraries are such lived-in places, aren't they? I mean the second-hand aspect of it, all those different fingers turning pages. Most comforting.'

'Yes,' said Harry 'Yes, that's the word. Comforting.'

'Of course,' Oliver continued, 'one could have that in a bookshop too, if one had a second-hand section.'

'I suppose so.'

Oliver peeled a section of paper from the muffin and examined it. He turned the muffin over and inspected its base. 'Bookshops must be browser friendly. Browsers always buy eventually, and they certainly drink coffee.' He nodded to himself. 'A coffee corner, and couches in which one can curl up.'

His hair, a spaniel mix of pale brown and blonde, swept back from his temples and fell to his shoulders. The dark grey irises of his eyes were ringed with a beautiful narrow navy band.

He was as slender as Harry was broad, but their heights were remarkably similar for all that – barely an inch between them, with Oliver the taller. The skin on his face was golden and smooth, and his cheekbones were wonderful, just wonderful.

'I should like to see you swim,' he said to Harry. 'I sense that the water is your true element. I should like to watch you glide through it like a seal.'

'These muffins are rather sweet,' he said later, 'which is not to take from them in the least. A little sweetness is one of life's great pleasures, don't you think, Harry?'

'Absolutely.'

'You may or may not be aware,' he said, much later, 'that I've just taken over the running of the bookshop for Maria.'

'No,' Harry said. 'I wasn't aware.'

'Maria has some personal issues which she needs to deal with, and in the meantime she's done me the very great honour of asking me to manage the bookshop in her absence. The arrangement is a little ... open-ended, and I feel it could continue for some time.'

'I see.'

'Yes ... I mention it because I find myself in the position of looking for an assistant, and I'm wondering if you, in your capacity as librarian, would be acquainted with any possible candidate.'

'Funny you should ask,' said Harry.

Smiling such a wide, happy smile. Ignoring the protesting sting of his healing scratches.

'Miep is nice,' Theo said. 'I never thought she'd be nice. Did she enjoy the play?'

'She did,' Ben said. He raised his glass and sniffed suspiciously at the champagne. 'And Gemima thought you were wicked.'

Theo narrowed her eyes at him. 'As in wicked stepmother?'

He laughed. 'As in very good. Don't you know anything?' He took a sip and grimaced. 'Why can't they serve a decent drink?'

Theo drained her glass. 'I think she should come and stay for a week when the play's over. Really get to know Chrissy.'

'Who – Miep?'

Theo punched him. 'Gemima.'

Ben caught her fist and opened it, and pressed her palm to his lips. He held out his glass. 'Have some more champagne,' he said, 'you wicked woman.'

'They're gone,' Judith said. 'They moved out.'

Maria lowered her tea. 'When?'

'Yesterday morning.'

'Was it hard?'

Judith bit her lip. 'Much as I expected.'

She wouldn't mention the car. It was all in the

503

past now.

Maria nibbled her muffin. 'Do you know where he's gone?'

'No.'

Neither of them said anything for a minute. They drank tea and ate muffins and looked around the room and saw all the tired, happy faces.

Then Maria, watching Ellen arguing with Edward, said, 'I've left Michael. I've taken Pat and left him.'

Judith drew her breath in. 'What? When did this happen?'

'Yesterday.' Maria pulled a piece from her muffin. 'Ellen came and picked us up and brought us home to my parents. That's why we were late coming to the rehearsal.'

'Lord, and there's me going on—'

'No, no, it's fine—'

'You should have said—'

'Not at all—'

They stuttered to a stop and drank more tea. Eventually Judith said, 'What will you do now?'

'Teach piano,' Maria said immediately. 'I've always wanted to do that. And I've got the perfect premises.'

'Where's that?'

'Above the bookshop. We've got two other floors that we never use. It all needs renovating, of course – it's full of clutter, boxes and things – but I'm going to get it cleared out and done up, and turn it into a flat for myself and Pat, and the new baby.'

'But—' Judith hesitated, 'I thought your husband owned the bookshop?'

'No – he bought it years ago as some kind of tax write-off, but he made it over to me when we got married, the whole building's in my name. I've put Oliver in charge of the shop, and he's delighted. I'm sure he's been dying to do things his way for ages. He'll probably make it far more profitable than I could.'

'Sounds great.'

'Yes and once the upstairs is ready, I'll advertise the piano lessons.'

'Good for you.'

'And what about you?' asked Maria. 'What are you planning to do with the rest of your life?'

'Actually,' Judith said, 'I was thinking of offering painting lessons. Just as soon as I can find a suitable premises.'

There was a pause, during which they both sipped tea.

'You know,' Maria said, thumbing away a drip that was running down the side of her cup, 'there's really plenty of room to have two completely separate spaces for classes above that bookshop. And Pat loves to paint.'

Judith tilted her cup so the tea ran towards the rim. 'Does he really?'

'Mmm. Music and art go so well together, don't they?'

'Perfectly.'

Another pause.

'I have to behave myself, with this baby,' Maria said then, 'but why don't you ditch the tea and have a glass of champagne?'

Judith smiled. 'You know, I think I might have a tiny one.'

'And maybe we could meet for a proper chat, once the play is over.'

'Definitely.'

'You were class,' Noah said.

'Yeah,' Aidan said. 'Class.'

'But it would be better if you were the killer.'

'Yeah – or the one who gets killed.'

'See those muffins over there?' Robert asked them. 'Bet you a euro each you can't find me one with chocolate chips.'

'Right,' he said as soon as they were out of earshot. 'Right,' he said again, getting down on one knee and rummaging in his pocket.

'Robert,' Caroline said, putting her glass down too quickly, almost knocking it over.

'Hang on,' he said, pulling out the box and fumbling it open.

'Robert, get up – everyone's looking.'

'Caro, will you marry me?' he asked. 'Please? Will you? I love you like crazy.'

'The boys are coming back,' she said. 'Get up, for God's sake.'

'Dad,' said Noah, 'there's no chocolate chip– Dad, why are you kneeling?'

'Will you?' Robert asked her. 'Will you just think about it at least?'

'Dad?'

'That's not fair,' she said, 'you can't just–'

'I know, I know,' Robert said. 'But I had to take a chance. Faint heart never won fair lady, and you told me you don't love him.'

'Robert...'

'Mum? Are you OK? Why are you crying?'

'Will you think about it?' Robert asked again. 'Will you just do that?'

Caroline brushed a hand across her eyes. 'God – alright, if it gets you off the floor.'

'Alright what?' Robert asked. 'Alright you'll marry me, or alright you'll think about it?' His knee was killing him, but he stayed down.

'Mum, are you getting married to Dad?'

Caroline took the ring from Robert and pulled it out of the box. 'When did you get this?'

'Today,' he told her, 'at lunchtime, in a hurry. We can change it.'

Her smile was watery, but it was there. 'In that case,' she said, 'yes.'

'Does that mean yes you'll–'

'It means yes I'll marry you, you impossible man. Now will you please get up?'

'Do we have to be page boys?' Noah asked.

Robert got awkwardly to his feet. 'You'd better look away,' he said to them. 'I'm going to kiss Mum now. It'll be very embarrassing.'

The applause started as he took her into his arms.

'I wanted to throttle you,' Ellen said, pulling cranberries from her muffin. 'Asking me why I limped before you'd even introduced yourself.'

'As I remember,' Edward replied, 'you used some choice language in your response.'

'Did I? Good.'

He frowned at her. 'You are without doubt the most irritating woman I have ever had the misfortune to meet. You're stubborn and hot-tempered. I have no idea why I'm so attracted to you.'

'*I'm* stubborn and hot-tempered?' Ellen smiled, trailing a finger along the back of his hand. 'Edward Bull, you have finally met your match. Anyway,' she said, 'you drive me mad too. You think you're always right and you're like an old woman about punctuality.'

'I see nothing wrong,' Edward told her sternly, trapping her finger within his grasp, 'with being on time. It's plain good manners.'

'Has anyone ever told you,' she said, 'that you look like Tommy Lee Jones?'

Edward smiled. 'Good Lord.'

'I know this great restaurant,' she told him, 'for when you take me out to dinner. After the play finishes.'

Edward sighed heavily. 'Yes,' he said. 'It seems we're headed that way, doesn't it?'

And apart from the odd row – and the occasional flying cup – they all lived happily ever after. More or less.

Curtain

Acknowledgements

Many thanks to Ciara Doorly and all at Hachette Books Ireland, to Faith O'Grady, to Annagh-makerrig, to Ann Menzies and Mags Hough, and to my family and friends, as always, for their support.

The publishers hope that this book has given you enjoyable reading. Large Print Books are especially designed to be as easy to see and hold as possible. If you wish a complete list of our books please ask at your local library or write directly to:

Magna Large Print Books
Magna House, Long Preston,
Skipton, North Yorkshire.
BD23 4ND

This Large Print Book for the partially sighted, who cannot read normal print, is published under the auspices of

THE ULVERSCROFT FOUNDATION